KT-545-611

RAITOR'S GATE

3 8014 05179 9374

MICHAEL RIDPATH
TRAITOR'S GATE

HEAD
ZEUS

First published in the UK in 2013 by Head of Zeus Ltd.

Copyright © Michael Ridpath, 2013

The moral right of Michael Ridpath to be identified as the author
of this work has been asserted in accordance with the
Copyright, Designs and Patents Act of 1988.

All rights reserved. No part of this publication may be
reproduced, stored in a retrieval system, or transmitted in any form
or by any means, electronic, mechanical, photocopying, recording,
or otherwise, without the prior permission of both the copyright
owner and the above publisher of this book.

This is a work of fiction. All characters, organizations, and events
portrayed in this novel are either products of the author's
imagination or are used fictitiously.

9 7 5 3 1 2 4 6 8

A CIP catalogue record for this book is available from
the British Library.

ISBN (E) 9781781851838
ISBN (HB) 9781781851807
ISBN (XTPB) 9781781851814

Printed in Germany.

Head of Zeus Ltd
Clerkenwell House
45-47 Clerkenwell Green
London EC1R 0HT

www.headofzeus.com

To Algy

Berlin
27 September 1938

Dearest Father,

By the time you receive this letter he will be dead. The newspapers will say that his assassin was an unknown German officer. It wasn't. It was me.

It is quite likely that I will also be dead. So I want to explain to you why I killed him.

When I was a boy you taught me that war is wrong. I listened to you then, but it was only when I had lived through eight months of hell in Spain that I knew what you meant. War is coming, and we have both seen how horrific modern war can be. Millions will die: this time it won't be just the young men; it will be the children, the women, the old, the innocent. I am an historian, trained to analyse economic and social causes for everything, but if ever in history there has lived an individual who through the force of his own will can destroy a continent, it is he. He is evil and he must be stopped: I am fortunate to be able to stop him.

I remember once we were on Yarmer Hill, overlooking Chilton Coombe, I was perhaps fourteen. You told me that my life would be a success if I left the world a better place than I found it. Well, I've tried to make a small difference over the last few years in Oxford, in Spain and now in Germany, and most of the time you and I have disagreed over my methods. But I hope, I pray, that in this last act I will have succeeded.

For all kinds of political reasons it is best that my identity be kept secret; I can trust you to do that. But I need you of all people to know what I have done.

Please give my love to Mamma and to Millie. I am sure they will understand. And to Charlotte and Reggie, of course.

In haste,
Your son,
Conrad

Prologue

July 1937

Thyme. Whenever Conrad smelled thyme, he thought of Spain. Not the Spain of matador and bull, of flamenco and guitar, of Goya and Velázquez, of castle and cathedral, but the Spain of death in the name of brotherly love.

In particular he thought of the sunrise at the beginning of his last week as a soldier, his nose brushing through the thyme as he crawled towards the crest of the ridge ahead of him. To his left, the metallic blue fingers of the dawn caressed the black humps that rolled towards Madrid thirty miles to the east. Behind him, in the distance to the north, loomed the heights of the Guadarrama Mountains, just distinguishable against the night. What lay ahead, over the crest of the next hill, Conrad had no idea. That was what he and his two comrades of the International Brigade had been ordered to discover.

Conrad had volunteered for the patrol. Dawn was his favourite time; the air was cool; tiny droplets of moisture hung on the leaves of the thyme and rosemary bushes; the hills were quiet, guile and cunning could keep you safe. The three of them, himself, David Griffiths, an old friend from Oxford, and Harry Reilly, a stocky stevedore from Liverpool, made a good team. Conrad was the best shot in the British Battalion, Harry was not much worse and David's eyesight and hearing were exceptional. They all looked after each other. Conrad

3

preferred operating against the enemy, the Fascists whom he had travelled a thousand miles to fight eight months previously, than worrying about the commissars, the secret police and the dogmatic generals on his own side.

They reached the crest of the hill. Below them lay a small valley, at the bottom of which ran a narrow ravine. A few yards beyond that stood an old stone chapel, and a cluster of ramshackle buildings, wreathed in a thin layer of mist hovering a few feet above the ground.

'Any sign of life?' Conrad whispered.

'There are people moving about down there,' David answered. He was holding one of the battalion's few pairs of binoculars to his eyes. The son of a Methodist preacher in the Rhondda valley, he was a wiry man, strong for his size, with a nut-brown face and a restless energy. At Oxford the energy had been channelled towards the cause of international socialism; here it was concentrated on killing fascists.

'Let's go and take a closer look,' said Conrad.

'If we wait ten minutes, we'll be able to see much better,' said David.

It was true. The blue fingers to their left had turned to red, and the darkness of the valley was lightening to a bluish grey. The mist was lifting.

Then, to their amazement, a single bell tolled from the chapel.

'Those are nuns,' said David.

Sure enough, figures emerged from the buildings and made their way towards the chapel.

The Republican forces had advanced swiftly over the previous two days against lacklustre opposition, and these nuns, safe behind Nationalist lines for months, had been caught out.

'No sign of the Fascists?' Conrad asked.

Before David could answer, they heard the crack of a rifle, then another and another. Pieces of stone flew off the cross on the chapel roof. The nuns screamed and ran into what they presumed was the sanctuary of the chapel.

Conrad and his two comrades leaped to their feet and hurried down the hill, but the chapel was a quarter of a mile away across the small but steep ravine. A group of about a dozen soldiers appeared, all carrying rifles. They wore the ragged medley of dusty clothing that was the uniform of the Popular Army. They began to cheer and run towards the convent. Conrad could make out the words: *'Putas de Dios!'* – 'Whores of God!' The hatred of many of the Spanish Republican soldiers towards the Church and the priests and nuns who served it was legendary. For them, the institution was inextricably connected to the Nationalists and to the landlords who had taxed the peasantry for generations. The hatred the foreigners could understand; the way it was expressed they could not.

As Conrad reached the edge of the ravine, he paused. 'Wait!' he called to Harry and David, who were already scrambling down. 'Let's stay at the top. It'll take too long to get up the other side.'

The soldiers were already dragging the women out of the chapel. One of the nuns was pulled down on to the ground by three of the men. A fourth was unfastening his trousers.

'Oye! Basta!' Conrad shouted. He stood up and waved. The soldiers paused for a moment. Two of them waved back and then the man standing over the nun dropped his trousers.

'Fire over their heads,' said Conrad. He aimed his own rifle at the wall of the stone chapel a few feet above the group of soldiers and nuns and pressed the trigger. Three sharp cracks rent the air as the three rifles discharged, and the man with his trousers around his ankles crumpled.

Shocked, Conrad glanced at David, whose face was grim and determined. 'The bastard deserved it.'

The nuns screamed and the soldiers reached for their own rifles. Conrad took aim and fired, as did Harry and David. Three more of the soldiers fell, and then the rest ran. David nicked one on the shoulder as he ducked through the scrub.

There was trouble the next day. The Russian commissar from the Popular Army brigade the soldiers had belonged to paid a visit to his counterpart in the British Battalion. He was a short balding man with a tiny paunch and the hint of a double chin, which set him apart from the scrawny soldiers around him. The commissar of the British Battalion, who was British himself, told the Russian to piss off. But the visitor had brought with him a soldier nursing a shoulder wound. As they were leaving the British Battalion HQ, this soldier caught sight of Conrad and nudged his commissar.

The Republican offensive pressed on towards the village of Brunete, but the Fascists quickly put together a stiff resistance. Two days later Conrad found himself a few miles further on, his body pressed flat in a shallow indentation he and Harry had scraped into the hard-baked soil. Ahead was a low bump, which had just earned the nickname Mosquito Hill because of the bullets whining all around it. The previous day the British Battalion and the American Washington Battalion had thrown themselves in useless waves at the hill, ably defended by the Nationalists. The bodies lay in front of Conrad, scattered about the brown earth, already putrefying in the sun. Many of them had been his friends, his comrades.

The sun blazed, turning the ground in front of the hill into a nightmarish oven of death. There were shell-blasted scraps of thyme bushes even here, but in the middle of the day their aroma was overwhelmed by the smell of rotting flesh and human excrement. The noise was overpowering: the relentless crash of shells from the Fascists' guns, interspersed with the crackle of small-arms fire and, in the all-too-brief moments of quiet, the buzzing of thousands of flies dancing from corpse to corpse.

Conrad was tired and he was thirsty. Everyone was thirsty. The streams shown on their maps had turned out to be dry, and the Republican Army's logistical capabilities were not up to bringing enough water to the front to slake the thirst of all its soldiers.

To their left, a Spanish Popular Army brigade was moving up to support yet another attack. It was the unit from which the soldiers who had tried to rape the nuns had come. Once they were in position, the order would be given for the British Battalion to attack again. These days it was always the International Brigades or the anarchist units who were thrown into the offensives, with the elite communist units held back from the worst of the fighting.

The order came to advance. Although Conrad was exhausted, as soon as he was on his feet adrenalin spurted through his veins and he ran, crouching low, dodging from left to right, Harry by his side, David slightly ahead and to the left. The Popular Army brigade had machine guns and they were spraying bullets in the general direction of the Nationalists on the hilltop.

Conrad threw himself down behind a small boulder and rested his rifle on it. He fought to control his breathing and his rapidly beating heart as he aimed at a head two hundred yards up the hill. The marksmanship of the average Republican soldier was appalling, not helped by their ancient weaponry, much of which dated from the previous century. But Conrad's rifle was a new German-made Mauser K98k that he had lifted a few months before from a legless Fascist soldier groaning on the battlefield at the Jarama River, and Conrad knew how to use it. There was no wind, but he allowed for range, and pressed the trigger. The head jerked backwards and disappeared.

'Come on!' David, who was squatting down beside him, set off up the hill. He had covered barely five yards when he was hit. In the back. He was thrown forward and landed on his face. Conrad crawled over to his friend. The bullet had gone through the heart; David was dead. Conrad turned towards Harry to tell him to watch out, but he was too late. Harry was lying a few yards away, face pressed down against the hard earth, his back a bloody mess.

Conrad pulled himself to his feet and began a crouching run. He felt a bullet tear into his upper arm; there was a flash of pain and then numbness. That bullet too had come from behind. He turned and darted back towards the boulder, throwing himself down on the side facing the enemy. All around him the remaining soldiers from the British Battalion stormed the hill.

Conrad peered around the stone back towards the Popular Army brigade's lines. Fear and adrenalin had turned to fury. If he had had his own machine gun he would have turned it on the Spanish brigade and blasted them to hell. Harry and David were two noble, brave men, who had given up their lives for Spain, to save Spain from fascism, and this was the thanks they had received.

But Conrad didn't have a machine gun, only a rifle. And it wasn't just the Republican Spanish who were firing. Nationalist machine guns were raking the hillside and their mortars were dropping shells around Conrad. Then, over the crash and crack of the battlefield, he heard the sound that the International Brigade had grown to dread. Aircraft engines.

Three aircraft, German Messerschmitts from the Condor Legion, flew low over the hill, strafing the attacking infantry; they had already knocked out all the Republican tanks. The Germans and Italians had won control of the skies over Brunete, which made the assault on Mosquito Hill even more foolhardy.

The attack faltered, and Conrad saw his comrades first dive to the ground and then try to make their way back to their own lines. Those that could move, that is. Many lay still on the mountainside, others groaned and screamed in pain and fear.

Conrad raised his head above the stone, preparing to sprint back down the hill. A rifle bullet ricocheted off the rock. In the midst of the battle, the Spanish brigade had a sniper zeroed in on him, someone with a rifle as good as his.

The Messerschmitts wheeled around for another run.

Stuck on the open flank of that hill, his face pressed against the hot earth, Conrad realized he had a choice of how he could die: a Nationalist machine gun from up the hill, a Republican sniper from below, a German aeroplane from the sky, or, if he was really lucky, one of the International Brigade's own machine-gun units lined up just behind the lines to catch any deserters. And if by some miracle the war didn't kill him, it would destroy his soul, just as it had destroyed the souls of so many of the men on both sides blasting away at each other all around him.

A few months before, while defending Madrid, Conrad would have been willing to die for the cause he believed in so passionately.

But no longer.

He had to get out of there. Not just from behind the boulder, but from Brunete, from Madrid, from Spain, from the whole damned war.

PART ONE

June 1938

One

It was still possible to have fun in Berlin, even in 1938. You could go out to a nightclub, you could drink champagne, speak of old times, drink more champagne, perhaps say more than you should. In more normal countries in more normal times the consequences of such a night might have been a sore head and apologies for the rash words of the night before. In Nazi Germany the consequence was death.

Conrad de Lancey was looking forward to the evening. He had arrived by train from the Hook of Holland that morning, dropped his things off at his hotel and spent the afternoon wandering from the former Imperial Palace past the grand buildings that lined Unter den Linden, through the Brandenburg Gate to the Tiergarten, where he had lost himself amongst the trees and ponds.

After a miserable year spent licking his wounds, he was glad to be out of England.

He had escaped from Mosquito Hill. Unable to go forward or back, he had run sideways, away from the Spanish brigade and towards the retreating Washington Battalion on his right. He had successfully mingled with the American walking wounded staggering back from the front. His luck held out when he managed to hitch a lift to Valencia with an outfit known as 'the Scottish Ambulance Unit', commanded by a formidable nurse wearing a voluminous tartan kilt. From there he stowed away on a ship bound for Marseilles. A week later, his arm in a sling, he was back in Oxford.

He had hoped to return to his old life: his unfinished thesis, his pretty cottage in Manor Road and his beautiful wife. But he came home to find Veronica gone and everything changed. As autumn became winter, the cottage, which Veronica had professed 'divine' when she had moved in, and 'a pokey hovel' when she had moved out, had become a damp, chilly rebuke, a daily reminder of warmer, happier times.

When Veronica had first left him, Conrad had felt shocked, numb. After a couple of weeks the numbness had been replaced by a slow, burning anger. He had tried to ignore it, to pretend it wasn't there. Whenever his friends or his family tried to speak to him about her, he parried with finely honed banalities.

Spain hadn't helped – those memories of the rotting corpses of his comrades on Mosquito Hill, of the desperate faces of the bombed-out orphans of Madrid and above all of the cruel betrayal of the idealistic young workers by the commissars and the politicians which had led to bullets in the backs of Harry and David. A noble cause had been corrupted into a hell of violence, cruelty and death.

Back in Oxford, he tried to work on the thesis for his D.Phil., about Prussia's war with Denmark in 1864. This little war, which had comprised two campaigns of a few weeks each, had eaten up four years of his own life, and he was sick of it. Oxford was damp and miserable without Veronica. When one morning in December Conrad had spied an advertisement in *The Times* for a teacher at a prep school in the depths of Suffolk, on a whim he had applied.

He was there for the beginning of the Lent term in January, covering for a member of staff who had been badly injured in a car smash. He laid low for a term and a half, not seeing anyone, his family, his friends and certainly not Veronica. He enjoyed teaching small boys French and Latin, and the isolation helped. But when the teacher he was covering for returned to school for the second half of the summer term, Conrad turned down the headmaster's offer of a permanent position.

For almost a year he had ignored all those issues that had been so important to him that he had risked his life for them: peace and war, socialism and fascism, the disaster that was engulfing Europe. But he had had enough of skulking in the lanes and water meadows of Suffolk. He decided it was time to face up to what was happening in the world.

So he bought a one-way ticket to Berlin.

It was a warm night, but unlike London, which had been shrouded in low grey cloud when Conrad had left Liverpool Street station the previous day, the air here was fresh and clean. Even at this hour the Kurfürstendamm was busy; tall blue-uniformed traffic policemen expertly marshalled the cars, trams and buses swishing along the street. It had only just got dark, and the pavements were alive with people flitting in and out of the pools of light emanating from the shop fronts, cafés, restaurants, cinemas and theatres. Many wore uniforms: greenish-grey for the army, brown for the Party functionaries and black for the SS. Many didn't. All of them had a sense of urgency, a sense of purpose.

Conrad paused under a street lamp to consult the note Joachim had sent to his hotel, including directions to the club. A young man, barely more than a boy, wearing a sharp suit and a thin moustache was leaning against an iron poster column a few feet away. He hissed something to Conrad under his breath. Conrad smiled politely and went back to his note. Just then a fashionably dressed lady approached, sniffing loudly. The youth smiled and the two disappeared. Clearly some transaction had occurred or was about to occur, but Conrad wasn't entirely sure what it was.

With a jolt he noticed the advertisement revealed on the poster column, a grotesque caricature of a man with a beard and a hooked nose, holding out a handful of coins and grasping a map of Germany under his arm. It was advertising an exhibition called *Der Ewige Jude* – The Eternal Jew.

Conrad walked a few steps further along the Ku'damm and turned off along a side street. Within a few yards he came across an illuminated sign of a jolly-looking cockatoo. He descended the neon-lit stairs and plunged into a dark, warm atmosphere of smoke and alcohol, of music and chatter. The place was nearly full and, as Conrad scanned the crowd, he spotted Joachim at a table near the back. Conrad wound his way through the tables towards him and Joachim leaped to his feet, his face breaking into a broad grin as he held out his hand.

Conrad shook it warmly. His cousin was pudgier than when they had last met, and his slicked-back hair had thinned. He was dressed very properly in evening clothes, but his cheeks were shining and his white tie was slightly askew. Conrad noticed an open bottle of champagne on ice on the table, and he suspected it wasn't Joachim's first.

'I'm sorry I'm a little late,' said Conrad, in German.

'I've been here a while,' said Joachim, in English, with a grin. 'It is wonderful to be back in Berlin after freezing Moscow. I know these places are a bit tame, but there is enough of an atmosphere about them to remind me of the good old days.' Joachim's English was excellent, but his accent was unique: a mixture of Germanic precision and the affectation of a 1920s Oxford aesthete.

Conrad scanned the dance floor and was relieved to see that the couples dancing were of mixed sex. Conrad had visited the notorious Eldorado Club in Berlin with Joachim in 1929 at the tender age of eighteen. To say that he had been shocked would be an understatement. 'I imagine the Nazis have closed all your favourite old haunts.'

'Many of them,' said Joachim. 'But there are still some interesting places to go. You just have to know where to look. Have a glass of bubbles, old man. It's filthy stuff these days, I'm afraid, but you get used to it after a couple of glasses.'

Joachim Mühlendorf was Conrad's cousin, a diplomat in Germany's embassy in Moscow who was on a week's leave in Berlin. He was one of the few people with whom Conrad still corresponded, if only on an irregular basis, and when he had heard that Conrad's move to Berlin coincided with his own leave, he had cabled Conrad insisting that they meet. Conrad was happy to agree: Joachim was always good company.

Conrad's mother came from Hamburg, and after the war the de Lanceys had often visited her family there. Of all the cousins, Conrad and Joachim had got on best together. This surprised their parents: Conrad was athletic and a keen shot, while Joachim was pale and had a perennial cold. But Joachim was a voracious reader and had a sharp intellect, and it was this that had interested the younger cousin. Their friendship grew when Joachim came to stay with Conrad's family in London for a few months after an unexplained difficulty during his last year at his Prussian boarding school.

Joachim poured Conrad a glass of champagne. 'What brings you to Berlin? I thought you had dedicated your life to educating the inky-fingered.'

'Not my life, just a term and a half,' said Conrad. 'I wanted to come here and see what's happening. And perhaps write about it.'

'Write about it?'

'Yes. I did a couple of pieces for *Mercury* when I was in Spain, and they said they would be happy to take some more from Berlin.' Conrad hesitated. 'I also thought I'd try a novel.'

'Oh, like that chap Isherwood. I met him once, you know. A charming man.'

'Not exactly like him. It's about an Englishman in Berlin in 1914. The coming of the last war.'

'The war to end all wars?'

'Yes, that one,' said Conrad.

There was the other reason why Conrad was in Berlin, of course. And Joachim picked up on it.

'I was sorry to hear about Veronica.'

Conrad shrugged.

'It was such a shame I couldn't come to your wedding. I'd just been posted to Moscow so I couldn't get away. I would have loved to have met her. At one moment she sounded absolutely wonderful, the next a complete nightmare.'

Conrad smiled ruefully. 'I suppose she is both.' He was grateful for Joachim's sympathy, but he didn't want to talk about Veronica. At least not quite yet.

Joachim smiled in understanding. Then something caught his eye. He frowned and leaned forward. 'Don't look now, but there is a man behind your right shoulder staring at us. And I don't think it's because he wants to pick one of us up.'

Conrad didn't look. 'You think he's Gestapo or something? I suppose that's to be expected in Germany these days, isn't it? I am a foreigner, after all.'

'It's worse in Russia,' Joachim said. He stopped a passing waitress. 'A packet of cigarettes, please.'

When the waitress returned a moment later, he passed her a generous tip. 'Do you know that man over there, the one with the rabbit teeth? Is he a regular?'

The waitress looked up with the barest flick of her eyes. 'No, he hasn't been in before.' Then, understanding, she said: 'Don't worry, he can't overhear you. I have just served him: he's deaf.'

'Ah,' said Joachim. 'That's nice to know.'

Conrad looked around the club. The Kakadu was busy. A line of barmaids was frantically working at a large semi-circular bar to keep the customers supplied. Conrad smiled to himself as he noticed that they alternated between blonde and brunette, everything just so, everything in its proper pattern. A stunning blonde woman on the dance floor caught Conrad's attention. She was wearing a long figure-hugging evening gown with the rear cut away leaving her buttocks bare.

'I'm sure she'd dance with you if you asked her nicely,' Joachim said with a grin.

'Perhaps not this evening,' said Conrad. 'But it is a nice view.'

'I thought you'd like this place,' said Joachim. 'I met your friend here a couple of nights ago. Theo von Hertenberg.'

'I didn't know you were in touch with Theo!'

'I'm not really. That was the trouble. I've only met him through you, that time I visited you in Oxford, and then when you came to Berlin a couple of years later.'

Conrad smiled. 'I remember the Oxford visit and I'm sure Theo does. I will never forget you declaiming Goethe from my window in Front Quad. It was all I could do to stop you falling out.'

Joachim smiled. 'I was a little tight, wasn't I?'

'You were. You also weren't wearing very much.'

'It was a warm evening. I hope you didn't get into *too* much trouble on my account.'

Conrad had, but it was a long time ago. 'So why did you want to see Theo?'

'I had something I wanted to discuss with him, something

I'd heard in Moscow. Unfortunately, he brought a couple of girls along. Perfectly nice girls, but they rather got in the way of a frank discussion. Anyway, I seem to have offended him.'

'How?'

'I suppose I was a bit indiscreet. Hertenberg became quite huffy and more or less threw me out.'

'I'm sorry about that,' said Conrad.

Joachim shrugged. 'I *was* a little drunk. But I was speaking in English, and the girls didn't understand. I'm sure there was no one listening.'

'For all his enlightened ideas Theo is a Prussian at heart,' Conrad said. 'He disapproves of people behaving badly. He can't help it.'

Joachim leaned back in his chair. He carefully transferred the cigarettes from the packet the waitress had given him to a silver case engraved with the Mühlendorf family crest. The procedure complete, he offered one to Conrad before lighting one of his own.

'Do you trust him?' Joachim asked, looking closely at Conrad.

'Theo? Yes. Absolutely.' There was not a trace of doubt in Conrad's voice.

'Have you seen him recently?'

'Not for five years now. Not since I was over here in 1933. But we were very close at Oxford.' Theo was a Rhodes scholar, the first to arrive at Oxford from Germany since the war. Conrad and he had quickly become friends. It wasn't just that they shared a mixed heritage – Conrad's mother was German and Theo's grandmother American – nor that they both embraced the intellectual fashions of the time: the Labour Club, pacifism, home rule for India. They seemed to share the same view of the world, or at least they had seemed to then. Conrad was looking forward to seeing him in Berlin. Theo had always been a source of good-natured sanity; it would be interesting to see what he made of the insanity all around him. Besides, a night on the town with Theo was always fun.

'You know he has joined the army now?' Joachim said.

Conrad nodded. 'I know: he wrote to me a couple of years ago and mentioned he had joined the reserves. It seems quite unlike him.'

'It might have been a ploy to avoid signing up for the Nazi Party,' Joachim said. 'I tried that dodge myself, but the reserves wouldn't have me.' He tapped his chest. 'It's my heart. I get these palpitations.'

'So what did you do?'

Joachim shrugged. 'I became a Party member. I had to if I wanted to become a diplomat.'

Conrad couldn't help showing his surprise. Joachim had been a convert to Marxism in the 1920s, several years before it was fashionable in England.

'Don't look so shocked,' said Joachim. 'It doesn't mean anything.'

'Of course it means something,' said Conrad. 'How can you be a member of such a vile organization, even if it is just for the convenience of your career? That's a terrible reason.'

'You're quite right, Conrad,' Joachim said. 'I am a morally corrupted individual who deserves every ounce of your disapproval. But the question is not am I a Nazi, but is Theo one?'

'I doubt it very much,' said Conrad. 'I haven't seen him for years, but he was my closest friend at the university. His views on right and wrong are deeply entrenched. I would be very surprised if he had become a Nazi, a genuine one.' Although when Conrad had spent a month in Berlin in the spring of 1933 just after the Nazis had come to power, Theo had seemed complacent about Hitler. To Conrad's disgust he had said that someone had to bring order back to the country; it was just a pity the new Chancellor was so common and vulgar. As far as Conrad was concerned, the least of Hitler's sins was that he was 'common'. But Conrad couldn't conceive of Theo as a follower of the man.

'That's good to hear,' said Joachim. 'I had made up my mind in Moscow that Theo was the right person to speak to once I got here. After the other night, I thought perhaps I was wrong. But if I trust anyone, I trust you, and if you think he's all right...'

A group of three girls squeezed past their table. One of them, a tall brunette with a suggestive swing of her hips, paused to ask Conrad for a light. As he obliged, she murmured her thanks, dark eyes under long lashes briefly meeting his, and joined her friends at a table not too far away.

'I'm impressed. It's good to see married life hasn't dulled your talents,' Joachim said.

Conrad ignored him. 'Anyway, what did you want to talk to Theo about?'

'Have you heard of General von Fritsch?

'Yes. He was commander-in-chief of the army, wasn't he? Resigned a couple of months ago. Ill health or something?'

Joachim snorted. 'They accused him of being born on the seventeenth of May.'

Conrad frowned. 'I don't understand.'

'Seventeen five. Article 175 of the Penal Code.'

'Is that the one dealing with homosexuality?'

'The very same,' said Joachim. 'I know it well. But the Gestapo were framing him. They had an elaborate story about him picking up a male prostitute at the Potsdamer Station. There was a secret trial in March and von Fritsch was acquitted, but he resigned anyway. I understand that the army is still very upset about it.'

'I never heard about that.'

'Of course not,' said Joachim. 'But it caused quite a stir in the army, or so I am told.'

'And that's what you were talking to Theo about?'

'That. And something else I heard in Moscow, something even more interesting.'

Conrad raised his eyebrows.

'Oh, look, he's leaving,' said Joachim. The deaf man with the rabbit teeth was indeed on his way out of the club. 'I'm glad he's gone. Look, Conrad, are you planning to see Hertenberg over the next few days?'

Conrad nodded. 'I was intending to get in touch with him tomorrow, in fact.'

'Could you do that? And when you do, could you tell him I'm sorry about the other night and I really must speak to him before I go back to Moscow next week. Tell him I have some friends who can help him.'

'Help him do what?'

'He'll know what I mean. Please. It's terribly important.'

Conrad examined his cousin closely. He thought Joachim and Theo made unlikely conspirators, a view that seemed to be shared by Theo. But it clearly mattered to his cousin, and Theo could make up his own mind whether he wanted to speak to Joachim. 'All right,' he said. 'I will.'

'Thanks, old man.' He refilled Conrad's glass.

'Now. Tell me about Veronica. You said in your letters it was all a little unexpected.'

'That's an understatement.'

'You do have a tendency to understate these kind of things,' Joachim said.

Conrad smiled. 'I do, don't I?'

'It's all very well keeping a stiff upper lip, but if it was me who was walked out on, I would be furious.'

Conrad glanced at his cousin. He hadn't spoken to anyone properly about Veronica. He told himself and others when they asked that he didn't want to burden them. But Joachim had shared so many of his own confidences with Conrad when they were younger.

'Actually, it wasn't much fun,' he began.

Joachim was a good listener. Conrad must have been talking for ten minutes when he became aware of two shapes hovering over the table. Two men looked down at them, both wearing leather trench coats and gloves.

'Herr Mühlendorf?'

Joachim's eyes widened in fear when he recognized who they were. 'Y-yes?'

'My name is Kriminal Assistant Dressel of the Geheime Staatspolizei,' said one of the men. He had a hard, pinched face, close-cropped red hair and freckles. 'We would like you to accompany us.'

'Where to?'

'You will find out,' said Dressel. 'And you,' he said to Conrad.

'But I am a British citizen,' said Conrad.

'May I see your papers, please?' The Gestapo officer held out a gloved hand, his face impassive.

Conrad was aware of people at the neighbouring tables staring at them. The band was playing on resolutely, but aside from the music, the chatter in the club had died down to a murmur.

Conrad reached into the inside pocket of his dinner jacket and handed the man his passport. There was something immensely reassuring about the stiff blue document with its gold coat of arms and its demand on the inside page that His Britannic Majesty requested and required that foreigners keep their hands off his subjects.

Reassuring for Conrad, but not for Joachim. His cousin was sitting frozen at the table. There was still fear in his eyes, but also determination. Conrad saw his glance flick towards a door at the back of the club, only a few feet away. Despite their fearsome reputation, Conrad was pretty sure that the Gestapo would not risk harming him, a foreigner. But Joachim with his gossip about wayward generals? His best, his only chance of escape was in the next few seconds.

And it was up to Conrad to give him that chance.

The gloved fingers flicked through the pages clumsily. 'You speak German very well.'

'Thank you,' said Conrad, although it was more of an accusation than a compliment. Also he had only said a couple of words.

Dressel thought for a moment. 'You come with us.'

This was his chance. Conrad pulled himself to his feet, knocking over the chair behind him. 'I beg your pardon,' he said, drawing himself to his full height so that he looked down on the Gestapo officer. 'I will do no such thing.'

The man stared at Conrad. 'You look like a spy. You sound like a spy. You are coming with us.'

'This is outrageous!' said Conrad. 'I don't know what you think Herr Mühlendorf has done, but I can assure you he is a man of the utmost integrity. And as for myself, I am a British citizen! I demand...' He paused, shaking, switching up a gear from outraged Englishman to furious German. 'I demand that you contact my embassy at once! At once, do you hear!' He snatched his passport back from Dressel's fingers.

Dressel's colleague reached out and placed a glove on Conrad's sleeve. Conrad angrily shook it off. 'Take your filthy hands off me!' he shouted, and pushed the Gestapo officer hard in the chest so that he took a step backwards. Dressel grabbed Conrad's other arm and Conrad shoved him too. Conrad saw out of the corner of his eye a pistol bearing down on his skull. He managed to duck so that it only caught him a glancing blow, but it was enough to send him to his knees.

He heard a bang, and he and the two Gestapo officers turned to see the back door to the club swing open. Joachim had gone.

'After him!' snapped Dressel, and the two men rushed for the door, leaving Conrad on his knees in a pool of spilled champagne.

Smiling, Conrad pulled himself to his feet. He touched his temple, which was wet with blood, but the dizziness in his brain was already clearing. He stumbled for the front entrance, the other patrons staring after him open-mouthed, the waiters making no attempt to stop him. He spilled out into the warm night air and climbed the steps to the street. A green van was parked directly outside the club and he could hear the sound of running feet to his left. Without looking that way he turned right and walked hurriedly down the street.

He had gone about ten yards when he heard the sound he was dreading: 'Halt!'

He kept moving, but then there was a sharp crack and the whine of a bullet as it ricocheted off a lamp-post in front of him. The sound brought back the dusty battlefields of Spain. He stopped, turned and raised his hands.

Dressel ran up to him, panting and waving a pistol. 'Now you are coming with me!'

He was handcuffed, shoved down the street and bundled into the back of the green van. Fifteen minutes later he was dragged out on to the pavement beside a grandiose grey Wilhelmine building. There was no sign advertising what lay within, but Conrad could see a number eight beside the imposing entrance.

It was 8 Prinz-Albrecht-Strasse, the headquarters of the Gestapo.

Two

The entrance hall was a large room with a vaulted ceiling and high domed windows, watched over by two SS guards and a pair of crimson swastika banners. As Conrad climbed the stairs he was told to keep to the wall with his escort on the outside, presumably so that he wouldn't throw himself over the banisters. On the third floor he was taken along a corridor and shown into a tiny waiting room. He sat on a bench, and a tall guard took a seat beside him. He waited.

Exhilaration that Joachim had escaped faded. Now Conrad was inside their notorious headquarters, his initial certainty that the Gestapo would have to release him untouched seemed optimistic. He had no idea what the Gestapo would do to him; he tried to dismiss images of torture chambers and concentration camps from his mind.

He pulled himself together. It was Joachim they wanted, not him. He was innocent, he was no spy; they would release him – as long as he could maintain an aura of confidence. He would deny everything, and they would have to let him go. After all, His Britannic Majesty requested and required it.

At least Joachim was free.

After about three-quarters of an hour a large, ungainly man appeared, wearing steel-rimmed spectacles and a scruffy, ill-fitting suit. 'Herr de Lancey?' he said to Conrad, holding out his hand.

'Yes.' Conrad rose to his feet and shook it.

'My name is Kriminalrat Schalke.' He smiled. It was a strange, lop-sided grin, which exuded what seemed to be genuine friendliness. 'Come through.'

Conrad followed Schalke into an office, or rather interview room. Schalke sat on one side of the desk and Conrad sat on a chair a few feet back on the other. A female stenographer came in and settled herself at a machine on a table just behind Conrad.

Schalke leaned back, smiled and opened his hands. 'Herr de Lancey. It was very foolish of you to assault two of my officers.'

'I know,' said Conrad. 'And I am sorry.' The time for uncontrolled histrionics was over; he needed to be cooler now. 'But they were arresting me without cause. I objected. I still object.'

Schalke smiled again, that appealing uneven grin. 'Without cause? Surely the cause is obvious.' The man had the slow adenoidal twang of a Saxon, Conrad noticed. He also had a very slight stutter.

'Not to me,' said Conrad.

'You were discussing a plot to overthrow the Führer with a member of our diplomatic corps.'

'I was doing no such thing,' said Conrad. He made no attempt to hide his surprise.

'You were. Our man saw you.'

'The man with the buck teeth? The man who was pretending to be deaf? He was too far away, even if he could hear.'

'Oh, he wasn't pretending,' Schalke said. 'He is deaf. He's an accomplished lip-reader.'

Schalke smiled again.

'In that case he will know that we didn't discuss Hitler at all,' Conrad said.

'But you did discuss General von Fritsch.'

'We did.' A thought occurred to Conrad. 'Does your man speak English? Or rather lip-read in English? It must be very difficult to lip-read in a foreign language.'

Schalke seemed to accept Conrad's point. 'So, what did Herr Mühlendorf tell you?'

'I demand that you let me go,' Conrad said as evenly as possible. 'I'm a British citizen. I demand to see someone from the embassy.'

'I think you are a spy,' said Schalke, reasonably. 'It is quite possible to be a British citizen and a spy.'

'I am no such thing!'

'Then why were you discussing a plan to overthrow the Führer? And for that matter why do you speak such perfect German?'

'I am good at languages,' Conrad said.

'Very good,' Schalke said. He picked up Conrad's passport and opened it. 'It says here you were born in Hamburg. The seventh of March 1911.'

'That's true,' Conrad admitted. 'My mother is German: Joachim Mühlendorf is my cousin. But the family moved to Britain in 1914.'

Schalke frowned. 'A family of traitors.'

Conrad ignored the insult.

'And what is this? The *Hon.* Conrad William Giles de Lancey?'

'My father is a peer. A viscount.'

'Noble traitors.' Schalke put the passport down. 'Will you tell me what you and your cousin were discussing?'

'No. Absolutely not.'

'And who is Johnnie von Herwarth?'

'I have no idea.'

There was silence as the Gestapo officer studied Conrad through his wire-rimmed glasses. His blue eyes were not cold or cruel, but intelligent, warm, almost friendly. Conrad sat in silence. Then the big man rose to his feet. 'Joachim Mühlendorf was brought in ten minutes ago. He didn't get far; they caught him hiding behind some dustbins. A cat gave him away, a good National Socialist cat.' Schalke laughed at his little joke, a high-pitched giggle that seemed incongruous coming from such a large man. 'Some of my colleagues are just making him comfortable now. You can wait in here while I go and ask him some questions. I am sure he will be more forthcoming than you. An hour or two of intensive interrogation should suffice.'

'I demand that you inform the British Embassy of my presence here!' Conrad called after the man's back as he left the room. The stenographer rapidly typed out these last words and then followed her boss.

After all that, they had caught Joachim! Conrad shuddered as he thought of what his cousin would be going through somewhere else in the building. Joachim wasn't exactly tough. Once the Gestapo put pressure on him, he would talk, Conrad was sure of that. And after he had talked, there was not much Conrad could do for him.

He thought about his own interrogation. Would they torture him? If they did, what kind of torture would they use? How good was his protection as a British citizen?

He had no idea who on earth Johnnie von Herwarth was, nor about a plot to overthrow Hitler. If that was what Joachim had discussed with Theo at the Kakadu, no wonder Theo had been concerned. He just hoped that the Gestapo would believe in his own ignorance.

And what about Joachim's message to Theo, that he wanted to see him and that he had friends who could help him? Joachim was hardly tough: if his cousin cracked under interrogation, which was very likely, he would tell the Gestapo all about it.

Conrad decided there was no point in denying the message if it was raised by the Gestapo, but he wouldn't volunteer the information until that point.

It sounded as if Theo himself would be in trouble pretty soon and there was not much Conrad could do about it.

Conrad had been loath to tell the Gestapo who his father was, he always hated to do that, but in this case, once they realized his father was not just a peer of the realm but a former Cabinet minister, they would have to release him. Wouldn't they? The key thing was to convince them that he was not a spy.

Because if he failed, there would only be one outcome. Somewhere he had read that they beheaded spies in Germany.

As Klaus Schalke walked along the familiar corridor from one interrogation room to the other, he considered the British prisoner. He had not expected a full and frank explanation; there would be plenty of time to extract that. What he had been seeking in the interview was a preliminary assessment of the man. He discounted the bluster: it disguised a calm intelligence. De Lancey could be a spy. His fluency in German and his mother's background would be convenient for an agent.

There would be time enough to find out. For the moment he had to consider Mühlendorf. He paused outside the interview room. Inside he could hear grunts and muffled screams. Unlike most of his colleagues, Klaus did not enjoy the physical aspects of interrogation. Despite his size, he was not particularly strong, and he was known more for his clumsiness than usefulness with his fists. That was Dressel's talent.

When he had first joined the Gestapo Klaus had avoided interrogations and focused on the organization and collation of information, something at which he excelled. For this he had been appreciated, not least by Reinhard Heydrich, the head of the Gestapo, who understood that the organization's effectiveness relied on its ability to gather information about any and all of its citizens, not its skills in beating them senseless.

But it was impossible to steer clear of the interrogations altogether, and, much to his surprise, Klaus found that he was quite effective at conducting them. Not only that, but he enjoyed them. It wasn't the blood and the screaming and the broken bones that pleased him, although he was getting used to that, it was the feeling of power. To see someone who had been in a position of authority – a university professor, a civil servant, a policeman, a priest – sitting before him steady and dignified, to assess him, to identify his weak spot, to press hard on that weak spot until the man was cowering in front of him, debasing himself in any way he could think of to make Klaus like him, gave Klaus a thrill that was almost sexual.

Mühlendorf should not be difficult. They had a fair amount of information on him, from the Gestapo informers in the embassy in Moscow, from sources in Berlin and also from Department II-H, which dealt with homosexual affairs. Meisinger, the Kriminalrat in charge of the department, had given Klaus some useful information. These pansies were usually easy to break. Often they were accomplished gossips who knew a lot and were eager to impart that knowledge to avoid a concentration camp. Klaus could see no reason why Mühlendorf should be any different. Which was why he had brought him in.

The noises in the interview room had ceased and Klaus walked in. Joachim was lying on the floor, groaning. A strong light from the desk illuminated him. His face was pale and there was blood on his cheek, but from that angle Klaus could not see how much damage had been done to him. Klaus glanced at Dressel, who had been assisted by two muscular black-uniformed sadists. Dressel shook his head; the prisoner had not yet said anything of interest. Klaus and Dressel had a good working relationship. Dressel enjoyed beating the shit out of prisoners, but never went too far. He knew of Klaus's squeamishness, but he was careful not to comment on it: he was intelligent enough to realize that Klaus was rising fast in the Gestapo hierarchy.

Klaus seated himself at the desk. 'Get up, please, Herr Mühlendorf,' he said quietly.

The man on the ground groaned and hauled himself up on one elbow to stare at Klaus. He blinked; the light was too bright for him to see his interrogator properly. The two uniformed thugs lifted him to his feet and pushed him backwards on to the chair. He screamed as his backside touched the seat, and tried to stand, but the guards forced him down again. Unseen by the guards, Klaus winced. Why was it that when dealing with homosexuals these men could not leave their prisoners' arses alone?

'You may stand if it is more comfortable,' Klaus said.

The prisoner stood up. They had stripped off his tailcoat, but his white bow tie still hung loose around his neck: one half of it now soaked a deep red. His face was a mess. Nose broken, blood streaming down his upper lip, which was split, and a front tooth missing. It almost made Klaus sick to look at him.

Klaus glanced down at the Department II-H file in front of him.

'Now, Mühlendorf, on the fifteenth of March 1936 do you remember meeting a man known as Bayern Seppl in the Viktoriapark at about ten-fifteen at night?'

'That's a long time ago,' the prisoner replied, his words slurred by the split lip. 'I can't possibly remember what I was doing on that day.'

'Let me make it easier for you,' said Klaus. 'It was your second night in Berlin on leave from Moscow. Does that help?'

Joachim hesitated, and then spoke quietly. 'I didn't know that was his name, but I do remember that meeting.'

'And did you indulge in unnatural acts of a homosexual nature with Bayern Seppl?' Klaus asked. According to Meisinger's file, he had been spotted by a former male prostitute and blackmailer who had been happy to talk.

Joachim nodded. 'Yes, I did.'

Klaus smiled to himself. This was going to be easy. He ran through three other hurried liaisons that Joachim had been involved in during his brief periods of leave from the Moscow embassy. Klaus had to admire Meisinger's thoroughness. Joachim denied none of them.

'Excellent,' said Klaus. 'Now, tell me about this plot to overthrow the Führer.'

Joachim licked some blood from his split lip. 'Certainly. I heard a rumour in Moscow that a plot was afoot. I was curious, so when I returned to Berlin, I asked my friends.'

'I see,' said Klaus. 'And from whom did you hear this rumour?'

'From Vassily Dashkov in the Soviet Foreign Office.'

'Not from Johann von Herwarth?'

'No. Certainly not. I never discussed the matter with him.'

'Do you have any details about this plot? Who would be involved?'

'None,' said Joachim. 'And I don't know who would be involved. The army, presumably, upset by the way the Gestapo set up General von Fritsch.'

'General von Fritsch was not set up by the Gestapo,' Klaus corrected him.

'Forgive me,' said Joachim. 'Of course not.'

'Who in the army?'

'I have no idea,' said Joachim. 'That was why I was asking Hertenberg the other night. I thought he might know something, but if he did, he wouldn't tell me.'

'What are the army planning to do?'

'Once again, I have no idea.'

Klaus raised his eyebrows. 'You realize that given what you have admitted about your activities over the last few years, we can place you in "protective custody" for violating Article 175 of the Reich Penal Code?'

'Protective custody' was the legal mechanism whereby the Gestapo could lock someone up without formally charging him. The fiction was that the suspects had to be taken into custody to prevent them from committing future crimes. The prisons of the Third Reich were full of convicted criminals, the concentration camps with citizens in protective custody. All in all it was probably better to be a convicted criminal.

'I know that,' said Joachim, somehow managing to inject a note of defiance in his voice.

Klaus was puzzled. This was not going as he had expected. By now Joachim should have been willing to cut a deal. He should have been eagerly explaining exactly who had told him what, and probably throwing in some useful titbits for Meisinger's files at the same time.

But he wasn't doing that. He was holding out. And from the look of defiance on his face he would hold out for some time longer. He was hiding something – something more than a rumour, Klaus was sure of it.

Klaus asked more questions, about the Moscow embassy, about the rumoured plot against Hitler, about Johnnie von Herwarth, about General von Fritsch, about Conrad de Lancey, about Theo von Hertenberg, with no result. The guards on either side of Joachim were itching to hit him again, but they knew Klaus wouldn't let them, at least not yet.

Klaus realized the time had come to exert more pressure. 'Can you swim, Mühlendorf?'

'Yes,' the prisoner answered cautiously.

'Excellent. Have you ever found yourself in trouble – you know, out at sea, or in the middle of a large lake far from the shore?'

'No.' Still cautious.

'So you don't know what it's like to drown?'

'No,' said Joachim, and Klaus thought that he caught just a hint of fear.

'Well, now's the time to find out.' He signalled to the guards, who dragged a metal bathtub over to the prisoner. It was heavy – it was full of water.

They stripped off Joachim's blood-spattered dress shirt exposing a flabby, battered torso, and forced him to kneel over the tub.

Klaus moved around the desk until he was standing over him. 'Look at me!' he commanded.

The guard pulled back Joachim's hair so that they were staring at each other. Klaus saw hatred, defiance, and that hint of fear. Good. He nodded to the guards, who plunged Joachim's head into the water for about thirty seconds. When they pulled him out, Klaus shouted a question: 'Who else is involved in this plot?'

Joachim gasped for air, but before he had a chance to answer he was back under water. This was repeated three times, until they paused to allow Klaus to shout more questions. Joachim coughed and spluttered but didn't answer.

Next he was under for a minute at a time. At the third plunging he swallowed water. Still no answer. Now two minutes, longer than a man in Joachim's state could possibly hold his breath.

He writhed, stiffened, bubbles rose to the surface and then he went still.

'Get him out,' Klaus ordered. He wasn't worried; this was all part of the procedure. The guards lay Joachim on the ground and began mouth-to-mouth resuscitation. It didn't usually take long to revive a prisoner, and once he had drowned once he was normally reluctant to drown again.

The guard was blowing hard into Joachim's lungs. After half a minute or so, he glanced up at Dressel. 'There's something wrong.'

Dressel knelt beside Joachim and felt his chest. No movement in the lungs. Then he grabbed his wrist and frantically searched for a pulse. He glared at the guard. 'You fool! His heart has stopped. Find a doctor!'

Conrad waited. And waited. He imagined Joachim cowering behind some bins in an alley, the wail of the cat, the discovery. It had probably been foolish to help Joachim escape, but he had had at least to try. Now he would have to face the consequences.

But it was Joachim who would be suffering at that very moment. For nothing more than spreading gossip. Conrad felt a flash of anger. His cousin was harmless; he wasn't a threat to the Nazi state, he couldn't be. But the Nazi machine of brutality and violence would grind him up like so many of its other weak and innocent citizens.

At last he heard footsteps in the corridor, and prepared him–self for the next stage of his interrogation. It was Dressel, the red-haired officer who had arrested him, and he looked harassed. 'Come with me,' he said and, accompanied by two guards, led Conrad along the corridor and down some back stairs to the basement.

Conrad shivered. It was noticeably colder down here. By this time it was late; he wasn't sure how late because they had taken his watch. He was led along a brick corridor lined with cells from which emanated snores, muttering and groans. Dressel paused outside an open door.

'Get in!' he commanded.

'You can't lock me up,' Conrad said. 'I demand to see someone from the embassy. Have you even informed them that I'm here?'

'In!' he repeated, and shoved Conrad through the door. The guard slammed it behind him.

Conrad looked around the small room. A table, a chair, a wooden bunk without blankets, a high tiny window at ground level with the world outside and a single light bulb burning from the ceiling.

Conrad began to pace. The British Embassy was only round the corner and a couple of hundred yards up Wilhelmstrasse, but it felt as if it was on another continent. No one would even know he was there. The hotel would probably inform the police if he didn't return in the morning. A fat lot of good that would do. Theo knew he was coming to Berlin, but it would take a few days for him to wonder why Conrad had not been in touch. Only Joachim knew where he was. Conrad shuddered. Poor Joachim.

Some graffiti caught his eye, scratched into the wall. 'This is a murder cellar' and 'Down with Hitler'. Conrad wondered where the writers of those words were now. Were they dead? Or were they in one of those mysterious concentration camps, which were the subject of so much speculation and rumour?

As the night wore on he tried to suppress his fear. Spies in Germany were beheaded, he knew. But he wasn't a spy. All he had to do was convince the Gestapo of it. He quit pacing, and lay down on his bunk, still dressed in the dinner jacket he had worn to the Kakadu, huddled into a ball against the cold.

It reminded him of those nights in Spain before an offensive, lying awake on the cold ground, trying not to think of the battle the following day, of the risk of death or, worse, of being horribly maimed. He could almost smell the thyme. He had developed his own brand of optimistic fatalism back then, a belief that whatever would be would be, but that *he* was going to survive, whatever the odds against it. It might have been illogical, but it had worked. He couldn't banish the fear. All his comrades were afraid: fear was good; fear sharpened the senses and quickened the legs. But some men had gone beyond fear; they were the ones with death in their eyes, and they never lived more than a few days.

Sometime in the small hours he heard steps along the corridor and the sound of someone or something being dragged. Was it Joachim? Then the voice cursed in a coarse Berlin accent. It wasn't Joachim, but some other poor blighter. There was the sound of a blow, a cry and then a cell door clanged shut.

Half an hour later, more footsteps, rapid this time, purposeful, coming down the corridor towards his cell. As they neared, he heard a voice he recognized. He sat up on his bed to face the door.

It was flung open, and there, erect in the smart field-grey uniform of a lieutenant of the Wehrmacht, stood the familiar figure of Theo von Hertenberg.

Three

'Thank God you're here,' said Conrad. He should have known that it would be Theo and not the British Embassy who would rescue him.

'Be quiet!' Theo shouted. Behind him were two uniformed guards and Dressel. 'Follow me!'

Conrad was taken upstairs, his black bow tie, his watch, his passport, keys and wallet returned to him. All this time Theo ignored him, but went through the paperwork of his release with Dressel, who seemed distinctly unhappy. Within a few minutes they were out on the street.

'Get into my car,' Theo ordered. A sleek silver Horch convertible was waiting on the opposite side of the street from the Gestapo HQ.

Conrad did as he was bid, and Theo pulled away. It was only when they were a good way down Wilhelmstrasse that Theo relaxed. 'Sorry about all that shouting,' he said. 'I needed to humour these Gestapo boys: they like that kind of thing. Are you all right?'

'Yes. Yes, I am.'

'Did they hurt you?'

'No. They didn't touch me. Got a cigarette?'

Driving with one hand, Theo fumbled in the pocket of his uniform with the other for a cigarette case. Conrad took it gratefully and lit up. He hadn't seen Theo for five years, but his friend had changed little, at least physically. He was tall and slim with delicate, high cheekbones and a rather long pointed nose; even the fine duelling scar along his jawline seemed to have been carefully crafted rather than slashed. There were small changes: his high forehead had become higher as his dark hair receded, and creases around his mouth had become lines. And of course he was wearing the uniform.

'Thank you,' said Conrad. 'I knew I would be glad to see you in Berlin, but I had no idea how glad.'

'It was lucky I was able to get there in time.'

'You know they've got Joachim Mühlendorf as well? Couldn't you spring him too?'

'I'm afraid Mühlendorf is dead, Conrad.'

'No!' Conrad was stunned. Torture he had expected. But not death. 'They... killed him?' He could barely take in what he had been told. 'I thought they might rough him up a bit, but not that. Don't they have trials and that kind of thing in this country any more?'

'He died of natural causes. A heart attack.'

'You don't believe that, do you?'

'Actually, I do. They were pretty angry about it. They had just started interrogating him and hadn't got anything out of him yet.'

'The poor devil.'

'I'm sorry, Conrad.'

They drove on in silence as Conrad struggled to absorb what had happened to his cousin. After all the death he had seen in Spain he should have become inured to it, but he wasn't. He wasn't at all.

Five minutes later the car pulled up on a dark road a few yards off the Tiergarten. It was dawn and the birds in the bushes and trees of the park were making a racket. Conrad checked his watch: a quarter to five.

'Whisky or breakfast or both?' Theo asked.

'First whisky and then breakfast,' said Conrad.

'Come on.' Theo led him in the side door of an imposing villa and up the stairs to his expensively furnished apartment. He poured Conrad a stiff whisky and went through to a small kitchen where he began to fry bacon and eggs.

Conrad gulped the whisky down, the spirit burning through his body. Joachim. Poor bloody Joachim.

The bacon sizzled. Theo, the army officer, looked faintly ridiculous wielding a frying pan.

'I can't get used to seeing you in uniform,' Conrad said.

'Don't knock it. If I wasn't wearing this, I wouldn't have been able to get you out.'

'But I don't understand *why* you are wearing it.'

'It seemed the best option,' Theo replied. 'I was trying to pass my law exams but it was made clear to me that that would be impossible unless I joined the Nazi Party. That I wasn't prepared to do. But if you're in the army, then you're exempted from joining the Party, so I did my training and became a reservist. And guess what? Last year they called me up. So now I am a lawyer in the War Ministry wearing a uniform.' Theo prodded the rashers of bacon. They smelled delicious: Conrad realized he was hungry. 'Anyway, you wore one in Spain, didn't you?'

Conrad snorted. 'A uniform would be overstating it,' he said. 'And that was a big mistake.'

Theo glanced at Conrad. 'I was surprised you went. You used to believe that war was wrong whatever the cause.'

'It seemed like a good idea at the time,' said Conrad. 'It wasn't.'

The uniform was so unlike Theo. It wasn't that Theo's background wasn't warlike. Far from it. Theo's family came from Pomerania, part of the old Kingdom of Prussia. Most of his ancestors had been officers in the Prussian army, from the von Hertenberg who had commanded a division under Frederick the Great at Rossbach in 1757, right down to his father who was promoted to major general after his exploits at Tannenberg in 1914. Theo himself had been a keen fencer when he was at the University of Heidelberg; he had been a member of the renowned Vandalen student corps, in which role he had sustained the duelling scar. But like so many of the other undergraduates of that time, when he arrived in Oxford as a Rhodes Scholar he consciously reacted against the values of his upbringing.

In the early 1930s Oxford was changing: Oxford bags were out; grey flannel trousers were in. The decadence of the bright young things of the twenties was giving way to a new, serious breed of undergraduate, dismayed at the poverty and unemployment they saw all around them and determined to do something about it. Which wasn't to say that Theo and Conrad hadn't drunk themselves stupid on many occasions; they had just done it after meetings of the Labour Club or lectures on Indian independence. At such times Theo had a tendency to muse on the poetry of Rainer-Maria Rilke or the philosophy of Hegel, musing which impressed some but which Conrad was convinced didn't quite make sense. But since Conrad had usually had a few drinks too, he couldn't prove it. Any of Theo's friends then, of whom there were a great many, would have been surprised to see him in the uniform of the Third Reich.

'How did you know I had been arrested?' Conrad asked.

'I got a call from a friend in the Gestapo.'

'I was afraid they would be after you. I'm sure Joachim must have told them about seeing you in the Kakadu the other night.'

'It's difficult to arrest serving army officers,' Theo said. 'Even for the Gestapo. Here you are.' He handed Conrad a plate, and they both sat at the small kitchen table.

'Mm,' said Conrad as he took his first mouthful. 'Thanks, Theo, this is wonderful.'

'So Mühlendorf told you about the evening in the Kakadu? He really made a fool of himself.'

'He more or less admitted that. He had a message he wanted me to pass on to you.'

'Which was?'

'Tell Hertenberg I'm sorry about the other evening. Tell him I must see him before I go back to Moscow and I have friends who can help him. He didn't say what his friends could help you with.'

'Or who they were?'

'No. What did he tell you in the Kakadu?'

'Oh, nothing, really. Just some wild rumours he had heard.'

'About a plot to remove Hitler?'

Theo frowned. 'Did he tell you that?'

'No, it was the Gestapo who asked me whether I knew anything about a plot.'

Theo's frown deepened.

'Is there anything in it?' Conrad asked.

'Of course not,' said Theo sharply. 'There are always rumours like that, spread by people with vivid imaginations who know nothing. People like Mühlendorf. First the SS is behind the conspiracy, then it's the army, then it's Göring or Goebbels or even the Kaiser. There's never anything in any of them.'

'What about Johnnie von Herwarth? Who is he?'

Theo leaned back in his chair and lit a cigarette. 'Conrad, it's really best if you forget all about what Mühlendorf said to you. There was nothing in it, it was just gossip, and he shouldn't have repeated any of it. He was indiscreet; it got him killed. Sadly, that happens in this country these days.'

'But why did he want to speak to you in particular?' Conrad persisted. 'He hardly knew you. He said something about deciding when he was in Moscow that you were the best person to talk to.'

'I don't think that's something you should worry about,' Theo said.

'He was my cousin, Theo. And he's dead. So I probably should worry about him.'

'I'm sorry he's dead, Conrad. But I had to vouch for you just now to the Gestapo. So, for my sake, forget all this happened. Don't talk to anyone in this country about it, either. And certainly don't write about it. Do you understand, Conrad? It's important.'

Conrad did understand. Germany was a dangerous place, even if you were a well-connected diplomat like Joachim. He had no idea what strings Theo had had to pull to get him released, and he had no desire to jeopardize Theo's safety. 'I imagine you had to go out on a limb for me, Theo. Thank you.'

Theo smiled. 'When you've finished that have a hot bath, and then bed.'

Conrad felt filthy and exhausted after the night's events. 'I will. Thanks, Theo.'

But even though he owed his freedom to Theo, he knew that he could not simply push what had happened to Joachim out of his mind.

Four

'Ashes to ashes, dust to dust.' The pastor repeated the familiar prayer in unfamiliar German words as he scattered earth on to the coffin six feet down in the frozen earth. Conrad hunched his shoulders in the stiff breeze that blew in from the Elbe, bringing with it stinging drops of rain. They were in the small, exclusive cemetery next to the small, exclusive church where Mühlendorfs had been christened, married and buried for generations.

A miserable day for a funeral.

Conrad closed his eyes and thought of the Joachim he had known since he was a boy. He could almost hear his cousin talking excitedly about the latest book he had read. Joachim had introduced Conrad to the adult realm of ideas with an enthusiasm and vigour that Conrad found impossible to resist. He didn't want to resist. Shakespeare and Goethe; Kant and Locke; Keats and Schiller; Newman and Luther; Bentham and Marx; Tolstoy, Dostoevsky and Balzac; Joyce, Kafka and Mann: they read them all and discussed them all. It was Joachim who had first lent Conrad the *Communist Manifesto*, and who ensured that when the socialist creeds swept Oxford University in 1930, Conrad was already well versed in the necessary texts.

Without Joachim, Conrad's life would have been different. Poorer.

The pastor's words stopped and Conrad opened his eyes. There were very few mourners there: a dozen members of

Joachim's family and no more than a half a dozen others, one of whom was Dressel, the Gestapo officer. The Mühlendorfs had tried to keep the ceremony a quiet family affair. They were ashamed of their son in life and even more ashamed of him in death.

The cognac flowed freely at the gathering afterwards in the tasteful Mühlendorf mansion, which clung to the wooded slopes of the hill above Blankenese, a former fishing village on the north bank of the Elbe. The conversation, following the tension at the graveside, was light and brittle, as was the laughter. Conrad would have cut the reception if he could, but he was duty bound to represent his mother, so he decided to stay for an hour, and then he would escape to the station and the train back to Berlin.

He felt a touch on his elbow. It was his uncle Manfred, a bulky man with a neatly trimmed, pointed beard. 'Let's get away from here,' he said, and he led Conrad out into the garden.

The rain had stopped, but the breeze was still blowing. Below them was the broad highway of the Elbe, dotted with ships big and small, old and new. Ship-owners like Manfred Mühlendorf enjoyed living here: they could watch their vessels moving back and forth to the great port of Hamburg, earning good money in front of their very eyes. A dark shower cloud was scudding in from the North Sea to the west, like a giant ball, rolling up the thin bars of sunlight reflecting off the river in front of it.

'You were a good friend to my son,' Uncle Manfred said, his voice catching. 'I always thought you were a good influence on him.'

'He was my cousin. And he was a good influence on me.'

'You know what I mean.'

'Yes, I know,' said Conrad. 'He was a brave man, at the end.'

'Brave?' said Uncle Manfred, puzzled.

'You know I was there when he was arrested?'

'Yes.'

'Well, he was arrested by the Gestapo because he was over-heard by one of their agents gossiping about a rumour he had picked up in Moscow. There was probably nothing in it. But they arrested him anyway and tortured him and he died.'

'But they said he was discovered in a well-known haunt for homosexuals with another man...'

'I know what they said, but that's not what happened. I was there. Do you believe me or do you believe them?'

Manfred looked closely at his nephew. 'I believe you.'

Conrad stopped and faced his uncle. Manfred Mühlendorf was a powerful man. 'So what are you going to do about it?'

'What do you mean?'

'I mean, are you going to let the state kill your son without kicking up a fuss?'

'What can I do?'

'I don't know,' said Conrad. 'But I do know that you can do something. It's only because people like you don't do anything that these bastards can get away with it.'

Uncle Manfred frowned, but he was listening.

'You have contacts in the government, don't you? This country has been turned into one great armaments factory. Your ships must carry some of that material.'

'They do. Quite a lot of it.'

'Then make a fuss, Uncle. Joachim was a brave man. He deserves it.'

As he sat on the train from Hamburg to Berlin staring out of the window over the endless North German Plain, Conrad wondered whether Manfred Mühlendorf would do something. He hoped he would. It would only be a gesture, he wouldn't be able to bring

Joachim back to life, but a gesture would be important. Conrad had known that the Third Reich was brutal: that was why he had come to Germany, to see that brutality at first hand. Well, in that he had succeeded. But he couldn't understand how the Germans had let this Third Reich emerge. He knew them well: they were a cultured, moral, law-abiding race. True, some of them had tendencies to militarism, but Marx and Engels were German, as were Bach and Beethoven, and Goethe and Rilke.

And now they were standing by and watching their country imprison, torture and kill their neighbours, their friends, even their children.

But what could they do? What could Conrad do? He had come to Germany to observe and to write, but now he wanted to *do* something, to show that he at least thought that Joachim's death was wrong, that it shouldn't go unnoticed, unpunished.

He thought about his cousin's last days. He was beginning to wonder whether Joachim's gossip had been entirely innocent. Joachim had sought out Theo, a man he scarcely knew, to tell him a rumour. Why Theo? Then there were Joachim's friends who were willing to help Theo. What friends? And help him do what?

Perhaps this mysterious Johnnie von Herwarth was one of these friends. And perhaps there was more to the plot to remove Hitler than Theo made out.

Theo clearly knew more than he had been prepared to tell Conrad. Also, Theo's contacts within the Gestapo seemed to be remarkably good. Conrad supposed that anyone in Germany could have a 'friend' in the Gestapo, but a friend who was willing to contact Theo at three o'clock in the morning?

It didn't make sense. Not Theo. If anyone could be trusted to keep his head in modern Germany, to keep a healthy distance from Nazism and all its vile ideas, it was Theo.

And how the hell had the Gestapo found out about Joachim's indiscretions in the first place?

It was the implication of that last question that bothered Conrad the most.

Klaus Schalke stepped out of the door of 8 Prinz-Albrecht-Strasse and walked the few metres around the corner to the Prinz-Albrecht-Palais on Wilhelmstrasse. This opulent building, which had served as the Berlin home of members of the Prussian royal family, was now the headquarters of the Sicherheitsdienst, or the SD, and housed the office of Reinhard Heydrich, who was head of both the SD and the Gestapo.

Klaus was apprehensive. Although he knew that he was one of Heydrich's favourites, he also knew he wasn't safe. Like most people, there were stretches of his past life that might appear unsound in the wrong light. No one in Nazi Germany was safe, not even members of the Gestapo.

It had been a bad week. Klaus was worried about his mother, usually so energetic, who had fallen ill yet again and hadn't been able to shake a general lassitude for a couple of months now. The doctor said there was nothing wrong with her but Klaus was sure there was. He didn't know what he would do if anything happened to her, anything... well... final. He knew he wouldn't be able to bear it.

Klaus hated his father: a small man, meticulous and nasty, who had resented his son's size and sloppiness, and had beaten him regularly. But his mother, bigger than his father, warm and loving, had always been there to comfort him. He couldn't imagine life without her.

He still had not received a reply to the carefully crafted letter he had sent the week before to his angel, the only other woman in his life, and he was beginning to fear that it would remain unanswered like all the others. He had really hoped that this time... but he was being foolish. As always.

And now this.

Klaus was sent straight into Heydrich's office. Heydrich was sitting at his desk studying a file Klaus recognized. '*Heil Hitler!*'

'Sit down, Schalke,' Heydrich snapped.

Klaus's fears were justified: his boss was not happy. As he did as he was bid, he somehow managed to trip over the edge of the rug in front of Heydrich's desk and lurched into the chair with a thump and an ominous sharp crack. Clumsy at the best of times, he seemed to find it impossible to control his limbs when he was nervous. He pushed his glasses back on to his nose and Heydrich's glare slipped into focus.

For someone in such a powerful position Heydrich was young: he had become head of the Gestapo at thirty and was still only thirty-four. He was tall with a high forehead, small restless eyes and full lascivious lips. He had long slender hands: he was an excellent violinist. Like Klaus, he had a disturbingly high voice. He exuded a unique aura of delicate violence. Unlike Klaus, women found him handsome, or at least those who liked their men with a hint of danger did.

There were several good reasons why Heydrich liked Klaus. Klaus understood the importance of information: of gathering it, of sifting it and of using it. And he was capable of finding ingenious solutions to difficult problems. In fact it was this skill that had brought Klaus to Heydrich's attention when Klaus was a junior lawyer in the Berlin prosecutor's department working on some of the Gestapo's cases.

Heydrich suffered from persistent rumours about his ancestry; his grandmother's name was Süss, which sounded Jewish. One of Heydrich's henchmen who knew Klaus's abilities also knew he had been to university in Halle, Heydrich's home town, and so asked him to help. At that time, when most of the professional classes had to show documentary evidence of their Aryan ancestry if they wanted to keep their jobs, forged documents were easy to procure. The Gestapo's plan was simply to forge the Süss grandmother out of existence. But Klaus advised against this: people who knew the Heydrich family in Halle knew about Frau Süss; denying her existence would simply leave the head of the Gestapo vulnerable to more rumour. Klaus's suggestion was to make an already complicated family situation more complicated. Of course Frau Süss existed, of course she was Heydrich's grandmother, but she had only taken the name Süss as a result of a second marriage to a locksmith, who anyway wasn't really Jewish. A couple of subtle alterations to documents were required, an ancient birth certificate was mislaid – nothing too blatant. The trickiest bit had been changing a date on a tombstone.

Heydrich was impressed. Not just with the idea, but with the mind that had produced it. So he offered Klaus a job in the Gestapo. It was an offer Klaus could not very well refuse. Since then he had done all kinds of awkward jobs for Heydrich, including accompanying him for nights of debauchery on the town, nights which his boss relished but Klaus found embarrassing and frankly disgusting.

'How could you have let this happen, Schalke? Didn't you know that this man had a weak heart?'

'I am very sorry, Herr Gruppenführer. We had no way of knowing. There was nothing on file.' At least there wasn't now. Klaus had located the reference to Joachim's heart condition in the army medical report which had denied him entry to the reserves. This he had swiftly removed.

'I have had von Ribbentrop on the telephone to me. And worse than that, Göring.'

'I can understand the Foreign Minister,' Klaus said. 'But why Göring?'

'Mühlendorf's father owns a shipping line in Hamburg. His ships transport most of the Reich's iron ore down from Sweden. He goes hunting with Göring – they are best friends. And he is kicking up a fuss.'

'That is unfortunate.' Von Ribbentrop was of no real consequence, but Göring was not someone you wanted to cross. Although the Gestapo was universally feared in Germany, it was by no means universally powerful. In the Third Reich power was disseminated among many institutions. Heydrich's Gestapo was only one of these. There was the Party, the Wehrmacht, Göring's Luftwaffe, Goebbels's Propaganda Ministry, the Finance Ministry, the industrialists and businessmen. The civil service, including the Foreign Office, and the judiciary retained some influence. Even Himmler and the SS, the Gestapo's parent organization, were not all-powerful. No single individual was in Nazi Germany, except perhaps the Führer himself. And he liked to keep things that way.

'Unfortunate? It's not unfortunate. It's the inevitable result of your bungling! Why couldn't you have been more careful with Mühlendorf? You knew he was a diplomat.'

'I should have been, Herr Gruppenführer. But I am convinced that he was hiding something.'

'What about the Englishman, de Lancey? Is he a spy?'

'I don't know. We have let him go. But we will keep an eye on him.'

Heydrich examined the file on his desk, which was open at Klaus's report on Mühlendorf. 'So what do you think he was hiding? Do you believe there really is a plan to overthrow the Führer?'

'There might be.'

'From where? Within the Foreign Office?' Heydrich snorted. 'What can they do? Send a cable to the Führer humbly requesting his resignation?'

'Possibly within the Foreign Office. Possibly the army. You know how unhappy they are about von Fritsch.'

'Do you have any proof?'

'Not yet. But I can look for it.'

'The generals believe they are responsible to no one but themselves; they haven't yet understood that it is their duty to serve the National Socialist state.' Heydrich looked at Klaus sharply. 'We have to be very careful about the army. I don't want you going around arresting soldiers: there will be no end of trouble.'

'I understand, Herr Gruppenführer!'

Conrad was determined to register his own protest at Joachim's death. But what could he do, a lone foreigner in a country where the whole might of the state was focused on the suppression of protest? He had seriously considered marching into 8 Prinz-Albrecht-Strasse and yelling at that big Gestapo oaf. Even if he was arrested in the process, it would make him feel better and his detention might get some publicity. But he knew that would be at best pointless, at worst dangerous. So he went to the British Embassy, just a little further up Wilhelmstrasse from the Gestapo headquarters.

There his demands to see the Ambassador were deflected by a charming Third Secretary of about his own age. Conrad's plan was to complain about his own treatment with the hope of drawing Joachim's death into the resulting outcry. But the Third Secretary explained that there was to be no outcry. Although Conrad's arrest did indeed sound unwarranted, he had been treated well, he hadn't even been interrogated let alone physically harmed, and he had been released as soon as the Gestapo had recognized their mistake. As for Joachim Mühlendorf, he was a German citizen and it was not British policy to interfere in the treatment of German citizens by the German authorities.

The Third Secretary maintained his calm no matter how hard Conrad pressed him. In the end Conrad gave up, frustrated, defeated.

Back at his hotel, he pulled out his typewriter and bashed out an account of his arrest. For an hour he thumped the keys until his fingers hurt. He read through the result: powerful, passionate, shocking. It lacked the dryly observed insights that the editor of *Mercury* liked in his magazine, but Conrad would force him to publish it anyway. And if Theo didn't like it, to hell with him.

To hell with him? As Conrad stared at the article he knew that its publication could get Theo into serious trouble. He had promised Theo not to write about what had happened; he had to keep that promise. He tore up the sheets of typescript and went to bed.

Five

The next day Conrad spent in the 'Stabi', as the Staatsbibliothek on Unter den Linden was called, armed with a new exercise book and notebooks he had scribbled in during his time at the prep school. He had spent three weeks in the library in 1933 researching his thesis on the Danish war. He was fond of the old place; it seemed one of the few institutions left in Berlin still free of Nazi influence. True, the Friedrich-Wilhelm University next door had been purged of non-Aryan and otherwise unsound professors and twenty thousand books had been burned in front of the opera house over the road, but the Stabi itself still contained tens of thousands of volumes written before National Socialism had ever been conceived.

He found himself a quiet desk, opened the exercise book and began writing. He had decided to write in longhand and type his work up later. He had been mulling over the first chapter for weeks, and he was pleased how easily it flowed.

The idea of writing a novel in Berlin had come to him during the Easter holidays, which he had spent in Suffolk. His plan was to write about a young Englishman who had married a German woman and lived in Berlin in 1914. One of the major characters would be a Prussian friend, an army officer. The novel would be about how a family could be blown apart by the prospect of war, and the difficulties that the Englishman and the Prussian faced as they realized they would soon be fighting each other.

Conrad was aware of the parallels with his own life: his father in Hamburg in 1914, and his own friendship with Theo. But that was the point. He hoped that by writing the book he would begin to sort things out in his mind.

In Spain he had seen how war corrupted the good and the bad, the socialists and the Fascists. Yet although Spain had given him a hatred of war, it had also given him a taste for action. He couldn't stay in Suffolk any more. In Berlin he would be able to see for himself how the world was tearing itself apart. And by writing his novel here, perhaps he would understand it a bit better, or at least understand himself.

Although none of that would help Joachim.

At about half past three he called it a day, his head buzzing with what he had written. He strolled out into the courtyard of the Stabi and paused by the fountain, enjoying the June sunshine and the crisp Berlin air. Creepers criss-crossed the old grey façade like a thick beard on an old grandfather's face. The splashing of water from the fountain drowned out the hum of the traffic outside.

'Lovely building, don't you think?'

Conrad turned in surprise at hearing English spoken. Next to him was a short, middle-aged man with owl-like glasses resting on a pointed nose and a friendly smile. He looked very English.

'Yes, I suppose it is,' Conrad replied.

'De Lancey, isn't it?' The little man held out his hand. 'My name's Foley. Captain Foley.'

Conrad shook the hand, feeling slightly bemused. 'I'm with the embassy here,' Foley said. 'I heard you had arrived in Berlin, so when I saw you here I thought I would introduce myself. Do you fancy a stroll? I'm just going back across the Tiergarten to my office.'

'All right,' said Conrad, curious about what the little man might have to say. Perhaps the embassy was going to do something about Joachim after all.

They set off along Unter den Linden, a bustle of cars, trams, buses and bicycles and the overladen brightly coloured wheelbarrows of street vendors selling everything from sausages to books. To Conrad's eyes the street looked bare without its linden, although skinny saplings popped up at regular intervals, replacements planted a couple of years before, after the original trees had been ripped up to dig the new S-Bahn line. This end of the street was graced with grand buildings: the library, the opera, the university, and a veritable army of statues, with Frederick the Great rising massively on his horse in the middle of the road. A band of Hitler Youth streamed past; boys of nine or ten wearing swastika armbands and brown shirts and shorts. Conrad was glad to see that their marching step was pretty ragged, and they still acted more like a bunch of chattering schoolboys than the fanatical automatons they were being groomed to become.

'Do you know Berlin?' Foley asked.

'I came here for a few months to research my thesis,' Conrad said. 'My mother is from Hamburg; I was actually born there. We left when war broke out.'

'I was studying philosophy in Hamburg in 1914,' said Foley. 'It's a wonderful place. But I was slow to leave: damned nearly didn't get out. Your father is Lord Oakford, isn't he? Arthur de Lancey as he was then.'

'That's right.'

'I came across him during the war. Not in the trenches, although I did my stint there. Like him, I caught a bullet and ended up working for the general staff. Unlike him, I didn't earn a VC catching it.'

'That was military intelligence, wasn't it?'

'That's a rather grand name for what we were doing,' Foley said. He glanced up, his mild eyes meeting Conrad's through his spectacles.

For a moment Conrad wondered whether the man was trying to tell him that he was still in intelligence. It seemed highly unlikely. Foley looked to be in his fifties, a nondescript pen-pusher if ever there was one. Conrad shook himself; he was imagining it. His own father had left the Intelligence Corps in 1919, never to go near it again. Foley must have done the same.

They passed the junction with Wilhelmstrasse, a few yards down which stood the British Embassy. 'I thought you said you worked in there?' Conrad asked.

'That's a simplification,' Foley said. 'I'm actually the Passport Control Officer. My job is to grant visas to anyone wishing to visit Britain. Or anywhere else in the Empire, including Palestine. Our office is on Tiergartenstrasse. It's another lovely building; my predecessor bought it for a song in 1920.'

They walked through the tall columns of the Brandenburg Gate and entered a construction site. In front of the Reichstag building, still empty since the fire in 1933, stood the Siegessäule, a two-hundred-foot-high monument built in the 1860s to commemorate Prussia's victories over Denmark, Conrad's very own war, and Austria. It was known by irreverent Berliners as the 'Siegesspargel' or 'Victory Asparagus'. Now the whole edifice was clad in scaffolding. And the road through the Tiergarten had been transformed into a straight, ugly scar, bordered on either side by the stumps of recently felled trees.

'This is Hitler's latest grand plan,' said Foley. 'He's going to move the Siegessäule to the middle of the park and create a broad avenue from there to the Brandenburg Gate for his army to march along. In the meantime all this work is an infernal nuisance; it really fouls up the traffic.'

They crossed the road into the park, weaving through the stationary cars whose engines growled with impatience. 'You must be quite busy at the moment,' Conrad said. 'I imagine there's plenty of demand for visas.'

'Rather. There seems to be no end to the queues. Jews mostly.' He sighed. 'Sadly we reject most of the applicants.'

'Why?' asked Conrad.

'Quotas,' said Foley. 'Strict quotas, and getting stricter all the time. I could issue my annual quota of visas many times over, I could tell you. I ask for more, but they give me less. There's unemployment in Britain and Arabs are rioting in Palestine, so there's no room for more penniless Jews.'

'I suppose it's understandable,' said Conrad.

'No. No, it's not,' said Foley, a flash of anger in his eyes. 'We have to help these people or many of them will die. I know of a number of cases of applicants we have rejected going to concentration camps. Many commit suicide. Most Jewish Germans have been blind to what has been happening. Until very recently Germany was the most hospitable country in Europe for Jews. It was a sanctuary for displaced Jews from the East, from Poland and Russia. Jews are some of the most educated and influential people in this country, which is why they are a popular target for the Nazis. Most of them just could not believe that this current storm of anti-Semitism wouldn't blow over. But now they realize it's getting worse, especially since the invasion of Austria in March. And it will get worse still.'

'I see what you mean,' said Conrad. 'And there's nothing you can do for these people?'

'We do what we can,' said Foley grimly. 'But it's never enough.'

They plunged deeper into the park, leaving the piles of earth and jumble of construction equipment to their right. The Tiergarten was originally a royal hunting forest on the edge of old Berlin, but in the nineteenth century it had become a haven of quiet in the midst of the metropolis. Spindly trees closed around them and the roar of the machinery became a hum. Sunlight dappled the path beneath their feet.

'Well, Captain Foley?' said Conrad. 'You've got me here. What do you want to say to me?'

Foley smiled. 'Oh, just that if you hear anything that you think might be of any use to His Majesty's Government I'd be grateful if you could let me know. I'll pass it on to the right people in London.'

'I take it you have heard about my arrest the other night?'

'Yes. And what happened to your cousin Joachim Mühlendorf. A terrible thing, but all too common these days.'

'And are you going to kick up a fuss?'

'I am sure that the Third Secretary explained to you the embassy's position. And you understand that I—'

'If you can't help me, why should I help you?' Conrad interrupted.

'You have friends here. Is there anything you think we should know?'

Conrad thought about Joachim's gossip about General von Fritsch and a conspiracy against Hitler. No doubt Foley would be very interested in all that. But he didn't see why he should report conversations with his friends to someone he had only just met. '"We" being who exactly?'

'"We" being the British government,' Foley said. 'Your government.' He touched Conrad's arm. 'Let me make something clear. I'm not asking you to become a spy or anything like that. There's nothing cloak-and-dagger about any of this.

It's just that war between our country and Germany sometime in the next few years is becoming a distinct possibility, and the more information we have about them, the better. All I'm asking is that you keep your ears open. Especially around your friend Lieutenant von Hertenberg.'

'Theo? Why are you interested in Theo?'

'He's just one of many people we are interested in.'

'You're asking me to spy on my friends?'

Foley stopped. The frozen air rose in a cloud about his lips. 'I'm asking you to do your duty. Just as your father did his duty in the war.'

'I'm not my father, Captain Foley, and I'm not going to be your damned spy,' Conrad snapped. 'Now if you don't mind, you go your way, and I'll go mine.' A narrow path wound into the trees on the right, and Conrad took it, leaving Foley standing behind him.

Conrad strode furiously through the woods. Foley was trying to manipulate him, use him in the same way he had been used in Spain. The mousy little spymaster was trying to enmesh him in exactly the kind of intrigue he had been writing about only that morning. *Realpolitik*, the cynical diplomacy of the balance of power, secret agreements and alliances, feint and counter-feint, the whole ghastly dance that had led to war twenty-four years before and might lead to war again. And then there was Foley's facile assumption that because his father had fought so bravely in the last war Conrad would mindlessly follow orders towards another one.

Conrad's pacifism ran deep. It was his father who had instilled a hatred of war into him. Arthur de Lancey had joined up in 1916, an older replacement for the wave of enthusiastic young subalterns who had been wiped out in the first two years on the Western Front. He had fought well, winning a DSO at the Somme in 1916 and a Victoria Cross a year later at Passchendaele, when he and a lance corporal had captured a German machine-gun position and held it against fierce counter-attacks until the rest of his company arrived. To Conrad as a boy this had seemed impossibly brave, and he was desperately proud of his father the war hero.

But the war hero had been changed by that day. His arm was badly mangled and had to be amputated. The scars in his mind were much worse. He was overcome with bouts of depression and irritability where he would fly into a rage with his wife or his children for no apparent reason. These bouts were unpredictable, and they could last a day or a month, but they were in stark contrast to the much longer periods of normality when he was wise, kind and approachable.

He developed a passionate opposition to war in all its forms. After the armistice he became involved in international pacifist organizations, and spent time and money in supporting the Quaker Emergency Committee, which helped starving children in post-war Germany. As Conrad grew older, he came to admire his father's idealism; indeed it paved the way for his own whole-hearted support of socialism when he was at Oxford.

But Lord Oakford, as he had become on the death of Conrad's banker grandfather in 1931, had been desperately disappointed in his son when he had gone to Spain. For Conrad it had been an agonizing dilemma. Like his father he believed that killing people was wrong, even in a just war. But he also came to believe that fascism was evil, and that unless it was stopped it was an evil that would swallow the whole continent of Europe. It fell to the idealists of the world, young men like Conrad, to stop it, to draw a line in the sand. Conrad wasn't alone; many of the Oxford undergraduates who had voted against King and

Country in 1933 set off with him to fight and die for Spain three years later. But for Lord Oakford, the case was much clearer. War was wrong and Conrad was wrong to go and fight in one.

It hadn't seemed like that at first. When he had first arrived in Spain, Conrad had been invigorated by the spirit of comradeship and egalitarianism he had found in the International Brigade, indeed throughout the whole Republican Army. Trade unionists, socialists, communists, anarchists, professional soldiers, peasants, students and even schoolchildren from all over Europe and from every corner of Spain had joined together to fight fascism. And over the winter of 1936–7 they had succeeded, defending Madrid heroically. It was a heroism of spirit as much as a heroism of military prowess and Conrad was proud to be a part of it. Conrad came from a background of extreme privilege and had spent half his life feeling extreme guilt about it. Now, fighting shoulder to shoulder with some of the poorest and most generous people he had ever met, he felt fulfilled for perhaps the first time in his life. He was good at it too.

But things had changed. War took these young idealists and corrupted their humanity: the incident Conrad had witnessed of the rape of the nuns was but one tiny event among thousands. The Republican Army was ill-disciplined and ill-organized and facing defeat, so the Soviet-backed communists took matters in hand. The improvements in military training and discipline were no doubt necessary. But as the spring of 1937 turned to summer, the Republic fought its own civil war. A new secret police force threw men of doubtful political allegiance into prison, many foreign volunteers among them. The commissars thrived on talk of a fifth column of fascist-inspired traitors and a new category of enemy they invented, the 'Trotskyist-Fascists' who were everywhere, all in the pay of General Franco. When they found them, the commissars shot them, even when, like

David and Harry and Conrad, they were attacking the enemy at the time.

Conrad knew now his father had been right. But Conrad still hated fascism, and in leaving Spain he felt he had left a job undone. The epidemic of collective insanity had started in Italy, spread to Germany and Spain, and was threatening France and even Britain.

That was why he had come to Berlin: he couldn't bear sitting in England, kicking his heels, while the Nazis ran amok in Central Europe. Here the epidemic was at its most virulent; here he could observe it at close quarters. But he was beginning to think that perhaps he should do more than simply watch it and write about it. Maybe he should do something to restrain it. Exactly what that something might be, he had no idea, at least not yet.

But he wasn't spying for His Majesty's bloody Government, that was for sure.

Six

That evening Conrad telephoned Theo from his hotel. Captain Foley's interest in his friend had aroused his own suspicions. There were too many unanswered questions surrounding Joachim's death, questions that only Theo could answer.

Theo sounded wary on the telephone.

'I need to speak to you,' Conrad said. 'Can we meet this evening?'

'I'm afraid that will be a little difficult. I am giving a small dinner party tonight.' Still wary.

'Oh come on, Theo. I can look in afterwards. It's important.'

Conrad could sense Theo's hesitation. But then his tone became more welcoming. 'I tell you what, why don't you come to dinner? It would be good to introduce you to some of my friends. Eight o'clock at my apartment.'

There were eight for dinner, including Conrad. In addition to Theo there was a lawyer, an officer in the cavalry, and four women, one of whom was clearly Theo's girlfriend, a pretty blonde girl named Sophie. The food was good: Theo's cook obviously knew not only how to prepare food, but also how to procure it, an increasing problem in Germany in 1938 as the nation's resources were concentrated more on guns than butter. A couple of excellent bottles of hock soon got the conversation flowing. Conrad found himself seated next to another blonde, just on the heavy side of statuesque, named Maria von

Tiefenfeld. She declared herself an Anglophile and insisted on speaking in English, although her English was much worse than Conrad's German.

'I love English gentlemen,' she said. 'They are so much more cultured and well-mannered than the Germans. German men are so brutish, with their duels and their drinking.'

Conrad smiled in a way that was, he hoped, both cultured and well-mannered.

'You remind me of Mr Alec Linaro, the racing driver,' Maria said. 'Have you heard of him? Perhaps you know him?'

The smile that had been flickering on Conrad's lips disappeared. 'Yes. Yes, I do, actually. The resemblance has been pointed out before.'

'Now he is a fine English gentleman,' Maria said. 'I met him at the Nürburgring Grand Prix last year. You must be very brave to drive a car so fast around the racetrack, is it not so? But he is charming at the same time. Do you think not?'

'I suppose so.' Maria had a point. Conrad had first met Alec Linaro at a dinner party two years before. He was indeed brave, charming and very good-looking. He was married to the daughter of an earl, but that hadn't stopped him from paying great attention to Veronica. They had bumped into him on a number of occasions over the following year, during which time his charm had increased.

Maria then began to tell a long story about going with Linaro to visit the Rhine valley after the race. Conrad didn't follow it, beyond getting the strong impression that Maria had spent at least one night, and probably several, with the dashing racing driver. His mind was tumbling, spinning in its own painfully familiar vortex.

'I prefer jockeys, myself,' said a voice on Conrad's right in German.

In relief, Conrad turned to the woman sitting on his other side, a friend of Sophie's named Anneliese. 'And why is that?'

'They must have empathy with an animal, not just a machine. That seems a greater skill.'

Maria snorted in disagreement, and turned to Theo.

'That's a very good point,' said Conrad, unable to keep the gratitude out of his voice.

'I take it you and Mr Linaro don't get on,' said the woman, with a smile in her eyes. She was dark with short curly hair, a snub nose and a pretty, lively face.

'Very perceptive.'

'Not so very. You would have to be blind not to see the discomfort you were in.' Her eyes flicked towards Maria and back to Conrad. They were green, intelligent, ironic. 'Despite your great culture and perfect manners you couldn't quite hide it.'

Conrad smiled. 'Was it that obvious?'

'So what did he do? Crash your car? Get your sister pregnant? Steal your last bottle of whisky?'

'He did steal something, actually.'

'Oh,' said the woman, understanding. 'Wife or girlfriend?'

'Wife.'

'Oh.' A look of genuine sympathy flashed across her face. 'That's not much fun.'

'No.'

Conrad had the impression that Anneliese was examining him. It was a sensation he rather enjoyed, especially since she seemed to like what she saw – although a hint of mischief flickered in her eyes, so he could not be sure.

'You're not really English, are you?'

Conrad laughed. 'I am, actually.'

'What do you mean? You speak German without an accent and de Lancey sounds French to me.'

'Huguenot. My ancestors left France a couple of hundred years ago. And I am pretty good at languages. But I can assure you I am English.'

'Well, you *look* German. An Aryan *Übermensch* if ever I saw one.'

Conrad looked for irony in her eyes and found it. It was true: he did look German. He was tall, square-shouldered with fair hair, although his eyes were grey rather than blue.

'My mother is German,' Conrad admitted. 'And I was born in Germany, although I only lived here a couple of years. But I don't think I'm exactly what Nietzsche had in mind.'

'What did I tell you?' Anneliese said. 'You're German.'

Conrad was needled. He felt English. He *was* English. He opened his mouth and then closed it, suddenly infuriated by the way she was enjoying his discomfort. She smiled and touched his arm.

'I'm sorry,' she said. 'You would probably be better off speaking to Fräulein von Tiefenfeld.' She sipped her wine, suddenly serious. 'Theo told me what happened to your friend Herr Mühlendorf. I'm sorry.'

'Cousin.'

'Was he your cousin? Oh, yes, Theo did tell me that. Apparently he had a heart attack in Gestapo custody.'

'I'm sure his heart didn't stop unaided,' Conrad said bitterly.

'I'm sure it didn't,' said Anneliese. Her expression was full of sympathy, so much sympathy that Conrad suddenly felt uncomfortable. He hadn't lost all of his English reticence. 'I met him only a couple of nights before.'

'At the Kakadu?'

'That's right. He seemed very nice. But he was a bit drunk.'

'That sounds like Joachim. We were actually there together the night we were arrested.' Conrad decided to do some gentle digging. 'He said that he had talked to you about Johnnie von Herwarth,' he said, stretching the truth slightly.

'Yes. Do you know Johnnie?'

'No. Do you?'

'I only met him once. He's an old friend of Theo's. It was a couple of months ago. He was on leave from the embassy in Moscow; he works there with Herr Mühlendorf.'

'Of course. Joachim also said that he discussed some other things with Theo?'

Anneliese frowned. 'They did have a conversation in English,' she said carefully. 'I didn't understand it.' Conrad realized he had gone too far. This was the Third Reich after all, and he and Anneliese had only just met.

A peal of laughter came from the end of the table. Theo's girlfriend, Sophie, was getting a little tipsy. She was small with a blonde bob and big blue eyes. Very pretty, which was not surprising, knowing Theo. 'How do you know Sophie?' Conrad asked, changing the subject.

'We trained together,' Anneliese replied. 'We are both nurses.'

'Oh?' Conrad raised his eyebrows. 'So Theo met her in a hospital? I didn't realize he had been ill.'

Anneliese laughed. 'No, not a hospital, a nightclub. Despite the films, hospitals aren't very romantic places. We may be angels by day, but by night we are something quite different. Or at least Sophie is.'

'But not you?'

'I keep her company.' She frowned. 'Like you, my past is a little complicated.' Conrad realized that unlike him she didn't want to talk about it, and so he didn't press her. 'I like Sophie, although we are very different. Originally, I went to medical school. I came top of my class; I was set on becoming a doctor like my father.'

'What went wrong?'

'I was forced to spend some time away from university. And when I wanted to return, they wouldn't let me back.'

'Why not? I thought German universities were quite flexible about that sort of thing. People are always hopping from one to another.'

'Well, it turns out that I'm Jewish.'

'I see...' said Conrad. 'Actually, I don't quite see. Didn't you know you were Jewish?'

'I never considered myself Jewish. In fact, I used to go to church every now and then with my mother. But my father's family are Jewish. He's an atheist, or he would call himself a humanist. He thinks organized religion has done more harm than good in the world. He was quite upset when my mother started taking me to church – I think it went against some agreement they made when they were married. And my grandparents, who do go to synagogue every Saturday, explained to me that I can't be Jewish because my mother isn't.'

She sighed. 'But that's not what the law says. The law says that because two of my four grandparents are non-Aryan, I am non-Aryan, and that means I can't qualify as a doctor.'

'That's outrageous!'

'Of course it is. But it wouldn't be any more outrageous if I was one hundred per cent Jewish, would it? And the Nazis' anti-Semitism is there for all the world to see. Hitler hardly keeps it a secret, does he?'

'No. You're right. But I suppose it's one thing to read about anti-Semitic laws in the newspapers, it's another thing to see them at first hand. What about your father? Is he still allowed to practise?'

Anneliese laughed, a hollow laugh.

Conrad felt the unease. 'What?'

'My father's in prison. Although he tells me there is plenty of work for him to do there.'

'My God! What is he in there for? Being a doctor?'

'More or less. Late one evening we got a telephone call from a neighbour. There had been a car accident in front of her house and one of the drivers was seriously injured. I was living at home at the time, and I rushed out in the car with my father. The man was in a bad way; he had severed an artery in his leg and was losing a lot of blood. My father and I bound up his leg and drove him to the local hospital. He needed a blood transfusion, and the hospital was only a small one and it didn't have any stocks of the man's blood type. But my father's was a match, so he donated some of his own blood to keep the patient alive until they could get some more stocks from another hospital.'

'Did the driver survive?'

'Yes, unfortunately.'

'Unfortunately?'

'He was a minor official in the local Labour Front and an ardent Nazi. When he recovered, he was shocked to discover that he had Jewish blood in his veins. So shocked that he reported my father to the authorities. Father was arrested, tried for "race defilement" and imprisoned.'

'The swine! Would he have survived without your father's blood?'

'No, not a chance. I went to the trial. The man said that he would rather be dead than know he was carrying around Jewish blood in his veins for the rest of his life.'

'Idiot!'

'The strange thing is, I think he genuinely meant it. It is frightening how these Nazis can lose touch with reality, with common sense.'

'I can't believe it,' said Conrad, shaking his head.

'You will get used to it.'

The maid cleared their plates and produced some cheese, both German and French, once again demonstrating the hunter-gathering skills of Theo's cook. But no Stilton. Anneliese took some Mainzer sour-milk cheese and Conrad some Brie.

'When is your father due to be released?' asked Conrad.

'In a couple of weeks.'

'That must be a relief.' Conrad looked to Anneliese, expecting to see a smile, but she was concentrating on the cheese in front of her, chasing it around her plate as she tried to spread it on a slice of bread. Conrad realized he had said something wrong. 'Is there a hitch of some kind?'

Anneliese bit her lip. Her self-assurance seemed to crumble away in front of Conrad's eyes. 'You could say that.'

'What do you mean?'

'You see, the release is the most dangerous time of all. The Gestapo often wait outside the gates to arrest the prisoner as he walks free. They take him into what they call "protective custody" and throw him into a concentration camp. It's much worse than prison.'

'But why would they do that to your father?'

'To protect the Aryan population from his blood,' Anneliese muttered bitterly. 'Herr and Frau Schmidt could be innocently driving along the road, have an accident, go to hospital and wake up Jewish. They must be protected from this risk.'

'Do you know for sure the Gestapo will do this?'

'I've heard they are intending to. It was a high-profile case, as I'm sure you can imagine. Himmler himself took an interest.'

'I'm so sorry. Is there nothing you can do? Can that really be legal?'

'It is legal. My one hope is if I can get him a visa to leave the country. Sometimes the Gestapo let prisoners do that. If he's abroad he can hardly be a risk to German blood, can he? I've been trying for the last month. The problem is it's so difficult to get a visa.'

'Have you tried Britain?' asked Conrad.

'Yes. In fact that was our first choice; my father has a cousin there. But there are queues and quotas. The same goes for Palestine – the British administer the visas for there too. The United States, France... they are all cracking down. But I haven't given up yet. I will not let him end up in one of those camps. I will not!'

Conrad thought about Foley, of the conversation he had had with him in the Tiergarten. Faced with the immediate distress of Anneliese, his earlier distrust of the man seemed irrelevant, capricious even.

He broke the silence. 'I know the Passport Control Officer at the British Embassy,' he said. 'Or at least I met him this morning. Would you like me to have a word with him?'

Anneliese smiled, hope flickering in her eyes. 'Would you?'

'I can try. It might not work.'

'Please do,' she said. 'Please, please do.'

Seven

Conrad had no opportunity to speak to Theo alone until the other guests had all left. Anneliese had given him her telephone number so that he could get in touch with her if he had any luck with Captain Foley.

Theo glanced around the apartment. André, his cook, was chivvying the maid to clear up the mess. 'It's a nice night. Let's go for a walk.'

'All right,' Conrad said, and followed his host out into the street. The air was pleasantly cool. They walked up to the Tiergarten and then headed west, the trees and bushes looming darkly beside them.

'Sorry about that,' said Theo. 'You never know who is listening these days.'

Conrad raised his eyebrows. 'The cook? Or are you worried about microphones? Why would they want to bug you?'

Theo shrugged. 'Who knows? But it always pays to be careful.'

'That was an excellent dinner,' Conrad said. 'Thank you for inviting me at such short notice.'

'I was lucky to find André,' Theo said. 'You obviously got on well with Anneliese.'

'I like her.'

'So do I. She's an intelligent woman. And she has had a difficult time.'

'She told me about her father. It's an appalling story.'

75

'There's that. And other things.'

'It all sounds quite mad.'

'It is,' said Theo. 'As you spend more time in Germany you will see lots of things like this. And it's important to remember that they *are* quite mad – not just mad, wrong. If you are not careful you grow accustomed to the madness, it loses its ability to shock, it becomes acceptable. And you become one of the madmen.'

'I don't understand how the people put up with it,' Conrad said. 'Ordinary people, not the fanatics. Germany used to be full of ordinary people.'

'We are all sleepwalking,' Theo said. 'Sleepwalking to oblivion.'

This sounded like the Theo Conrad knew, not the Theo wearing an army uniform. That still made Conrad uneasy, as had Captain Foley's curiosity about his friend. Conrad realized he had no clue about what Theo did apart from working in the War Ministry. Theo had implied that he acted as a lawyer there, but Conrad wasn't exactly sure what a lawyer did in the army. Perhaps Theo was actually involved in something else entirely: drawing up invasion plans for Czechoslovakia, or organizing Germany's rearmament programme. Both of these seemed most unlike him.

Conrad remembered a summer night at Oxford. It was in their second year: he and Theo had been working their way through a bottle of port in Conrad's rooms. They had just drunk a toast to Algy, as was their custom. Algy was Algernon Pendleton, whose name was engraved on a mahogany plaque fixed above the door of Conrad's rooms, together with the year he had arrived at the college, and the year he had been killed at Ypres. Many, if not most, of the rooms in Conrad's college commemorated their former occupants in this way.

'You know,' Theo had said, 'we shouldn't let them do that to us.'

'What, fight each other?'

'Yes. They shouldn't be allowed to order you to kill me, or me to kill you.'

'They shouldn't,' said Conrad. 'But one day they probably will.'

'Let's promise to refuse if they try. Not just promise. Swear it.'

'Right oh,' said Conrad, slouching in his armchair. 'I swear it.'

'No, we need more than that,' said Theo. He went over to Conrad's bookcase and found a Bible. 'Put your hand on this and swear it.'

Conrad hesitated and then rested his palm on the book. 'I do solemnly swear that I will not let anyone tell me to go and kill my good friend, Theo von Hertenberg.' He glanced up at Theo. 'All right?'

'Very good. Give me the book.' Theo returned to his chair and holding the book in the air, repeated the oath in German. He placed the Bible on the floor by his chair.

The two friends sat in silence for a long time. They were half drunk and the oath had been made in an atmosphere of mock sincerity. Yet they meant it. And seven years later, Conrad meant it still. It wasn't just a personal thing between Theo and him: their friendship represented the antipathy their generation felt towards massacring each other. It was a kind of moral progress to match the technological progress they saw all around them, a conviction articulated in the famous vote at the Oxford Union two years later supporting the motion that 'This House will under no circumstances fight for its King and Country'.

But over those seven years Conrad had changed: he had married and fought in Spain. And what had Theo been up to?

Their correspondence had been desultory since Conrad had last visited Theo in Berlin in 1933, and petered out completely when he had gone to Spain. At the time, Conrad had put that down to his own preoccupations. But now he wondered whether Theo didn't want to be seen to be writing to a member of the International Brigade. Understandable, perhaps, but disappointing.

They turned south, crossing the dark silent ribbon of the Landwehr Canal and entering streets of shops and people. They passed through a crowd spilling out of a brightly lit cinema on to the pavement, searching for taxis. An enormous picture of Frederick the Great was emblazoned over the pseudo-Grecian façade, which glowed an eerie luminescent blue in the lights.

'Anneliese told me who Johnnie von Herwarth is,' Conrad said. 'You didn't say he was an old friend.'

'I didn't, did I?' said Theo dryly. 'Did Anneliese say anything about that evening with Joachim?'

'Not really. Apart from that he was drunk.'

'Good,' grunted Theo.

They turned back along quieter residential streets towards Theo's apartment. Unease gathered around them, like mist in the night. Conrad was obviously grateful to Theo for rescuing him. But Theo hadn't been able to save Joachim, and he didn't show much sign of caring about that much either. Joachim was just another innocent German chewed up by the Nazi machine. Of course Theo's response wasn't unusual, it was the classic reaction of his countrymen to brutal murder by the state. Look the other way. Talk about something else. Well, Conrad wouldn't look the other way. There were things about Joachim's death that didn't make sense, and Conrad was going to make sense of them, whether Theo liked it or not.

'Was there any truth in what Joachim said?' Conrad asked. 'About a plot to remove Hitler?'

'I've told you,' said Theo. 'It was just a wild rumour.'

'Like you told me you didn't know Johnnie von Herwarth?'

'I said no such thing. I just didn't answer your question.'

'Semantics,' Conrad said. 'Lawyer's semantics.'

'Well, at least it's not a soldier's semantics,' said Theo, with half a smile.

'Theo, he was my cousin. I have a right to know what was going on.'

Theo walked in silence for a minute. Conrad could tell he was thinking, and let him. Eventually he spoke. 'The lawyer in me says you have no prima facie right to know, Conrad. The citizen of the Reich in me tells me the less you know, the better. But you are my friend.'

There was something ominous in the way Theo spoke. 'And?'

Theo took a deep breath. 'It is quite likely that Joachim Mühlendorf was a Soviet spy.'

'That's absurd!' said Conrad. 'Joachim is the last person in the world I would imagine as a secret agent.'

'Never a bad qualification,' said Theo.

'I don't believe you.'

'Don't you? You knew him much better than me. Is it possible that he was ever a communist?'

'Not in any formal sense,' said Conrad.

'But he had communist beliefs?'

'Yes,' Conrad admitted.

'And is it possible that he still had those beliefs when he died?'

Conrad took a moment to consider the question. 'Yes, I suppose so. Although he was a member of the Nazi Party.'

'I don't know whether he was recruited in Moscow, or some time before. But if Mühlendorf was a spy, it would help to be a Party member to do his job.'

Conrad frowned, thinking. It *was* possible. Despite his extra-vagant behaviour, Conrad knew that Joachim's socialist beliefs ran deep. And Joachim would love the idea of people like Theo assuming he was a superficial lightweight when actually he was leading a secret life spying against the Nazi regime. But Conrad wasn't going to admit as much to Theo. 'So are you trying to tell me it was perfectly justifiable that the Gestapo killed him?'

Theo paused before answering, as they overtook a couple sauntering along the pavement. The street was quiet and their voices carried in the still night. Theo lowered his. 'No. But I am saying he was an enemy of my country. A Bolshevik.'

'And is Bolshevism so much worse than Nazism?'

'Conrad,' Theo said wearily. 'He was spying for a foreign power. He was betraying his own country, *my* country. And yes, Bolshevism is evil. I spent three weeks in Russia after I went down from Oxford, just to look around, see what the workers' promised land was really like. And it's hell, Conrad, really. It dehumanizes people. You must have seen that in Spain?'

'Perhaps,' said Conrad. 'But Nazism dehumanizes people too. Is that why you supported Hitler when I saw you here in 1933?'

'I never supported Hitler,' Theo said. 'It's true that in 1933 I thought that Hitler was the lesser of two evils and someone had to put some order into the mess that Germany had become. I thought Hitler wouldn't last more than a couple of years. But I was wrong. Like everyone else, I was too complacent.'

Conrad couldn't help himself asking the question that had been foremost in his mind over the previous few days. 'Theo. Are you a Nazi?'

'Of course I'm not a Nazi!' Theo snapped. 'Don't be so damned suspicious.'

They had reached the Landwehr Canal again; a half-moon

was reflected in a strip of silver shimmering on the otherwise black water. They were at the point where Theo turned one way and Conrad the other to get back to his hotel.

Theo halted. 'Look, I asked you to forget about Joachim. I meant that. And it's very important you do as I ask, otherwise the Gestapo will think you are a Soviet spy also. And that would not be good for your health.'

'I was thinking about my interrogation,' Conrad said.

'Conrad—'

'No, listen,' said Conrad with impatience. 'The Gestapo officer asked me about Johnnie von Herwarth, and he asked me about the plot against Hitler, the one that you say doesn't exist.'

'So?'

'So, Joachim hadn't mentioned either of those two things to me that evening. Which means that someone at the Kakadu that night with you and Joachim must have told them.'

'Perhaps their lip-reader was watching us?'

'Joachim spoke to you in English, didn't he? It must be very difficult to be a bilingual lip-reader. Think how hard it must be for a deaf person to learn a foreign language. Face it, Theo. It's much more likely that someone at your table informed the Gestapo.'

'That doesn't make sense,' Theo said. 'It can't have been Sophie; she speaks no English, and besides she disappeared to the Ladies once Joachim started talking to me. Anneliese was there, but she doesn't speak English very well, either. And, as you heard tonight, she is the last person who would be helpful to the Gestapo.'

'Precisely,' said Conrad. 'Which leaves just you and Joachim. And it wasn't Joachim.'

Eight

It was early evening at the Adlon Hotel, the cocktail hour. A quartet played a gentle waltz, although no one was dancing yet. All around voices murmured in conversation, interrupted by the rattle of ice cubes in a cocktail shaker. The Adlon, standing on Unter den Linden only a few yards from the Brandenburg Gate, was the grandest hotel in Berlin. Everyone who was anyone coming through the city stayed there. Conrad had already spotted Lord Lothian, a former Cabinet colleague of his father's, scurrying out of the lift. In the last ten years the mix of visitors had changed: fewer film stars and opera singers, more diplomats and journalists.

Conrad had come straight from the Stabi, where he had spent the day reading about the assassination that had started the Great War. He had decided to insert a prologue into the novel: a description of Gavrilo Princip shooting the Archduke Franz Ferdinand. The story fascinated him; Conrad had not realized how huge a part luck had played in the outcome.

The Archduke, heir to the throne of Austria–Hungary, was visiting Sarajevo with his wife Sophie. Seven members of Young Bosnia, armed with weapons provided by the Black Hand, a Serbian secret society, planned to assassinate him. As the Archduke's motorcade made its way through the city, the first assassin couldn't get a clear shot. The second managed to get close enough to lob a bomb at the Archduke's car, but missed, seriously injuring the occupants of the car behind. Although shaken, the Archduke went ahead with a reception at the town hall, and then decided to visit the injured in hospital.

By this time the conspirators had given up, and one of their number, Gavrilo Princip, went into a shop to buy some lunch. As he came out he was astonished to see the Archduke's car reversing up the street, having taken a wrong turn. Princip promptly dropped his lunch and shot the Archduke, killing him and starting a world war. He then swallowed a cyanide pill, which he vomited straight back up, and was restrained before he had a chance to shoot himself.

A nice first chapter.

The Adlon was a favourite haunt of foreign correspondents, and Conrad had arranged to meet a contemporary of his at Oxford, an American journalist living in Berlin named Warren Sumner. Although Conrad hadn't known him very well at the university, he had always rather liked him, and he thought he might be a good source of information for articles for *Mercury*.

He tried to listen as Warren conducted a passionate argument with a journalist from the English *Daily Mail* about the strength of the Czech defensive fortifications. The subject would be a good one for *Mercury*, but Conrad's thoughts drifted to Joachim and Theo.

He was still trying to come to terms with the idea that Joachim had been a Soviet spy. The more he thought about this piece of news, the less surprising it was. He realized he wasn't shocked; on the contrary, he was proud of his cousin. Conrad had no sympathy with Stalinist Russia, especially since he had seen the Soviet attempts to suborn the Republican Army in Spain, but he admired the way that Joachim had stood by his principles and done what he could to oppose the Nazis. He supposed that Joachim, used to leading one kind of secret life, was good at leading another.

What he found very difficult to accept was the possibility, fast becoming a probability, that Theo was responsible for Joachim's arrest. That was something Conrad really didn't want to believe.

'Darling! Imagine bumping into you!'

He turned to see a very familiar face beaming at him.

'Veronica! What the hell are you doing here?' Conrad asked before he could stop himself.

'It's an hotel, Conrad. I'm staying here.'

'With Linaro?'

'No, he's back in Hampshire with Katherine and the kids, poor darling.' Lady Katherine Linaro was a pretty if rather dull woman and Conrad felt sorry for her: with Veronica as a rival she didn't stand a chance. 'Aren't you pleased to see me?'

'Not especially.'

He heard a cough next to him. Warren was staring at Veronica, with his whitest, most gleaming smile. Conrad couldn't blame him. His wife was beautiful, tall, with red hair and high cheekbones and a poise that was both aloof and alluring at the same time.

Reluctantly, Conrad introduced them. On hearing the words 'my wife' Warren's eyebrows shot up.

'Would you excuse us, Warren?' Conrad asked and moved Veronica away from the group towards a fountain supported by a circle of wrought-iron elephants. The trickle of water was magnified in the splendid lobby, the circular ceiling of which stretched high upwards past five sets of landings to a glass cupola.

'Why are you in Berlin?' Conrad asked.

'I'm keeping Diana company. You remember Diana Guinness?'

Conrad certainly did. Born into the aristocratic but eccentric Mitford family, she had married a charming man who was an heir to the Guinness brewing fortune, but had dumped him in favour of Sir Oswald Mosley, leader of the British Union of Fascists.

'Oh, a meeting of the "Wayward Mistresses' Club", is it?'

'Don't be so vile, Conrad, it doesn't suit you. Anyway Diana and Tom are married now.'

'Tom?'

'Oswald Mosley. Diana calls him Tom. So do I. And it's an enormous secret. They got married eighteen months ago here in Germany with Adolf Hitler as a witness. Imagine that!'

'Quite the society wedding.'

Veronica's eyes gleamed. 'In fact, Diana has gone round to the Chancellery now to watch a film with Hitler. *The Lives of a Bengal Lancer.* It's his favourite. "Uncle Wolf", she calls him.'

'And you didn't join them?'

'Oh, he's such a common little man. Not really my sort of person.'

'I see.'

'And I wasn't invited. But never mind. You can take me out to dinner. Diana took me to this wonderful little place the other night with the Goebbelses; we could go there.'

'No, Veronica.'

'Oh, come on, darling, please! I do have something I want to talk to you about. And you have to admit, it's easier to talk here in Berlin in neutral territory without other people around.'

She gave him a smile full of enthusiasm. Her eyes shone with mischief. When they had first met the mischief had been beguilingly innocent, now it was knowing.

Conrad sighed. Although he remained bitter at the way she had treated him, he still had an urge to talk to his wife. 'All right. Let's go. I'll just make my excuses to Warren.'

He had met the Honourable Veronica Blakeborough in the summer of 1934 at a ball he had been reluctantly dragged to by an old school friend. It was her coming-out season; she was barely eighteen, red-haired with a beautiful cream complexion and a lithe slim figure. She was infused with an innocent wickedness that Conrad found intoxicating. She must have liked him, for she fiddled her dance card to ensure that she spent most of that evening dancing with him.

Conrad wangled an invitation to the next debs' ball, at a grand house in Berkeley Square, and he danced with Veronica again. This time she had a 'scheme'; it was the first of many that Conrad was to experience. Her idea was to sneak out to a nightclub one of the other debs had told her about, the 400, and be back before her aunt noticed she was gone. So they escaped; they danced, they smoked, they drank champagne, they laughed and then they returned to Berkeley Square, her chaperone none the wiser.

Conrad was besotted. And she was fascinated by him. She found his socialism intriguing, his disagreements with his father inspiring. Conrad suspected they were too young to get married – he was still only twenty-three, and she was far too young – but he also knew that he would never meet another woman like her. So despite, or probably because of, their parents' opposition, Conrad and Veronica were married in her village church in Yorkshire in May 1935.

After their marriage, Veronica had become an immediate hit with London society, and she and Conrad were invited here, there and everywhere. Veronica was surprised by Conrad's modest cottage in Oxford, but accepted his explanation that since the family bank had nearly gone bust in 1931 his income was significantly less than it might otherwise have been. Veronica didn't care; there were plenty of people to stay with. Conrad enjoyed the social whirl; he found the contrast with the hours spent studying in Oxford libraries invigorating. He knew that it was really Veronica everyone wanted to see, but they were all perfectly pleasant to him. Some of them he would even count as his friends. His one regret was that he never seemed to get enough time alone with his beautiful young wife.

A thought that had obviously been shared by Alec Linaro.

The 'wonderful little place' that Veronica knew turned out to be Horcher's, one of the most sumptuous restaurants in Berlin, and a favourite of prominent Nazis. Indeed, in the midst of the white tablecloths, shining silver and gleaming crystal sat Field Marshal Göring himself, splendid waiters in red waistcoats and black knee-breeches buzzing around him. The Fat Boy was tucking into a small fowl of some kind, a napkin jammed under his chin to prevent his tightly stretched white uniform getting spattered with sauce.

They were seated at the other end of the room, and ordered jugged hare and claret. Conrad did his best to resist Veronica's charm, but under the influence of the food, the wine and Veronica's laughter, he slowly unbent to the point where he was almost enjoying himself. After a couple of abortive attempts by Conrad to mention Linaro, which Veronica completely ignored, the racing driver was forgotten.

They lit cigarettes over coffee. Göring's table at the other end of the restaurant erupted into laughter.

'You know he wears make-up?' Conrad said.

'No!' said Veronica her eyes widening. 'But he's a general!' She peered across towards the far table. 'His face does look a little flushed.'

'That's not flushed, it's rouge. A touch of lipstick. Eye-liner. Warren told me this evening.'

'Poor Conrad,' Veronica said. 'It must be hell for you in Berlin.'

'You mean with all these Nazis everywhere?'

'Are you still a Red?'

Conrad frowned. 'I'm not sure. My faith in the cause was jolted pretty badly in Spain. But I still feel that there is too much of a gap between rich and poor. That there must be ways of organizing society which don't involve leaving millions of workers and their families unemployed and starving. I still feel there is too much injustice in the world. And, I suppose, I still feel guilty that I am one of the privileged elite living very comfortably on a private income.'

'Oh, you are too harsh on yourself. You always were. You did volunteer to go and get yourself killed for people you didn't even know. That was pretty brave.'

'Stupid perhaps,' said Conrad.

He remembered the day in October 1936 when David Griffiths had excitedly announced that he was going to join the International Brigade fighting the Fascists in Spain. Veronica had thought it a terrific scheme and that they should both go: it would be fabulous fun. Conrad could fight and she could do something heroic with the Red Cross.

At first Conrad had rejected the idea: it offended the pacifism he had absorbed from his father. But David was passionate and persuasive. Conrad shared David's fear that fascism would engulf Europe, and admired his friend's courage in wanting to do something to stop it. How could Conrad sit back in his cosy cottage in Oxford while his friends were fighting and dying a thousand miles away for a cause in which he himself believed utterly? And if fascism did sweep through Europe while he had done nothing, would the knowledge that he had stuck to his pacifist principles in safety while others had died for theirs be enough to salve his conscience? He had to go, even if it meant killing other people. Even if it meant dying. So David and he left for the training camp for international volunteers in Albacete, with Veronica promising to follow as soon as she could organize herself a position in the Red Cross.

Two weeks into his training, Conrad received a letter with the wonderful news that Veronica was pregnant. This meant, of course, that she would have to stay in England. She wrote to him every day, then twice a week, then not at all. The mail in Spain was intermittent at best, and Conrad assumed her letters had been lost, even though the other Englishmen in the International Brigade were occasionally getting theirs through. When he was on his way back to England he cabled her to let her know which boat train he was taking from France, but she wasn't at the station to meet him. It was only when he got home to Oxford that he finally found a letter from her saying she had run off with Linaro.

She had lost the baby: he had received a short letter about that. But he couldn't help wondering – if things had been different, he would be a father now, of a son or a daughter? And would she have stayed with Linaro – or rather, would Linaro have stayed with her? A heavily pregnant woman is not the ideal mistress to take to Le Mans or Monte Carlo.

If there really had been a miscarriage, of course. Perhaps she had visited a back-street doctor. Perhaps she hadn't really been pregnant. Or perhaps the baby wasn't even his.

'You know I really was rather beastly to you,' Veronica said.

'You were.'

'I'm sorry.'

Conrad had the impression that they were coming to the business part of the evening. But if Veronica wanted his forgiveness, she wasn't going to get it.

'I'm quite surprised you don't want a divorce,' she went on.

So was Conrad, but it was something he had tried not to think about. Despite everything he wanted Veronica back, the old Veronica, the mischievous young girl who loved him and who would never deceive him. If he thought about it sensibly he knew that that was impossible, that the innocent Veronica was long gone, if in fact she had ever existed. But he wasn't yet ready to think about it sensibly, to face up to the inevitable.

And he certainly wasn't going to admit as much to Veronica. 'Is Linaro getting one?'

'Not yet.'

'Do you want to marry him?'

Veronica smiled. 'Not yet.'

'Then why do you want a divorce?'

'You never know what may happen.'

'I see what it is. You want to be free to marry someone else at the drop of a hat, just as we did.'

'Oh, Conrad, you know our marriage is over. Do the gentlemanly thing. All you need to do is go off to Brighton with a tart, we hire a private detective who bursts in on you and Bob's your uncle.'

Conrad raised his eyebrows. 'You want me to be the guilty party?'

'That's the gentlemanly thing to do, Conrad. And you've never been anything less than a gentleman. That's what Bryan did with Diana.' Bryan was Bryan Guinness: gentleman, devoted husband and cuckold.

Conrad shook his head. 'No, Veronica. I am not going to Brighton with a tart.'

'Oh.' She looked downcast. 'Well, be a dear and think about it, will you?'

The dinner ended on a cool note. When they left, Göring was still enjoying himself with his Luftwaffe cronies.

Conrad searched for a cab, but there was none, so they set off down the street to the next corner. It was quiet: the only people on the street were a group of four members of the SA with swastika armbands around their brown coats shaking tins, seeking donations for a Nazi charity, and laughing loudly. The SA, or Sturmabteilung, were the stormtroopers of the Nazi movement. They had been the strong arm of the Party during its rise to power, the muscle on the streets; their brown-shirted members had pride of place at the front of Nazi parades. That was until the Night of the Long Knives in June 1934, when Himmler's black-shirted SS had launched a coup against the SA, murdering most of their leaders. Now it was the tall blond SS supermen who strutted alongside the Führer, leaving the beefy thugs and bruisers of the SA to beg for alms and break Jewish shopkeepers' windows.

As Conrad and Veronica approached them, the laughter stopped. Veronica's grip on Conrad's arm tightened. One of the stormtroopers thrust out a tin and shook it. There was a strong smell of beer about the group, and also an air of suppressed excitement. Conrad was tempted to ignore them, but whether because of the presence of Veronica, the quietness of the street or the air of menace about the group, he dropped a few coins in the tin.

'*Heil Hitler!*' slurred one of the men.

'*Heil Hitler!*' said Veronica.

'I do wish you wouldn't say that,' Conrad protested in English as they hurried on.

'Oh, come on. It's just like *bonjour* in French, isn't it?'

'No, it isn't.'

About fifty yards further down the street, they came across a couple more stormtroopers, waving a tin under the nose of a professorial-looking gentleman in his sixties with a grey beard and a monocle.

'I'm sorry, I have no money,' the man who looked like a professor said in a shaky voice as Conrad and Veronica walked past. 'I left my wallet at home. I was just going for a walk.'

'Are you a Jew? He's a Jew, Fritz!'

There was something in the way that the man stiffened that led the two SA men to think that their suspicion was confirmed. Conrad paused. 'What's going on?' whispered Veronica, who didn't understand German.

'It doesn't look good,' said Conrad. He approached the stormtroopers, taking out his wallet. He extracted a note.

'Would you allow me, sir, to make a contribution on your behalf?' Conrad said to the professor, stuffing the note in the tin.

'Thank you, sir, but we need a contribution from this Jew.' The bigger of the two was speaking; he had a beer belly, close-cropped grey hair and meaty fists.

'But I've given you something for him,' said Conrad.

The stormtrooper grabbed the professor by the collar and shoved him up against the wall. 'You Jews are so tight,' he growled. 'Just a few marks for the honest German poor, that's all we're asking for.'

'But I have no money. I tell you, I have no money!' The professor's voice rose in panic and his eyes were wide with fear, a fear which seemed to feed the aggression in the stormtrooper.

'All Jews have money,' the thug growled.

'Put him down!' Veronica's voice rang out clear and English. 'Let him go, you brute.'

The stormtrooper hesitated, not sure how to treat a tall beautiful Aryan woman giving orders in a language he didn't understand.

'Don't worry, madam,' said the professor in heavily accented English. 'This is not your problem.'

The SA bully swung his fist into the professor's stomach and he doubled up, his monocle swinging from its cord.

In a flash Veronica slapped the stormtrooper hard across the face. 'Stop that at once!'

The other stormtrooper, smaller but meaner-looking, spoke in German. 'Leave us alone, *gnädige Frau*, or we will arrest you.'

Conrad touched Veronica's arm. 'Let's go,' he said.

Veronica glared at the second stormtrooper. 'Go away, you horrid little man,' she said. And then she slapped him too.

A red weal appeared on the pale skin of the smaller man. His eyes, which had been blurred with drink, focused in anger. He swung his right fist at Veronica.

Conrad caught it. 'Steady now,' he said.

The man swung his left, hitting Conrad rather feebly in the side. The bigger man dropped the professor and grasped Conrad's shoulder.

'Run, Veronica!' Conrad shouted. She grabbed the hand of the old professor, kicked off her high-heeled shoes and set off barefoot down the street. Conrad thrust his knee between the legs of the smaller man and wriggled free of his larger comrade. The big stormtrooper swung clumsily at Conrad's head. Conrad ducked and jabbed upwards at the stormtrooper's nose, which erupted in blood.

The group of four Brownshirts further down the road had heard the commotion and were running to help. Conrad turned and sprinted.

He had seen Veronica dash into a narrow side street, and he followed. He spotted her and the professor disappear down some steps leading to a basement. 'Stay there!' he shouted as he ran past.

It was a short street and Conrad had a good lead, so he slowed enough for his pursuers to see him rounding a corner at the far end. They followed, rushing past the basement where Veronica and the professor were hiding.

Conrad ran on, ducking from left to right down side streets and alleys. He was a fast runner and his followers soon gave up. When he was sure they were no longer on his tail, Conrad waited five minutes and then cautiously jogged back to Veronica's hiding place.

He looked over the railings down into the well. Half of the small space was illuminated by a street lamp. In the shadows of the remaining half a cigarette glowed.

Conrad descended the steps. Veronica was alone. 'Where's the Jewish professor?'

'Oh, he's gone. You know he really was most ungrateful. He said we were stupid to cause so much trouble and all that would happen was that we would get him thrown into a concentration camp.'

'He's probably right,' said Conrad.

'Probably. But it was rather fun, wasn't it?' Even in the dark Conrad could see Veronica's cheeks were flushed and her eyes gleaming.

He couldn't help returning her smile.

'You were so brave, taking on those two brutes,' she said.

'Well, thank you.' Conrad gave a little bow.

'You should have stayed to beat up the rest.'

'There were a few too many of them.'

'Not for you, darling.' Veronica dropped her cigarette. She was leaning against the wooden door of a basement. There was a strong smell of damp coal dust. Footsteps scurried by on the pavement above. 'Conrad?'

'Yes?'

'Kiss me.'

So Conrad kissed her.

They pulled apart. 'That was nice,' said Veronica. 'Now, let's get my shoes and you can take me back to my hotel.'

Confused and angry with himself, Conrad led Veronica up the steps to the side street. As they turned the corner on to the street where they had met the stormtroopers, they saw a bundle crumpled on the pavement.

Conrad ran. It was the professor, blood seeping from his temple and the corner of his mouth, his face lying in splinters of glass from his smashed monocle. Conrad took off his jacket to make a pillow and shoved it under the professor's head.

'Oh, God!' said Veronica.

The man's eyelids fluttered and he tried to say something. Conrad bent close to his mouth to hear. The words were in English.

'Tell your wife... tell your wife her own business to watch.'

Conrad turned to Veronica. 'Get an ambulance!' he shouted. 'How do I do that?'

'There's a telephone box at the end of the street over there. Here's the money.' Conrad fished some coins out of his pocket and flung them at her. '*Krankenwagen*. Ask for a *Krankenwagen*!'

But the man had died before Veronica had even reached the telephone box.

Nine

Theo hurried along the corridors of the offices on the Tirpit-zufer, nodding and saluting as he passed uniformed colleagues on the way. He hadn't quite told the truth when he had claimed to Conrad that he worked in the War Ministry. The War Ministry was indeed next door, on the Bendlerstrasse, but this particular set of corridors and cubbyholes was the domain of an organization known as the Abwehr. The Abwehr was the German secret service, and it was quite successfully secret: few Germans and even fewer foreigners knew of its existence. And it was the head of the Abwehr, Admiral Wilhelm Canaris, who wanted to see him.

Canaris's offices were on the top floor of the building with a view over the Landwehr Canal, in this part of Berlin an elegant stretch of water lined with chestnut trees and ornate residences. The admiral was waiting for him, together with Colonel Hans Oster, the head of Section Z of the Abwehr and Theo's direct boss. Section Z was responsible for administration and organization. Although this might sound the most bureaucratic of the various departments, it was actually one of the most influential. Oster was the man Canaris turned to when he needed something done, and, increasingly, Oster would turn to Theo.

Canaris smiled and bade Theo sit down. There was a pleasing informality about the Abwehr, Theo thought. Although staffed solely by military officers, they treated each other courteously and with respect, a culture that had been reinforced when Canaris arrived as the new chief in 1935. The admiral was a small, mild-looking man with white hair and a sallow skin. In the war he had had a lively naval intelligence career in South America and then in Africa, where, in addition to picking up useful skills and languages, he had contracted malaria. Theo thought of his chief not as a high-ranking German officer but rather as a cosmopolitan in a uniform. Canaris was fond of quoting the motto of the founder of the Abwehr, Colonel Nicolai: 'Secret work must always be the preserve of the gentleman. When this ceases to be the case, all is doomed to failure.'

Colonel Oster was not quite as subtle as his boss, but was just as intelligent. He was a dashing, good-looking officer who wore the Iron Cross First and Second Class and the Knight's Cross with Swords, decorations he had won on the Western Front. After the war he had served under General von Hertenberg, which was how he had first come across Theo. On a visit to his former commanding officer's Pomeranian estate, Oster had been introduced to Theo and immediately recognized his talents. Over a period of nearly a year, Oster had persuaded him to join the Abwehr.

Oster seemed to know everyone and everything, and he had a knack of inspiring loyalty and trust in his fellow officers, both senior and junior. Theo liked and respected him, and the sentiment seemed to be reciprocated. There had been a scandal several years before when Oster had been stripped of his rank after having an affair with the wife of a senior officer, but Canaris had reinstated him and the two men worked well together.

'Ah, good morning, Hertenberg,' Canaris began. 'We have confirmation about Mühlendorf.' As Canaris spoke, a dachshund trotted over from a basket in the corner and hopped on to his lap. The admiral stroked the dog absently.

Theo raised his eyebrows. 'From the Gestapo?'

'No. From Moscow. He was seen speaking to a senior officer in the NKVD a week before he left for Berlin.'

'Just as we thought. And that explains one thing that never quite made sense to me.'

'What is that?' asked Canaris.

'Why he didn't talk. I know the Gestapo didn't get very far in their interrogation, but Mühlendorf knew what he was in for. If he really was just a diplomat purveying gossip he would have given the Gestapo everything they wanted and more right away. He was holding out on them; he had something to hide.'

'Do you think he had heard anything specific?'

'About a plot against Hitler?'

Canaris nodded.

'No,' said Theo. 'And especially not if he was a Soviet spy. He was on a fishing expedition. He told de Lancey to tell me that he had friends who could help. Perhaps he was referring to the Soviets.'

'Perhaps,' said Canaris. 'Is there any chance that de Lancey is a Soviet spy also?'

'I would be very surprised,' said Theo.

'Tell us about de Lancey,' said Oster, speaking for the first time. 'We are really quite interested in that man.'

So Theo told them.

The Tiergartenstrasse, as its name suggested, ran along the southern perimeter of the park. Conrad knew he was getting close to number seventeen when he saw a queue snaking along the pavement beside the brand-new pink-stucco Italian Embassy. He followed the line towards a fine eighteenth-century sandstone building and was stopped by a large Yorkshireman in a commissionaire's uniform, displaying a row of medals from the Great War.

'I'd like to see Captain Foley, please,' Conrad said in his best English accent. 'My name's de Lancey.'

Conrad waited as the commissionaire disappeared. One of his colleagues was dispensing tea from a trolley to the line of supplicants. They were pinched, desperate-looking people, some well dressed, some in little more than rags. Many of them appeared Jewish to Conrad, although he might have been mistaken. He wasn't convinced that you could always identify a Jew simply by looking at him, and he didn't like the Nazi assumption that you could.

Conrad was tired. He had spent half the night at police head-quarters in the Alexanderplatz. Veronica had suggested that they leave the dead professor where he was, but Conrad had insisted on waiting for the police. He was not going to walk away and pretend that nothing had happened, however much trouble that might cause. The grizzled sergeant who had taken down the details of the incident grasped the situation immediately, and explained that since Conrad and Veronica had not actually seen the SA men beat up the professor, it would be impossible to bring charges against them successfully.

It turned out that the professor wasn't actually a professor, but a Jewish schoolteacher from Charlottenburg who had been giving a private lesson close by. The police sergeant refused to give Conrad the teacher's address so he could speak to the man's family. Although frustrated by the sergeant's unwilling-ness to help, Conrad recognized that he was simply trying to keep two foreigners out of trouble. After initially weeping softly to herself on the pavement, Veronica had pulled herself together and sat through the rest of the night in silence, her face cast in a mask of cold haughtiness. She rebuffed Conrad's gestures of comfort. Conrad knew his wife was in distress, but he also knew she wouldn't admit it, even to him. It was three o'clock before Conrad deposited her at the door of the Adlon and said goodbye. He had no desire to see any more of her while she was in Berlin.

The Yorkshire commissionaire reappeared, and at his 'Follow me, sir' Conrad crossed a courtyard and climbed some steps into an entrance hall. Inside, it was mayhem; here the queue bunched and heaved and became an insistent mob. Conrad was ushered up the stairs into an inner office on the first floor. Foley was sitting at his desk, in front of which stood a tall, well-dressed businessman.

Foley leaped to his feet and held out his hand. 'Ah, good morning, de Lancey. This is Herr Trencholtz.'

The businessman turned to Conrad. 'Delighted to meet you,' he said in perfect unaccented English, holding out his hand. Conrad shook it.

A spaniel appeared from under the desk and sniffed Conrad's trousers.

'One moment, de Lancey,' Foley said, returning to his desk. 'Have a seat. We won't be long here.'

Conrad sat down and fondled the spaniel's ears. Foley examined the German businessman's passport and a visa application next to it. He studied the paper and then the man in front of him. He picked up a red pencil and drew a line through the application. 'I'm sorry, I'm unable to grant you a visa,' he said to the man, in German.

The businessman replied in rapid angry English that he had received an invitation from Imperial Chemical Industries and that the British Home Office had granted a permit on his behalf.

'Yes, I have read the permit,' said Foley, once again in German. 'It entitles me to grant you a visa, but it doesn't oblige me to.'

'But why haven't you?' protested Herr Trencholtz. 'There must be a reason.'

Foley smiled politely. 'I'm terribly sorry, but I'm afraid we don't discuss the reasons for our decisions. Matter of policy, you know. Now, good day.' He ushered the man, still protesting, out of his office. The businessman was nearly a foot taller than him. He returned to his desk and stuck a pipe in his mouth. 'What did you think of him, then?'

'He seemed perfectly respectable to me,' said Conrad.

'Too respectable. A spy if ever I saw one,' said Foley. 'We don't need his type in Britain.' He smiled at the spaniel, which was leaning against Conrad's trousers, rhythmically thumping his tail. 'I see Jonny likes you, that's a good sign. Did you know that Jonny is a good Aryan dog?'

He put his hand in a small bowl on his desk and the dog pricked up his ears. 'Come on, Jonny, show the gentleman you are an Aryan. Say "*Heil Hitler*".'

The dog leaped on to its hind legs, lifted up its right paw and gave two sharp barks. 'Good boy,' said Foley and tossed him a lump of sugar. 'Now, what can I do for you?'

Conrad explained Anneliese's father's predicament. Foley listened carefully, pulling on his pipe.

'Dr Werner Rosen, did you say? I remember the case; it was highly publicized at the time. Shocking. And I think your friend is right to be concerned. He's just the sort of man the Gestapo would throw into protective custody.'

'Can you help him?'

'Did your friend explain how the system works? Does he have enough money for the Capitalist Certificate?'

Anneliese had explained this to Conrad. In order to be eligible for a visa to Palestine an applicant had to show proof that he had at least a thousand pounds available to him when he arrived there. Even for wealthy Jews this was a problem, since it took months or even years to get the foreign exchange cleared through the Reichsbank. For the likes of Dr Rosen it was an impossibility. The family's savings were non-existent.

'I'm afraid not. What about Britain? Can you get him a visa for England?'

Foley shook his head. 'The British Medical Association have been complaining about the number of Jewish doctors entering the country. They say that British medicine has nothing to gain from new blood and much to lose from foreign dilution.' Foley's voice was laced with contempt. 'They sound almost as bad as the Nazi who complained about the blood transfusion in the first place, don't they?'

'He wouldn't have to practise as a doctor—'

Foley raised his hand to halt Conrad. 'Believe me, if there was a way I could let even half of those people out there into Britain, I would. But I can't. I ask for more visas but the Foreign Office doesn't give me them. And with all the Arab unrest in Palestine in the last couple of years, they are not happy taking in more Jews there, either. I'm in a very difficult position here; we all are. We have to decide who stays and who goes, and we have to be fair to everyone, however impossible that is in reality. Dr Rosen's case is compelling, but so are all those other cases. I can't let one applicant through because he has a British friend who will speak up for him. It's not just.'

'Would it be any different if I had gone along with your request to spy for you?' asked Conrad.

'Do you have something you want to tell me?' Foley sat

back in his chair, puffing at his pipe in a slow rhythm, and waited.

Conrad took a deep breath. 'As you know, I was arrested two weeks ago. By the Gestapo.'

'Go ahead, old man.'

Foley listened closely as Conrad described the evening in the Kakadu, Joachim's gossiping, and then his arrest, interrogation and death.

'I'm sorry about your cousin,' said Foley, when Conrad had finished. 'I hear so many of these stories and each is terrible in its own way; all the victims have friends, families.'

Conrad gave a brief nod of acknowledgement.

'Do you think the plot is just a rumour?' Foley asked.

'I have no way of knowing.'

'What about von Hertenberg? What's his view?'

'He thinks it's just gossip.' Conrad decided not to mention Theo's theory that Joachim was a spy. It would only encourage Foley's suspicions of his friend.

'And you don't believe him?' Foley was studying Conrad's face intently through those owl-like glasses.

'Can you do something about Dr Rosen?' Conrad asked.

Foley frowned. 'I'm hoping to get another small batch of visas through from London next week.'

'He's due to be released next week.'

'I can't promise anything, de Lancey,' said Foley with a sigh. 'I really can't.' He studied Conrad. 'What you've told me is very useful. But I would like to find out some more about your friend von Hertenberg.'

'Why?' asked Conrad. 'He says he's a lawyer in the War Ministry. What possible interest could that be to you?'

'I think he's more than just a lawyer.'

'Well, what is he then?'

Foley shook his head. 'I can't tell you more than that.'

'I'm afraid I'm not inclined to spy on my friend,' said Conrad. 'Especially if you won't tell me why I should.'

'Oh, I can tell you why you should,' said Foley. 'The politicians back home may talk until they are blue in the face, but you and I both know that the Nazi regime is evil and the one way that Hitler will be stopped is by war. It might be this year, it might be in five years' time, but at some point our country will be fighting this one.'

Conrad was listening.

'God knows, I love Germany,' Foley went on. 'I've lived here for nearly twenty years, and I hate war. But it's going to happen. And when it does happen, unless Britain is a damned sight better prepared than she is at the moment, we will lose. That doesn't just mean that the Germans will win, it means that the Nazis will rule Europe. Whatever our misgivings, it's up to all of us to do everything we can to stop that happening.'

Conrad shook his head. 'Theo is my friend,' he said, and got up to leave. 'Please do all you can for Dr Rosen.'

Foley stood up and saw Conrad to the door of his office. 'Think about it,' he said, as he shook Conrad's hand.

As Conrad left the Passport Control Office, he did think about it. He brushed past the queue outside and jumped on to a cream-coloured bus heading east towards Unter den Linden and the Stabi. He climbed up to the upper deck and stared out at the green treetops of the Tiergarten.

There was no doubt in Conrad's mind that if he helped Captain Foley the chances of Anneliese's father getting a visa for Britain would be much higher. He was sure Foley really did have strict limits on the number of visas he could issue, but as long as some were available, Dr Rosen would get one. If Conrad did nothing the poor man would rot in a concentration camp. There might be thousands of others like him in Germany, but Conrad couldn't do anything to help them. He might be able to help Dr Rosen, to do something useful for once.

Anneliese would be very grateful. True, he had found her company fun, stimulating – more than that, exciting. But he was married and still faithful to his wife. He wished he hadn't kissed Veronica. How could he allow himself to be manipulated by her still? Perhaps he was wrong to be wary of seeing other girls; perhaps the sooner he did so the sooner he would escape Veronica's influence over him.

But how could he spy on Theo, his friend? Or was Theo his enemy? Conrad's conversation with Theo after the dinner party had crystallized a series of little inconsistencies into solid suspicion. Yes, Theo counted Conrad as a friend. That was why he had put pressure on his friends – *friends*, for God's sake – in the Gestapo to release Conrad. Why he wanted Conrad to forget about Joachim and avoid more trouble with the Gestapo. Oh, yes, it looked as if Theo was being loyal to his old friend. But it also looked as if he had sold out Joachim.

Theo obviously wasn't an innocent lawyer in the War Ministry. He knew more than he was letting on: it was distinctly possible that he had passed on Joachim's tittle-tattle in the Kakadu to his friends in the Gestapo. And now Joachim was dead.

Perhaps this was a chance for Conrad to do something about Joachim's death. Find out exactly what Theo was up to, and, yes, if necessary use him. Because if Theo had caused Joachim to be arrested he deserved more than to be spied upon.

The bus crept towards the Potsdamer Platz, a maelstrom of metal spinning around a flimsy traffic tower on four spindly legs. It was the bustling centre of modern Berlin, criss-crossed with tarmac, rails and overhead wires, the magnificent façade of Wertheim's department store rising massively off to the left and the Columbia-Haus, a curved modern office block, loomed on the right.

Conrad looked out at the gleaming new Germany and felt the anger rise in him: the anger born out of his frustration at what had happened in Spain, his inactivity in England afterwards, at the battering to death of Joachim and the Jewish schoolteacher, at the way the dictators, the torturers, the murderers, the burners of books, the destroyers of liberty were taking over Europe and no one was stopping them. No one!

He remembered what Theo had said about how the Germans were sleepwalking to oblivion. Theo was dead right. He glanced at the couple in the seat next to him: he was middle-aged, portly with a fine walrus moustache and a watch chain straining across his bulging waistcoat; she was small, wide, with flabby cheeks and kindly eyes. Respectable, law-abiding sleepwalkers.

That was the old Theo speaking. The Theo Conrad knew and understood. He hated the idea that that Theo had gone. Conrad had lost so much over the previous year: his wife, his socialist ideals, his cousin; he was in danger of losing his belief in humanity. And yet Conrad *did* believe in humanity: it was an essential optimism about the goodness of the ordinary human being that kept him going. If Theo of all people had become a Nazi then that belief, that optimism would be severely damaged, perhaps irreparably. And without it, there was darkness. Conrad was not easily frightened, but that darkness scared him.

He had to know who Theo really was.

The bus swished along Leipziger Strasse past Göring's new Air Ministry, a stark, swastika-embossed limestone pile guarded by tall iron bars and an eagle perched on top of a squat pedestal. Two Luftwaffe soldiers goose-stepped in an absurd pas de deux outside.

Was there any truth in what Foley was saying about the inevitability of war? Conrad feared there was: he felt his old confidence that peace could be preserved slipping away. But he had to cling on to it. If the politicians, if the people, could just keep their heads and not do anything stupid, war could be averted. Well, that might be a possibility in Britain, perhaps, or France, but what of Germany? Would Hitler keep his head? Would all those Nazis strutting around in their uniforms? Would the massed crowds at the Party rallies?

Conrad was not going to abandon the possibility of peace just because of glib platitudes from a minor Foreign Office functionary about duty and his father's bravery. The Great War had shown up the idiocy of blind patriotism. Foley was trying to manipulate him into participating in just the sort of diplomatic games that had ignited that conflict. Trying to get him to compromise on his pacifism in order to fight the Nazis. Conrad had done that once before, in Spain, and it hadn't worked. Should he really do it again?

Despite the evidence, Conrad couldn't quite bring himself to believe that Theo had shopped Joachim to the Gestapo. Perhaps there had been microphones in the Kakadu, or a lip-reader with really good eyesight who could understand English, however unlikely both of those possibilities seemed. He didn't know for certain, either, that Dr Rosen would be released if he cooperated with Foley. But Conrad did know that once he undertook to be a spy for the British government against his best friend he would have taken an irrevocable step, become a different person, a person he didn't want to be.

As the bus lurched to a stop on the corner of Friedrichstrasse and Unter den Linden, and Conrad stepped on to the pavement, he came to a decision. It would be wrong to try to trick Theo into giving him secrets, that would be betraying their friendship. But if he asked him straight out, then it would be up to Theo whether to help him or not. He had no idea what Theo's reaction would be. Theo might have joined the German army, but he had always had a strong sense of justice and an equally strong dose of common sense. He must realize that Hitler was wrong – worse than wrong, evil. There was a chance, a good chance that he would be sympathetic to Conrad's suggestion.

And, either way, Conrad would find out who Theo really was.

The woman getting off the bus after Conrad had no idea of the turmoil simmering in the Englishman's brain. She was just doing her job. She was in her early thirties, smallish, wearing a brown hat and shapeless raincoat and carrying a shopping bag, one of thousands of such women in Berlin. Her job was made easier by Conrad's preoccupation. And it was a job well done: Conrad's visit to the British Passport Control Office would be sure to interest her superiors.

Ten

Conrad had been waiting on the Bendlerstrasse outside the War Ministry for an hour and a half. He lit another cigarette and checked his watch – it was half past six. Conrad was pretty sure he hadn't missed him, but he didn't know how late Theo might work. And of course he didn't really know whether Theo worked in the War Ministry at all; that was what he was here to confirm. If he didn't see Theo that evening, he would try Gestapo headquarters on the Prinz-Albrecht-Strasse the following day.

He turned away from the entrance to the ministry and looked down the street to see the tall figure of Theo striding towards him from the direction of the Tirpitzufer, the road that ran along the Landwehr Canal. Theo was almost upon him before he recognized his friend. 'Conrad! What are you doing here?'

'I wanted to talk to you and so I thought I would wait for you to leave your office.'

Theo glanced up at the imposing grey block of the ministry building. 'Well, this is a damn silly place to wait. We'll be seen.'

'Does that matter?' said Conrad. 'We are friends after all. What's strange in us meeting?'

'Do you realize we are being watched?'

Conrad looked up and down the street. There were three people waiting at a bus stop about a hundred yards away. A woman, a round old man and a tall man with an umbrella and hat. At that distance it was difficult to see any of the three closely.

'The tall man by the bus stop?'

'No, the woman,' Theo said.

'Is she watching me or you?'

'Well, she's watching both of us now, isn't she?'

'Let's walk to your flat then,' said Conrad. 'I have something I want to say to you.'

Theo paused to light a cigarette. 'If you want to say something important, it's better we don't go to my flat.'

'Oh, the microphones.'

'It's always safest to assume they are there. Let's go down to the canal.'

'What about our tail?'

'She won't get close enough to hear.'

They crossed the Tirpitzufer and walked along the path next to the Landwehr Canal, under the chestnuts. Above them was the new Shell building, an elegant nine-storey edifice whose smooth white curves looked effete compared to the strong square slabs of Nazi construction sprouting up all over Berlin.

Conrad hesitated as he prepared to tackle Theo on Foley's request, but it was Theo who brought the subject up before Conrad had a chance. 'So you've been to the British Passport Control Office?'

'Yes. I wanted to speak to the people there about a visa for Anneliese's father. You know he's in prison?'

'By "the people" you mean Captain Foley?'

'Yes, I do,' admitted Conrad. 'But how did you know I've been there?'

'And do you know that Captain Foley is head of the British Secret Service in Berlin?'

'I guessed as much,' said Conrad. 'Is it you who has been having me followed? Don't you trust me?'

For the first time since they had met that evening, Theo smiled. 'Yes, actually, I do trust you. About the big things, anyway.'

'What do you mean?'

'I mean, I trust your instincts, your beliefs. You're a good man, Conrad, an honest man, someone who believes in right and wrong and who will stand up against injustice when you see it.' Theo's voice was warm, but it was warmth tinged with a touch of sadness. 'That's why I think you should go back to England.'

'But why?' said Conrad. 'You said yourself the people of this country are sleepwalking. So are the people of my country. Do you want me to join them?'

'They weren't all sleepwalking,' said Theo. 'When the Nazis came to power and Hitler usurped the constitution, there were many people who looked the other way, myself included, I'm ashamed to say. But there were some, hundreds – no, thousands – who stood up and shouted that what was happening was wrong. Students, workers, trade unionists, writers, civil servants, lawyers, artists, schoolteachers, academics, pastors. People like you.'

'Well, it seems there aren't enough of us,' said Conrad.

'The cemeteries are full of you,' said Theo. 'And the concentration camps. You asked whether I trusted you; well, I don't trust you to keep yourself out of a graveyard.'

'They won't touch me,' said Conrad. 'I'm a foreigner, and a well-connected foreigner at that.'

'Oh, believe me, Conrad, if they really want to, they'll touch you. They won't be stupid enough to arrest you and put you on trial. A bullet in the back of the head is all it needs. Perhaps your body will never be found. Go home, Conrad. Please.'

They came to a little bridge over the canal and crossed it, heading back towards Bendlerstrasse. A barge nosed quietly through the dark water. Conrad spotted the woman following them, now facing them on the other side of the canal. She turned and dropped her shopping bag, spilling a couple of items on to the pavement, and stooped immediately to pick them up.

Given what Theo had told him, Conrad wondered whether he should continue with his plan. But now he needed to know more than ever whose side Theo was on.

'You said you are not a Nazi,' he began. 'And that you think the Nazis are mad.'

'What if I did?' said Theo.

'I don't know what exactly you do at the War Ministry, but if you come across any pieces of information that are interesting, you might pass them on to me? Something about Joachim's plot to overthrow Hitler, perhaps?'

Instantly Theo stopped, as if he had been struck. He glanced quickly at Conrad with an expression of shock and surprise; then he took a deep breath and walked on, staring straight ahead, his jaw set, the duelling scar stretched taut.

'Theo?' Conrad said, searching for a response and getting none. 'You could choose what to give me. Just things that might damage Hitler.' They walked on in a silence that was rapidly becoming unpleasant. 'Theo?'

'You're asking me to spy on my country,' Theo muttered.

'I'm asking you to help stop Hitler starting a war.'

'No,' Theo said. 'If a war starts between our two countries, which is highly likely, you're asking me to help Germany lose it.'

'If a war starts it will be Hitler who starts it,' Conrad said.

'I can't believe this!' Theo said. 'What right have you got to ask me to betray my country?'

'I'm not asking you to betray your country,' Conrad said. 'Just to stop the Nazis.'

Theo's eyes were alive with anger. 'Look, Conrad. I thought you were on the side of peace and against war. I thought you were for the international brotherhood of man. I thought you swore that you wouldn't let anyone order you to kill other people.'

'Yes,' said Conrad, swallowing. 'I believe in all that.'

'You can either be in favour of peace, or you can be on the side of your country against mine,' Theo said. 'What you cannot do is try to persuade me that spying for your country against my own is somehow backing the cause of international peace and harmony.'

'I decided to ask you straight out,' protested Conrad. 'I'm not trying to trick you or anything.'

'Captain Foley asked you to do this, didn't he?'

'Yes,' admitted Conrad.

'Why me? Why is he interested in me?'

'I don't know,' said Conrad. 'But I suspect *you* do.'

Theo snorted and shook his head. 'I was wrong when I said I trusted you. You, of all people, to become a spy.'

'All right,' said Conrad. 'If you don't want to tell me anything I understand.'

'You're damn right I don't want to tell you anything!' Theo stopped and faced Conrad. 'Look, I suggest you go back to your flat, pack your suitcase and get a train back to England. And until you do so, I suggest we don't meet again.'

He hailed a passing taxi, which pulled over. He climbed in and wound down the window. 'Go home, Conrad. If you want to stay alive, go home.'

Conrad trudged back to his hotel. The sky was grey and it began to rain. Conrad ignored it, moving slowly, not bothering to check whether the woman or some as yet unidentified colleague of hers was following him.

If Conrad had ever had any doubts that Theo was not simply drafting legal documents in a little office in the War Ministry, he had lost them now. Theo had put a tail on Conrad. He knew all about Captain Foley and the British Passport Control Office. And his contacts were good enough to tell him that Joachim was a Soviet spy.

Theo's accusations had struck home. Conrad didn't like his friend, or former friend, claiming that he had sold out his principles. That was the whole point of tackling Theo directly; if Theo really was as anti-Nazi as he claimed then he should have been all too eager to help Conrad.

But he hadn't been. And the obvious conclusion was staring Conrad in the face. Theo had become a dyed-in-the-wool Nazi who would ruthlessly betray first Joachim and then him.

The idea hit Conrad hard. It undermined not just his trust in Theo and his friendship, but his very understanding of the world. But, despite all the evidence, Conrad couldn't quite accept it yet. He had hoped the confrontation with Theo would bring certainty. Instead it had piled on further doubts.

At Oxford, Theo had enjoyed a reputation as a bit of an enigma. But Conrad had understood him – or thought he had. There were three opposing forces in Theo's character. There was the arrogant, upright Prussian, with his belief in order and duty. Then there was the romantic intellectual who liked to discuss poetry and ideology late into the night. And finally there was the charming, good-looking man-about-town who could drink his male friends under the table, and charm his female friends under the bedcovers. These aspects of his character seemed to be in constant conflict; at any time one or other was dominant, but the others were always there under the surface.

So who was Theo now? The Prussian patriot? The ideological Nazi? Although Conrad had seen him with flirting with the blonde girl, Anneliese's friend, at the dinner party, he seemed much more serious than Conrad had ever known him. None of this quite made sense.

Theo had been serious when he had warned Conrad about the dangers of staying in Germany, deadly serious. Conrad accepted that Theo had a point: he must be more careful how he behaved in Berlin, and he could not assume that just because he was a former British government minister's son he was safe. But Conrad wasn't going to run away. Joachim had followed his principles and died for them. Conrad had been prepared to die for his in Spain, and had seen too many of his brave colleagues give up their lives for an ideal. What was happening to people like Joachim, like the schoolteacher in the street, like Anneliese's father, like countless other Germans, was wrong and Conrad couldn't – wouldn't – run away from it.

Eleven

General Ludwig Beck, Chief of the General Staff, surveyed the remains of the dinner that he and twenty of his fellow staff officers had just consumed. Candlelight glimmered off silver candlesticks and cutlery, sparkled through crystal glasses and decanters, and gleamed in shimmering pools on the deeply polished wood of the dining table in the private room of the Esplanade Hotel in Berlin. The grey of the officers' uniforms and the black of the iron crosses adorning their necks flickered in shadows. Although they were relaxing after a good meal and plenty of drink, their sabre-scarred faces betrayed the intelligence, discipline and imagination that had made the German general staff the envy of the world for at least a century.

Beck hadn't eaten or drunk much of the food and wine. An austere, thin figure, he possessed an iron self-discipline, into which he had retreated after the death of his wife from tuberculosis in 1917 when they had been married only one year. Although a highly talented violinist, he hadn't played a note since that day. Unlike many of the men around the table, Beck was not from a Prussian military family: he was an intellectual from the Rhineland, widely read in philosophy, economics and French literature. He was the brains behind the army, the author of the highly praised *German Army Manual of Tactics* and the proud successor to von Moltke, who had planned the victory in the Franco-Prussian War, and to von Schlieffen, whose strategy had nearly led to a swift German triumph in 1914. A small man with an intense, intelligent face, his student duelling scar took the form of a swirl on his temple just behind his left eye.

They had spent the day in the best tradition of the Prussian general staff, playing a war game. This had tested 'Case Green', a German invasion of Czechoslovakia, with the French coming to the Czechs' aid. The results had been even worse than Beck had expected. The Czechs had thirty-four well-trained and well-armed divisions and a string of robust fortifications along their border with Germany. The German army had indeed prevailed against the Czechs, but it had taken them three months, during which time the French army had smashed the six German divisions facing them in the west, and swept across the Rhineland deep into Germany. The Germans lost; the French won. That was the inescapable conclusion.

Beck wasn't surprised. As a professional military strategist he was deeply suspicious of Hitler's plans. The previous November Hitler had called in his service chiefs for a conference at the Reich Chancellery and delivered a five-hour harangue on his scheme to win *Lebensraum* in Central and Eastern Europe. First Austria, then Czechoslovakia, then Danzig and Poland would be attacked to secure 'living space' for the German people, and all this would happen between 1938 at the earliest and 1943 at the latest. Beck hadn't been at that meeting, but General von Fritsch, the then commander-in-chief of the army, had been so incensed that despite being sworn to secrecy he had immediately rushed out to confer with his loyal deputy. Von Fritsch was convinced that the British, French and Russians would not sit idly by and watch Germany swallow up the eastern half of Europe. A world war would be the inevitable result, a war that Germany would lose. Beck agreed, and had spent the last several months firing off furious memoranda about the economic and military weaknesses of the idea: the memorandum was General Beck's weapon of choice. Since the humiliation of von Fritsch and his replacement by the much more malleable General von Brauchitsch, Beck had kept the memoranda flying.

As yet he had had no success.

Beck was still angry at the way von Fritsch had been framed by an unholy alliance of the SS, the Gestapo and Göring, with the tacit encouragement of the Führer himself. He was no admirer of Hitler, but he was a soldier who knew his duty. He saw his role as one of providing counsel, and if that was rejected, obeying orders. When one of his own subordinates had muttered that something must be done to avenge the humiliation of General von Fritsch, Beck had quoted his famous predecessor, Count Schlieffen: 'Mutiny and revolution are words that have no place in a German officer's vocabulary.'

Besides, von Fritsch had made it absolutely clear to Beck that it was of the utmost importance that Beck maintain his position as Chief of the General Staff and not allow himself to be outmanoeuvred into relinquishing it by Göring or Heydrich or any of the other of von Fritsch's enemies.

He took out a sheet of paper and glanced at the speech he was about to deliver summing up the lesson to be learned from the day. It was simple: the political leadership, meaning Hitler, must be made to understand the consequences of its policy towards Czechoslovakia. Defeat. Humiliating defeat.

He surveyed the officers round the table. Most, such as General of Artillery Halder, his deputy, were loyal to the traditions and principles of the German army. There were one or two, some of the younger men, Luftwaffe officers, who had been seduced by Hitler's overconfidence. But overconfidence didn't win wars, good planning did. If Beck knew anything about war he knew that.

He rose to his feet to propose the toast. In his youth, and in the time of his most illustrious predecessors, this would have been to the Kaiser. But not now.

He swallowed and raised his glass. 'Gentlemen. The Führer.'

Conrad saw Anneliese the instant she walked into the café. He watched her as she spoke a few words to the waiter, her eyes flashing as she laughed at his reply. She was lovelier than he remembered.

It had proved difficult to pin her down; the number she had given him belonged to a communal telephone, and she seemed to work odd hours in the hospital, but eventually he had got through and she had agreed to meet him for lunch at the Café Josty in the Potsdamer Platz. Dinner was out of the question because she was working night shifts.

She was shown to his table. She was dressed very properly in a dark green suit, white gloves and a small green hat, but there was still something alluring in the way she moved. Despite the Nazi strictures on women wearing make-up, she wore lipstick.

'I love this place,' she said. 'It's the best people-watching café in Berlin.' And it was true. Large plate-glass windows looked out upon the busy square, alive with people, bicycles, trams, buses and motor cars. Inside the café was crowded too, but it had a cosy feel to it. 'And they have all the foreign newspapers. Censored, these days, of course. But it's a good place to catch up on what's *really* going on in the world.'

'Have you just come from the hospital?'

'Not quite. I was working the night shift, so I've only had time for a couple of hours' sleep this morning. You must forgive me if I'm a bit dopey.'

'Busy night?'

'Very busy, thanks to Frau Grynszpan.'

'The ward sister?'

'No, a patient. She has had a hernia operation. But I've been her captive audience for the past week. She has a grandson she is desperate to introduce me to. I finally saw him last night.'

'What's he like?'

'Twenty and very shy, very earnest. And *very* polite. The poor man – his grandmother was staring at him hard the whole time he was talking to me. And I would swear that she told him what to say. The line that particularly impressed me was, "Do you like gefilte fish? It is my favourite food. I know where you can buy the best gefilte fish in Berlin."'

'Gefilte fish?'

'Jewish fish balls. They are disgusting. Or at least I think so; the Grynszpan family obviously doesn't.'

Conrad laughed. 'I hope you were kind to the poor boy.'

'Yes, I was. I agreed to go with him to the gefilte fish stand next Sunday, and Frau Grynszpan was so chuffed. Then afterwards, as he was leaving, I told him I had suddenly remembered I had promised a friend I would go to church with her that morning so I couldn't make it, but not to tell his grandmother as it would only upset her. You should have seen the look of relief on his face! I didn't realize I was that frightening.'

'Well, it sounds as if you were considerably less frightening than his grandmother.'

'But not the gefilte fish.' Anneliese shuddered and examined the menu. 'Fortunately there are none on offer here.' They ordered sausages. The problem with lunch in Berlin was that when you came down to it, the choice was always some kind of sausage or ham. Fortunately Conrad was growing quite partial to the various *Würste*.

'I spoke to Captain Foley of the Passport Control Office about your father,' Conrad said.

Anneliese's eyes lit up. 'And?'

'No luck.'

'Is there nothing you could do to persuade him?'

Conrad shook his head. 'I did try quite hard,' he said. He had decided he had better not describe exactly *how* hard.

The light in her eyes disappeared and her shoulders slumped. 'Oh, well. Thanks for the thought.'

'When is he due for release?'

'Next Monday.'

'Perhaps they won't rearrest him.'

'Oh, they will. I'm quite sure they will unless I can get him out of the country somehow.'

'Perhaps these concentration camps are not that bad,' said Conrad. 'No one seems to know for sure what goes on in them. An American journalist friend of mine has been to Dachau near Munich. He said it was a bit Spartan, but the inmates were well fed and quite cheerful.'

'Those weren't the inmates, they were the guards,' said Anneliese.

'No, Warren said—'

'They were the guards,' said Anneliese firmly. 'When they have visitors they lock up the inmates and put the guards in prisoners' clothes. I've seen them do it.'

'You've *seen* them?'

Anneliese sighed. 'Yes. You see I *know* what a concentration camp is like. And I couldn't bear it if my father ended up in one.' She bit her lip and a tear ran down her cheek. The change from her previous confidence caught Conrad by surprise. All at once he remembered Theo's comment about her, his suggestion that it wasn't just the treatment of her father that would cause her to hate the regime.

'I say, Anneliese. I'm... so sorry. You've been in one, haven't you? You know all about them. And I was sounding off on something I don't have the faintest clue about.'

Anneliese wiped her cheeks and smiled at him. 'Usually I try not to talk about it.' She sniffed. 'I think I mentioned I had to interrupt my medical studies—'

'If you don't want to say anything—'

'No, no, that's all right. I'd like to talk about it. I've nothing to be ashamed of. And I grilled you about your wife at dinner.' A smile reappeared for an instant, and then it was gone. 'When I was at university I became involved in politics, or rather my boyfriend did. His name was Paul and I was devoted to him. Everyone was; he was a natural leader. And he was a communist. This was in 1929 – before the Nazis came to power. He and I used to organize marches at the university. So did the National Socialists. A lot of them ended up as fights. But I thought Nazism was evil and communism was the only way forward for humanity. It seemed the natural extension of all my father had taught me: humanism, a distrust of religion, a desire to do something to help the poor and underprivileged, and also a form of self-discipline. I was eighteen, I was in love and I was an idealist – what is wrong with that?'

'Nothing,' said Conrad. 'In fact I rather wish I had known you then.'

'Well, we worked hard, Paul and I. We marched, we organized, we made speeches, we wrote articles, we published pamphlets. But despite all our efforts the National Socialists won the election in January 1933.'

'I remember. I was here in Berlin.'

'Were you here a month later, after the Reichstag fire? Hitler blamed it on the communists and rounded us all up. Paul and I were sent to concentration camps – separately of course. It was horrible, truly horrible. I was only there for six months, but never again.' She shook her head. 'Never again.'

Anneliese glanced at Conrad who was listening attentively. 'It was the guards that made those places evil. They could have been merely unpleasant, but the guards were the most appalling women: sadists; cruel, evil people. They took pleasure in making their charges' lives hell – worse than hell – and the camp system encouraged it. That was where I lost my belief in communism, my belief in the nobility of humanity. I realized that there is good and evil in the world, but in that place there seemed to be very little good. I could hardly bear it. Many of the others couldn't – some committed suicide and some just gave up, wasting away.

'Eventually they let me go, and that was when I tried and failed to return to the university and my medical studies. But they kept Paul in a camp. He had some very powerful enemies in the Nazi Party, especially a man called Baldur von Schirach who was head of the Nazi student movement. They never let me see him. I wrote to him all the time, but I have no idea whether he ever received my letters. Then one year, just before Christmas 1935... ' She hesitated. '... I received a box through the post, with the compliments of von Schirach.' She paused for breath. Conrad remained silent – he could tell she wanted to go on, even though it was difficult for her. 'It was a cigar box, with a swastika, Paul's name and the word "traitor" stencilled on the top. I shouldn't have opened it... it was stupid, I wasn't thinking clearly. I was just so upset. Inside were... inside were ashes.

'I broke down. I had a complete nervous breakdown. I was studying nursing at that stage. That's when Sophie and I became friends: she was so good to me. But it took me months to get over it.' She glanced at Conrad, her eyes moist with tears. 'What am I saying? I haven't got over it; I'll never get over it. And the idea of the same thing happening to my father? I just can't bear it. I won't let it happen: I can't let it happen.'

'It sounds as if Paul was a very brave man,' said Conrad.

Anneliese smiled, her wet eyes bright. 'He was. He was a wonderful man.'

'Sometimes, when you look at the madness of the Nazi regime, and you ask yourself how can the Germans put up with it, you forget that many of them didn't,' Conrad said, remembering Theo's words. 'Many of the best of them tried to stop it and have died for their efforts. None of us should forget people like Paul.'

Anneliese looked down at her half-eaten sausage. 'I'm sorry, I'm sure you weren't expecting a lunch like this, were you?'

'I suppose I wasn't.'

'Would you like to go for a walk afterwards?'

'Yes, I would,' said Conrad.

She led him into the Tiergarten, around the maze of lakes and footpaths until they came to a small enclosure full of rose beds, surrounded by a beech hedge, trellises, gazebos and wooden benches.

'Let's sit here for a bit,' said Anneliese. 'This is the Rosengarten, one of my favourite places.'

It was getting hot, so they found a bench in the shade. The garden was dominated by a thirty-foot marble statue of a woman in a flowing dress with a broad-brimmed hat and a fan. Anneliese explained she was the Empress Auguste Viktoria, whose idea the garden was. The conversation had flowed easily as they had meandered through the park, but now they fell silent. A nursemaid passed them, pushing a pram with one hand, a toddler in a little pre-Nazi sailor's uniform clasping the other. A breath of air rustled through the garden, the roses nodding a gentle welcome. Outside, beyond the protective cocoon of the trees, they could hear the hum of the vast city, the largest metropolis on the continent of Europe, the Third Reich's powerfully beating heart. But here, for a few minutes, they felt safe in their own small world of sanity.

'How well do you know Theo?' Conrad asked.

'Not that well. I see him occasionally with Sophie.'

'What do you think of him?'

'He seems decent. Honest. He's charming, of course. Sophie dotes on him.' Anneliese frowned. 'He seems very fond of her, but I don't like the way he treats her sometimes. I think he takes her for granted.'

'Do you know what he does in the War Ministry?' Conrad asked.

Anneliese shook her head.

'Does Sophie?'

'I don't think so. She doesn't really worry about that kind of thing. What are you getting at?'

'Do you think he might be in the Gestapo?'

'No,' said Anneliese quickly. She paused, thinking the idea over. 'No. He's far too straightforward for that. In fact, I would be surprised if he is a Nazi. He never says anything blatantly anti-Hitler in front of me, but it's the throwaway remarks he makes. He likes to call Nazi officials "golden pheasants", for example. But why ask me? He's your friend. You should know him best.'

Conrad sighed. 'Was,' he said. 'And now I'm not sure I know him at all.'

'What happened?' Anneliese asked.

Conrad hesitated. He realized his earlier reticence had disappeared; he needed to tell her. 'I did something very stupid. I asked my friend to spy against his country.'

'You did what?' Anneliese glanced swiftly around her in the

classic manner of a citizen of the Third Reich who knew that there were ears everywhere, even in this obscure corner of the Tiergarten. 'Why on earth would you do that?' she asked in an urgent whisper.

Conrad shrugged. 'Remember the British Passport Control Officer I told you about? The one who wouldn't help your father? It turns out that he is some kind of cog in the British secret-service machinery. He was the one who asked me.'

Anneliese's lower lip was trembling. 'Did you do that for me? For my father?'

'Partly,' said Conrad. 'Oh, I don't know why I did it. I really wish I hadn't now.'

Anneliese's face cracked. She seemed on the verge of tears. 'Thank you, Conrad,' she said, reaching out her gloved hand towards his. He held it.

They sat in silence, wrapped up in their own thoughts.

'Conrad?' Anneliese said at last

'Yes?'

'If we gave this Captain Foley a secret, a real secret, do you think he would help my father?'

Twelve

It was early morning: the two horses cantered down the broad avenue through crisp dew. Theo loved to ride in the Tiergarten at this time of day, with the rhythm of the hooves beneath him, the cool air rushing past his cheeks, the mare's breath billowing like steam around his ears, no one else around. A few metres in front of him Colonel Oster pulled up and turned off the avenue into a narrow path through the trees, back towards the stables on the Bendlerstrasse. Theo caught him up, horse and rider panting heavily. Although Oster was at least twenty years older than Theo, he was the better horseman, he was lighter and he was fit. He showed scarcely any sign of physical exertion, although his horse had worked up a good sweat.

'I wish we could do this all morning,' said Oster.

'Do you ever see General von Fritsch out here these days?' asked Theo.

'Not since he resigned. He's too humiliated to be seen in public, even on a horse in the Tiergarten.'

They passed a small pond and a rather grand statue of a minor composer of operas; the path was just wide enough to ride abreast. It was amazing how quiet it was here in the very heart of the city.

'An extraordinary thing happened to me the other day,' Theo said. 'I was approached by the British to spy for them.'

Oster turned to him, his eyebrows raised. 'Your friend de Lancey?'

Theo nodded.

'What did you say?'

'It took me by surprise; I wasn't expecting it at all. I felt insulted and I told him so. We left on bad terms.'

'You told me you didn't think he was a spy?'

'And I didn't. But we know that he went to the British Passport Control Office a few days ago. Foley has obviously got to him. I'm surprised, I thought Conrad's pacifism was stronger than that.'

Oster stared hard at his subordinate. 'So, Hertenberg. What shall we do with him, I wonder?'

Conrad glanced at the station clock. Six minutes past five and the evening rush hour was just getting into full swing. The vast Anhalter Station, one of the two largest in the city, was a baroque cathedral dedicated to the worship of steam. He had arrived a little early: if there was anyone watching, he wanted to appear to be hanging around waiting to meet someone on an arriving train. The clock was a small one for such a large station, and it was mounted above the main entrance. At this time of day people were bustling past him, the direction of the flow being mostly into the station and trains to Bavaria, Anhalt, Saxony and Czechoslovakia.

It had taken him an hour and a half to get from his hotel to the station, less than a mile away. After Theo's revelation that he had been followed to the Passport Control Office and then again to the Bendlerstrasse, Conrad wanted to make absolutely sure there was no one on his tail. He hadn't seen anyone, but he had tried a variety of dodges to make sure: lingering over a cup of coffee in a café and studying all the other customers, jumping on and off U-Bahn trains, walking slowly in one direction across the Pariser Platz and then turning on his heels to retrace his steps. He was as sure as he possibly could be that he was clear.

When Anneliese had asked Conrad that morning over a hurried cup of coffee at Café Josty whether he was still serious about helping her father, he had instantly answered yes, even though he knew there would be danger. Her instructions had been clear. Her uncle, who was employed by a company called Focke-Wulf, was working on the design of a new fighter aeroplane. He was in Berlin for a meeting at the Air Ministry and would be on his way home, catching a train from the Anhalter Station. Conrad was to wait for him at a quarter past five under the clock.

Conrad kept his eye on Platform Seven. He had checked a timetable, and there was a train that arrived there at five-sixteen. His plan was to wait until all the passengers were off the train, and then to leave the station disappointed.

The clock again. Eight minutes past. He was confident that Anneliese's uncle would accost him at exactly quarter past; a rendezvous this important would bring out the punctuality in any German. He checked for potential watchers: in the Anhalter Station at that hour of the day there were dozens of possibilities.

This was real, honest-to-goodness spying Conrad was involved in now. He realized that he was gambling every-thing, perhaps even his life, on Anneliese and her uncle being careful. They were only amateurs, like him. There were all kinds of mistakes they could make. He had to trust that their innocence had kept them out of the Gestapo's eyes. Except Anneliese wasn't really innocent: she was an ex-communist who had done time in a concentration camp. Perhaps they had a permanent watch on her.

Eleven minutes past. A man Conrad had suspected of being a Gestapo watcher folded up his evening newspaper and headed off to a train on Platform Four. Conrad was jumpy. It had been foolish to arrive early after all; the waiting was killing him. It was the longest ten minutes of his life.

Thrust deep into his overcoat pockets, his hands were clammy. He pulled them out and opened his tightly bunched fists to let the air cool his palms. He shouldn't have agreed to do this. He didn't know Dr Rosen; he wasn't sure he even knew Anneliese. For a moment he thought of just walking away. But he had given his word, and having done that he couldn't let Anneliese down. Anneliese's uncle had already taken a great risk to meet him; Conrad had to be there.

Fourteen minutes past. A fat man in a bow tie holding a rolled-up newspaper sauntered up to him. Conrad tensed, but the man sauntered past. A train whistle blew and steam billowed along one of the platforms.

'Excuse me, sir, would you like to read my newspaper? I have finished it.'

Conrad turned to see a thin man with glasses and a greying moustache holding out a copy of the *Frankfurter Zeitung*. He was licking his lips, and sweat glistened on his forehead. The paper was shaking.

Conrad took it. 'Thank you, that's very kind,' he said.

'Not at all,' said the man, touched his hat and walked briskly off towards Platform Eight, where the train was just about to leave.

His heart beating rapidly, Conrad moved towards Platform Seven where another train had just arrived and was disgorging its passengers. He tried desperately hard to concentrate on the passengers and not look around for watchers, or better yet, just turn on his heel and leave. The wave of hurrying men and women jostled past him, and then they were gone.

With a sigh of relief, he glanced at the now empty platform, checked his watch, shook his head in feigned disappointment that the person he had been supposed to meet had not been on the train, and turned for the station exit.

Turned, and walked straight into a big man in a raincoat. A smaller colleague stood next to him.

'Can I see that newspaper, please?' the man said, holding out his hand.

'No,' replied Conrad, indignantly.

'Gestapo,' the man said simply, opening his wallet to show his identification.

Conrad hesitated and then handed over the newspaper. 'Can't you people buy your own?' he said, allowing a heavy English accent to tinge his German. He didn't want his perfect German to arouse suspicions this time.

'Are you a foreigner?' the man snapped.

'I'm English.'

'May I see your papers?'

With steady hands, Conrad pulled his passport from his breast pocket and passed it to the officer, who examined it closely.

'Where did you get this newspaper?' the Gestapo officer barked.

'Someone just gave it to me. I assume he had finished with it. Jolly decent of him, really.'

'Do you know the man?'

'No. Never seen him before in my life. I did get a look at him, though. I could probably identify him if you wanted me to.'

'Don't worry, we know who he is.' The officer turned to his colleague, who was shaking the newspaper. 'Anything?'

'Nothing.'

The Gestapo officer grabbed the newspaper and leafed through it furiously, swearing under his breath. His face was reddening.

'If you're looking for the test scores, I don't think that paper carries it,' said Conrad. 'Last I heard Australia were two hundred and twenty for four.'

The officer glared at Conrad as if he were mad. 'Search him!'Protesting mildly, Conrad took off his coat and turned out his pockets. Nothing.

The officer pursed his lips in frustration. 'Take down his name and address,' he ordered his colleague. 'We'll be in touch if we need you.'

'May I have my paper back?' Conrad asked.

The Gestapo officer ignored him, and strode towards the station exit clutching the copy of the *Berliner Tageblatt* to his chest.

Thirteen

Klaus was tired. The previous evening he had accompanied Heydrich to Salon Kitty, a high-class brothel in a smart area of Berlin, staffed by beautiful and sophisticated women. The establishment's nine bedrooms were wired with microphones, and the idea was to entice foreign diplomats to come in and relax and then to listen to their pillow talk. The project had notched up some minor successes and Heydrich was very proud of the place, so proud that he frequently inspected it. Often he took Klaus with him, and Klaus was always careful to telephone ahead to make sure that the microphones were switched off for their visit. On such nights Klaus never made it home to bed until after two.

Klaus found it strange how little interest he had in the women at the salon. Sometimes, if he was drunk enough, he would give one of them a good seeing to, but mostly they just made him think of his angel. He wondered when he would forget her. It was nearly twelve months since they had split up and, if anything, his feelings for her were stronger than they had ever been. Never; the answer was never.

At least he had received a letter from his mother saying she was feeling much better. Worry over her health had been bearing down heavily on him for the last few weeks, and the relief was exhilarating. Perhaps on Sunday he would slip home and see his parents. He knew his father wasn't looking after his mother properly and it made him feel very guilty that he couldn't be home more. His father was such a pig, willing to be waited on hand and foot by his wife for all those years, and then when she became ill grumbling because she could no longer look after him rather than repaying her for everything she had done for him.

Klaus removed his spectacles, rubbed his eyes and picked up one of the files from the pile on his desk, flicking it open. More denunciations, this time by a butler who objected to his employer, a director of the Reichsbank, entertaining Jews to dinner. The day-to-day work of the Gestapo was relentless: the collation and analysis of the thousands of pieces of information that came in from informants and busybodies throughout the land, as well as from the Gestapo's own men. The information accumulated faster than the Gestapo could process it.

Klaus had discovered that two things were required to make sense of it all. One was a well-designed and efficiently maintained card-index system; the other was a team of clerks diligent enough to be accurate, but imaginative enough to make connections. One of the best of these was Gertrude Lüttgen, a mousy twenty-year-old pastor's daughter with an extraordinary memory and voracious curiosity. When she knocked on his door with the announcement: 'It's probably nothing, Herr Kriminalrat, but I was just wondering...' he always listened, however busy he was.

'Come in, my dear,' he said at her timid knock, with a friendly grin. 'What have you got for me?'

'It's a report from an incident yesterday,' Fräulein Lüttgen said, clutching a file tightly to her chest. 'Our officers were following an engineer from the Focke-Wulf aircraft factory whom they had been told had been acting suspiciously recently. On his way back from the Air Ministry he bumped into a man at the Anhalter Station and handed him a newspaper. Our officers searched the man, but couldn't find anything on him, so they let him go.'

'So?' Klaus wasn't impatient. Knowing Fräulein Lüttgen, he knew there would be more.

'So I thought I recognized the man's name. I checked and I was right. It was someone you interrogated a couple of weeks ago.'

'Who?'

'An Englishman named Conrad de Lancey.'

Conrad met Anneliese at the S-Bahn station at Potsdamer Platz. God, she was beautiful. It was strange, the more he saw her the more beautiful he thought she was. It wasn't her bone structure or her figure, it was something in the way she moved, in her smile, in the way her eyes flashed.

'What is it, Conrad?' she said. 'Are you all right?'

'Oh, yes, yes, I'm fine,' he said, trying not to sound embarrassed. 'Let's go.'

It was a hot day and the famous Berliner Luft, the crisp energizing air which made the city bearable in summer, had vanished. Despite the oppressive heat, they walked briskly towards the British Passport Control Office, Anneliese threading her arm through his.

'Oh, Conrad. I'm so glad you weren't caught,' she said. 'My uncle told me the train was stopped by the Gestapo at the first station outside Berlin, and he was hauled off. He thought he was done for. They told him they had arrested you, but fortunately he kept his nerve and said that he had just given you an old newspaper he had finished reading. They let him go in the end, but he was quite shaken and he says he'll never do anything like that again.'

'I don't blame him,' said Conrad.

'But why didn't they arrest you?' Anneliese asked. 'Did you escape somehow?'

Conrad smiled. 'I thought it wise to discuss your plan with Foley. Just as a precaution, he said he would provide some help. As soon as your uncle passed his paper to me, I walked into a crowd. One of Foley's men jostled me and switched newspapers. So whatever your uncle gave me went straight to him. A moment later I was stopped by the Gestapo. You should have seen their faces when they couldn't find anything!'

'But if they had found something you'd be in a cell now!'

'I know, but they didn't, did they?' Conrad said, squeezing her arm. 'The one problem was that we didn't know what newspaper your uncle would hand me. Fortunately the Gestapo never noticed that his *Frankfurter Zeitung* miraculously became a *Berliner Tageblatt*.' It was strange but despite the risk, or possibly because of it, Conrad had enjoyed the whole experience. He would certainly think twice about doing it all again, but it had been a sweet feeling to fool the Gestapo. 'And if we can get your father out of the country tonight it will all have been worthwhile.'

'Thank you so much, Conrad,' Anneliese said. 'Do you think Captain Foley will have the visa?'

'I hope so. I'm sure he will have done all he can to get it.'

'I'm trying not to get my hopes up in case I'm disappointed, but it's difficult not to.' And indeed there was eagerness in Anneliese's voice and in her step as they walked along Tiergartenstrasse. 'I will miss my father if he goes to Britain, but at least I'll know he'll be safe.'

The people queuing patiently along the street outside the Passport Control Office were wilting in the heat, brows glistening with sweat. The Yorkshire commissionaire recognized Conrad and led him through to Foley's office. The captain was pleased to see them, as was his dog, but Conrad sensed immediately there was something wrong. Perhaps because Foley was English and she was German, Anneliese didn't seem to pick up the same feeling.

'Congratulations to both of you,' Foley said in English with a smile. 'That information your uncle gave us was gold dust, pure gold dust.'

'I'm glad,' said Conrad. But as he said it he realized he wasn't. He hadn't really considered what usefulness the information would have for his country. It was Anneliese's father he was concerned about. Whatever he was doing, he wasn't doing it for Britain, he was doing it for victims of Nazism, individuals who were important to him: Anneliese, Dr Rosen, Theo, Joachim, and, he realized, ultimately himself. He was still wary of the kind of blind patriotism that required unquestioning loyalty to one's country's government: there was too much of that all around him in Berlin.

'Fräulein Rosen, I would be extremely interested in obtaining any further information your uncle may be able to provide.'

'I am sorry, Captain Foley,' Anneliese replied in halting English. 'He was quite afraid this time. I do not think he will help you again.'

'I quite understand,' said Foley, switching to German for Anneliese's benefit. 'But please just ask him to bear it in mind in future. If the situation in this country continues to deteriorate, he might change his position.'

'I will tell him,' said Anneliese. 'Now, have you issued the visa for my father, Captain Foley?'

'Yes, I have it here,' said Foley with a quick smile, touching a form in front of him.

'That's wonderful!' said Anneliese, glancing at Conrad. Seeing his expression, she looked at Foley. 'What? What is it?

What's wrong?' A note of panic rose in her voice.

Foley sighed. 'It's the exit permit,' he said. 'The Gestapo won't grant one.'

'But I've done all the paperwork! The passport, the tax-clearance certificate. It took me weeks to get it all together.'

'There's nothing wrong with the paperwork,' said Foley. 'Usually when there is a hiccup like this we can sort it out, inducements can be brought to bear. In this case I asked a good friend of mine to do all he could, and normally that's enough. But not this time. My friend says that someone doesn't want your father to leave the country.'

'No.' She whispered the word and her lower lip trembled. A single tear ran down her cheek. She sniffed. 'I'm sorry. I just thought... I hoped... I knew I shouldn't have counted on it but...'

Foley opened a drawer in his desk and produced a clean handkerchief, which he offered to her. Conrad realized he must be used to desperate weeping women in his office; he probably had a stack of them stowed away there. She dabbed her eyes. Conrad moved over to her and put his arm around her shoulders. She leaned into his body.

'Is there nothing you can do?' he asked.

Foley shook his head. 'I'm sorry. I've tried everything. The entry visa to Britain is good for six months, but without an exit permit it's useless.'

'I can't let him rot in a camp,' Anneliese protested.

Foley sighed. 'I appreciate the risk you both took to bring me this information, and I will continue to do what I can for your father. I have pulled people out of concentration camps before, provided we can get the exit permit.'

'Perhaps he won't be rearrested?' Anneliese looked at Foley hopefully.

'Perhaps,' he said. But all three of them knew it was unlikely. If someone had been concerned enough to block the exit permit, he would probably want to make sure that Dr Rosen went straight back into custody.

Anneliese pulled herself together. She stood and held out her hand. 'Thank you for all you have done, Captain Foley.'

'I'm just sorry it wasn't enough.'

They were just about to leave when Conrad hesitated. 'Captain Foley. You said "someone" doesn't want Dr Rosen to leave the country. Do you know who that "someone" is?'

'Yes, yes I do.' Foley examined a small notebook. 'It's a Gestapo officer named Klaus Schalke. He's quite the rising star, apparently, a favourite of Heydrich's.'

'Schalke?' said Conrad.

'Do you know him?' Foley asked.

Conrad glanced at Anneliese, who was clearly surprised by his recognition of the name. 'You could say that. We're not exactly best of friends. He was the one who arrested me. He let me go after my cousin died in custody, and I would have thought he had forgotten me, but perhaps he bears a grudge.'

'Who knows?' said Foley. 'Sometimes these people can be persuaded, but my contact was advised not to approach Schalke. He was told it might make things worse.'

'Can we speak to him?' Conrad said. 'Perhaps I can find out what he has against me, if indeed there is anything.'

'No!' said Anneliese.

'But I'm a British citizen—'

'If you've had a brush with him in the past you should keep well clear of him,' she said.

'Fräulein Rosen is probably correct,' said Foley. 'And Schalke's opposition might well have nothing to do with you. He's a Nazi, isn't he? Perhaps the idea of a Jew giving blood to an Aryan fills him with revulsion. These people have a very warped view of the world.'

Conrad shared Anneliese's gloom as they left the building. 'If this Gestapo officer blocked the exit permit because of me, I'm very sorry,' he said.

'Captain Foley's right; it probably had nothing to do with you,' Anneliese replied. But she avoided his eye as she said it. She was understandably upset, and angry, but Conrad didn't know whether her anger stretched to him.

'What now?' he said.

'My father's due to be released at three o'clock this afternoon. I was planning to meet him and give him his visa. Now I suppose I will go to see him be freed and then arrested again.'

'Can I come with you?' Conrad asked. 'I've heard so much about him, I'd like to see him. Of course if you'd rather not, I would quite understand.'

'No, please come. I'd like that. And after all you have done for him it would be good for you to see him, however briefly.'

They went straight to the Anhalter Station. Dr Rosen was in prison in the city of Dessau, about eighty kilometres to the south-west of Berlin. At twenty minutes to three, Conrad and Anneliese arrived in a taxi at the gates of a grim stone building. Anneliese threw herself into the arms of a middle-aged woman with wispy grey-blonde hair, who was standing watching the gates expectantly. It was even hotter in Dessau than it had been in Berlin, and the woman's hair was damp with sweat.

'Mama, this is Conrad de Lancey, an English friend of mine who helped me get the visa.'

The woman held out her hand to Conrad. She had kind blue eyes. 'May I see it?' she said, her voice eager.

'Yes you may, but, Mama, it's useless! We couldn't get an exit permit. The Gestapo wouldn't issue one.'

The woman staggered as if she had received a physical blow. 'Does that mean... Oh, *Liebchen*, look. The van.'

Sure enough, parked twenty yards along the road in the shade of a chestnut tree was a green van of the kind that Conrad had already been inside.

'They're here! The Gestapo are here!' Anneliese's voice was anguished.

They waited outside the gates for the next twenty minutes, the sun beating down on them, neither mother nor daughter willing to move into the shade. The street was like an airless oven, heat bouncing off the stone walls of the prison. There was no sign of movement in the van, and in the shade it was impossible to see whether it was occupied. But they knew it was.

At a couple of minutes past the hour, the heavy prison gate opened, and a small olive-skinned man in a baggy suit emerged.

'Papa!' Anneliese ran to him, followed by her mother. Dr Rosen held them both tight. Conrad stood back, but the doctor noticed him over the shoulder of his daughter and smiled. It was an extraordinary smile of strength and kindness. Conrad would never forget it. 'Oh, Papa, we couldn't get the papers! We tried, we tried so hard, but we couldn't get the papers!'

Two ordinary-looking men wearing pristine raincoats even in the mid-afternoon heat emerged from the van and approached the trio. Conrad was beginning to recognize the uniform of the plain-clothes Gestapo. The doctor stood up straight to meet them. Anneliese detached herself from him.

One of them presented the doctor with a sheet of typed paper. 'Dr Rosen. This is a protective custody order. Please come with us.'

'One moment, please.' The policemen stood respectfully aside as the doctor took the hands of his wife and daughter. 'Look after each other, won't you?'

'I will,' said Frau Rosen.

He turned to his daughter who was blinking back tears. 'Anneliese? Will you look after your mother?'

She bit her lip and nodded.

'I won't be long: they'll let me out soon.' Then he kissed them both.

The women watched bravely as one of the Gestapo eased him away, slipped handcuffs over his wrists and led him off to the van.

Then Anneliese cracked. 'No!' she screamed, and she sank to her knees. Her mother crouched down and held her. In that position they watched Dr Rosen being bundled into the back of the vehicle. A few seconds later it drove off, and was gone.

After a miserable afternoon with Frau Rosen, Anneliese and Conrad returned to the station and a train back to Berlin. Conrad took Anneliese back to her place, which turned out to be a room in a tenement building in the Scheunenviertel, the poor Jewish quarter. This was a part of Berlin that Conrad had never visited: bustling, narrow cobbled streets; small shops stuffed full of cheap goods; children everywhere running, playing and gawking; murky corner bars; high, crowded tenements, plaster peeling off the walls. And everywhere there was graffiti: cartoons of Jews beheaded or hanged, obscene inscriptions, or the simple word *Jude* in large clear letters. Several shop windows were boarded up, where the glass had been recently broken.

Many of the inhabitants, with their untrimmed earlocks and beards, wore traditional Jewish orthodox dress, and all around Conrad heard the unfamiliar sound of Yiddish. The people were from Eastern Europe, refugees from the pogroms of Russia and Poland, with little in common with the indigenous German-speaking Jews; even their religious observance was different. Anneliese said that when she had been forbidden to continue studying to become a doctor on account of her ancestry, she had decided to live amongst the community of which the state had decreed she was now a member, to surround herself with other people whose basic rights were inexorably being stripped away from them. Besides, the rent was low.

Anneliese's room was on the fourth floor. It was baking hot and she opened the windows on to the interior courtyard. At least the stove, a tall blue-and-white tiled contraption that dominated the room, was unlit. Everything was clean and tidy, with the exception of a single bookcase which was overwhelmed with volumes. On top of the wireless was a photograph of Anneliese with her mother and father and a tall thin young man: a brother. Everyone was smiling. Happier times.

'Conrad?' said Anneliese, in a small voice. 'Can you stay? Please?'

So Conrad stayed. They ate a simple supper of bread and soup, talked, and then he held her long into the night until eventually she fell asleep and, a few minutes later, so did he.

Fourteen

Conrad flicked through his copy of *The Times*, amused to see that the censor had blacked out the report from Berlin. After a good morning's work at his flat, he had dropped in to the Café Josty for a cup of coffee. He was beginning to rather like the place, and Anneliese was right: they did have a good selection of foreign newspapers. Outside, cars, bicycles, buses and trams swarmed around the green spindly traffic tower in the middle of the Potsdamer Platz. It didn't look big or strong enough to tame the mass of clanking, roaring machinery.

He was pleased with his new flat. Warren Sumner had helped him find it. It was located in a quiet square near Nollendorfplatz and decorated in a very modern style. The owner, a Jewish architect who was abandoning Berlin for Paris, was happy to leave the art and furniture in Conrad's care. Conrad agreed to pay the rent directly to him in Paris, which was a great relief to the man since the strict German exchange controls had prevented him from taking more than a tiny sum with him.

Conrad had spent the morning writing an article for *Mercury* on the difficulties German Jews faced trying to get visas to leave the country. He had toned down the outrage and anger that had suffused his first draft, and the resulting piece was more powerful for it. He felt he had made his point: the British government should let more Jews into Britain and Palestine.

Although he had mentioned the difficulties of doctors obtaining visas he had been careful not to refer to Dr Rosen directly. And he knew it would be foolish to sign the article under his real name: he needed a pseudonym. In Spain he had used 'Matador', but that was hardly appropriate in Berlin. After some reflection he had chosen 'Linden'.

The Times editorial urged that the Sudeten Germans be allowed a plebiscite to decide their own future, even though it might mean their secession from Czechoslovakia to the Reich. The Sudetenland was a mountainous strip of Czechoslovakia predominantly inhabited by German speakers. The Sudeten German Party, a pseudo-Nazi organization led by an odious man of cunning charm called Henlein, was vigorously protesting at the way the cruel Czechs were tormenting innocent Germans, and demanding that Hitler do something about it. There had been a scare a few weeks before, in May, that the Wehrmacht had been on the brink of invading, but swift mobilization of the Czech forces and strong words from Chamberlain, the British Prime Minister, and Lord Halifax, his foreign secretary, had seemed to deter Hitler. Now *The Times* was suggesting that Halifax permit the Sudetenland go to Germany without a fight.

Edward Wood, the third Viscount Halifax, was an old friend of Conrad's father from Eton. Conrad had first met him several years before when he had joined his father for a shoot on a Yorkshire grouse moor where Halifax was a fellow guest. Halifax was an imposing figure, six feet eight inches tall with a long, somewhat forbidding face. Despite the handicap of only having one functioning arm, for he had been born without a left hand, he was an excellent shot. But so too was Conrad, and Halifax had taken quite a shine to the Oxford undergraduate.

Lord Oakford admired Halifax, and was convinced that, despite his occasional tough words, his friend would never make the same mistake as his predecessor of 1914, Lord Grey, and allow Britain to be sucked into a continental war.

But Conrad was no longer convinced by his father's determination to secure peace at all costs. It was true that Czechoslovakia was a long way from England; that it would be difficult to persuade Englishmen to die for a distant country that was not even twenty years old. Yet Conrad had seen at first hand what Nazism could do. David Griffiths and Harry Reilly had died opposing fascism, and in Conrad's view their actions were noble, not pointless.

Conrad walked back to his flat deep in thought. As he rounded a corner he became aware of a commotion along the narrow street in front of him. A group of boys in light brown Hitler Youth uniforms were bunched around the front of a shop. It was a small hardware store. Conrad had been in there only the previous afternoon to buy a screwdriver and a hammer to make some basic repairs to the flat. He had been served by an old man with fluffy grey hair and a twinkling eye. A Jew: Conrad knew this because the word *Jude* had been scrawled across his shop window.

Conrad hurried to see what was happening. The windows of the shop were shattered and the boys, aged about ten to fourteen, were hurling spanners, wrenches, light bulbs and pots and pans grabbed from the shelves at two figures curled up on the pavement. One boy, the smallest, was attempting to whip the figures with a piece of electric flex. He was yelling regurgitated party slogans in a high-pitched voice as he lashed out: 'To hell with the Jews!' and somewhat oddly: 'Room for the Sudeten Germans!' A small crowd of half a dozen adults looked on.

'*Halt!*' Conrad shouted. The boys took no notice. Conrad forced his way through the small crowd, threw one of the boys to the ground and stood in front of the shopkeeper and his wife.

They were both groaning. A good sign. At least they were alive and conscious.

'I said, stop!'

The boys paused. The biggest, a strapping lad nearly six feet tall, was wielding a monkey wrench. 'Are you a Jew?' he snarled. 'Show us your nose!'

Conrad cuffed him hard across the face with the back of his hand. The boy dropped his wrench and held his cheek. The others lowered their hardware uncertainly. 'Piss off!' Conrad shouted. 'And don't come back!' He took a step towards a freckled boy wielding a frying pan. The boy broke and ran. The others hesitated and then followed him.

Conrad knelt beside the two old people, sprawled in a bed of broken glass. 'Are you all right?'

The woman sat up against the wall of the shop and nodded. The old man groaned faintly. There was blood running down his temple and his eye was swollen.

'Go!' a voice whispered in his ear. Conrad turned to see a fat middle-aged lady with the no-nonsense attitude of a school-mistress. 'Go, now, before the SA come. I'll look after these two.'

Conrad hesitated.

'Go!'

Conrad went, trotting down the street towards his flat.

Conrad stayed at home that night, cooking himself an omelette for supper. He didn't want to venture outside again that day. It was going to be difficult staying in Berlin, learning to walk on the other side of the street as schoolchildren beat up pensioners.

The phone rang as he was polishing off the last of the ome-lette. It was Captain Foley.

'I've got some good news for you, de Lancey,' he said.

'The exit permit?'

'I received a phone call this afternoon. We'll have it early next week.'

'Hurrah!' said Conrad. 'That was quick.' It was only three days since he and Anneliese had watched the green Gestapo van taking Dr Rosen into protective custody.

'Ours is not to reason why,' said Foley. 'Why don't you and Fräulein Rosen come to my office on Tuesday? We should have everything in order by then, and we can all go to fetch her father. He's in Sachsenhausen; it's a concentration camp just north of Berlin. Tell Fräulein Rosen to buy a train ticket for London for that night; we will have to get him out of the country right away.'

'Thank you, Captain Foley. Thank you very much.'

As soon as he had hung up with Foley, Conrad telephoned Anneliese. Her landlady, a busybody named Frau Goldstein, who had questioned him at length during his previous visit to Anneliese's room, answered the communal telephone and went to look for her. She returned a moment later to say that Anneliese was working at the hospital and therefore probably wouldn't be home until ten o'clock.

Conrad wanted to see her in person with the good news. He had tried to telephone twice in the last couple of days, failing to get her each time. He was finding it ever more difficult to keep her out of his mind. He enjoyed her company and her conversation; she made him laugh and there was no doubt she was physically attractive, and that attraction was working on him. But she was also a mystery: Conrad wanted to know more about what was behind those ironic green eyes. She had had a very tough few years and he admired her ability to cope with it on her own, but the vulnerability he could sense made him want to hold her, protect her, as he had on that night after they had returned from the prison in Dessau. He could imagine himself falling for her, falling heavily for her. Another reason to stay in Berlin.

But of course he was still married to Veronica, and that still meant something to him, if not to his wife.

At five to ten he took the U-Bahn to the Scheunenviertel and hurried to her tenement building. The streets were quiet that night – no sign of Nazi marauders, and precious little sign of the inhabitants themselves. He checked his watch: twenty past ten. Anneliese would be home but not in bed yet.

Frau Goldstein answered the door. She didn't want to let him in, but Conrad insisted, saying that he had some important news for Fräulein Rosen. The landlady argued for a moment and then shrugged her shoulders and let him pass, muttering to herself.

Conrad rushed up the stairs. There was a light under the door. She was in. He knocked.

No answer.

He waited and knocked again.

'Who is it?' It was her voice.

'It's Conrad. I've got some news.'

'Oh, Conrad, I'm very tired. Can you come back tomorrow?'

'I'll be quick. And you'll want to hear it, I promise.'

'Please come back tomorrow.' Then he heard a heavy tread on the floorboard inside the room. 'No!' Her voice rose in panic. 'Stop! Don't!'

The door was flung open, and there, smiling, with his collar unhooked and his shirt undone, loomed the large frame of Kriminalrat Klaus Schalke.

Fifteen

Conrad's first instinct was to slam his fist into the big grinning face. Then he heard a sob from inside the room and he felt a surge of revulsion. He knew why Anneliese was upset: she had been caught, caught in the most outrageous betrayal. At that instant he wasn't sure exactly how far that betrayal went, all he knew was that he wanted to get away from there as quickly as possible.

Schalke's grin broadened as he took in Conrad's confusion. 'Don't worry, *mein Liebling*,' he called over his shoulder. 'I think he's just leaving.'

Burning with anger, Conrad turned and blundered down the stairs and past Frau Goldstein, who had been listening in the hallway, into the street. He stood on the pavement, taking in great gulps of the cool night air. It was obvious what Schalke was doing there. It was also obvious why Anneliese had invited him: to get an exit permit for her father.

For a moment he thought he didn't know who Anneliese was, but then he realized that he did, that he had known all along. She was a single-minded, selfish woman who would do anything, *anything*, to set her father free. That was why she was with Schalke now. That was probably why she had been so friendly to him over the last couple of weeks. God, he had assumed that she had betrayed him by taking Schalke into her room, and probably into her bed. But she hadn't done that at all. To her, he and Schalke were equivalent: men who were weak enough to be manipulated to bring her what she wanted.

He thought of the message he had come to give her, about the exit permit for her father. Well, she knew all about that already, no doubt. But he didn't want to jeopardize the delicate bureaucratic dance that was needed to spirit her father out of the country. He pulled out an old envelope and scribbled a hasty note on the back that Anneliese should call Captain Foley.

He rang the doorbell, and Frau Goldstein answered immediately. She looked visibly distressed. 'Oh, Herr de Lancey, that girl is so stupid. Do you know who the man is?'

'I know, Frau Goldstein. And so does Fräulein Rosen. Now please give her this note.' He just wanted to get the message through to Anneliese; once he had done that he had no need to communicate with her ever again.

'I am so sorry, I wouldn't allow him in my house, Herr de Lancey, but you must understand that it is a mistake to make an enemy of men such as him. And when you telephoned I thought if I said she was working at the hospital you wouldn't come—'

'I understand, Frau Goldstein. The note.' He thrust the envelope into her hand and turned into the dark street.

The Friedrichstrasse Station was smaller than the Anhalter, and it was difficult for Conrad to find a spot from where he could watch Platform One unobserved. In the end he settled on a corner of the station café, through the window of which he could get a pretty good view. The train for Hanover and the Hook of Holland left the platform at 4.10 p.m., but Conrad gave himself plenty of time to settle in before any other observers arrived.

He had spoken briefly to Foley on the telephone the day before to confirm which train Dr Rosen was going to catch. Conrad was pleased about the doctor. The man had been treated barbarically and deserved a chance of a new life. He hoped that England would be kind to him. But his daughter. His daughter.

For the last few days Conrad had played in his head over and over again the time he had spent with Anneliese. He saw everything in a new perspective, with her as the cunning manipulator and himself as the dupe. Had she thought the hours spent with him tedious, but necessary if her father was to be freed? He had done so much for her. Risked his life to pass on secrets to Foley. Destroyed his relationship with Theo.

She had written him a note, which was now crumpled in his jacket pocket. He had read it so many times he had memorized its contents.

Dear Conrad,

I am terribly terribly sorry. You should never have had to see Klaus like that. I am sure you know why he was in my room: he has promised to arrange the exit permit for Papa. You might not know that Klaus and I have been acquainted a long time.

You have been unfailingly kind and considerate; such a help to me both spiritually and in arranging for my father's visa. You do not deserve what I have done to you.

I won't ask you to forgive me; I can't forgive myself. I am so pleased that my father will soon be free, but that freedom has come at a great cost. I hate myself, for what I have become, for what I have done to you, for what I have done with Klaus. When I was a student Paul and I started a long war against the Nazis. Now they have won. He is dead, and I – well, I may as well be. But at least my father is free.

Don't let them destroy you too, my dear Conrad.

Fondly,

Anneliese

It was hard to dismiss a letter like that. Conrad was tempted to feel sorry for her, but it was a temptation he resisted. Anneliese was trouble. Just as Veronica had been trouble. Both of them had exerted their magic on him; he had fallen for both: both had used him. True, Anneliese's goal had been nobler than Veronica's – Veronica basically wanted a good time and had become bored by Conrad. He had no idea what Anneliese really thought about him. Her letter said no more than that she felt guilty, which wasn't at all surprising.

He glanced at a menu. He wasn't hungry, but his mouth was dry so he ordered a beer. In the midst of the swirling mass of humanity, he spotted a Gestapo watcher, also positioned with a view of Platform One. He wasn't making much attempt to be unobtrusive, and he hadn't seen Conrad.

The line in the letter about being acquainted with Klaus for a long time puzzled Conrad. They seemed unlikely friends: Anneliese was a half-Jewish nurse; Klaus was in the Gestapo. He wondered what past they had shared together. Then his blood went cold. He remembered how he had accused Theo of informing on Joachim. What if it had been not Theo, but Anneliese?

Theo had ruled her out because he said she didn't speak much English and wouldn't have understood Joachim, yet Conrad had seen her speaking the language with Captain Foley. Come to think of it, the first words she had spoken to him had been after overhearing the blonde woman at Theo's dinner party talk about Linaro in English.

And she knew Klaus.

Joachim had died at the hands of Klaus Schalke. No wonder Anneliese was disgusted with herself.

Just then a small group hurried towards the train at Platform One. There was Foley, Dr Rosen – walking awkwardly, his head shaven under his hat – Frau Rosen and lastly Anneliese. Even in the week since Conrad had last seen him at the gates of Dessau Prison, Dr Rosen seemed to have shrunk. Foley helped him stow his suitcases on the train. He only had two: restrictions on Jews applied not just to how much money they could take out of the country, just ten marks, but also to their property.

The doctor shook hands with Foley, and hugged his wife and then his daughter. They were some distance away and the glass windowpane of the station café was between them, but as Anneliese held her father, Conrad thought that she caught sight of him watching them. Her eyes widened for a moment and then shut. A minute later, to the shrill cry of the guard's whistle and the clamour of steam, the train pulled out of the station. At least one man has escaped the Nazis, Conrad thought, and one man is better than none.

An oppressive gloom gathered about Conrad as he threaded his way through the commuters hurrying into the station. It wasn't just Anneliese who had manipulated him. Foley had told him something else when he had telephoned to confirm the time of Dr Rosen's train.

Theo von Hertenberg worked for the German secret service. Which meant Conrad was as naive a mug as ever walked the streets of Berlin.

PART TWO

July 1938

Sixteen

It was a beautiful July in Berlin. Relaxed crowds thronged the pavements in the sunshine, the girls in their summer dresses, couples dancing on café terraces, ice-cream vendors with their rainbow wheels and multi-coloured umbrellas doing a brisk trade. Neat baskets of geraniums and petunias shouted their presence from windows and balconies. There was a sense of optimism and purpose in the air.

But not for Conrad. He sought refuge in the Stabi and his novel, but didn't find it. It was hard to write about imaginary lives in Berlin in 1914 when Berlin in 1938 had changed his own life so deeply.

He was coming to terms with the realization that he had spent the first twenty-seven years of his life completely misunderstanding the world around him. It was if he had lived his life in a large, dimly lit room and suddenly switched on a bright table lamp. Under the stark light, deep shadows stretched everywhere he looked. He had assumed that most people were good, decent individuals, who said what they thought and felt, and whom you could trust. Of course everyone had some flaws in his or her character, but these were usually obvious and could easily be ignored. As a reasonably intelligent observer, he could spot the good and the bad.

Anneliese and Theo had taught him that this wasn't the case. He had never completely understood either of them, but he had assumed in his naivety that those parts of their characters that had remained a mystery to him represented confusion: in Anneliese a secret pain; in Theo a conflict between his own sense of justice and the insanity of the country in which he lived. But that wasn't the case at all. Both Anneliese and Theo shared the same secret: they were manipulating him. It wasn't as if he hadn't been warned. Veronica had taken advantage of his gullibility as well, but at least she had been less coldly manipulative; she just had a natural flair for getting what she wanted.

It wasn't just individuals whose shadows were now plain to see. It was whole countries; the world, even. He was beginning to realize that the Nazi insanity surrounding him might not be an aberration, but the way the world was. No one knew exactly what was going on in Soviet Russia, but it was probably just as bad there, if not worse. There was the ugly aggressive posturing of Mussolini's Italy, and if the Fascists won in Spain the vengeance they would inflict on those who had opposed them would be terrible. It probably wouldn't be much better if the Republicans were the victors. He had assumed, with so many, that there was still a chance that the Great War had indeed been 'the war to end all wars'. This, of course, was rot. That conflict had ushered in a period where glorification of power was everything and where another world war was a certainty. Well-meaning men like Lord Halifax or Neville Chamberlain had no chance of preserving peace. Hitler would manipulate them, just as he had manipulated everyone else.

He considered returning to England, but the idea dispirited him even more. He couldn't face Veronica, and Oxford and his still unfinished thesis on Bismarck's Danish wars didn't appeal. Besides, he hated the idea that he was running away. No matter how awful Nazism was, or how much of a mess it made of his own life or the lives of others, he was determined not to flee from it.

After a week or so lurking in the Stabi, writing and rewriting listless paragraphs and trying to ignore the self-satisfied *Volk* strutting around outside, he came home one evening to find an envelope waiting for him, the address in Theo's handwriting. It was an invitation to join Theo at his parents' house in Pomerania. There was to be a wedding, and Theo wanted to introduce him to the rest of his family. Conrad scanned it quickly, ready to crumple it up and throw it into the wastepaper basket, but the last sentence held him up: *If that oath we made to each other still means anything to you, as I believe it must, please come. There is madness in this world; together we must try to overcome it. It is our duty.*

In Conrad's frame of mind, no oath given while drunk many years before meant anything, and he failed to see how two young men could possibly have any effect on the insanity that was gripping whole nations. As for duty, that was the watchword of the manipulator. And yet...

That oath had meant something to Conrad once. Deep down, he knew it still did.

He pulled out some writing paper and replied to Theo. He would go.

Theo's family lived in a small village in Pomerania, about two hundred kilometres north-east of Berlin. It lay in the ancestral heartland of the Junkers, the Prussian landowners descended from the old Teutonic Knights who had formed the backbone of the German officer class since before the time of Frederick the Great. Conrad took a train to the Hanseatic town of Stettin on the Baltic coast, and then changed twice on to ever-smaller trains until he arrived at a village station. Theo was there to meet him in his silver Horch, and they were soon bumping along stone roads through open countryside with fields alternating between sparse golden rye nodding in the light breeze and close-cropped pasture.

Theo chatted away to Conrad as though there had been no rift between them, and in the sunshine, on the open road, Conrad found himself responding. They passed slowly through a village of brick barns and wooden houses, the smell of freshly baked bread wafting out of open doorways. A group of five or six girls dressed in milkmaids' skirts who were playing in the road with hoops scattered out of the path of the car. Chickens busied themselves in small gardens adjacent to the road, and on the roofs of several of the larger buildings were great bundles of sticks where storks were nesting. It was all very quaint and rustic, but to Conrad's eyes a bit primitive.

Theo seemed to read his mind. 'The soil here is very thin and sandy and the yields are not very good. Farmers do nothing more than eke out an existence. It's been a long time since owning an estate here was very profitable. Actually, I doubt if it ever was. That's why so many of the Junkers became professional soldiers or civil servants. They needed the money.'

They drove past a small stone church and turned up an avenue lined with lime trees, at the end of which was a low manor house of white stucco with a steep red-tiled roof. Theo stopped the car, bounded up the steps and opened the oak door. Inside was a cool dark hallway with grey flagstones, heavy velvet curtains and dim oil paintings of von Hertenbergs in various uniforms. A fireplace dominated one wall, and above it hung the head of a European bison. Dotted also around the walls was a veritable arsenal of arms and armour.

Within seconds figures emerged from doorways and down the stairs to greet the returning son. There was Theo's father, a large man with a walrus moustache and blue eyes that twinkled behind his monocle; his mother, tall, slim and refined; and a sister, just as tall, blonde and gorgeous. Theo's younger brother, a lieutenant in the army, was on manoeuvres in Thuringia near the Czech border and hadn't been able to get away for the weekend. They were all overjoyed to see Theo. There was much talk of the wedding; it was a female cousin from a nearby village who was getting married. She was a Bismarck, a Prussian name with which Conrad was very familiar.

They had coffee and cake on the terrace at the back of the house, and then Theo suggested that he and Conrad go for a walk in the pine forest that stretched along the low ridge beyond the garden.

Theo set off at a brisk pace. It was a hot afternoon, and the shade of the pine trees provided a welcome relief. They walked in silence for ten minutes. Now Conrad was very aware of the barriers between them: he recalled that painful conversation along the Landwehr Canal, that mutual betrayal.

They came to a break in the woods and a small, brilliantly blue lake. A heron was standing motionless on a fallen log, staring at the water. Bees danced among the little blue flowers around the shore. The two men paused, breathing heavily after their rapid walk. Tiny sounds surrounded the lake: the lap of water, the murmur of the bees, a rustle of air through the reeds and then a splash of a fish lunging for a fly.

'Why did you ask me here, Theo?'

'To meet my family.'

'Yes, but why?'

Theo picked up a small stone and threw it far into the lake. The sharp plop shattered the near silence. 'I want to talk to you, and here seems the right place to do it.'

'About our agreement never to fight each other?'

'Yes, I suppose so.'

'You're a soldier, Theo. You wear a uniform.'

Theo laughed. 'A lawyer warrior.'

'I know you are a member of the secret service. I'm surprised you have to wear a uniform. I would have thought it would be a raincoat and hat tipped down over your eyes, a bit like your Gestapo friends.'

Theo frowned. 'Who told you that? Foley?'

Conrad nodded.

'That was one of the things I wanted to talk to you about.'

'Oh, really?' said Conrad, his words heavy with scepticism. He laughed bitterly. 'So here we are, two spies on opposite sides stirring up a war. Although I think I've retired before I've even really got going.'

'Let's walk a bit further,' Theo said. 'There's something I want to show you.' And he led Conrad deeper into the trees. The forest seemed even darker here, and a carpet of fallen pine needles covered the path. The air was cool and laden with the scent of pine and earth and darkness. Out of the corner of his eye Conrad thought he saw something flitting between the tree trunks. He turned his head and it was gone. A deer perhaps? In an English wood, the further you walk the nearer you are to the other side. This ancient German forest felt very different; open fields could be many days' walk away for all Conrad knew, and with each step he was leaving civilization further behind him. All those old German myths about the woods that his governess had taught him when he was a boy, from Hansel and Gretel onwards, crowded around him.

'Actually, I think we are on the same side,' Theo said. 'Or we should be.'

'You're not going to try to get me to spy for your country, are you, Theo? I know I tried to get you to spy for mine, but it was pretty clear that was a mistake, and one I regret.'

'No, not for my country. For something more than that. For what you and I believe in.'

'I'm not sure what I believe in any more,' Conrad said. 'In fact, I'd almost say I believe in nothing.' He chuckled. 'Except if I did say that, you'd start quoting Hegel and Nietzsche at me.'

'I've stopped doing that,' Theo said. 'These days things are much simpler. It's really just a question of right and wrong. For me, my conscience and my faith tell me that everything I see around me is wrong.'

'I didn't notice much of your conscience or your faith when I was in Berlin in thirty-three. You didn't seem all that unhappy when Hitler came to power. I remember you saying that someone needed to sort the country out.'

'That's true. And like a lot of my countrymen, I was wrong. But unlike many of my countrymen, I realize that now. Being a lawyer, even a very junior one, I couldn't avoid seeing the travesties of justice all around me. There was the Night of the Long Knives in thirty-four when the state murdered hundreds of men in cold blood. They weren't innocent men, most of them, they were SA thugs, but General von Schleicher was a former chancellor, and General von Bredow was a friend of my father's, and head of the Abwehr. My uncle was on the list, but fortunately he was warned the day before and went into hiding.'

'Is he still alive?' Conrad asked.

'Very much so. In fact, he's coming to dinner tonight. But what really opened my eyes was a secret trial I was involved in a year later. The defendant was the commandant of a concentration camp, an SS officer. It all came out in court, all the vile things his men had done to the prisoners. One of their games I particularly remember. They would strip the prisoners naked and cover them with tar. Then they set the tar alight: the prisoners died a horrible death. The evidence of extreme cruelty was overwhelming and the commandant was convicted. It was a miracle the case came to trial: a combination of a bureaucratic cock-up on the part of the SS and a judge who had not yet been intimidated by the Nazis. Needless to say no similar case has been brought since then.'

'So why join the secret service?'

'An officer who used to serve under my father suggested it, Colonel Oster. The Abwehr is actually one of the very few institutions in Germany which can keep out of the gaze of the Nazis. There are some benefits to secrecy.'

'So this Abwehr organization is opposed to Hitler?'

'In a word, yes.'

'You don't expect me to believe that, do you?'

'Actually, I do.'

'Then why were you so offended when I asked you for information?'

'I thought you were asking me to betray my country, which is something I am not prepared to do. But what I *am* prepared to do is to work with you to stop Hitler starting a world war.'

'How can I do that?'

'You can pass on a message.'

'I've done enough of that sort of thing,' said Conrad. 'Unlike you, I don't feel a duty towards my country. All that talk of "duty" and "patriotism" during the last war was simply a way of inducing young men to voluntarily walk across open ground and be mown down by machine-gun fire. I don't want to play any part in that.'

'So you'll just stand on one side and let it happen then?' said Theo.

'I can hardly stop a world war by myself, can I?' Conrad said.

'You can try. You *have* to try.'

Conrad didn't respond. They walked on in silence until they came to a clearing in the woods. A number of small stones formed a ring in the middle, and nearby lay a mound. On the far side of the mound were two standing stones about eight feet tall.

'What's this?' Conrad asked.

'No one really knows. Some people think it's four thousand years old, some think it's much more recent. I used to come here all the time when I was a boy. It still draws me. Every time I come home I have to walk out here. They call it "Traitor's Gate".'

'Why's that?'

'A traitor was hanged there by those two stones in the fifteenth century. Or at least they called him a traitor. I'm not so sure.'

'Hmm.' Conrad's interest in historical puzzles was piqued, as he knew was Theo's intention. 'Who was this traitor?'

'A knight of the Teutonic Order named Otto von Schivelbein. Did you know that this area was passed to the Teutonic Knights by Brandenburg in about 1400?'

'No,' said Conrad. 'My medieval German history is a bit sketchy.'

'Well, it was. The Teutonic Knights were at the height of their power. Their lands stretched eastwards from here across East Prussia to what's now Estonia. But the Poles and the Lithuanians had formed an alliance against them. War was coming.'

'I think I knew that,' said Conrad.

'In 1409, Otto was sent to a secret meeting with envoys of King Wenceslaus of Bohemia, offering a bribe to Wenceslaus to persuade the Poles to back off. The local knights believed that part of the deal was to pass on this region to Poland. They didn't like that idea. So they ambushed Otto, took him along to this place, hanged him by those standing stones, and then disembowelled him. At least, that's how the story goes. So, to their descendants this place is known as Traitor's Gate.'

'But you don't think Otto was a traitor?'

'Nine months later the Battle of Tannenberg was fought – the first one, not the one my father took part in. The Teutonic Knights were soundly defeated by the Poles and the Lithuanians, and from that point on the days of the order were numbered.'

'And this Otto could have stopped that?'

'Maybe, maybe not. Who knows? But it seems to me it was worth a try.'

They sat on the mound. The sun was dropping in the sky, and the shadows of the two stones stretched towards them up the mound. The brief whispers of breeze had died down now. All was still.

'Theo?' Conrad said.

'Yes?'

'Was there anything in what Joachim said about a plot to overthrow Hitler?'

Theo waited before replying. 'Almost.'

'What do you mean?'

'Johnnie von Herwarth is an old friend of mine. He's a diplomat in our Moscow embassy. When Johnnie was in Berlin on leave, he and I had talked about how we could get rid of Hitler. It was idle chat, really, nothing more than wishful thinking. There is quite a lot of opposition to Hitler in the Foreign Office as well as in the Abwehr and the army. Nothing came of it, although for a moment earlier this year I thought something would. Mühlendorf was right; the Fritsch scandal did upset a lot of people in the army. But at the right moment, when Fritsch was exonerated, they didn't move.'

'Why not?'

'They couldn't organize themselves. They had high hopes

for General von Brauchitsch, the new commander-in-chief of the army, but he has turned out to be useless. There was no one to give the orders and without orders German officers are lost.'

'You sound as if you regret that?' said Conrad.

'I do,' said Theo bitterly. 'There might never be as good an opportunity again.'

Conrad considered Theo's response. If it was genuine, it meant that Theo was far from being a Nazi.

If it was genuine.

'I can see why you didn't tell me what you knew then, but why did you rebuff Joachim when he asked you about it?'

'He was much too blatant. If Johnnie really had confided in him he would have been more careful. It didn't feel right. And, as I told you, it wasn't right.'

'You mean because he was a Russian spy?'

'He was on a fishing expedition. It's quite possible that the Soviet government would try to help a coup against Hitler, but that's not the kind of help we want.'

Conrad smiled grimly. 'So you, me and Joachim, we were all spies.'

'I'm not really a spy,' said Theo.

'Aren't you?' said Conrad. 'What is this Abwehr organization then? Is it part of the Gestapo?'

'Oh, no. Far from it,' Theo said. 'Germany doesn't work like that nowadays. All the different institutions work separately in a kind of rivalry. Sometimes it's friendly, sometimes it's deadly, like the Night of the Long Knives. The Gestapo and the Abwehr leave each other well alone; we each stick to our own territory, although we do share information. We're very different organizations, though.'

'So you say. What about the "friend in the Gestapo" who told you Joachim and I were arrested?'

'The Abwehr have friends in every government department in Germany. People who keep us informed.' Theo looked at Conrad sharply. 'We're not Nazis,' he snapped. 'We don't torture people. We don't persecute Jews. We don't carry out assassinations. I can assure you that we behave with as much honour as your own secret service, probably more.'

'Ah, so it's the Red Cross that you are affiliated with,' said Conrad. 'How stupid of me not to realize that.'

Theo fought to control his temper. 'I'm telling you all this for a reason. Sometime soon, I don't know exactly when, we may ask you to pass on a message for us. When we do, I want you to remember this conversation.'

'What kind of message?'

'I can't say. Yet.'

'You're wasting your time, Theo,' Conrad said. Above the trees to the east the blue sky was concentrating into a dark grey. 'Is that a thunderstorm?'

Theo pulled himself to his feet. 'That's something you'll have to answer for yourself.'

Seventeen

There was a guest at dinner, 'Uncle Ewald', who had ridden over from his own estate some ten miles away. Conrad presumed he was the uncle who had been on the SS list during the Night of the Long Knives. He was a short man with receding hair, hard, uncompromising eyes and a neat moustache. He was seated opposite Conrad, and from the moment he entered the house Conrad was aware of his disconcerting stare.

On Conrad's right was an ancient lady, stooped, wrinkled but with bright brown eyes. She was Theo's grandmother, the general's mother. She insisted on speaking English to Conrad, and he was entranced by her accent, a clipped version of archaic American. She had come to Berlin when she was eighteen, in 1868, to study music. She had met Theo's grandfather six months later, fallen in love and married him, much to the amazement of her own family. She was careful not to specify exactly who they were, although they had houses in Newport, Rhode Island, and New York, and Conrad suspected that she, rather than the barren local farms, was the source of Theo's spare cash. She had only been back to her own country twice, once a couple of years after she was married, and again in the 1920s. She had, however, insisted that all her children and grandchildren should be proficient in English and study music.

All the while Conrad was speaking to the old lady, he was aware of Uncle Ewald's eyes staring at him across the table.

Finally he turned to meet the stare and smiled politely.

'Theo tells me your father used to be a member of the British government,' the intense man said.

'That's right,' said Conrad. 'He was a minister for about three years.'

'And why did he resign?'

'For a politician, my father has a rather well-developed sense of honour,' Conrad said. He had become used to such direct questioning in Germany, which he might have found rude over an English dining table. 'You may remember a few years ago that there were rumoured to be secret negotiations between the British and the French over Abyssinia. It was all highly embarrassing and our government denied all knowledge of it, which was plainly ridiculous. My father felt he couldn't continue to serve in a government which was lying about what it knew and didn't know, and so he resigned.'

'Good for him,' said Uncle Ewald. 'But what did his Cabinet colleagues think of that?'

'The Prime Minister at the time, that was Stanley Baldwin, was frustrated by the whole thing, but I think most of his other Cabinet colleagues secretly admired what he had done.'

'So he's still on speaking terms with them?'

'Yes, yes, I would say so,' replied Conrad hesitantly. He was beginning to wonder why this man was grilling him so persistently.

'Good.' Uncle Ewald attacked the pork knuckles on his plate with quick efficient strokes of his knife and fork. Conrad noticed a motif of a running fox on his cufflinks. 'What brings you to Germany, Herr de Lancey?'

'I'm writing a novel. It's set in Berlin, just before the beginning of the war. I thought it would make sense to write it here.'

'Hah! Very interesting. And whose fault was it?'

'Whose fault was what?' said Conrad. 'Do you mean the war?'

'I do,' said Uncle Ewald.

'Everyone's,' Conrad answered after a moment's thought. 'Britain, Germany, France, Austria, Russia, everybody.'

'Your compatriots didn't seem to think so at Versailles. They were of the firm opinion that it was Germany 's fault. And that we should pay for it, pay until our country was starving, and too impoverished to pay any more. How did they put it? They wanted to "squeeze us like a lemon until the pips squeak".'

'I agree that was pointless,' said Conrad. 'But all the countries of Europe paid the price, a higher price, in the millions of lives lost.'

'I take it you are not an enthusiast for war, Herr de Lancey?'

'No, I'm not. I don't think anyone in his right mind would start a modern war on purpose. But I fear there is a risk that we may all stumble into one, much as we did last time.'

'Do you think our führer is stumbling in that direction?'

The questions were becoming difficult, very difficult. And there was something in Uncle Ewald's manner that demanded more than polite platitudes in answer. 'He might be. But whatever I may think of some of Hitler's policies, I don't underestimate his intelligence. He's no fool. Hitler may want to expand German influence in Europe, but he will do it without war if he possibly can. What do you think?'

'I think you misunderstand him,' the Junker answered, still staring at Conrad. 'He is determined to start another war, unless someone stops him. What is your countrymen's opinion of him?'

'It varies,' Conrad said. 'There are a few that admire him, but not many: some misguided aristocrats and Oswald Mosley's Blackshirts. Some people think he's a joke, some think he's vulgar, some are afraid of him, some write him off as a mere demagogue.'

'I see.' And then Uncle Ewald asked the question that all foreigners in Germany dreaded, but which they rarely had to answer. 'And you. What do you think of our Führer?'

Conrad hesitated. His first response was to reply with non-committal politeness, but he knew that wouldn't satisfy the man opposite him. As the seconds passed, there was silence around the table and Conrad was aware of everyone looking at him, so he blurted out the simple truth. 'He's evil,' he said. 'He must be one of the most evil men the world has ever known.'

For the first time Uncle Ewald smiled. 'Have you ever read *Mein Kampf*?'

'I've tried,' said Conrad. 'I couldn't finish it.'

'You should. Because then you will know you are right.'

'Uncle Ewald has made us all read it,' said Kätchen, Theo's younger sister. 'And he's right. It's the most horrible, terrible stuff.'

'I even made an appointment with Hitler to discuss it with him just before he came to power,' Uncle Ewald said. 'I spoke to him for two hours. I couldn't quite believe that he meant it. But he did.'

Conrad looked around the table at the deeply Prussian family. He could imagine how it must have seemed suffocating to the younger Theo, and why he had fled to Oxford and its socialism to escape its clutches. But he could see they were all united in sharing Kätchen's sentiment, all of them including the bluff general and the ancient grandmother.

'Did you notice the flag on the church in the village?' Uncle Ewald asked.

'I didn't see a flag.'

'Precisely. It's one of only four churches in Prussia not to fly the swastika.'

'The swastika on a church?' Conrad said. That seemed a bit incongruous, even for the Nazis.

'The SA tried to make Uncle Ewald fly it,' Kätchen said. 'He chased them off with a gun. They arrested him and then he agreed to give the job to the schoolteacher. But he moved the flagpole to the middle of a pile of manure, and for some reason the teacher doesn't hoist it. Now we don't fly the swastika in our village either.'

Conrad thought of his own village in Somerset, and tried to imagine a swastika flying from St Peter's Church. It might happen one day if there was a war and the wrong side won.

After dinner they all moved through to the drawing room. With a little urging from his sister, Theo sat himself behind an impressive grand piano and began to play some folk songs that Conrad vaguely recognized. Kätchen sang along. In England after-dinner music recitals made Conrad cringe. If there was to be music, let it be a gramophone, over which people could happily chat or even dance. But here, on the edges of the Prussian forest, to spend an evening listening to music seemed the most natural thing in the world. Theo gave up his seat to Kätchen, who played a Beethoven sonata beautifully. Then she insisted that her grandmother play the violin.

The old lady refused, but Theo and his sister persisted, citing Conrad's presence. With a glance full of meaning, although at first Conrad wasn't sure exactly what meaning, the old lady agreed. Kätchen left the room and returned a couple of minutes later with a violin, which she handed reverentially to the old lady.

'It's a Stradivarius,' Theo whispered.

Somehow, incredibly given her bent, stiff limbs, the old woman began to play. Conrad thought he recognized the piece, a Bruch concerto. It was the saddest, most haunting music he had ever heard.

The listeners knew that the high spirits, the beauty must come to an end. With the frail chords echoing in their heads they climbed the stairs to bed.

The thunderstorm Conrad had seen brewing didn't burst upon the manor until the middle of the night, leaving the weather fresh and clear the following morning. The wedding was in a neighbouring village and Theo took Conrad in his car, although most of the rest of the family went by horse-drawn carriage. The ceremony took place in an ancient fortified stone church, not nearly large enough for all the guests. The church was dominated by a huge hand-carved wooden cross towering above the simple stone altar, which was bedecked with roses, lilies and larkspur.

The bride and groom arrived, fresh from the potato distillery, for the chief distiller was also the local registrar. Theo whispered to Conrad that after the brief civil service the registrar was obliged to present the couple with their own matrimonial copy of *My Struggle* by one A. Hitler. The perfect way to start a life together. The bride was dressed in traditional white, complete with veil, and the groom, like Theo a lawyer who had joined the reserves, was wearing his army dress uniform and also, oddly, his coal-scuttle helmet, even though the other guests in uniform wore peaked caps. Regulations, Theo said. At least it made the bridegroom easily identifiable.

The service was presided over by a chubby-faced pastor of about thirty named Dietrich Bonhoeffer, who gave a short but moving address about goodness and love surrounded by evil. Conrad had heard of him: he had been in trouble with the Nazis for his opposition to the government's attempts to Nazify the Protestant church in Germany. Afterwards there was a bridal procession through the park from the church to the manor house where the wedding feast was to take place, headed by the bride and groom. Conrad escorted Kätchen, and Theo one of the bride's sisters.

Here in the countryside there were none of the shortages of the town. The feast included an orgy of cream and cakes, and somehow the bride's family had managed to acquire an unending supply of champagne. After the dinner, with its silent toast to Wilhelm, King of Prussia and former Kaiser, there was music and dancing in an avenue in the park shaded by ancient chestnuts that joined overhead, forming a canopy. Father and daughter opened the dancing with a waltz, with all the guests clapping in time. There was a brief hiatus as the shy groom refused to take the floor with his wife for the second dance, a break in tradition which threatened to bring eternal shame on the whole proceedings, but fortunately Theo stepped in and whirled her around the makeshift floor

All the important families of the region were there: Herten-bergs, Bismarcks, including the former Prussian Minister of the Interior, Herbert von Bismarck, Kleists, of which Uncle Ewald was one, Wedemeyers and Schulenburgs. The older men wore lines of miniature medals across the chests of their morning suits. These Prussian families were large, and there were children everywhere. One imperious old lady seemed to preside over it all: Ruth von Kleist, Theo's other grandmother. Everyone showed her the utmost respect and even Conrad was introduced to her. It was a beautiful evening, and Conrad danced and drank and enjoyed himself among these strangers.

'Young man!'

Conrad, surprised to hear English spoken, turned to see Theo's American grandmother summoning him, a gleam in her eye.

'Yes, Frau von Hertenberg?' he replied.

'Call me Betty. And get me a glass of whisky, will you? Theo promised he would hide a bottle for me behind the elm tree.'

'Certainly, Betty.' Conrad found the bottle of Johnnie Walker in question, and two glasses. He poured one for himself and one for the old lady.

'Thank you, young man,' said the old lady with a wicked grin. 'Theo told me you were reliable. Bottoms up.' She downed the drink in one, and the grin became even more wicked. 'At times like this I wish my father was still alive. He loved a good party.' She blinked. 'Ooh. I think I need to sit down.'

Conrad escorted her to a chair. 'Now, do you see those two girls over there gossiping away?' She pointed to two girls, barely out of their teens, fresh-faced and glowing.

Conrad nodded.

'They are the Schulenburg sisters. Pretty as peaches, aren't they?'

'Yes, Betty, I would say they are.'

'Well, go and ask one of them to dance. I would recommend the little one. The tall one doesn't stop talking.'

Conrad did as he was bid. He ended up dancing with both of them, and then Kätchen, and then one of her cousins and then Kätchen again. Conrad was a good dancer and he had no shortage of willing partners. The movement, the music, the girls, the champagne put him in a really good mood. He was enjoying himself for the first time in a long time.

But the fact that, with the exception of Theo's grandmother, he was the only foreigner present, and also the only person whose family was not one of the close-knit circle of neighbours, struck Conrad as odd. He had noticed Sophie wasn't there, for instance.

'Tell me again why I'm here,' he asked Theo.

'It was Uncle Ewald's idea,' Theo said. 'But I'm glad you came.'

Conrad looked for Uncle Ewald, and saw him in earnest conversation with the matriarch, Ruth von Kleist, and the pastor. 'So am I.'

Theo raised his glass of champagne. 'To Algy.'

Conrad smiled as he remembered the little wooden plaque in his rooms at Oxford commemorating the undergraduate who had died at Ypres. 'To Algy.'

As Conrad sat on the small, slow train puffing its way through the Pomeranian countryside towards Stettin, he was still smiling. He had forgotten the bitterness of the last couple of weeks, if only temporarily. Of course, he knew why Theo had invited him. Had they met in a quiet Berlin bar there was no chance that Theo would have been able to persuade him of his sincerity. Even if Theo had introduced him to his superiors in the Abwehr, whoever they were, there would be nothing they could have said that would have dispelled the doubts in Conrad's mind. Theo did after all work for the secret service, and one thing all secret-service personnel must be experts in is deception.

But there was nothing deceptive about Uncle Ewald, about Kätchen von Hertenberg, about her father the bluff general, about the matriarch Ruth von Kleist, about the pastor Bonhoeffer, about the elderly grandfather of the groom who had proposed a gruff toast to the King of Prussia. When Theo said he wanted to stop Hitler, he meant it.

Conrad had no illusions about the Junkers he had spent the weekend among. As a historian he knew that they were about the most reactionary, conservative group of people in Europe. Whichever theory you subscribed to about the causes of the Great War, you couldn't hide from the fact that it was planned with enthusiasm by Prussian generals. He knew many of them had supported Hitler when he first came to power, seeing in him a bulwark against the much-feared Bolsheviks, and he was sure that many of them still supported their führer.

He thought of the mysterious clearing in the woods and those two standing stones, the 'Traitor's Gate'. Theo could agonize over whether that knight Otto had been a traitor or not to the Teutonic Order, or to the local knights, but to Conrad, the salient point was that he had died a horrible death as punishment for his scheming.

Conrad knew he was being manipulated again, and not just by Theo. The Abwehr, whoever they were, almost certainly knew what Theo was doing. As did Uncle Ewald, clearly. And what he was doing was trying to get Conrad to pass a message to the British government. He had no idea yet what the message would be, but he was sure that since Theo had gone to all this trouble, it must be an important one.

Conrad had had enough of being manipulated. He still didn't feel any sense of patriotic duty to spy for his country. Nor was he convinced that Theo had told him the whole story. The Abwehr would have to find another messenger.

Eighteen

Conrad's mind was still full of thoughts of his weekend as he took a taxi from the station back to his flat. As the cab turned off Kurfürstenstrasse into the little square where he lived, he saw a woman's figure beneath the old chestnut tree by the back of the church.

Anneliese.

The taxi pulled up in front of his building. As he climbed out she took two tentative steps towards him. He paid the driver, but when he turned back towards her she was walking rapidly away towards Nollendorfplatz. He thought of calling after her, but then he didn't.

He didn't sleep well that night, thinking about her. One moment he would be imagining her wicked smile, her laugh, her eyes. Then he would drift off to sleep and awake with another image of a half-undressed Klaus in his mind, so vivid that it took him a few moments to remember where he was, his heart beating rapidly in a mixture of shock and anger.

The following morning, as he stood waiting to cross Unter den Linden on his way to the Stabi, he saw her again. This time she walked purposefully towards him.

'*Heil Hitler*, Anneliese,' he said with a touch of cruelty.

'*Grüss Gott*,' she replied, using the old, banned, pre-Nazi greeting.

A gap appeared in the traffic, and Conrad stepped off the

pavement to cross the road.

'Wait!' said Anneliese, and touched his arm.

Conrad waited. 'Yes?' She looked thinner than when he had last seen her, and paler, and her eyes were dark smudges. Food was harder to come by in those days of 'guns before butter'. Perhaps that was the reason.

'Please let me talk to you, just for a few minutes. You don't have to say anything, you can walk off to the library afterwards, but please listen to me.'

Conrad sighed. 'All right.' In truth he didn't feel the anger he had expected on seeing her in front of him. He just felt numb.

They were right outside the Café Kranzler, and they got a table on the flower-bedecked first-floor terrace overlooking the street. They ordered coffee. Kranzler's still served real coffee, not the ersatz stuff that was on offer almost everywhere else, but in small quantities, barely half a cup each.

Suddenly the numbness left him and the heat of his old anger returned. Anneliese was just beginning to speak when Conrad interrupted her. 'You slept with that Gestapo bastard, didn't you?'

Anneliese held his gaze and blinked. 'Yes.'

'Just so he could get your father out of the country?'

She swallowed and nodded.

'And that's why you saw so much of me, wasn't it? Right from when we met at Theo's dinner party you thought I could be useful to you. Well, you were right, I was.'

Anneliese mumbled something that Conrad couldn't hear. 'What was that?'

'I said, I liked you. I still do like you. That's why I'm here.'

Conrad snorted and looked away at a tram swishing along the street below.

'Can I tell you about Klaus?'

'Why should I want to know about Klaus?'

'Please listen. Please.'

Anneliese was on the verge of tears. But beneath the misery, there was determination.

'All right,' said Conrad, reluctantly, reining in his anger.

'I first met him when I was a medical student at university. At Halle. He was studying law. He was one of Paul's most enthusiastic supporters. He came on all the anti-Nazi demonstrations with us; he helped distribute leaflets. I knew he liked me then, I could tell, but he worshipped Paul and he knew I was unattainable. He was already in Berlin as a junior lawyer when Hitler came to power, so he avoided being picked up with Paul and me and the others.

'I saw him in Berlin later, when I was training to become a nurse. When Paul was killed Klaus was nice to me. Kind, gentle, genuinely considerate.'

'He was a Gestapo officer, for God's sake!' Conrad said.

'Not then, he wasn't,' Anneliese said. 'He had joined the Nazi Party, but you had to to pass the law exams. You remember, Theo told us that. Anyway...' She fiddled with the saucer of her coffee cup. 'Anyway, I needed someone like him to comfort me. We became engaged.'

'What!'

'He was a good man. Or I *thought* he was a good man. I didn't love him, of course I didn't love him, I still loved Paul, but that didn't matter because I knew I would never love another man anyway, and I wanted so desperately to be looked after, and Klaus wanted so desperately to look after me.'

'How romantic,' said Conrad, but even to him the bite of cynicism in his voice jarred.

'Then he was asked to join the Gestapo. And he said yes.'

'I'm surprised they took him: a former communist agitator.'

'You would be amazed at the number of good socialists who have become good National Socialists in this country,' said Anneliese bitterly. 'They just don't ask each other too many difficult questions.'

'But wasn't it a clue that perhaps he wasn't a very nice man?'

'We argued about it. I am half-Jewish after all, and at that stage it was clear that would be a problem for him as much as for me. But Heydrich had asked him personally, so it was impossible to refuse. And...' She fiddled with the saucer again.

'And?

'And he said he would get my father out of prison,' Anneliese said with a note of defiance. 'And he would have done too, if only Himmler hadn't taken a personal interest in the case.'

Conrad raised his eyebrows.

'In the end I broke off the engagement. I didn't love him and I never would love him, and that mattered. And I couldn't live with someone who was in the Gestapo, however kind he was to me personally.'

'What you mean is he couldn't get your father out of jail and so he was no more use to you. Until this year, that is.'

Anneliese shook her head.

'Did you tell him about Joachim?' Conrad asked.

Anneliese frowned. 'No! Of course not.'

'It's a bit of a coincidence that it was Klaus Schalke who interrogated him, isn't it? A couple of days after you had overheard him telling Theo about a plot to get rid of Hitler. You told me you didn't understand what Joachim was saying, but I know you speak English.'

'You're right, I did understand Joachim, but I didn't know Theo that well, and I didn't know Joachim at all, so it seemed safer to claim ignorance. That's just the kind of talk you don't want to overhear in Germany. But I absolutely did not speak to Klaus about it. At that stage I hadn't spoken to Klaus for months.'

'So it wasn't just another dodge to get your father out?'

A tear fell down Anneliese's cheek. 'I know what you think of me, and the awful thing is mostly you are right. I think I'm contemptible too. I know you don't want to see me again, of course you don't. At the time I thought it was worth doing anything, *anything* to get my father out of the concentration camp. I did a lot of things I bitterly regret now and I hate myself for them. Believe me, I hate myself so much more than you hate me.'

'That doesn't make sense,' said Conrad.

Anneliese took a deep breath. 'One of the things I most regret – no, *the* thing I most regret, is losing you. You saw what was happening to my father and did your best to help him. You risked your life for a man you didn't know because the way he was treated was unjust. When I was with you the world seemed normal; I felt like a normal human being. And now you've gone... Now I've treated you so badly...' She stumbled, and bit her lip.

Conrad was about to say something cutting, but the words never left his lips. He looked straight into her eyes. He saw pain and misery but also defiance. His cynicism suddenly seemed ugly when faced with Anneliese's honesty.

She got to her feet. 'There it is then. I've said it. What I came here to say. Goodbye, Conrad.'

And she was gone.

Conrad spent the whole morning in the Stabi staring at a blank sheet of paper. He just couldn't get Anneliese out of his mind. He felt an almost overwhelming urge to rush around to her room, take her in his arms and tell her that he forgave her. But it was an urge that he fought against, fought against and conquered.

The bitterness and resentment that he felt about the way she had treated him still burned, and he had no intention of casting off that protective shell in a moment of weakness. These days you could trust nobody. He had relented with Theo, and he would probably suffer the consequences. He wasn't going to give in to Anneliese. There was bound to be something she wanted from him, maybe a visa for herself. Yes, that was it: she wanted to go to England to join her father. Well, he wasn't going to be made a fool of again. He wasn't going to be hurt again.

Later on, back at his flat, he was listening to Bruch's violin concerto on his gramophone – the piece that Theo's grandmother had played – when he had a visitor. It was Sophie. He was struck by how pretty she was, with her short blonde hair, delicate mouth and big baby-blue eyes.

'What a surprise!' Conrad said. 'Come in. Can I get you a drink?'

She asked for a sherry, and he mixed himself a whisky and soda.

'Nice music,' she said, taking the drink.

'Theo's grandmother played it over the weekend. Have you met her?'

'I haven't met any of Theo's family,' Sophie said, a touch of bitterness in her voice.

'Really?' said Conrad, realizing he had put his foot in it.

'He knows they would think I wasn't good enough for him. A nurse and the daughter of a fishmonger from Friedrichshain.'

'Nonsense,' said Conrad.

'Oh, come on, you know it's not nonsense. You have a class system in your country, don't you? You are the son of a lord, it's easy enough for you to ignore it. Not so easy for me.' She sighed. 'And not so easy for Theo either.'

Conrad couldn't argue with that. 'I'm sorry,' he said. 'It

shouldn't be like that. Theo shouldn't be like that.'

Sophie smiled at him. 'You wouldn't care, would you?'

Conrad smiled. 'I'd like to think not. Actually my parents thought my wife was totally unsuitable and I married her anyway. Sadly they were right.'

'So you'd marry Anneliese even though she's half-Jewish?' Sophie asked.

Conrad laughed. 'There are very many reasons why I *wouldn't* marry Anneliese, but the fact that she is half-Jewish is not one of them. What about you and Theo?'

It was strange to be asking his friend's girlfriend about marriage, but there was a pleasingly intimate honesty about Sophie that encouraged him.

'That will never happen,' Sophie said.

'Yet you stay with him?'

'I love him,' she said. 'I know that the best I can hope for is to be his girlfriend. Or, more accurately, his mistress. But I can't imagine life without him.'

'He's very lucky,' Conrad said.

They sipped their drinks, listening to the Bruch.

'I've come to speak to you about Anneliese,' Sophie said.

'I guessed as much.'

'She has been miserable since you saw her with Klaus.'

'And so have I.'

'I'm sure you have,' said Sophie. 'A few days ago I thought she was going to kill herself. I caught her taking a batch of tranquillizers from the hospital. Stealing them. She said she couldn't sleep, but I could see she was lying. Anneliese wouldn't steal for something like that. It was something more... final. And she did try once before, several years ago.'

'Are you trying to make me feel guilty?' Conrad said defensively. 'Unless I talk to her, she'll kill herself? Is that it?'

'No, no. You're not responsible. She is and she knows it and that is precisely the problem. But she did what she did for love of her father. Most girls don't love their father that much, I know I don't, but for Anneliese he is the most important person in the world. She worships him – you can tell that whenever she talks about him. I'm not defending what she did, but I do understand it.'

'Did she ask you to come?'

'Absolutely not,' Sophie said. 'She would be mortified. As far as she is concerned there is no chance that you will ever have anything to do with her again.'

'Well, on that we are in agreement.'

'She has told Klaus that she won't see him any more.'

'Lucky man,' said Conrad. 'But look, why *are* you here?'

'You see, the thing is...' said Sophie, glancing down into her empty glass, before looking at Conrad with those large frank blue eyes. 'The thing is, she loves you.'

Conrad snorted. 'She hardly knows me.'

'And I suspect... well, I suspect that you love her. Am I right?'

Conrad wanted to protest, but suddenly he couldn't find the words.

'I'm sorry. I must be going. I apologize for intruding on you like this. You must think me an interfering busybody. But Anneliese is one of the people I am fondest of on this earth and she has had a very difficult time these last few years. So, I think, have you. Goodbye, Conrad.'

Four hours later, Conrad found himself on the corner of the quiet cobbled street where Anneliese lived. Everywhere was silence; no one dared venture out in this area late at night these days, apart from the Nazi thugs, of course. A drawing of a man hanging from a gallows was scrawled across the window of the little cobbler's opposite Anneliese's tenement building.

Conrad could feel the indecision creeping up on him. He had walked rapidly the whole way from his own flat, urging himself on, but now he was almost at his destination, uncertainty tugged at his sleeve, and whispered a name in his ear. His heart was beating fast. The urge to go ahead and do what his heart told him to do and damn the consequences was almost overwhelming. It was an exhilarating feeling, but he had felt it once before, when he had proposed to Veronica. 'Veronica,' the voice whispered. 'Remember Veronica.'

But Anneliese was different. She had to be different. If it turned out she really was just like Veronica, life would be unbearable. The world would be unbearable.

Shaking off his doubts, he strode along the street to the door of the building and knocked. Two minutes later, amongst loud muttering and grumbling, the door was opened by the landlady, in dressing gown, slippers and curlers.

'Good evening, Frau Goldstein, I'm very sorry to trouble you so late at night—' Conrad began.

Frau Goldstein's frown turned into a smile. 'Herr de Lancey! A pleasure to see you again. Fräulein Rosen is upstairs. And she is alone.' Conrad smiled quickly at the landlady and climbed the stairs. On the landing, outside Anneliese's door, he hesitated. He remembered the last time he had been there, Klaus Schalke's heavy tread, his big body appearing in the doorway in front of him.

What the hell was he doing?

He knocked.

He heard movement inside the room, and knocked again.

'Who is it?' The voice sounded tired.

'Conrad.'

The door opened slowly, and there was Anneliese, in a dressing gown. She looked pale and nervous, almost frightened as she saw Conrad's frown.

He smiled.

Her eyes studied his and the apprehension melted away. A smile spread across her own lips. 'Conrad,' she said and fell into his chest. He held her, tight, so very tight.

Nineteen

After that night Conrad and Anneliese spent every spare moment together. It was easy for Conrad; his visits to the Stabi became less frequent, but the time he spent there was much more productive. Suddenly his novel began to flow.

For her it was more difficult; she had her shifts to do at the hospital, but Conrad was happy to adjust his life to fit around hers. They just didn't get much sleep. Any distance between them was banished. They made love all the time, that first night with a manic desperation, afterwards with humour, with languor, with tenderness, with whatever mood took them. It was like nothing Conrad had experienced before. It was wonderful.

Most of the time they stayed in Anneliese's little room in the Scheunenviertel; it was more efficient since Anneliese didn't waste precious time travelling to and from the hospital. Frau Goldstein was pleased with this turn of events, and was always effusive in her welcome to Conrad. But whenever Anneliese had a day off they would switch to Conrad's flat.

Sometimes they would venture out for forays into the Tiergarten. They would always head for the Rosengarten, where the roses were in full bloom and the benches filled with lovers like them, and then go on to one of the *Zelte*, the semi-permanent restaurant tents on the banks of the Spree, and dance on the terrace to Strauss waltzes.

When they weren't making love, they talked. It was one long conversation, which they picked up where they had left off whenever they were interrupted by the need to sleep or for Anneliese to work. It was the uncontrolled ramblings of two minds, darting from subject to subject in a manner that made sense only to them. They talked about everything: music, sex, books, dreams, their childhood, politics, food, God. Anneliese recovered her sense of humour, luxuriated in it. She even told Conrad funny stories about Paul and her time in the concentration camp. She talked about her father, about her brother Franz, who was in Bavaria learning to fly in the newly formed Luftwaffe, and her mother, who, thanks to Foley, had just left for London to join her father. The only part of her life she didn't discuss was Klaus Schalke.

Conrad spoke of his own family and friends, but he barely mentioned Veronica, only when she was an unavoidable walk-on character in a story. This was for two reasons: he was still married to her and that made him guilty, and shoved to the very back of his mind remained the fear that in abandoning himself to Anneliese he had laid himself open to the same kind of pain that Veronica had caused him.

They were in Conrad's bedroom. It was nearly midnight, but it was still warm. They were lying naked on top of the sheets, and Conrad was tracing with his finger the shape of the bars made by the moonlight through the blinds on Anneliese's stomach. He felt very happy. She saw and she smiled.

Then he remembered an item he had seen in the newspaper that morning. A new ordinance had been announced that would force all Jews to adopt the first names 'Israel' or 'Sarah'. It followed hard on the heels of other ordinances that had decreed that all Jewish passports would have to be stamped with a 'J' and that Jewish cars would have to carry special number plates. Jews were no longer allowed to visit a theatre, to go to the swimming pool or certain parks, to own a radio or even a pet. This ratcheting up of anti-Semitism in legislation reflected what was happening on the streets, where random round-ups and beatings of Jews were becoming ever more common. Before the invasion of Austria in March it had been inconvenient to live as a Jew in Germany. It was swiftly becoming impossible.

'What is it?' asked Anneliese, sensing the thought.

'Are you going to leave the country?' he asked her. 'Join your parents in London?'

'I don't think so,' she said.

'Why not?'

'I think I'm old enough to live by myself, don't you?'

'This Jew-baiting is getting worse.'

'But no one thinks I'm Jewish. I don't look Jewish.'

'Oh, come on, Anneliese. With all these new regulations, they'll have you walking the streets with a J tattooed on your forehead before too long.'

'I'd much rather be here with you.' Anneliese stretched out her hand and stroked his thigh. Her breast moved into the bars of moonlight and shadow. Conrad touched it. She smiled again.

'I'm worried about you.'

'You shouldn't be,' said Anneliese. 'I'm the great survivor.'

'Seriously,' Conrad said. 'I couldn't bear it if some Nazi thug beat you up, or they threw you into another camp.'

Anneliese rolled on to her back and laughed.

'What's so funny?'

'I've been thinking about that. A week ago I thought that no one would care. Apart from my parents and my brother, of course. But I thought I should stay in Germany and take whatever punishment God wanted to give me – I deserved it.'

'That's ridiculous.'

'It didn't seem like it then. It seemed perfectly logical.'

'That was last week. What about now?'

Anneliese stroked his cheek. 'Now I just want to think about this moment, this minute with you. Not about next month or next year.'

'But you must think about the future, before it's too late. For my sake, you must get out of this insane country.'

'For your sake?' said Anneliese with a smile.

'Yes,' said Conrad.

They kissed.

'Yes,' he repeated.

She shook her head. 'I can't.'

'What do you mean, you can't?'

'When I asked Captain Foley for a visa for my mother, I asked for one for myself too. I wasn't going to, but my mother insisted.'

'Good for her.'

'Captain Foley said there was no chance.'

'Why?'

'I'm a communist. Or I was a communist.'

'That shouldn't matter.'

'Oh, but it does. Captain Foley is explicitly forbidden from issuing visas to communists.'

'That's outrageous!'

'Possibly. To be fair, no other country is too enthusiastic about us either.'

'Isn't there anywhere else you could go?'

'It's getting harder all the time. Captain Foley suggested Shanghai; it's about the one place you can still get a visa for as a German Jew. Oh, Conrad, would you like me to go to Shanghai? I'd much rather be here with you.'

'I'll talk to him,' Conrad said.

'You can try if you wish,' Anneliese said. 'But I think I'm stuck here.'

Conrad tried to do as Anneliese said she was doing, think of just the minutes, the hours they were spending together. But he couldn't help thinking about the future, the near future. And it scared him.

In the chestnut tree in the square outside Conrad's flat a nightingale was trilling a complicated aria of its own composition. In the middle of the square, next to the tree, was the red-brick Church of the Twelve Apostles. Although it was a cloudless night and a full moon, and although there were street lamps around the square, there were numerous niches and crannies in pitch-black shadow. In one of these stood Klaus.

He had been standing there for three hours, ever since he had followed Conrad and Anneliese back from the neighbourhood restaurant in which they had eaten their supper. It had been a long evening. He had waited outside St Hedwig's Hospital in the Scheunenviertel for Anneliese, and had followed her to her building. Even though she looked tired, she had walked fast. He had watched for a quarter of an hour, and then she had appeared, changed out of her nurse's uniform, and scurried off towards the U-Bahn, a small smile on her face. What little pleasure did she have to smile about?

Klaus had lagged well behind her. Although he worked for the Gestapo, he had no experience of following people. His size and his clumsiness made him an appalling choice of watcher; he had other skills of more use to his employer. But Anneliese was tired and preoccupied and Klaus was certain she hadn't seen him.

As she had turned into the little square, Klaus knew for sure where she was going. He had had Conrad followed earlier that summer and he knew his address. He bit his lip in frustration and pounded the wall of the church with his fist. A tear ran down his cheek. That night, of all nights, he needed to see Anneliese.

Eighteen hours earlier his mother had died. It had been quick. The doctors had thought she had beaten the mysterious ailment that had plagued her over the previous year, but all the time the cancer, for that was what it turned out to be, must have been eating away inside her, undetected. She had only begun to feel ill again a week before. The deterioration had been fast. Klaus had managed to get the day off, and by great good fortune had been at her bedside in her little house in Halle when she had died. His father was downstairs, reading the newspaper. He had smiled when Klaus had told him the news, actually smiled. Klaus had long suspected that his father had hated his mother throughout their long marriage, but it was only then that he had realized it was true. Klaus wanted to hit him, but even at that moment he was scared of the small old man. Those vicious beatings he had received throughout his youth had left him cowed and in awe of his father. So he stormed out of the house, his heart full of grief and anger. Why couldn't the old bastard have contracted cancer instead of her? He had a disgusting rasping cough, which always ended with him spitting up great gobs of mucus. He'd been doing that for years. He should be dead, not Klaus's mama.

He knew it was foolish to think about Anneliese while he was in that frame of mind. When she had dropped him the reason was clear enough; once her father was out of the country he was no longer any use to her. He had never accused her of that obvious truth for fear of alienating her. He wanted her to love him, not hate him.

The problem was that those few days when she had been his again had transformed his longing for a lost love into an obsessive desire. If his life was to have any meaning at all, he had to be with Anneliese.

He had tried explaining this to her, but she had been stubbornly firm. Indeed that was one of the things that Klaus loved about her: her wilful independence. He remembered, he would always remember, seeing her shouting slogans on those communist marches, her blouse tight over her breasts as she raised her fist, her hair tangled in the wind and the excitement, her face alight, not with hatred or rage, but with a passionate idealism. He had done nothing on those marches but stare at her. However impossible it seemed at the time, with her and Paul so obviously in love, and he a great shambling oaf whom she pitied, he knew that one day, one day she would be his. All he had to do was wait.

And she was his, for a while. It had started on the day she received Paul's ashes through the post in a cigar box. That was before Klaus had joined the Gestapo, when he was still a humble lawyer in the Berlin Prosecutor's Office.

Anneliese had telephoned him late in the evening to tell him; Klaus had after all been a friend of Paul's at university. It was an extraordinary telephone call: there was no grief, no hysteria; her voice was devoid of emotion, dead. When Klaus offered to come and see her the following morning, she said she wouldn't be there and hung up.

Klaus had thought it over for a minute and then dashed round to her building in the Scheunenviertel. The landlady tried to refuse him entry, saying there was no sound from her room and she must be sleeping, but Klaus barged upstairs, and after banging on her door, broke it down. As he expected, she was lying fully clothed on her bed with an empty medicine bottle on her bedside table.

He had picked her up, slung her over his shoulder and run

the five hundred metres to St Hedwig's Hospital. He was in time: they pumped her stomach, and she lived.

He had stayed with her all night, and the following day packed her into his small Opel to take her to the little village that he used to visit on summer holidays with his mama. It was in the mountains of Silesia, near the Czech border. The woman who ran the guest house remembered him: Klaus was memorable even at fourteen – he had been a great clumsy giant at that age. Klaus and his angel spent a glorious week together while she recovered. He had to lie to his office, claiming that his mother was ill. She was too ashamed of what she had tried to do to get in contact with her own parents, at least at first. It was idyllic: the mountain, the lake, the trees, the cows heading out to the steeply sloped pastures after their morning milking, the slow peace of the village. Eventually the week had to end, Klaus had to return to work, and Anneliese insisted on going back to her family, but over the following weeks and months Klaus looked after her. Nothing was too much trouble for him. He seemed to give her the sense of security, of comfort, of reliability that she needed. She improved in front of his eyes.

The day he had asked her to marry him had been the most frightening of his life, and then the most joyful when she had said yes. A few months later she broke it off. Although heartbroken, truthfully he wasn't surprised; he had always known that she had only agreed to marry him in a moment of weakness.

This summer she had come to him once more. And she would again, in time. He thought of her as his angel, but actually he was her guardian angel, faithfully coming to her aid. It was hardly an equal basis for a relationship, but this was not a relationship of equals. He wasn't worthy of her; he knew that. But if he was patient, patient and watchful, she would need him again and he would be there. It was their destiny.

So he had tried to force himself to stay away and wait. But it was difficult and that night, the day after his mother had died, it was very difficult. Especially now that he had seen her with the Englishman. How he detested that man! He so badly wanted to storm in there, arrest de Lancey and take her in his arms. But he knew that if he did that he would switch from guardian angel to bitter enemy, and it would be harder than ever to win her back.

No, there was nothing to do but stand outside the church, listen to the nightingale and watch the darkened windows of de Lancey's flat.

Hatred welled up inside him, mixing deliciously with love and grief.

Twenty

Conrad strolled up Bendlerstrasse, past the purposeful bulk of the War Ministry, and stepped out of the bright sunlight into the cool of the lobby of the Casino Club. Despite its name, the Casino Club was not a glitzy gambling den but rather an ancient establishment in which the Prussian aristocracy could gather while they were in Berlin. Theo's father and grandfather had been members.

Conrad had slept very little the night before, and he was light-headed, but in a thoroughly good mood. How Anneliese was going to cope with a long day at the hospital he had no idea.

He was shown through to the bar where Theo was waiting for him, looking tense. Conrad was pleased to see him: he realized that in his mind Theo had been reinstated to the category of 'friend'.

They shook hands. A waiter instantly appeared, and Theo ordered them both whisky and sodas.

'Nice place,' said Conrad, looking around the room. Half the men in the bar were in uniform; half were in suits. Most had the stiff, upright bearing of the Junker as opposed to the roly-poly solidity of the Berliner burgher. The walls were adorned with large oil paintings and smaller prints depicting past Prussian kings and German emperors, with some celebrated field marshals thrown in. Heavy silver knick-knacks were scattered over tables and bookcases. On the surface, the place was similar to a

London club, but it had an atmosphere of crisp formality rather than of comfort and relaxation.

'Not quite as nice as our old quarters,' said Theo. 'We had a lovely building in the Pariser Platz until last year when the Nazis kicked us out. It's been taken over by the Minister for Armaments and Munitions. But at least this is just over the road from the War Ministry, so it's very handy.'

Taking his whisky, Theo looked Conrad up and down and smiled. 'You look well. I mean, you look exhausted. But happy.' He frowned. 'If I didn't know you better I would guess that you were getting your wicked way with some poor girl.'

Conrad grinned broadly.

'Is it anyone I know?'

Conrad nodded.

'Not Anneliese?'

'That's right. I've been seeing a lot of her this past week. An awful lot.'

Theo frowned. 'What about her Gestapo boyfriend?' Conrad had told Theo about Anneliese and Klaus Schalke in Pomerania.

Conrad saw Theo's expression and felt a surge of irritation. 'It's over, I'm sure of it.'

'You have to be very careful of a man like that,' Theo said.

'Obviously,' Conrad said. 'But it's not as if I have anything to hide these days.'

'Well...'

'Oh, I see,' said Conrad. 'That's what this is about. The message you want me to deliver.'

A small figure moved briskly into the bar. 'Hello, Uncle Ewald,' Theo said. 'You remember Conrad de Lancey?'

'Of course,' said the Junker. He was smartly dressed for the city in winged collar, club tie, tiepin and waistcoat. He clicked his heels, bowed and held out his hand. Conrad shook it, with a little bow of his own.

'I must be going, Conrad,' Theo said. 'I have something to attend to over the road. But Uncle Ewald is anxious to treat you to lunch.'

Conrad accepted his fate, and, abandoned by Theo, he followed Ewald von Kleist through to the club dining room. The waiter showed them to a small table in an alcove at the back of the room.

Lunch was stilted at first as von Kleist made curt small talk, but in the interests of making things bearable Conrad asked him about politics, and the landowner became quite animated as he discussed Germany's history and its future. He was a right-wing monarchist who wanted the Kaiser back, just as Conrad had expected, but one who was driven by a fierce sense of justice. What he saw going on in Germany was wrong and he was going to say so, whatever the cost. He was enough of a realist to know that the cost would be high.

After lunch they retired to the library, and von Kleist ordered coffee and cigars. There was no one else in the room, save a portly old gentleman snoozing into his newspaper. Von Kleist identified him as a landowner from Silesia who invented business in Berlin every couple of months so that he could escape his wife and go to sleep in an armchair in the club for a week.

Von Kleist got down to business. 'You know that Hitler is determined to invade Czechoslovakia?' he began.

'Everyone expects it,' Conrad answered.

'He has made the general staff draw up detailed plans for an invasion before the first of October.'

'I'm not surprised.'

'The generals' evaluation of the situation is that if Britain and France stand by Czechoslovakia there will be a long, bloody war that Germany will lose.'

'You would lose? Interesting. But would Britain and France stand by Czechoslovakia?' Conrad asked.

'That's precisely the question!' von Kleist said. 'At the moment France has guaranteed Czechoslovakia's borders, and Britain has undertaken to join France in any war with Germany. In practice the French will follow the British lead. The British made encouraging noises of support to the Czechs when the Czechs mobilized in May. But the French and the British are sending out mixed messages. Your ambassador seems very pro-German. Your foreign secretary, Lord Halifax, seems much more eager to negotiate than to fight.'

The coffee came, with a humidor, and von Kleist paused to light a cigar. 'I can understand that. We tried that tactic too, here in Germany. When my friend Franz von Papen was chancellor in 1932 he thought if he dealt with Hitler as a responsible politician Hitler would behave responsibly. Six months later, Hitler was chancellor. Hitler is used to dealing with weak adversaries: he doesn't believe that the British will stand by Czechoslovakia. He believes he can invade that country with impunity, just as he invaded the Rhineland and Austria. He needs to know he is wrong.'

'I'm not so sure he is, unfortunately,' said Conrad.

'We must encourage the British to stand by Czechoslovakia.'

'And how will you do that?'

Von Kleist cleared his throat. 'In answering your question I might be signing my own death warrant. But I trust you. My nephew trusts you.'

The hard eyes stared at Conrad. He resisted the temptation to look away. 'Go ahead,' he said.

'By telling the British government that if they do, and if

Hitler insists on invading anyway, we will remove him.'

'Remove him! You mean you'd launch a coup?'

'We would arrest him and replace him with an interim administration that would negotiate a fair peace with Britain, France and Czechoslovakia.'

'But what will the German people say? You know how popular Hitler is.'

'The people fear war. We couldn't do this now. We can only act if we can plausibly say that we are keeping Germany out of a war like the last one: long and bloody that we will ultimately lose. Which is why Britain must stand by Czechoslovakia, and why we must wait to move until Hitler has ordered the invasion.'

Von Kleist puffed on his cigar. The fox on his cufflinks peeked out of his sleeve. 'Of course there is a chance that if Britain does stand unequivocally next to Czechoslovakia, Hitler will back down and there will be no war.'

'But you don't think that's likely?' said Conrad.

'Do you?'

'By "we", whom do you mean?'

'There are quite a number of us. Senior officers in the army, the Abwehr, the Foreign Office, the police.'

'And these men will go along with your plans?'

'They are not my plans, they are theirs.' Von Kleist smiled. 'And Theo's. He is a bright and energetic young man.'

Conrad's pulse quickened at what he heard. It sounded too good to be true. If the Germans really could remove their dictator then there would be no need for a war, and the senseless violence in Germany would stop. It sounded as if opposition plans against Hitler were much further advanced than Theo had suggested. Joachim was right all along. But of course Joachim was dead. 'They are all taking an enormous risk,' Conrad said.

'Is it such a risk, when the alternative is a war that will be bloodier than the last one? As so often is the case, the greatest risk lies in doing nothing.'

'Have you planned a date?'

'Hitler intends to order the invasion sometime in September. We will need to move just before that.'

'Two months away. And whom do you want to tell my government all this? Me? I'm not sure I have the credibility.'

'No, that role falls to me,' von Kleist said. 'I intend to travel to London sometime in the next two or three weeks. I would like to speak to some important members of your government. We need someone we can trust to arrange the trip. That's you.'

Conrad raised his eyebrows.

'You must be careful to whom you speak. It's probably best to contact the government ministers either directly or through your father. Whatever you do don't go through your secret service.'

'Why not?'

'Admiral Canaris tells me that it has been penetrated. Awkward reports would come through to him, my name and yours would be placed on files, the information would be difficult for the Abwehr to ignore. He also says the British secret service are not to be trusted: they betray their agents if it is useful to them. But you should have direct access to the people I want to contact.'

'I suppose so,' said Conrad, imagining trying to discuss all this with his father.

'Will you do it?'

Conrad's initial thought was to say 'no'. He had already decided he wanted to keep out of any international intrigue Theo might try to enmesh him in. But the enormity of what von Kleist had told him made him hold his tongue.

Von Kleist, who had been hunched forward conspiratorially throughout this conversation, leaned back into his armchair and sipped his brandy. He was willing to give Conrad time to think.

The idea that this man and the officers who stood behind him should actually want Britain to come to the aid of their enemy seemed illogical, even absurd. But the more Conrad thought about it, the more sense it made. Of course it was a high-risk strategy, it made defeat for Germany much more likely if there was a war, but that just showed how determined von Kleist and his friends must be to avoid one. There was no doubt they were serious about toppling Hitler.

Conrad still didn't feel any sense of patriotic duty to spy for his country. Nor did he want to be manipulated by Theo or Foley or the Abwehr. But whatever else you could say about the Junker sitting opposite him, he wasn't manipulative. He was an honest, straightforward, brave man of integrity who was prepared to risk his life to save Europe from mass bloodshed. This was presumably why he had been chosen as an envoy; the man had credibility.

Conrad wanted to end Hitler's evil regime, the regime that had twisted truth, spread hatred, tortured and murdered. The regime that had destroyed Joachim Mühlendorf and would one day destroy Anneliese.

Suddenly everything slotted into place. Conrad hated war. He hated Hitler. Here was a chance to do something that might make a real difference. David Griffiths and Harry Reilly had been willing to die to stop fascism overwhelming Europe. In the struggle between sanity and insanity he couldn't be a bystander. While there was a chance, even a small one, that von Kleist's mission could avert a war, he had to take it. Otherwise, he couldn't live with himself.

'I'll do it,' he said.

* * *

Anneliese came to his flat that night. She was exhausted after a full day at the hospital on top of several nights of inadequate sleep, but despite that they stayed up late into the night, in bed, talking.

'How was your lunch with Theo?' she asked. Conrad had told her they were meeting that day.

'I only saw him briefly,' Conrad said. 'He palmed me off on to his uncle Ewald.'

'The man you met in Pomerania? That was a bit cheeky of him.' During their week-long conversation, Conrad had told Anneliese all about his weekend with Theo's family. 'Ah, I understand,' she said. 'He wanted to give you "the message".'

Conrad nodded.

'Was it something to do with Joachim's plot?'

'I'd better not say. But if their plan works, there won't be a war.'

'That would be good,' said Anneliese. 'You are right to help them. I know it goes against your resolution to keep yourself out of political intrigue, but you can't step away from an opportunity to do something like that. It becomes a duty.'

'I thought that,' said Conrad. 'But a duty to whom? To my country? To your country?'

'No,' said Anneliese. 'To right. To justice. To everyone, English, German, Czech, French.' Then she smiled. 'To us.'

'That's exactly it,' said Conrad. 'It feels as if I am doing this for you, for us.'

'Just be careful,' Anneliese said.

'Oh, I think my part in this is fairly safe,' Conrad said. 'But they want me to go back to England to speak to my father. I'll probably leave in the next couple of days.'

'Will you be coming back?'

'Of course,' said Conrad, leaning over to kiss her. 'The tricky bit will be persuading my father to help.'

'Surely he wants peace? He doesn't like Hitler, does he?'

'Oh, no. But he and I disagree all the time, often violently. It's become almost a habit. It wasn't always like that, but it has been for the last several years. Since I married Veronica, anyway.'

Until he had gone up to the university, Conrad had idolized his father, stung by criticism during his father's bad moods to strive to earn praise once the storm had passed. But at eighteen, faced by his father's increasing unreasonableness, Conrad started to stand up to him until it became a point of pride to oppose him.

That's when things started to go wrong for the de Lancey family. First came the death of Edward, Conrad's elder brother, in a climbing accident on the slopes of Mont Blanc. Then the banking crisis of 1931: Gurney Kroheim, the family merchant bank, was heavily involved in Germany, and would have gone under during the run on the banks there had it not been for a rescue engineered by the Bank of England. The humiliation of this contributed to Conrad's grandfather's death six months later, and his father's unpredictable temper worsened, becoming an almost intolerable burden on the family.

It was Conrad's conversion to socialism, instigated by Joachim and encouraged by Oxford, that had driven a wedge between him and Lord Oakford, who had been a Conservative MP from 1924 until he succeeded to the title in 1931. The gap had simply been widened by Conrad's marriage to Veronica.

'At least your father saw through her,' Anneliese said. 'He must be perceptive.'

'We'll see,' said Conrad. 'I wonder if you will ever meet him?'

He had said this without thinking, as both of them had said

so much without thinking over the previous days, but it was a question whose answer had all sorts of implications.

'I'd like to,' said Anneliese, carefully.

Conrad raised himself on to his elbow. 'If I was able to persuade Foley to come up with a visa for Britain for you, would you go through all the paperwork and leave here?'

'Would you be here or there?

'If you were in England, then I would be in England too.'

Anneliese paused and then smiled. 'Yes. Yes, I would. That would be nice.' Then she frowned. 'But don't get my hopes up. It won't happen. Captain Foley was very firm.'

'Captain Foley is always firm,' Conrad said.

Twenty-one

Opposite the Passport Control Office at 17 Tiergartenstrasse was a large marble statue of Richard Wagner, sitting imperiously above three desperate Valkyries. Beyond that, a narrow path stretched into the trees. There Conrad met Foley and his dog. The three of them started off; the little man set a brisk pace, but for all his energy he looked tired. The spaniel was eagerly sniffing, checking which dog had come by that morning and leaving his own calling card on every other tree.

'Thank you for meeting me out here,' Foley said. 'It really is the best place to talk in Berlin. These days the park is full of diplomats and embassy officials like myself.' He touched his hat as they passed a dapper man in morning coat and winged collar in earnest discussion with a disreputable-looking German.

'The Third Secretary at the Italian Embassy,' he said. 'See what I mean?'

'You must be busy these days,' said Conrad.

'Very busy,' said Foley with a sigh. 'The queues get ever longer and the visas ever more restricted. They will let almost no one into Palestine now. I don't know if you heard about the conference at Évian a couple of weeks ago? It was supposed to lead to an international agreement that every country would take in their fair share of Jewish refugees. Instead they are all trying to outdo each other in barriers to immigration. No one wants to be a soft touch. It's like a trade war, only much, much crueller.'

'What will happen to those Jews who can't get out of Germany, do you think?'

Foley sighed. 'It will get worse.'

'How much worse can it get?'

'Never underestimate the determination of the Nazis, or their ability to go further than anyone thought possible,' Foley said. 'They'll round them all up and lock them up in the concentration camps. And then one day a Nazi bureaucrat will calculate that it's too expensive to feed them all.'

'What – they'll starve?'

'Perhaps. Or perhaps they'll shoot them.' Foley shook his head. 'I hope to God I am wrong.'

They were walking towards the noise of construction in the middle of the park, where the Siegessäule was halfway resurrected in its new location, the Grosse Stern circle. With a couple of excited barks, the spaniel shot off after a squirrel.

'Come here, Jonny!' called Foley, and after a couple of wags of his tail at the bottom of a birch tree the dog returned to his master.

Conrad thought of the queue outside the Passport Control Office and then he thought of Anneliese. 'Thank you for getting Frau Rosen out.'

Foley smiled. 'That one wasn't difficult. She is "Aryan" after all, and her husband was already in Britain.'

'But you couldn't do anything for Anneliese herself?'

Foley looked at Conrad sharply. 'Are you seeing her again?'

Conrad smiled. 'Yes.'

'Good,' said Foley. 'I like that girl. She has a lot of spirit, a lot of guts. But she is a communist. Or was. And that rules her out.'

'Is there nothing you can do?'

Foley shook his head. 'No, I'm sorry, de Lancey. There really isn't.'

'What if she was a spy? One of your agents? Surely you have agents who are ostensibly communists or Nazis or whatever?'

'She isn't.'

'Isn't she? Didn't she give you that information about the new fighter aeroplane?'

'Yes, she did. The information was first class, which is why I arranged for a visa for her father as I promised. But she made it clear that that was all we could expect from her uncle.'

'And that's all she can expect from you?'

'I'm afraid so, old man. I'm sorry.'

They walked on in silence, Conrad biting back his anger. There had to be a way, damn it.

Of course there was a way.

'What if I was a spy?' he said. 'What if in order to recruit me you had to grant her a visa? Couldn't you justify that?'

'Look,' said Foley. 'I know how desperate you are to get Anneliese out, and I would love to be able to help, I really would, but I can't be a party to you fabricating something. I would have to make a case in a written report to London. It would have to be real information.' Foley stopped and stared up at Conrad. 'Is it?'

It would be so easy to do. Tell Foley about Uncle Ewald's visit to England. He would probably find out soon enough anyway. The only problem was that Conrad had given his word to von Kleist, which Theo would consider the same as giving his word to him. And perhaps there was something in the Abwehr's concern that the British secret service had been compromised. By telling Foley he might be risking the trip, threatening Ewald von Kleist's safety and his efforts to stop a war.

But Anneliese's safety was already threatened. Conrad respected Ewald von Kleist, but he loved Anneliese.

Yet they were only two people in the middle of a continent of millions that was on the brink of tearing itself apart.

'Yes?' Foley asked.

Conrad took a deep breath and shook his head. 'There's nothing,' he said.

Foley nodded. 'I hate bargaining over people's lives like this,' he said. 'I do want to help you; I want to help her. But I can't. I am sorry.'

He turned and hurried back the way he had came, Jonny trotting along behind him. Conrad wandered on through the Tiergarten. He had tried. But had he tried hard enough?

If the worst happened to Anneliese, Conrad would go through life knowing that he had had the opportunity to save her and had decided not to. That was something he didn't know if he would be able to bear.

He might have to.

A hundred metres behind him a young man in a lightweight suit whipped out a notebook, checked his watch and jotted something down. He saw Foley head one way and de Lancey the other. As per the orders he had received from Kriminalrat Schalke that morning, he followed de Lancey.

Theo entered the Chief of the Abwehr's office and saluted. It was the old-fashioned army salute: the first time Theo had met him and barked out '*Heil Hitler*' Canaris had gently but firmly reached out and lowered Theo's outstretched arm. Oster had just laughed. Theo had only been in his job for a week when he had attended a meeting where Canaris, with a straight face, had told his staff to give the *Heil Hitler* salute to any flock of sheep they might be passing in case there was a high-ranking Party official among them.

The office itself was remarkably bare for an admiral. The rug was severely worn, and in a corner was an iron camp bed. The only pictures were two portraits: one of Colonel Nicolai, the founder of the Abwehr, and the other of Admiral Kanaris, its present chief's namesake and one of the heroes of the Greek War of Independence. On the desk stood a scale model of the *Dresden*, the cruiser in which Canaris had served as an intelligence officer during the last war, and in which he had led the Royal Navy a merry dance all around the coasts of South America.

'Well done, Hertenberg!' the admiral said, smiling broadly. 'Von Kleist has just been in to see me. Your friend de Lancey has agreed to arrange the meetings for him in London.' Colonel Oster was sitting by Canaris's desk, smiling. Both of them were smoking large cigars. 'Von Kleist was impressed, by the way.'

'De Lancey is a good man,' said Theo. He was relieved. He had stuck his neck out in suggesting Conrad, especially since he hadn't been absolutely sure that his friend would go along with Uncle Ewald's request.

'And you are certain he has the contacts?' Canaris asked.

'His father does, I'm sure of that. And de Lancey himself knows Lord Halifax.'

'Von Kleist made him promise not to go through the British secret service,' the admiral went on. 'We know he has been speaking to Foley. Are you confident he won't mention this to him?'

'De Lancey is a man of his word, excellency.'

'Good,' said Canaris. It was an irony that within the Abwehr, ostensibly the centre of guile and deception within the Third Reich, honesty and integrity were highly valued. To Theo, it was what made the organization a tolerable place to work.

Canaris waved his cigar towards a pile of papers on his desk. 'General Keitel is on holiday and I have been covering for him. It's clear from all this that you were right, Oster. Hitler is serious about invading Czechoslovakia; it's not just a bluff.'

'Is there any indication of the exact date?' Oster asked.

'Before October the first. It could be any time in September. Hitler has asked me to help Henlein stir up trouble in the Sudetenland.'

'So are we going ahead with the coup?' Theo asked.

Canaris smiled. 'We must be prepared. If the British do as we ask and stand by Czechoslovakia, and if Hitler still insists on invading, as I think he will, then we must move against him.'

Theo hesitated. 'What will we do with him, excellency? After the coup.'

'We arrest him and then we try him.'

'Won't that be a risk, excellency? Letting Hitler live. He will be a focus for all those who oppose us, and there will be quite a few of them. The SS, the Gestapo, the Party members.'

'I know what you are suggesting, Hertenberg,' said Canaris sternly. 'And I don't like it. Killing an unarmed man is murder. It is exactly the kind of behaviour we are trying to stop. It is the wrong way to establish a new regime that will enshrine the rule of law as paramount. Do you understand me?'

'I understand,' said Theo. He was disappointed. He knew that Oster agreed with him. If a coup was to be successful, Hitler had to be killed on the first day. He admired Canaris for his scruples, but in this case they were a luxury that the plotters couldn't afford.

'How are your soundings going, Oster?'

'They are going well,' the colonel replied. 'We have widespread support. Most of the generals will join us; they are still furious at the way von Fritsch was treated. But if they are to get their junior officers to follow them, they need legitimacy. A leader. Someone from whom they can take orders.'

Theo and Oster had discussed this problem endlessly. With a decisive leader the army could have moved in March when General von Fritsch had been falsely accused. But von Brauchitsch, his successor as commander-in-chief, had been the model of indecision, and Beck, while just as outraged as his brother officers, had been reluctant to take action. Oster was the organizing force behind the plotters, but he was only a colonel. Canaris was an admiral, but the chief of the secret service was hardly the right person to legitimize a revolt. It had to be someone from the army. Not just a general, but a senior general.

'Beck,' said Canaris. 'Without Beck we have no chance.'

'That's right,' said Oster.

'I've read his memoranda,' said Canaris, nodding towards the papers on his desk. 'They are very persuasive: an invasion of Czechoslovakia will lead to a world war that we will lose.'

'I know,' said Oster. 'But he is still hesitating.'

Canaris puffed at his cigar. 'Keep working on him, Oster. If we are going to succeed, he *must* be persuaded.'

'Is this chair free?'

A jolt of fear ran through Conrad as he recognized the voice. He was sitting in the Café Josty, reading *The Times*. He looked up from his newspaper to see Klaus Schalke towering over him.

'No, it isn't,' he said.

Klaus smiled, and sat in the chair anyway. It creaked under his weight, and his knee knocked the table, tipping over a salt cellar. Conrad replaced it.

'Cigarette?' Klaus held out a cigarette case. Conrad shook his head, and Klaus lit one.

Conrad stared hard at the Gestapo officer. The fear was gone as soon as it had come, an involuntary reminder of the night of his arrest.

'Do you like Berlin?' Klaus asked.

214

Conrad ignored the question. He knew he should be wary; Anneliese had hinted at how obsessed Klaus was with her, and Klaus was no doubt extremely unhappy about Conrad seeing her. But Conrad wasn't going to be intimidated by that, and he trusted Anneliese when she said she had no intention of seeing Klaus again. In Klaus he didn't see a rival for his lover's affections; he saw a murderer.

'Why did you kill my cousin?'

'I didn't kill him. He had a heart attack while he was waiting to be interrogated.'

'Waiting? While he was being tortured, you mean.'

'I have no doubt he was under a lot of stress,' said Klaus. 'He had a lot to hide.'

Conrad snorted. 'You killed him.'

Klaus's eyes met Conrad's. He shrugged.

'You don't deny it?'

Klaus smiled. 'What happened to your cousin was an unfortunate accident. And it's unlikely to be the last.'

'What do you mean?'

'I mean that it is time for you to leave Berlin, Herr de Lancey.'

'That's strange, because I was planning to fly out tomorrow morning.'

Klaus raised his eyebrows. 'I'm very pleased to hear that. I take it you have no intention of returning?'

'I may,' Conrad said. 'I have some research to do for the novel I am writing.'

'I would advise against it,' Klaus said.

'You will find it difficult to arrest me,' he said. 'Do you know who my father is?' The time had come for name-dropping.

Klaus smiled. 'I certainly do. Viscount Oakford, former Cabinet minister, director of the merchant bank Gurney Kroheim, friend of half the most powerful people in your country. And of course you are quite right; if I were to arrest and charge you there would be all kinds of tedious protests. But that's not what I would do.'

'I'm glad to hear it.'

'No. If you did return to Germany, what I would do is grab you, stuff you in the back of my car, take you to some woods somewhere and shoot you in the back of the head.'

'I don't like being threatened by petty bureaucrats,' said Conrad, ostentatiously raising his newspaper and beginning to read. 'Now bugger off.'

'You are making a big mistake if you don't take me seriously.'

Conrad didn't look up. 'I said, bugger off.'

He heard as much as saw Klaus get up and leave. He only looked up when he heard the door of the café bang shut. He watched Klaus, almost a head taller than the crowd, as he pushed his way through the Potsdamer Platz towards Leipziger Strasse and Gestapo HQ.

If Klaus had been trying to rattle him, he had succeeded. Conrad was very glad that he was taking that aeroplane to London. But he did intend to return. And when he did, he was sure that Klaus would be there, waiting for him.

The two officers, the colonel and the general, emerged from the trees of the Grunewald, the forest that lay on the western fringes of Berlin, and trotted their horses along the shore of Lake Havel. It was a hot, sticky day, but a breeze blew in from the water, which was dotted with sailing boats taking advantage of the sun and the wind. Jutting out into the lake on their left was the Schwanenwerder, the small promontory which was packed with summer houses that used to be owned by Berlin's rich Jews, but which now had almost entirely been taken over by the Nazi hierarchy.

For all the apparent formality of the Wehrmacht, there was a certain intimacy amongst its officers, especially those who had served together before the great expansion of the armed forces after 1933. It was possible for a mere colonel like Oster to provide advice to the Chief of the General Staff, and for that advice to be listened to with respect and friendship. Oster had taken to dropping into Beck's office at the Bendlerstrasse, but as their conversations had progressed they had begun once a week to ride together through the Grunewald, well out of range of curious ears.

'Has Hitler responded to your memoranda, Herr General?' Oster asked.

'Not in any well-thought-out way,' Beck replied. 'What he did say was "I'm not asking my generals to understand my orders, but to obey them!"' There was bitterness in Beck's voice. 'But it's my duty as chief of staff to explain the military situation to the Führer. And the war game we played last month clearly shows that Case Green will not work. We will lose a war against Czechoslovakia if it receives the support of France and Britain.'

'Does the Führer think the West Wall will hold the French?'

'He insists it will. But it has barely been begun. He wants it ready by October, but that's impossible; it will take another two years to construct, at least. Which means, of course, that if we attack Czechoslovakia we will not have enough divisions to defend the Rhine from an attack by the French.'

'What about von Brauchitsch?'

'Oh, von Brauchitsch understands the military situation very well,' Beck said. 'Although I doubt he is putting the case forward strongly enough. If I can only get the other generals to back me, we might be able to stop him.'

'How far will you go?' asked Oster.

Beck's piercing eyes examined the other. He knew it wasn't an innocent question. 'I have told von Brauchitsch that if all the advice and warnings of the leaders of the Wehrmacht continue to be ignored, then we have a duty to our country and to history to resign our posts. All of us. Hitler cannot invade Czechoslovakia without his senior generals.'

'Can't he?' asked Oster.

'Of course he can't,' protested the general. 'It would be madness.'

'It seems to me that our führer is a little mad. Or, to put it another way, by going further than would be expected of any rational man he has seized whatever he has wanted so far. The chancellorship, the destruction of the Weimar constitution, the Rhineland, Austria. We should be prepared for him to take the path which seems madness now.'

They trotted away from the lake shore and turned on to a quiet track through the pine forest.

'When you say "be prepared", what do you mean?'

'I mean that if, despite all your reasoned advice, despite the threat of his generals to resign, he persists in starting a war with Czechoslovakia, we should be prepared to remove him.'

Beck didn't answer. They came to a decent stretch of grass verge, straight and wide, and he urged his horse on to a gallop. Oster followed him. As the path narrowed again, Beck slowed up. Horses and riders burst into a sweat in the heat.

'You know, Oster, it is so difficult. You, I, General von Brauchitsch: we have all sworn that cursed oath. It is not easy for us, as honourable German officers, to ignore it. When I was told I had to take it I nearly resigned my commission: I wish now I had.'

'If you had, you would be of much less use to your country now,' said Oster. But he accepted Beck's point. The oath of a

German officer was more than a ritual in an initiation ceremony. It was the contract of honour that bound army and country together. It was why German soldiers had died so bravely in so many wars. To a lawyer, the law is the ultimate arbiter of right and wrong, but to a soldier, it is honour.

In earlier oaths the German officer had sworn loyalty to the King of Prussia, then the Emperor of Germany, and then, in the time of the Weimar Republic, to the Fatherland. But the new oath, taken by the whole army in 1934, bound the soldier in an obligation of honour to Hitler in person: *I swear by God this sacred oath, that I shall render unconditional obedience to the leader of the German Reich and people, Adolf Hitler, Supreme Commander of the Wehrmacht, and at all times be prepared as a brave soldier to lay down my life for this oath.*

Men like Beck, having sworn such an oath, had to be prepared to die for it.

'I *will* get him to see reason,' Beck said. 'I shall keep the pressure up on von Brauchitsch and the other generals. Hitler can't fight a war without an army.'

'And if he doesn't see reason?'

Beck looked Oster straight in the eye. 'Then we do it your way.'

Twenty-two

Conrad was met at Castle Cary station by Tyndall, his father's chauffeur, in the shooting brake. It had been a long day: an early morning flight from Berlin's Tempelhof Aerodrome to Croydon, then through London to Paddington. It was late afternoon, and the sun shone out of a sky dotted with small puffs of cloud on to the green English countryside. According to Tyndall it had been a wet summer, and indeed the fields looked remarkably lush for July. They drove down ever-narrower roads winding in and out of small valleys and tiny villages. After nearly two months living in Germany, Conrad was struck by how disorganized everything was, how the villages and their buildings followed no set pattern, how the road network seemed random and meandering. The sky was smaller here among the rolling hills; there were copses and woods rather than forests, small quiet streams rather than great continental rivers, and a general lack of purpose in the inhabitants as they ambled along roadsides. This time of day was rush hour for the bovine community, and three times they found themselves trundling behind a herd of cows on their way in for the evening milking.

Chilton Coombe was not a grand house, but it was a beautiful one, with a long history, originally built in the sixteenth century. Honeysuckle, vines and a pink rose climbed up the faded red brickwork. A lawn sloped down to a rock garden and a small pond. The house and garden nestled in a narrow valley scored into the flank of a small range of hills overlooking the flat Somerset levels, which stretched as far as the ancient domed hills of Glastonbury and its tor to the north and Cadbury to the west. Conrad's grandfather had bought the house and surrounding estate fifty years before and although Conrad had lived in London for most of his childhood, he had looked forward to the long holidays spent there with his brothers and sisters. His father had inherited the estate in 1931, and since then his parents had divided their time between there and their town house in Kensington Square.

From the moment he walked into the hall he could tell from the atmosphere that his father was in a good mood. Millie, his tall, rangy, 22-year-old sister, almost skipped as she hugged him welcome. His mother's forehead was wrinkle-free as she kissed him, and his brother Reggie's grin was vacuous and uninhibited.

A few moments later Lord Oakford himself appeared from his study. Tall, with a spare frame and a stoop, his hair was still sleekly black, but his moustache had flecks of grey. The left sleeve of his jacket was empty, the permanent reminder of how he had won his Victoria Cross. He grinned when he saw Conrad, and his restless eyes quickly assessed his son. 'Wonderful to see you. How was your flight?'

'A bit bumpy. Some of the other passengers were sick.'

'Oh, yuck,' said Millie. 'Aeroplanes sound such beastly machines. Don't they smell, with all that vomit and the engine oil and everything?'

'Millie, really,' said her mother. 'I do wish you would take the boat train, Conrad. It's much safer. Did you read about that plane crash last year when Prince Christopher of Hesse died with half his family? Dreadful. And he was flying from Germany to England.'

'It's perfectly safe, Mamma,' said Conrad. 'I couldn't spare much time, so I thought it best to fly.'

'And what are you doing that makes life so busy?' asked his father.

'Perhaps that's something we could speak about later, Father.'

'How intriguing! I look forward to it. Meanwhile, nip upstairs and get changed and we'll have a drink before dinner.'

Dinner was a lively affair. Conrad's mother and sister bombarded him with questions about Germany and the Nazis. He tried to describe Berlin to them, the uniforms, the speeches, the violence, the hatred, the fear and the complacency. Lord Oakford listened carefully and Reggie not at all, occasionally trying to pull the conversation around to local affairs. Reggie was a crashing bore. In most families he would have been banished to the army, but given Lord Oakford's strong views on war he remained in civilian life. Ostensibly he was managing the small estate, although in practice he was annoying the hell out of the three tenant farmers and the gamekeeper. He was a year younger than Conrad and distrusted him and his politics. Conrad knew that Reggie was desperately worried that as the older surviving brother, Conrad, not Reggie, would eventually inherit Chilton Coombe. It was something that Conrad didn't think about. To him, the role of eldest son and heir was still held by Edward, even though he had been dead eight years.

Millie and Conrad had always got on well. She was lively, amusing and really quite beautiful in a gangling kind of way. Conrad knew of at least three proposals of marriage she had turned down, and was confident that, unlike him, she would wait until the right person came along. Conrad's other sister, Charlotte, was already married and expecting a baby.

Conrad was in a good mood as he made his way up to bed, having extracted a promise from his father to walk with him up Yarmer Hill the following morning. The apprehension he had felt on the train down to Somerset had been replaced by optimism that he would get a good hearing.

They set off after breakfast up through the orchard behind the house, Lord Oakford as always striding ahead, with his faithful yellow Labrador, Monty, scouting the ground to left and right. The remains of the morning mist hung low over the saturated levels, with the Tor and the other extraordinary hills emerging from it like islands. The sun was already burning strongly; the mist would be gone within an hour.

'Have you seen Veronica?' his father asked.

'I bumped into her in Berlin,' Conrad admitted.

'How is she?'

'You mean is she still with Linaro?'

'I suppose I do, yes.'

'She is. You were right about her, Father. I know that's obvious now, but it wasn't to me then. I'm sorry I didn't listen to you.'

'It was your mother who was right about her,' his father said. 'I was just the messenger. You were in love; you couldn't tell. Has she asked you for a divorce yet?'

'Yes. She expects me to be the guilty party.'

'And what did you say?'

'No.'

'Pity.'

This last remark struck Conrad as a little odd. He had always assumed his parents disapproved of divorce.

'You should give her what she wants,' his father said. 'There's a lot of righteous tosh spoken about divorce. But you both made a mistake; you may as well start again with a clean slate. Unless you want her back. Do you want her back?'

'Six months ago I would have said yes like a shot,' said Conrad. 'Now I'm not so sure.'

'Met someone else?'

'Yes,' said Conrad. 'Yes, I have.'

'Jolly good. Very glad to hear it.'

Conrad was surprised but rather gratified by his father's intrusion into his private life. It made a pleasant change to feel that they were both on the same side, rather than his father attacking Veronica and him defending her. He wondered what his father would think of Anneliese, if he ever met her. He suspected that he would rather like her.

They were walking uphill through a birch wood along the edge of a small stream. They emerged into open pasture at the top of Yarmer Hill. Here were the mounds and ditches of some ancient fort, a favourite place for Conrad and Edward to play when they were young. Lord Oakford sat down at the spot where he had sat with his sons and indeed with his own father many times before. From the hill there was a magnificent view down to the house below and across the flat grassland criss-crossed by dykes and hedges. The mist had lifted to be replaced by a higher haze, through which Glastonbury Tor was barely visible.

Conrad was reminded of that other ancient place, deep in the Prussian forest behind Theo's home a thousand miles to the east. The place Theo called Traitor's Gate.

'So, if it isn't Veronica, what have you come here to talk to me about?' asked his father.

'I met someone in Berlin,' Conrad said. 'He asked me to arrange a trip for him to London. And I need your help.'

Conrad told his father all about Theo and von Kleist and the latter's proposed mission to London. His father listened closely.

'I suppose you want me to arrange some meetings for him?' he said when Conrad had finished.

'Yes. It should be done directly and not through official channels. Apparently our secret service is leaky.'

'Who told you that?' Lord Oakford asked sharply.

'Von Kleist.'

'And how the hell would he know about our secret service?'

'Good question,' said Conrad. 'But he was confident that if the secret service found out about it, so would the Gestapo, eventually.'

'Hmm.'

'He should see Lord Halifax, and possibly the Prime Minister. I know you could arrange something with Halifax.'

'I could, but should I?' said Lord Oakford.

Conrad had feared that question. 'Yes, I think you should. I think it's in our country's best interests. In everyone's best interests.'

'I'm not so sure,' said Lord Oakford.

Conrad's heart sank. 'Why?'

'Two things. Firstly I don't think we should start a world war over the Czechs, however poorly they are treated. We should only fight if we have tried every last avenue of peace, and if our own country is threatened directly if we don't. Secondly, this von Kleist fellow sounds to me like a traitor. You are asking me to help a traitor. And not just me, the British government.'

'When you meet him, you'll see that whatever Ewald von Kleist might be, he certainly isn't a traitor. He's a brave and honourable man. He wants what he believes to be the best for his country.'

'You said this man is a monarchist?'

'I believe he is.'

'So he wants to carry out a revolution. Remove an elected leader and replace him with the Kaiser, the man who started the last war.'

'Hitler might have been elected originally, but he is an

225

absolute dictator now. No one is going to get the chance to vote him out of office.'

'Possibly,' said Lord Oakford. 'But you've spent the last few months in Germany. He's popular, isn't he?'

'Yes, he is. But it's a popularity based on propaganda. And he won't be so popular when he leads the German people into a war they believe they will lose.'

'So say your friends.'

'So say my friends,' admitted Conrad. 'But he's an evil man, you know that, Father. The world would be much better off without him.'

'You may think that, I may think that, but what right have we to intervene in another country's affairs to decide what leader they have?'

'But, Father, we are on the brink of a disaster as bad as 1914! Possibly worse.'

'Precisely,' said Lord Oakford. 'But once we start threatening Germany with war, there will be one. We have to offer them peace and give them every opportunity to take it.'

'But Hitler will take whatever he wants until we say "no",' Conrad said. 'If it's not Czechoslovakia, it will be Poland, or Russia, or France. The only way to avoid war is to get rid of the man.'

Conrad had successfully managed to avoid raising his voice to his father until that moment. Lord Oakford seemed to realize that the tension was rising, and to tacitly agree with his son that the issue was too important for the differences between them to be allowed to have an effect. He sat on the grass, his chin resting on his one good hand, looking out over the levels. Conrad sat in silence next to him, waiting. He knew his father wanted to say something.

'I've never told you how I lost my arm, have I?' he said.

'No,' said Conrad. His heart quickened. When he was a boy, he had been obsessed with finding out as much as possible about his father's most heroic moment, and bitterly frustrated at his father's reluctance to discuss it. Now, finally, he was to find out.

'I should tell you. I've always known there would be a time to tell you, and this is it.'

'All right,' said Conrad.

'You know how reluctant your grandmother was to see me join the army?' he began.

'I do,' said Conrad. Conrad's grandfather had astutely married the boss's daughter, from the Quaker family that had founded the bank. While Conrad's grandfather's Anglicanism had prevailed in the upbringing of Conrad's father, his grandmother's Quaker ethics had quietly permeated the family.

'Well, I was quite determined, and although the army told me I was too old at the time war broke out, after they had wiped out a generation of young officers they turned to me. What you probably don't know is how excited I was to be a soldier. I felt younger, invigorated, alive. Even in battle, which at that stage of the war was pretty beastly, I enjoyed myself. I was scared, certainly, but I was thrilled also. I was a good soldier, a good leader.

'Then my friends started dying, chaps I knew who had joined other regiments, my brother officers. Replacements would come up, and then they would die, sometimes after only a few days at the front. For a while, quite a while, I thought I could cheat death, but then I realized that it would catch up with me, that my death was inevitable. It was just a matter of time.

'Even then, I still took each day as it came. I saw men around me crack, but I kept on fighting. If anything I became braver. I was going to die for my country: I knew it and I accepted it. I thought a lot about your mother, and about you and Edward and the others. But all around me better men than me were dying: why should I escape?

'Then one day at Passchendaele we were pinned down by the Hun. They had counter-attacked and were in danger of pinching off a salient held by a battalion of the Gloucesters. Directly in front of us, on a slight rise in the ground, lay a German machine-gun post. It was in a commanding position, pinning us down and cutting off any chance the Gloucesters had to retreat. We sent a company in to try to overrun the position, but they were all wiped out.

'I volunteered to try to take the post by stealth. I set off with only six men, in the hope that the fewer of us there were, the less chance there was that we would be spotted. Battalion HQ ordered up a small artillery barrage, enough to give us cover, not enough to warn the Hun that something was up. We crawled our way closer and closer. We were about twenty yards away, when one of the Germans shouted out a challenge. I yelled back to him in my best Hamburg accent that we were wounded, and that we needed stretchers, quickly. There was a lot of shouting, and as a half-dozen stretcher-bearers scrambled down towards us, we charged the post. They were taken by surprise. We were lucky: a couple of well-placed grenades, some lucky shots, and we took the emplacement. But they killed four of us.

'So there was just me and Lance Corporal Roberts, a tough little dairyman from Frome. Anyway, we manned the machine gun and turned it towards the German lines. By that time my arm was shot to pieces.

'They came at us, wave after wave of them, and we mowed them down. I don't know how many men we killed. Dozens, maybe a hundred. It was a horrible sight, seeing all those bodies falling through the sights of the machine gun. I remember feeling more like a manic murderer than a soldier. But however many we killed, more came on. Roberts bought it, a shot in the throat. It was a devilish job firing the machine gun myself with one arm, but I managed somehow.

'There was a lull, while they regrouped. They must have thought there was more than one person facing them. My own company hadn't realized what had happened, I learned later that despite urging from some of the other officers, the company commander got himself in a blue funk and refused to order an attack to relieve me.

'I knew the Germans would come and I knew they would get me. It was a question of how many of them I would kill before they did. I was surrounded by bodies, British and German. Some were still alive, groaning. There was one boy who had died only about five yards in front of the position. He looked about sixteen, but he must have been a little older. He had buck teeth and surprised blue eyes. He reminded me very much of little Willi Müller in the post room at the bank in Hamburg. Because of the way he had fallen those eyes were staring straight at me. He was quite dead, but he was accusing me.

'Time stood very still. I was no longer scared. In my mind I was already dead. But suddenly I knew I wasn't going to take anyone else with me. The scores of broken bodies that littered the field of fire in front of me were no longer enemy soldiers, but young men I had killed: sons, husbands, perhaps some fathers, post-room boys. If I close my eyes now, I can still see them, the grotesque shapes they formed as they fell. I knew I wasn't a murderer, that I wasn't evil, but I also knew that if I was going to die, it wasn't going to be while I was in the act of killing other human beings.

'So I stood up and I walked towards the German lines. Not with my hands up, not carrying a gun, just walking. I kept expecting a bullet to hit me, but there was nothing, no firing, nothing. I kept going until I got to the German trenches. They were empty; the Germans must have scarpered. Then I sat down. I don't remember anything else. Apparently D Company found me sitting on the parapet, staring back towards our own lines. It didn't take the medics long to chop off my arm. But it took months for them to repair my mind.' He snorted. 'Well, they never did. You know that.'

Conrad sat in silence next to his father.

'I never killed anyone after that,' he said. 'I was hoping none of my sons would. And now you want to start another war.'

'We both want the same thing, Father,' Conrad said. 'It's just that I am convinced that the best way of preventing war is to help von Kleist. You must trust me, Father. You must help him.'

Silence.

Conrad could feel as much as see his father's body tense. His jaw muscles tightened, his fingers rubbed at his moustache in an unnaturally fast rhythm. Conrad knew what would happen next. He had known from the moment his father had started talking about the trenches, but he had been too transfixed to stop him.

'Father?'

Lord Oakford muttered something through clenched teeth.

'I'm sorry, I didn't hear that.'

'I said: You little shit!'

'Father, I—'

'All those good men who died in Flanders, you couldn't give a fuck about them, could you?' Lord Oakford's eyes were suddenly blazing. 'You've forgotten what they suffered – you never knew what they suffered, you took it all for granted. You just want to start another little fight, Bolshies against the Nazis, Britons against the Germans. Well, I won't let you, do you hear? I won't let you.' He was shaking with anger, his eyes glittering with an unnatural excitement.

'Father, that's not quite fair—'

'I would have thought if there was one thing I have taught you it is that we must never *ever* fight another war. Why can't you and your friends understand that? It must never happen again. It may be that evil men like Hitler get away with more than they deserve but at least millions of young soldiers won't die.'

Conrad felt the anger rise within him. His father's words stung. They were so unfair! He knew that he should ignore them, that they were a result of the damage his father had suffered that day in 1917, which was as real if not as visibly obvious as his empty sleeve. But this was a time when he needed his father's support. The stakes were so much higher than just the relationship between them. Without his father's support Conrad did not know how he would persuade the likes of Lord Halifax to listen to von Kleist. Lord Oakford's sudden emotional occupation of the moral high ground had become a ritual in their arguments, as if his wounds and his Victoria Cross gave him a right to it. This right had never been challenged before, but Conrad realized that he had to challenge it now, before it was too late.

'You're a coward, Father.'

'I'm *what*!' Lord Oakford's eyes blazed in fury. No one had ever called him a coward. He was self-evidently not a coward, which was why he was such an effective pacifist. For his son to accuse him of cowardice—

'You're a coward. There are brave men in Germany, friends of mine, who are willing to risk death to stop Hitler. They need your help. They know that it is inevitable Hitler will start a war, and when he does it will be a horrible one. You know that too

– you know war is coming, that's why you are in such despair. Well, do something about it. Take a risk too. It might not work, but it will be better than sitting back and letting Hitler destroy Europe unopposed. I thought you more than anyone would have the courage to act. I see I'm wrong.'

'Your impertinence is insufferable. I will not listen to this.' Lord Oakford scrambled awkwardly to his feet with his one good arm. 'I'm going back. Don't come with me. And I want you out of the house by luncheon!'

'You're running away, Father!' Conrad called as he watched Lord Oakford hurry down the hill, the sleeve of his left arm flapping. Monty, after a plaintive glance at Conrad, loped after him.

He had no idea how long his father's black mood would last now it had been ignited. Past experience would suggest that it could be over in a day, but in this case Conrad thought that highly unlikely. A week was average, although a month was a possibility. Either way, his father would stick by his command that he leave the house by luncheon. Wearily, Conrad followed him down the hill into the wood.

When he got back to the house, the atmosphere had already changed. Reggie passed him in the hall on his way out and glared at him. 'You had to pick a fight with him, didn't you? He's been fine for three months; you show up and you set him off. I'm surprised you have the front to come here at all.'

'Go to hell, Reggie,' said Conrad wearily, and climbed the stairs to his room to pack.

Ten minutes later there was a soft knock on the door. It was his mother, a frown firmly set on her forehead.

'Oh, Conrad, did you have to?' she said, sitting on his bed.

'I'm sorry, Mamma. I didn't do it on purpose, although I half expected it to happen.'

'Do you always have to provoke him? The rest of the family steer clear of certain subjects. If you could only do that too he wouldn't explode every time you came to visit and we would see so much more of you. I'd like that, Conrad.'

Conrad smiled at his mother. She had been a stunning woman when she was younger. As a grown man, Conrad had seen photographs of her from that time in a new light. From his boyhood he remembered a maternal smile and the warm comfort of her embrace; the photographs showed a striking beauty with a full figure and big seductive eyes under long lashes. Now in her fifties, she had put on weight, but she still had an air of quiet vitality about her.

'I would like it too, Mamma. But this time I really did need to talk to him about the war, the coming war. I needed him to listen.' He told his mother all about von Kleist and Theo.

'They make sense to me,' his mother said. 'I am amazed by how meekly my fellow countrymen put up with that monster. I'm glad there are some people in high places who will stand up to him. We must help them.'

'That's what I thought. But Father told me about the day he won his VC. And then he just became totally unreasonable.'

'He told you about that?' Lady Oakford said, her frown deepening. 'No wonder he is upset. I didn't think he would ever talk about that again.'

'I can see why he doesn't. And I understand why he wants to avoid a war.'

'But isn't this the best way to do that?' Lady Oakford said.

'I think so. And I had hoped to convince him, but he wouldn't listen. In the end I called him a coward.'

'You did what!' Lady Oakford looked shocked.

'He knows I'm right, Mamma, but that will just make him more upset. It will take a lot of bravery for him to admit to himself and to me that he is wrong about appeasement and Hitler should be got rid of. But now I'll have to approach Lord Halifax myself. I believe he likes me well enough, but you know how grand he is. I'm not sure he'll listen to me.'

'I could write to him, if you like.' Conrad was surprised to see his mother blush. 'He's such a cold fish it's hard to tell, but I've always thought he had a bit of a thing for me.'

Conrad laughed. 'Mamma! Now there's a thought. Thank you, it might help. Now, I'd better get Tyndall to take me to the station.'

'Where will you be going in London? You're welcome to stay at Kensington Square, of course.'

'I think I'd better not,' said Conrad. 'It would just aggravate Father when he found out. I'll stay at the club.'

His mother rose and embraced him. 'I'm glad to see you trying to do something.' He felt dampness on his cheek. She pulled back, her eyes wet. 'Oh, Conrad, I hope there won't be another war with Germany,' she said. 'I don't think I could stand it if there was.'

The strange thing was she said it in German, a language she hardly ever spoke to him any more.

In London, Conrad installed himself at his club. The first and most important person for him to approach was Lord Halifax. He knew he could rely on his mother to fire off a letter to him that evening, but he would have to wait until Halifax had received it before trying to contact him himself.

Somehow Veronica tracked him down. There was a note waiting for him at his club telling him he should ring her when he arrived in London. This he did, and she suggested that they meet up at the Café Royal for cocktails.

She was, of course, looking stunning, in a blue dress he didn't recognize, pearls and the exquisite sapphire earrings that his parents had given her. But she left him unmoved.

'You seem a little jollier than last time I saw you,' she said, sipping her gin and it.

'Do I?'

'You're not learning to love the Nazis, are you?'

'Certainly not,' said Conrad. 'Things are getting worse. Much worse.'

Veronica leaned back in her chair and smiled. She was an astute reader of human emotions, especially Conrad's. 'I know what it is.'

'Really?' said Conrad.

'What's she like?'

'Who?' Conrad had no intention of discussing Anneliese with his wife. But he did offer her a cigarette and then a light.

'Well?' said Veronica, her eyes amused.

'Well what?'

'Do you want that divorce now?'

Conrad was about to give his usual answer, but he stopped himself. Veronica noticed his hesitation but held her peace.

Why not? thought Conrad. Why the hell not? His life would undoubtedly be better not being married to Veronica. And there was Anneliese. Perhaps one day, somehow, he would be able to get her out of Germany.

'All right,' he said.

'Oh, darling!' Veronica leaned over the little table and kissed him on the cheek. 'But you will do the gentlemanly thing, won't you?'

'I suppose so. Although I have no idea how to go about it.'

'Don't worry, Diana told me all about it.' Veronica grabbed her bag and rummaged in it. 'Go and see this man,' she said, handing him the card of E. S. P. Haynes, Solicitor. 'He'll sort it all out.'

'Well, he'd better get his skates on. I'm going back to Berlin in a few days.'

'Go and see him tomorrow, will you please, darling? Diana says he's frightfully efficient.'

Conrad frowned at his wife. 'You seem very keen on all this. Are you working on one of your schemes? You think once we are divorced you can get Linaro to leave his wife, don't you?'

'Oh, Conrad, you always assume I am so *calculating*.'

'I wonder why,' said Conrad. He felt sorry for the Linaro family. They stood no chance against Veronica.

'Look! Here are Tom and Diana.'

Conrad turned to see the handsome figures of Diana Guinness, as she was still generally known, and Sir Oswald Mosley making their way through the crowd, heads turning to follow them.

'I must be going,' Conrad said, downing his drink.

'Oh, do stay and have a drink with them. Just one.'

But the idea of talking to a fascist here in Britain, still a land of innocence and freedom, made Conrad's stomach turn.

'I'll see your man tomorrow,' Conrad said. He was about to add the word 'darling', but it stuck in his throat.

The train cut through the South Downs as it sped its way northwards to London. Opposite Conrad sat Mae, a pretty but dull girl originally from Swindon who had moved to London to seek her fortune. She was reading a paperback; they had used up all their conversation before Redhill on the way down to Brighton the day before.

Conrad had a hell of a headache. He had started drinking

on the train down the afternoon before, and continued all evening, a lethal combination of whisky and champagne. Mr Haynes had insisted on champagne as being more emblematic of two lovers off to have an illicit good time. The hotel Mr Haynes recommended seemed to know the score; there was no need for a private detective, it was sufficient to give the chambermaid who brought them breakfast in the morning a memorably large tip. Mae had offered to earn her money in the traditional way, but seemed relieved when Conrad had declined. She was happy enough; she had started the latest Agatha Christie on the way down, and should have it finished by the time they reached Victoria.

The night had been bizarre and idiotic, but it did make some sense. No journalist would find much of a story in the charade, whereas if he had taken on the role of plaintiff and cited Linaro as co-respondent in court the newspapers would have been full of it. Conrad wouldn't have cared, he would be in Berlin, but it would have been unpleasant for Veronica and especially so for the Linaro family.

The whole thing was so frightfully, dismally, seedily British.

The worst of it all was, of course, Anneliese, the woman with whom Conrad would much rather have spent the night. If only Conrad had told Foley about Ewald von Kleist's visit, then perhaps Anneliese would be on her way to England. Or at least be getting her documents together.

But he couldn't have done it. Von Kleist's trip was just too important, more important than him or even than Anneliese. And he had given his word.

His word. The word of an English gentleman. Did that really matter so much?

After paying Mae, Conrad took a cab from Victoria Station back to his club, and turned his thoughts to how he would approach Lord Halifax, assuming he would have received and read his mother's letter.

But at the club, the porter had a telegram waiting for him: 'SPOKE TO YOUR FATHER STOP HE PROMISES HE WILL ARRANGE TRIP STOP PLEASE SEND LETTER WITH DATES AND CODE FOR REPLY STOP LOVE MAMMA.'

Conrad had to restrain himself from letting out a whoop. His mother had done it! Somehow she had persuaded his father to change his mind, and that while he was in the depths of one of his vilest moods. She had understood how important von Kleist's trip was; despite her serene exterior it was always a mistake to underestimate her determination.

He went through to the library and composed a quick letter, laying out the dates of the trip and suggesting a little code by which his father could let him know whom von Kleist would see. It was clever of his mother to remember that any letter sent to him in Germany would be liable to interception.

Then he went to Thomas Cook's in Piccadilly to book himself a flight back to Berlin for that afternoon. The divorce would have to wait.

He stood waiting in the queue and thought about Klaus's threat. There was no doubt he was taking a risk returning to Berlin. A big risk. As the lady in front of him argued about the cabin she had booked on the *Queen Mary* to New York, he considered turning around and walking out of the travel agent.

But he couldn't do it. Too much was at stake: too many brave men were relying on him. He would just have to hope that Klaus's threats were bluster, and that his father's status did provide some protection after all.

Finally satisfied, the lady moved away and Conrad stepped forward. 'I'd like to book a flight to Berlin. For today if possible.'

Twenty-three

Conrad rang Anneliese as soon as he arrived back at his flat, and he could tell from her voice that she was as happy to hear from him as he was to speak to her. She suggested he come right round.

After they had made love, they talked. Conrad told her about his trip to Brighton, which Anneliese thought very funny, although she did ask a number of penetrating questions about Mae. What they didn't do was discuss the implications of a divorce.

'I saw Foley before I left,' Conrad said. 'To try to persuade him to get you a visa.'

'No luck?' Anneliese asked.

'No.'

'I thought not. It doesn't matter. I'm just glad he got my parents out.'

'It *does* matter,' said Conrad. 'I...' He paused. He didn't know what he was going to say. He didn't know how to say it. That he had had the chance to secure Anneliese's freedom and he had chosen not to take it.

'What is it, Conrad?'

He took a deep breath. 'I could have told Foley about Ewald von Kleist's visit to London. Then he might have got you a visa.'

'No, you couldn't,' said Anneliese.

'Yes, I could. If I had told him about their plot to get rid of Hitler he would have bitten my arm off. You'd be on your way to England.'

'You couldn't have told him. You gave your word. And the Gestapo might have found out about the trip and stopped it.'

Conrad touched her cheek. 'But you would be safe.'

'No.' Anneliese shook her head. 'Listen to me, Conrad. As one who has done things she has deeply regretted to get people out of this damned country, I'm telling you you couldn't tell Foley. You shouldn't tell Foley. I wouldn't want you to.'

He pulled her over to him and held her.

They stayed like that for several minutes, wrapped up in their own thoughts, in each other's thoughts.

Then she shuddered.

'What is it?' he asked.

She pulled away from him and sat up on the bed, her knees hunched up to her chin. 'You know, I saw Klaus while you were away. The night before last. He came here.'

'Why did you let him in?' said Conrad feeling a surge of jealousy.

'He's Gestapo, what choice did I have?'

'Sorry,' said Conrad. 'What did he want?'

'He knows about us,' Anneliese said. 'I got the impression he'd been watching us. He tried to play it cool, but I could tell he was as jealous as hell. He warned me to stay away from you. He said you had been seen speaking to a British spy, so he must have seen you with Captain Foley. I said I didn't believe him, but it scared me. He said he would always look after me, and that I could always go to him for help.'

'Does he want to get back together with you?'

'I'm sure he does, but he didn't say it. I think he's hoping that if I'm in enough trouble I'll go back to him. But I won't. Never.'

Conrad stroked Anneliese's hair. 'You must be careful of him.'

'So must you.'

Conrad hadn't intended to tell Anneliese about his confrontation with Klaus the day before he had left for London, but now he felt he had to.

'Why didn't you tell me this before?'

'I didn't want to scare you.'

'Well I should be scared! We should both be scared.' She jumped out of bed and went over to her window, looking down on to the street.

'Can you see anyone?' Conrad asked.

'No. Wait, yes! No, it's just a shadow from the tree. I don't know... there could easily be someone hiding down there. Klaus will be bound to find out we are seeing each other sooner or later.' She turned to Conrad, biting her lip. 'What should we do? I'm frightened, Conrad.'

'You shouldn't be. He won't hurt you.'

'Yes, but he *will* hurt you. God, I dread to think what he might do to you.' A tear ran down her cheek. 'These damned Nazis. They go for everyone I love. Paul. My father. You. I couldn't bear to lose you.'

Conrad moved over to her and held her tight.

'You should go back to London right away,' Anneliese said.

'I have to stay here in Berlin for a few more days,' he said. 'I need to help Theo and his friends. And I couldn't just not see you.'

He let her go and looked at her, standing naked by the open window, her skin a pale blue in the Berlin night. She was so beautiful.

'It's too dangerous,' she said. 'We must keep away from each other. At least for a few days. We must be *very* careful.'

Conrad sighed. 'All right. But it's going to be difficult.' He smiled at her. 'And in that case we had better make the most of the time we have.'

Anneliese kissed him. A moment later they were entwined on the bed.

Just over a hundred miles away, in the city of Halle, Walter Schalke was preparing for bed. He was a little drunk – well, very drunk, having spent the evening at Wilhelmer's bar down the road. The bedroom was a mess; dirty shirts and underwear lay on the floor, and the grimy sheets were unmade from the morning. After his wife had died, Walter had employed a house-keeper who had done a lousy job and annoyed the hell out of him. So he had sacked her. He was finding it harder than he expected to find a replacement at the rate he was offering. These women were so greedy!

Life hadn't been quite as worry-free as he had expected after the old bat had kicked the bucket. There was no nagging, which was a relief. But there were a million and one small things that she had left undone, things that Walter didn't have the time or inclination to sort out. Bills, cleaning, clothes-mending, that kind of thing. Lazy sow!

There was a loud knock at the door.

'Who is it!' shouted Walter, pleased at the loudness of his own voice.

More knocking.

'All right, all right,' he said, putting on his dressing gown and staggering down the narrow stairway.

He opened the door. Two men barged in, one of them grab-bing him. 'Gestapo!'

'What do you want?' Walter asked belligerently.

'To search your house,' replied one of the men, pulling out a pistol.

'Put that away!' growled Walter. The man dug the gun into his ribs, making him launch into a bout of violent coughing.

The other man opened and closed doors, banging and crashing in first the kitchen, then the parlour, and then upstairs in the bedroom.

'What's he doing?'

'Searching the house.'

'Why? What's he looking for?'

'We've had a tip-off that you have been distributing subversive material.'

'That's ridiculous!' said Walter 'I'm a Party member, have been since 1929.'

The man appeared from the bedroom with a sheaf of mimeographed paper. He handed it to his colleague, who scanned it quickly. 'Come with us!' he said.

'What's that? I've never seen those before in my life!' Walter protested.

The policeman took no notice. 'Come on,' he said.

'Wait! My son is in the Gestapo,' the old man protested. 'He's a Kriminalrat in Berlin. He works directly for Heydrich himself. You should give him a call.'

One of the Gestapo exchanged glances with the other and shrugged. 'Go ahead,' he said.

'Hold on a moment,' said Walter. 'I'm not paying for the call myself.'

'In that case come with us.'

'No. All right, wait a minute.'

Walter found Klaus's office number and called the operator. He was put through.

'Klaus? It's your father. Can you tell these two baboons to leave me alone?'

He handed the telephone to the senior of the two Gestapo officers and smiled. 'He wants to talk to you.'

The man muttered down the telephone; Walter couldn't quite hear the conversation. Then, his expression blank, he handed the receiver back to Walter.

'Well, Klaus? Did you sort them out?' Walter demanded.

'I'm sorry, Father. They say they have found some incriminating documents in the house. I'm afraid that in the circumstances there is nothing I can do.'

'What! You know I'm a good Nazi! You tell them that!'

'We may not see each other again, Father,' said Klaus, his voice calm. 'So, goodbye.'

'You bastard! You put them up to this didn't you? You—'

'I love you too, Father. *Heil Hitler.*' Then the telephone went dead.

Ranting with anger and confusion, Walter was led to a car outside. He was pushed into the back alongside two young SA men in uniform. One of them he recognized from the next street but the boy refused to acknowledge him.

Half an hour later, a few kilometres outside the city, they turned down a narrow track into a forest. After five hundred metres the car stopped. The SA men fetched spades out of the boot, and the Gestapo officer, brandishing his pistol, told Walter to walk.

He was still cursing his damned swine of a son when the bullet smashed into the back of his head. He died instantly.

Conrad approached the British Embassy on Wilhelmstrasse with a mixture of trepidation and excitement. He had received a note from Ivone Kirkpatrick, the First Secretary. Conrad assumed that his father had made the necessary appointments for von Kleist, and Kirkpatrick would have the details for Conrad to pass on. Conrad had expected a coded letter directly from his father, but he supposed that once the Foreign Secretary and the Prime Minister were involved it was natural for messages to go through the Foreign Office. In any event he was anticipating this visit to be more fruitful than his earlier meeting with the Third Secretary to complain about his arrest and Joachim's death.

He stopped suddenly and turned, hoping to catch a watcher. There were several people on the street, none of whom gave him a second glance. He had been looking over his shoulder constantly ever since he had returned to Berlin, checking for Gestapo. He hadn't spotted anyone, but of course that didn't mean there was no one there. But he had kept his promise to Anneliese to stay away from her at least for a while. It was intensely frustrating to know that she was here in the same city as him, but that he couldn't see her, talk to her, hold her.

The embassy was a grand building with four imposing columns framing the entrance, adjoining the Adlon Hotel on the corner of Unter den Linden. It had originally been built as the city palace of a Berlin speculator who had gone extravagantly bankrupt, and Her Majesty's Government had stepped in to buy the place on the cheap. Fountains splashed in the marble entrance hall and, deeper within, the decor had the hushed, rather shabby splendour of the mature British Empire. Conrad was shown through to a sitting room, which was really a waiting room, and five minutes later the trim figure of Ivone Kirkpatrick appeared, neat in winged collar and morning suit, sporting a bright red carnation.

'Mr de Lancey, good of you to come. The Ambassador will see you now.'

'The Ambassador?' Conrad said. He had assumed that the kind of message he was expecting would be best delivered by a lower official.

245

'Er, yes. He was anxious to speak to you himself.'

Several yards of plush carpet and four turns along a corridor later and he was ushered into the Ambassador's office, complete with large desk and picture of King George VI. The Ambassador himself looked up, but did not get to his feet. 'Ah, Mr de Lancey. Sit down.'

Conrad sat in one of the two chairs facing the Ambassador's desk. Kirkpatrick took the other one.

Sir Nevile Henderson was a tall, elegant man with a little jet-black moustache, as fastidiously dressed as his first secretary. He had been British Ambassador in Berlin for a year, since when the tone of British diplomacy towards the Third Reich had changed noticeably. He was a sociable man, even for a diplomat, and he got on famously with the leading Nazis. He was a frequent hunting guest of Göring. He had caused quite a stir when, soon after his arrival, he had given a speech at the Kaiserhof Hotel to the German–English Society where he had said that he hoped that his own country would learn much from National Socialism. Not surprisingly, this remark had been widely reported in Germany and discussed at great length among the expatriate community in Berlin. Conrad knew his father couldn't stand the man – they had been contemporaries at Eton. Conrad feared that the feeling might be mutual.

'I have been discussing with London a proposed visit of a friend of yours,' Henderson began.

'That's right,' said Conrad.

'Ewald von Kleist. A monarchist.'

'And a staunch opponent of Hitler,' Conrad added.

'London asked for my advice, and I gave it to them. In my view it would be a grave mistake if anyone in the British government were to be seen speaking to this man.'

'I think the idea is that they wouldn't be seen.'

'Secret negotiations would be just as bad,' Henderson said. 'In fact worse. The government here would find out about them eventually.'

'But von Kleist has an important message to deliver,' Conrad said. 'And it is vital that it is heard at the highest level.'

'Ah, yes. And what is that message?'

'That's for Herr von Kleist to deliver, not me, your excellency.'

Henderson glanced at Kirkpatrick and tutted. 'I know you are here in Berlin in a private capacity, Mr de Lancey, but your father is, or was, a figure of some importance and you must be seen to be behaving in a seemly manner.'

'What do you mean?'

'For a start, it is your duty to follow the British government's line.'

'Which is?'

'To avoid holding discussions with extremist opposition groups.'

'And that's government policy?' Conrad said.

'It certainly is. Also in the current climate you should be careful how you conduct your personal relations.'

'Whatever do you mean by that?'

'I mean that you have been seen consorting with a Jewish communist.'

'I don't see what that has to do with you, or anyone else for that matter,' Conrad said, his voice laden with indignation.

'It has everything to do with me,' the Ambassador said. 'It is a provocation to our host government. In the current delicate situation between our two countries the last thing I want to have to do is waste time and diplomatic capital on young men who should know how to behave themselves.'

'I will see whom I want, when I want.'

'This isn't a free country, de Lancey. You know that.'

Conrad stood up to leave. 'So who will Herr von Kleist be meeting in London?' he asked.

'No one, I trust,' said Henderson. 'Now, good day.'

'*Heil Hitler,*' said Conrad before he could stop himself, and quickly left the room as the Ambassador's expression turned from disdain to outrage.

Conrad was fuming as Kirkpatrick led him back to the entrance. 'Is that man actually a member of the Nazi Party?' Conrad asked him.

'The Ambassador is very well attuned to the circumstances in present-day Germany,' Kirkpatrick said.

Conrad snorted.

They reached the imposing entrance hall of the embassy. Kirkpatrick shook Conrad's hand. 'The Ambassador did tell you to do your duty, didn't he?'

'By which he meant following the British government's line. His line,' Conrad said bitterly.

'I'm sure there was no need for him to point that out. One's conscience can usually tell one quite clearly enough what one's duty is, don't you think? And I would have thought that the British government could require nothing more from its citizens than that they do their duty.'

Conrad paused and examined the First Secretary's face, which was a picture of diplomatic inscrutability. 'Thank you for the advice, sir.'

'A pleasure. Good luck, Mr de Lancey.' When Conrad stepped into the street the edge of his fury had been taken off. It was good advice. It was the right advice.

When he got home there was a letter waiting for him, the name and address in his father's handwriting. He opened it with trepidation.

Dear Conrad,

I am really very sorry the weather was so bad when you were staying with us. It's much better now. Your mother was right, as always.

Bad news about the wedding. Uncle Claude can't come and neither can any of his family, not even Great-Aunt Mabel. I'm not sure who's behind their decision, I don't think it's Uncle Claude, but you just can't tell.

The good news is that Charlie has said 'yes' – you can always rely on him. I've also invited Richard Valentine, whom I think you know, and Graham Leigh, whom you probably don't.

I was up in London yesterday and saw Graham for dinner at Claridge's. He's looking forward to the wedding.

Hope you are still coming,

Yours ever,

Father

Conrad smiled. It wasn't as bad as he had thought. The first sentence was the nearest thing to a direct apology he had ever received from his father. 'Uncle Claude' was Lord Halifax and 'Great-Aunt Mabel' was the Prime Minister, Neville Chamberlain, an old woman if ever there was one. Obviously his father had been unable to discover the hand of Sir Nevile Henderson behind the refusal of any Cabinet minister to meet von Kleist.

Charlie was good news. That was the codename for Winston Churchill, still the most forceful and articulate member of the House of Commons even though he had been out of government for ten years. The other two were not one of the twenty or so names that Conrad had listed when he had made up the code. In that eventuality Conrad had suggested that his father use the initials of a fictitious guest as a clue. 'RV' was obvious: Sir

Robert Vansittart, an old school friend of his father's and a former under-secretary at the Foreign Office. That was good: he could be relied upon to pass on von Kleist's message to the government. It took Conrad quite a while to work out whom 'GL' referred to, until he realized it was George Lloyd, Lord Lloyd, another Eton contemporary of his father, and a prominent Conservative politician. The reference to Graham meant that von Kleist's first meeting would be dinner at Claridge's with Lord Lloyd.

His father hadn't done badly. With those three establishment figures, von Kleist's message should get through. Once the British government knew about von Kleist's plans they would be bound to stand by Czechoslovakia. Then when Hitler ordered the invasion he would be overthrown and the whole continent of Europe would breathe a sigh of relief. And he, Conrad, would have played a small but important role in that.

He felt a warm glow of pleasure. Finally he was doing something, something David Griffiths and Harry Reilly would be proud of.

Conrad saw Theo that evening in an odd little bar off Nollendorfplatz. It was called Billy the Kid, and there was a plaster statue of a Red Indian at the door and a mural of a wagon train along one wall. But it was all rather gloomy and tatty, the wood was just as dark and stained as in other neighbourhood bars, and the locals were Berliners through and through. The only gesture to the Wild West theme were the caustic comments the drunken regulars would address to the Red Indian on their way out into the street. They called him 'Big Chief Fritz', and seemed very fond of him.

Conrad had taken an hour to travel the short distance from his flat to the bar, hopping on and off buses, walking in circles around small blocks and doubling back unpredictably: he wanted to make absolutely sure he wasn't being followed. No one. Definitely no one. Nevertheless they chose a table in the far corner of the bar and made sure that there were no likely lip-readers nearby. They also spoke in English.

Although Theo was eager to hear what Lord Oakford had organized for his uncle, Conrad noticed a distinct coolness about him. This puzzled Conrad: he thought they had ironed out their differences. He told Theo about the letter from his father and about his interview with the British Ambassador. Theo was clearly unhappy that von Kleist wasn't going to see either Chamberlain or Halifax, but Conrad assured him that they would hear von Kleist's message through Vansittart and Churchill.

Theo downed his beer and ordered another one. 'We've picked up a disturbing report,' he said. 'Apparently a prominent German politician is planning to travel to London soon for talks with the British government.'

'That's not good,' said Conrad.

'You told Foley, didn't you?'

Conrad shook his head. 'No, Theo. And I asked my father to make sure that the British secret service was kept in the dark.'

'Was it in exchange for a visa for Anneliese?'

'I thought about it, but I didn't talk to him. I give you my word.'

'And I am supposed to accept that? Your word?'

Conrad couldn't help smiling at the irony. 'Yes, Theo, you are supposed to accept my word. I promised I wouldn't betray your uncle, and I haven't. Even though I dearly would have liked to, I didn't.'

Theo looked closely at his friend and then returned his smile. 'All right. So where did the leak come from, do you think?'

'I have no idea. The embassy? I told you I spoke to the Ambassador himself. He is not very happy about this trip.'

'Well, bugger him.'

'Precisely,' said Conrad. 'Is your uncle still going?'

'Oh, yes,' said Theo. 'It would take more than certain death to put off my uncle.'

As Conrad walked the short distance home from the bar, it occurred to him that he could have told Foley about the visit after all.

He turned into Zietenstrasse and a man in a large overcoat walked straight into him, almost knocking him to the ground.

'I say!' said Conrad. 'Watch where you are going.'

'Oh, excuse me, I am awfully sorry,' said the man in English. 'Captain Foley's compliments, and he asks Fräulein Rosen to get in touch with him at the earliest opportunity.'

Before Conrad could reply the man had gone, walking rapidly down Bülowstrasse. Conrad hadn't even registered his face.

Then the man's words sank in. Foley had changed his mind and found a way to grant Anneliese a visa. There could be no other reason why he should suddenly want her to get in touch with him.

Yes. That was it. That must be it!

He had to tell her, right then. He had promised that he would be careful about seeing her again, but it was late and it was dark. The streets were almost empty – Conrad was positive he wasn't being followed.

Glancing around one more time to check for non-existent watchers, he hailed a passing cab and headed for the Scheunen-viertel.

Twenty-four

Klaus watched the taxi pull up on the cobbled street outside Anneliese's tenement block and saw Conrad climb out. Anger welled up inside him. He fought to control it. He had been waiting for four nights: he would have to wait just a little longer. He walked as inconspicuously as he could around the corner and made a quick call from the telephone kiosk. Then he returned to his station.

The time passed slowly as he stared at the light in her top-floor window. It was a warm night, and he was overdressed in his leather coat. A couple of times he saw her silhouette; she was checking for watchers. At eleven-fifteen the light went out. At eleven-thirty Dressel and another Gestapo officer named Fischer arrived, ready for action. Klaus nodded to them and they hurried off. Klaus kept his eyes on the window. Sure enough, after two minutes the light flashed on, and he could hear Anneliese's scream. The street didn't stir. The inhabitants of that neighbourhood had learned long ago to roll over when they heard a scream in the middle of the night.

Half an hour later Conrad was led into the familiar entrance hall of 8 Prinz-Albrecht-Strasse and up the grand staircase. But on this, his second visit, he was much more worried. He was in the power of the man who hated him most in the world, and that man had all the talents and techniques of the Gestapo at his disposal to give vent to his hatred. He hadn't yet seen Klaus, but he knew that he would be lurking in the background close by. He had decided that come what may, he wouldn't tell Klaus anything about von Kleist's plans or the plot to overthrow Hitler. He realized the probable consequences of that decision. Over the next day or two he would experience more excruciating pain than he could imagine, followed by death.

On his first visit to the Gestapo headquarters as a genuinely innocent British citizen he had had faith that he would be rescued by the embassy, although in the end it was Theo who had stepped in. This time, Klaus would have taken pains to make sure that that didn't happen.

Conrad waited for about half an hour on a bench in a little room, crammed next to an SS guard, before one of the Gestapo who had arrested him arrived and led him away to an office.

He sat in a small wooden chair facing a desk. Behind him the door opened, and as he turned a fist caught him in the mouth. He looked up to see Klaus rubbing his red knuckle, breathing heavily.

'Stand up, de Lancey!'

Conrad stood up. Klaus swung clumsily and hit him in the abdomen a couple of inches below the solar plexus. Conrad could see the blow coming and tensed his stomach muscles. He managed to remain standing straight. Klaus hit him again and again, until Conrad finally doubled up. Then Klaus pushed him to the ground and kicked him in the back and the head. Everything went black.

When he woke up he found himself held upright on the chair by the other Gestapo officer. He wasn't sure how long he had been unconscious, probably only a few seconds, because Klaus was still breathing heavily. Conrad's torso and head ached, but he tried to ignore it, to pretend that he was somehow removed from his body. He knew the pain would get a lot worse before the night was over.

'Do you know why you are here?' Klaus asked him.

'No,' Conrad mumbled.

'Racial defilement. You were caught having sexual relations with a non-Aryan woman. You know that this is forbidden in Germany?'

'Oh, come on, Schalke, that isn't a rule that you take any notice of, so why should I?' said Conrad.

Klaus hit him again in the face. Conrad decided to stop goading his interrogator.

'And don't think your friend Hertenberg is going to ride in here at the last minute like the U.S. cavalry,' said Klaus. 'He doesn't know where you are; we have kept your presence very quiet. By the time the Abwehr find out you are here it will be too late. For you.'

'What about the British Embassy?' said Conrad.

Klaus laughed. 'I believe you spoke to the British Ambassador recently. From what I know of him, he won't be very sympathetic to a British citizen who breaks such important local laws.'

'My father was a government minister,' said Conrad. 'You cannot imprison and torture me without my government objecting.'

'Of course we can,' said Klaus. 'We don't always throw our prisoners into prison or a concentration camp where your diplomats can find them, you know. Quite often we just take them into the woods and shoot them. That's what we will do in your case. When we have finished with you here.'

Conrad looked at Klaus's implacable face and realized that a bullet in the head in the woods was inevitable. It was a question of whether he could avoid compromising the conspiracy before he received that bullet.

'You were seen speaking to a Captain Foley last week in the Tiergarten. What was that all about?'

'I wanted to thank him for getting a visa for Anneliese's father and mother.'

'Did you really need to go for a walk in the park to do that?'

'I was intending to see him in his office. Captain Foley suggested the walk. I think he was finding the office a bit claustrophobic.'

'Liar!' Klaus screamed, his face reddening. 'Captain Foley is the British secret-service representative in Berlin. You know that! Everyone in this city knows that!'

'No, I don't.'

'Of course you do!' shouted Klaus and belted him again across the face. Conrad felt blood in his cheek, but his teeth were still all intact. For such a big man, Klaus didn't really hit that hard.

Klaus stood in front of Conrad, shouting. But Conrad wasn't listening. He was damned if he was going to accept his trip to the woods. There had to be a way out. He realized that small lies, deceit and misdirection wouldn't work; Klaus would be expecting them. What he needed was a big bold lie. In a flash one came to him. But he needed to let it slip out slowly if he was to persuade the Gestapo.

Klaus stopped shouting and pulled himself together. In a voice pitched at a more normal level, but still heavy with menace, he repeated his question. 'So, what were you saying to Captain Foley?'

'I suggest you ask Lieutenant von Hertenberg that,' Conrad said.

Klaus grinned and shook his head. 'Your friend is not going to discover you were here until it is too late.'

'I am working for the Abwehr,' Conrad said.

Klaus snorted. 'Horse shit.'

'As you know Theo and I are old friends. You also know that my mother is German, I was born in Germany – in fact I consider myself German. I think that the Führer is leading Germany in absolutely the right direction.'

'You are English, de Lancey. Your father is English, you have spent nearly all your life in England.'

'That's also true,' said Conrad. 'But there are many English-men who think the same way I do, especially those in the upper reaches of society. Adolf Hitler is the only hope Europe has of stemming the tide of Bolshevism.'

'I've been watching you over the last few weeks. I haven't seen you showing any enthusiasm for National Socialism.'

'Of course not,' Conrad said. 'Theo was quite explicit that I should be seen to disapprove of the Nazis while I am here. A basic precaution.'

'You expect me to believe that you are a spy? For Germany.'

'Of course. I would have thought Theo explained that when you released me the last time I was here.'

'He didn't explain anything like that to me,' said Klaus.

'Ah,' said Conrad.

Klaus shook his head. 'This is absurd. So what were you discussing with Foley?'

'I cannot say.'

Klaus smiled and hit him again. 'Once we get to work on you we'll find out.'

'Why don't you just contact the Abwehr?'

'That's not going to happen,' said Klaus. 'But if you are spying for the Third Reich, you can tell me all about it. I do work for the Gestapo, after all.'

'The Abwehr were very specific that I shouldn't discuss what I was doing with any other department.'

'And why not?'

'You see, it's quite... political.'

'I'm not listening to this. I think we should just take you out to the woods and shoot you now.'

'I'm getting somewhere, you know,' Conrad said. 'With Foley. In another week or two I might... Let's just say that what I am working on is much bigger than you or me or Theo von Hertenberg. And some very senior people know that.'

'I don't have time to listen to all of this,' Klaus said, his eyes narrowing under his glasses.

'I'll tell you what,' said Conrad. 'I'll speak to Heydrich.'

'Heydrich! Why him?'

'Because he will understand what I am doing. And because I think I can trust him.'

'Are you mad? Heydrich will have you for breakfast. Anything you have to say, you tell me. Now stand up!'

Conrad pulled himself to his feet. Klaus grabbed him, pushed him hard against the wall, and then beat the hell out of him. The last Conrad remembered he was sliding down to the floor.

He must have been out for more than a few seconds this time, because when he woke up, Klaus was no longer in the room. He felt battered and bruised; his head ached and his vision was blurred. With difficulty he got to his feet. One of the Gestapo officers who had arrested him was watching him with amusement. Conrad recognized his red hair and freckles: he remembered him from his first arrest when he had introduced himself as Dressel.

Conrad made his way over to a chair. 'I don't think your boss likes me,' he said.

Dressel smiled. 'It was a mistake to mess around with his girlfriend.'

'He does seem in a bit of a bad mood today.'

'Yes, it's a real treat for me to see him beat you like that. He usually doesn't take such a personal interest in his prisoners' comfort. That's my job.'

'He looks as if he enjoys it,' Conrad said.

Dressel laughed. 'For such a big man, he really isn't very effective.'

'Oh, I don't know,' said Conrad.

'Let me show you,' said Dressel. 'Stand up.'

Conrad stood up.

'Now, lift up your shirt and turn around.'

Conrad did as he was bid. He heard a brief swish, and then there was the sharpest, most excruciating pain in his kidney. He fell to the ground and, despite himself, groaned. After a couple of minutes he sat up and then vomited.

'See what I mean?' said Dressel. 'I'm afraid the Kriminalrat just doesn't have the technique. Never mind. It will be my turn soon. And then you'll tell us all we need to know.'

Conrad pulled himself back on to the chair. For some reason it seemed important to be seated, rather than sprawled on the floor. It gave him some control. 'Where is your friend the Kriminalrat?'

'He'll be back.'

'He's making a big mistake,' Conrad said. 'I know he hates me. But it won't look good for him when Heydrich finds out what he has done. Or for you for that matter.'

'I'll take the risk.'

'Look. I didn't tell Schalke this, but the Abwehr believes that the British secret service has penetrated the German government at the highest levels. The very highest.'

'Oh, yes?' said Dressel, doubtfully. But Conrad could tell he was listening. 'You mean one of our ministers is a spy?'

'It looks like it. We don't know yet. Which is why I still have work to do.'

'You expect me to believe that?'

'Yes. I know Schalke won't. But Heydrich might, once he has spoken to Admiral Canaris. You know who he is?'

'Yes, I do,' said Dressel. 'But you know what will happen to you if Canaris says he has never heard of you?'

'Do you know what will happen to you if he has?'

Dressel looked doubtful. 'I know you are loyal to your boss,' Conrad said. 'But he has clearly lost his sense of perspective. For both your sakes, find a way of letting Heydrich know I'm here. Then we'll see.'

Dressel stared at Conrad. Then he picked up the telephone and barked a quick order. A moment later an SS guard came into the room and Dressel was gone.

Conrad sat on his chair and waited. His vomit was splattered over the floor behind him. It stank. He thought about Anneliese, her joy when he had told her that Foley wanted to see her, and then a few minutes later the look of fear and horror on her face as he was marched out of her room, her plea to him to come back and his promise to her that he would. Well, he would do his best to keep that promise.

After half an hour, Klaus came in, with Dressel, followed by two guards carrying a metal bathtub. They placed it a few feet from Conrad and returned with buckets of water. No one said anything until the tub was three-quarters full.

'You know this is how your cousin died?' said Klaus.

'I thought he had a heart attack.'

'He did. After we drowned him. He was lucky, really. Now, are you sure you don't want to tell me anything more about what you were saying to Foley?'

At that moment the door was flung open and a tall young

man wearing the black uniform of an SS Gruppenführer came in. Klaus, Dressel and the guards snapped to attention. Conrad recognized the high forehead and the wide-lipped mouth of Heydrich.

'Is this the man?' Heydrich said to Dressel in a surprisingly high-pitched voice. Dressel nodded. Klaus shot a bitter glance at his deputy and gave up his chair to Heydrich. The Gestapo chief shone the desk lamp into Conrad's eyes. Conrad could barely see the man, just his long, almost feminine fingers resting on the desk.

'Herr de Lancey,' Heydrich said. 'You have been caught having sexual relations with a Jew. In this country that is a serious crime. If you are wasting my time, you will be shot without delay. I don't care who your father is. Do you understand?'

'Yes,' said Conrad. His mouth was dry or, to be more precise, his tongue was: there was still quite a lot of blood in both cheeks. There was something in Heydrich's calm self-assurance that spoke of power, absolute power, the power to maim, torture and kill, the power to get what he wanted. But fear sharpened Conrad's wits and his determination.

'You claim you are working for the Abwehr?'

'That's correct. I suggest that you confirm this with Admiral Canaris himself.'

'And what are you doing for them?'

'Can I speak to you alone?' Conrad said.

Heydrich paused, and then turned to Klaus. 'Leave us!' he snapped. When the guards, Klaus and Dressel had all left the room, he turned back to Conrad. 'Well?'

'We believe, or at least the Abwehr believes, that there is someone at the highest levels in the German government passing secrets to the British. By getting close to the British secret service, they hope that I will be able to find out more.'

'Ridiculous,' said Heydrich. 'Who is this man?'

'We don't know for sure yet, but the evidence is pointing towards one suspect.'

'And who is that?'

'I cannot say.'

'You cannot say because you do not know.'

'I cannot say because if I am right, the consequences for the Third Reich would be very grave. And I may be wrong.'

'Tell me who it is, and I will speak to Admiral Canaris.'

Conrad hesitated. He had to pitch this just right. 'I know that the Abwehr would not want me to tell you.'

Heydrich snorted. 'That may be true, but they are not here, are they? And I am.'

'All right,' Conrad said. 'I will tell you. But don't for God's sake tell the admiral I did so.' He paused. 'It's Göring.'

'Göring! Working for the British! Absurd. What evidence do you have?' But Conrad could tell that some part of Heydrich rather welcomed the idea. The rivalry between the SS and the Fat Boy was well known, ever since Himmler had snatched Göring's Prussian police force, put Heydrich in charge of it and created the Gestapo. Which was why Conrad had selected him as his putative traitor.

'I really can't tell you my evidence. And it is by no means conclusive.'

'Why should I believe you?'

'Telephone Canaris.'

Heydrich switched off the light. Still dazzled, Conrad couldn't see Heydrich's expression. But he could feel him gathering his thoughts. 'Wait here,' he ordered.

So Conrad sat and waited, watched over by two SS guards. It might work. Canaris was clearly aware of von Kleist's visit, and would know of Conrad's part in it. Conrad had never met the Chief of the Abwehr, but he assumed that given his position he was almost certainly a man of intelligence and some deviousness. When he received Heydrich's telephone call he would probably realize what was required of him. Of course he wouldn't necessarily go along with it, he might decide that it was safer to abandon Conrad to the Gestapo. It was his choice: Conrad's life was in his hands.

An hour later, Dressel came into the room. He was smiling. 'Well, your story has been confirmed. You can go. And I should apologize for any inconvenience we have caused you. The Herr Gruppenführer asked me to wish you luck and to keep him informed. We'll take you to see the doctor and get you cleaned up a bit before you leave.'

'Thank you. And thanks for listening to me, Dressel.'

'Not at all,' said the Gestapo officer. 'But I would lay off Schalke's woman from now on if I were you.'

'You idiot, Schalke! You have balls for brains!'

Klaus had been expecting the summons to Heydrich's office. He did his best not to flinch in the face of his boss's ire. 'Yes, Herr Gruppenführer!'

'I mean if he was some young university student that would be fine, but this fellow has connections. And you knew that.'

'I felt his conversations with the British secret service were suspicious.'

'Oh, come on, Schalke, I was the one who got to the bottom of that, not you!'

'You cannot believe him, surely, Herr Gruppenführer?'

'Admiral Canaris does, and that is good enough for me. If it turns out de Lancey has been stringing the Abwehr along, it's their problem not ours. And I do not want you to make it ours!'

'No, Herr Gruppenführer.'

'For an intelligent man, you can be very stupid, Schalke. You know as much as anybody how vulnerable we are after the von Fritsch business. The Gestapo doesn't need any more enemies at the moment. So keep well clear of him and keep well clear of her. Do you understand me?'

'Yes, Herr Gruppenführer!'

'Good, because I will *not*' – Heydrich slammed his fist on to his desk – 'have the Gestapo undermined by the foolish actions of its officers.'

'I understand, Herr Gruppenführer.'

Heydrich leaned back in his chair. His frown eased and his lips broke into a lascivious grin. 'She must be quite some girl.'

'She is.'

'But she's Jewish?'

'Half-Jewish.'

'That's a big problem right there, Schalke. You know what you need?'

'What's that?'

'You need to get laid. There's a new cute little Austrian girl at Salon Kitty I should introduce you to. Paulina. She says she likes big men.' Heydrich winked. 'Let's go tonight, eh?'

Klaus forced himself to smile. He was lucky that Heydrich was feeling so understanding, and he had to respond positively to it. 'That's a very good idea, Herr Gruppenführer. You're right. It's probably just what I need. Thank you.'

'Excellent,' said Heydrich and turned to the papers on his desk.

'*Heil Hitler!*' said Klaus, and left the office.

He knew he had been lucky to get away with a rebuke. Heydrich and Canaris were totally different men, but they had a strangely close relationship. As a nineteen-year-old naval cadet Heydrich had served on a training ship commanded by Canaris, and they had seen a lot of each other since then. They lived almost next door to each other in Schlachtensee and Heydrich would often visit the Canaris household to play the violin accompanied by Frau Canaris on the piano, while the admiral cooked a Spanish dish. Klaus knew also, because Heydrich had told him, that Canaris was trusted and respected by the Führer, who admired and was a little intimidated by his cosmopolitan sophistication. If de Lancey had Canaris's protection he was untouchable.

That was depressing. Maybe he should shoot de Lancey himself. But although he would certainly not be formally prosecuted by the authorities, Heydrich would know that he was responsible and his career in the Gestapo would be over. He would probably be dead himself within a week.

And now that de Lancey had been released, Anneliese would know that Klaus was behind his arrest. His plan had been to blame other Gestapo officers and to tell her that he had set out to free de Lancey but had been too late. She would never believe that now; in fact she would hate him. He realized that she would never be his again.

The thought bore on him like an enormous dark weight. With his mother gone and Anneliese lost to him, what was the point of living? Maybe he *should* shoot de Lancey and then himself. Why had Anneliese rejected him? He loved her more than this Englishman did; he probably loved her as much as Paul had. Paul had been a great man; Klaus had always known that. But de Lancey? All right, he was good-looking and Klaus wasn't; as far as Anneliese was concerned, that was probably enough.

Bitch!

Bitch? How could he think of his angel as a bitch?

Because he was angry with her, bitterly angry. If he couldn't have her, then no one else would, not de Lancey, nor any other smooth-talking gigolo she might come across.

* * *

The passengers waited patiently in the cabin of the three-engined Lufthansa Ju-52 on the apron outside the great semi-circular terminal building at Tempelhof Aerodrome, among them Conrad. All of them had gone through the painstaking formalities at customs and passport control where papers were checked and questions asked, especially of the Germans on board. Each German traveller had to be sponsored by a ministry, have their allowances for foreign money stamped by the Reichsbank, and show an invitation from a foreign friend who would bear their expenses while abroad, all of which was noted in the Gestapo files. There were no simple tourists any more.

Theo had seen no reason why von Kleist's visit to London could not go ahead. Apparently, Canaris had been impressed by Conrad's ingenuity and had been quite happy to go along with the deception. He much preferred that to Conrad bravely refusing to talk until he eventually gave everything away under torture. To reassure the Gestapo of his cover, Conrad had stayed in Berlin a few days, even meeting Foley. Conrad assumed that Foley knew about von Kleist's visit, but neither of them mentioned it. Foley did, however, confirm that Anneliese's exit visa was in place once her other documents were ready. Conrad avoided seeing her; there was no point in provoking Klaus, and with luck they would soon be together in London.

The steward had announced that there was a brief delay while they waited for another passenger. Out of the window Conrad noticed an open-topped Mercedes containing a German general and a civilian speeding along the tarmac towards the aeroplane. It screeched to a halt, the general climbed out and briskly shook the hand of the civilian, who rushed up the steps. The soldier was General Paul von Kleist and the civilian his cousin Ewald. The last passenger safely on board, having circumvented all of the departure formalities, the door shut and the aeroplane taxied to the runway. A minute later it was airborne and on its way to London.

General Beck sat and stared at his desk, unfamiliarly clear apart from a fountain pen and a single sheet of paper bearing the title of the Chief of the General Staff.

It had been a humiliating couple of weeks. In the end von Brauchitsch had bowed to the weight of Beck's memoranda and called a meeting of the generals at army headquarters in the Bendlerstrasse. He had read out Beck's latest paper pointing out the absurdity of Hitler's proposed invasion of Czechoslovakia and asked for comments from the assembled officers. General Adam, the oldest and most respected general present, had spoken about the West Wall defences of which he was in charge, and emphasized that they could never withstand a determined French attack. The other generals, with the exception of two, had agreed that the Führer's strategy was dangerously flawed. The two dissenters were von Reichenau and Busch. Beck had torn a strip off Busch for suggesting that a German general's duty was to blindly obey his führer.

But then von Brauchitsch had let the meeting lapse without reading out the speech Beck had prepared for him inciting the generals to threaten mass resignation. Afterwards, Beck was furious; von Brauchitsch avoided him.

Ten days later Hitler had gathered the same generals together at Jüterbog to watch the Wehrmacht's artillery demolish some concrete bunkers that were supposed to represent Czech fortifications. The whole thing was a sham and Beck told him so. The gunners had had weeks to prepare and so had their ranges exact, and the concrete was nowhere near as thick as that in the Czech fortifications.

Hitler ignored him. Not only ignored him; he humiliated him. Either Busch or von Reichenau must have told Hitler about the generals' meeting, because after dinner he spoke about the weakness of his general staff. He implied that they were cowards, that Beck was a coward. And at some point during the day he told von Brauchitsch to forbid Beck from writing any more memoranda.

Von Brauchitsch, his superior, had lost confidence in him. Hitler had lost confidence in him. He was being asked to plan a war based on a ludicrous strategy that would lead to certain defeat. His situation was intolerable. There was only one honourable course open to him.

He thought of all his conversations with Oster over the summer. Perhaps a coup was the only option left, but he knew he couldn't lead it from his present position of weakness.

He glanced up at the portrait of his predecessor, Field Marshal Helmuth Count von Moltke, exuding austere intelligence and self-confidence. The humble Ludwig Beck had never done his office justice after all.

He pulled the single sheet of paper towards him and began to write.

Dear Colonel General,

It is with the greatest regret...

Twenty-five

The taxi dropped Conrad off at the gates of Chartwell, Winston Churchill's country house in Kent. He walked up the short drive and rang the bell on the front door.

'Mr de Lancey!'

He turned to see a short round figure approaching him in a blue boiler suit wielding a trowel in one hand and a cigar in the other.

Churchill jammed the cigar between his lips, held out his hand and shook Conrad's. When he was younger Conrad had attended a couple of dinner parties at which Churchill had held forth, and he wasn't sure whether Churchill would remember him, but the great man's smile was friendly, almost familiar.

'Been in a motor smash?' he said, looking at Conrad's battered face.

'Slight disagreement with the local police in Germany,' Conrad said. 'Don't worry, it's all sorted out now.'

Churchill grinned. 'Come along with me,' he said through teeth clenched around his cigar. 'I'm building a wall by the kitchen garden. I should be writing, but I thought I would just finish this row. I'm up to my neck in Ancient Britons, Angles, Saxons and Jutes. I thought I had shot of them when I left school, but they have come back to haunt me.'

'I thought you were working on *Marlborough*,' Conrad said. 'I've read the first three volumes, and I'm rather looking forward to reading the final one. When will it be published?' Although the first Duke of Marlborough was not exactly Conrad's period, he enjoyed Churchill's writing.

'Harrumph,' said Churchill, but he was grinning as he puffed on the cigar. '*Marlborough* is nearly finished. This is *The History of the English-Speaking Peoples*, a foolish project I promised to my publishers years ago. Bill Deakin is providing me with some valued assistance. He tells me you know each other?'

'Yes, I know Deakin,' said Conrad. Bill Deakin was a young don at Wadham, someone Conrad both liked and admired. Churchill's habit of taking on and firing historical assistants was legendary amongst the academic community and Deakin had been brave to accept the post. 'Until a couple of years ago I was working on my own thesis at Oxford. German history.'

'A dark subject,' said Churchill. 'And getting darker by the day. Tell me, how is your father? I don't see as much of him as I would wish.'

'Very well, I think. He spends a lot of time in Somerset these days.'

'An admirable man,' Churchill said. 'Of course I disagree with him on appeasement, but he was the only one of that Cabinet to do the right thing over the Hoare–Laval pact. They should all have resigned.'

They reached the wall, a half-completed line of red bricks surrounding the kitchen garden. It was a warm day and Churchill was sweating. He plunged his trowel into a bucket and smoothed the mortar along the wall, before carefully aligning a brick against a piece of string. The brick didn't look very straight to Conrad, but he decided not to point this out to Churchill.

'I saw Herr von Kleist on Friday with Randolph,' Churchill said. Randolph was Churchill's son. 'I took him for a drive around the estate.'

'What did you think of him?'

'I like the man. He said he's a patriot and I believe him. He says that the ordinary Germans do not want a world war. Do you think that is true, Mr de Lancey?'

'I believe so, sir. Oh, they love their uniforms and their military parades, but Germany lost twice as many men as we did in the Great War.'

'And do you think that Herr von Kleist has the support amongst the general staff that he claims?'

'Once again, I believe so. I have met his family in Prussia and they are implacably opposed to Hitler. I think it is difficult for some of them; they have such an entrenched sense of duty that to oppose the head of state is something they will only do as a last resort. But they believe they are reaching that point.'

Churchill grunted. 'Herr von Kleist says that General Beck requires a letter from the British government committing to support Czechoslovakia in the event of an invasion, so that he may show it to his supporters. A secret letter to someone who has declared opposition to a sovereign government is, of course, impossible for a serving minister to write. But I have discussed the matter with Lord Halifax, and I have drafted something which I hope will suffice. Would you be good enough to see that it gets to Herr von Kleist on your return to Berlin?'

'Certainly,' said Conrad. 'Can you persuade our government to take von Kleist seriously?'

Churchill wiped his brow and sat on his steps. 'I can try,' he said. He frowned, his fleshy cheeks drooping. 'Here I am, an old man without power and without party, what advice can I give?'

'You must tell them what you think,' Conrad said. 'They might disagree with you, but they have to listen to you.'

'I take it you don't accept your father's views on appeasement, then?' he said.

'Not any more.'

'Very good,' said Churchill. 'Tell me, Mr de Lancey, do you think Herr Beans will fight the Germans if they do invade?'

Conrad frowned for a moment before he realized Churchill was referring to Edvard Beneš, the President of Czechoslovakia. They spent a fascinating hour discussing Central European politics before Conrad returned to his waiting taxi, Churchill's letter for von Kleist and General Beck safe in the inside pocket of his jacket.

Conrad sat in the first-floor drawing room of his family's home in Kensington Square, sipping a cup of tea. He was staying there while he was in London, rather than at his club, and his father had just come up to town to sound out those of his old Cabinet colleagues who were still languishing in the capital in August. It was a hot day, and the windows were open, letting in the occasional sound of a car driving around the square and the more persistent hum of traffic from the High Street a hundred yards distant.

'Your face is a bit of a mess,' said Lord Oakford.

Conrad touched his cheek. 'Actually, it's healing quite well.'

'Who did it? Winston?'

Conrad laughed. 'No. Although he did greet me brandishing a trowel. It was the Gestapo.'

'Did they hurt you? I mean, beyond what I can see?'

'Not much, fortunately. I managed to put them off the scent just as they were getting into their stride.'

'Be careful, my boy.'

'I will, Father.'

There was an awkward moment as Lord Oakford peered closely at his son. Then he seemed to relax, sitting back in his chair and sipping his tea. 'So, how is Winston?'

'Building a wall,' replied Conrad. 'He said some nice things about you. About your resignation.'

Lord Oakford chuckled wryly. 'It is a sad thing when the most notable event of one's time in government is one's departure from it.'

'I think he, like you, is frustrated at being out of things.'

'Who said I was frustrated at being out of things?' said Lord Oakford.

Conrad smiled. 'Just a guess, Father.'

'Well, I'm not completely out of touch,' Lord Oakford said. 'I had luncheon with Edward today at White's. He knows all about your man von Kleist's visit; Van, George Lloyd and Winston have given him a full report.' Edward was Lord Halifax, and Van was Sir Robert Vansittart, the foreign-policy expert.

'I wonder if they all said the same thing?'

'Probably not. Van is a bit suspicious. He seemed to think von Kleist wanted to grab half of Poland.'

'Oh dear. And Halifax?'

'He doesn't quite know what to think. He has authorized Winston to send a letter—'

'Which I have here,' said Conrad, patting his jacket, which was lying on the arm of the sofa.'

'Be careful with that,' said Oakford.

'Don't worry, I will.'

'But you know Edward. He worries about it not being quite "proper". And I have to say, I know what he means. It's dashed tricky dealing with renegade aristocrats.'

'It's the only way,' said Conrad.

Lord Oakford frowned. 'I hope you are right.'

Conrad sipped his tea. 'And what about the Prime Minister?'

'He's fishing at the moment. In Scotland.'

Conrad snorted. 'While Europe is about to burst into flames?'

Lord Oakford shook his head. 'I know, I know, but he was asked to Balmoral by the King, and he could hardly decline. I was at Cliveden over the weekend. There was a lot of talk about what we should do with Germany, as usual. Geoffrey is adamant that appeasing Hitler is the only way.' Geoffrey was Geoffrey Dawson, editor of *The Times* and an old friend of Lord Oakford. 'Nearly all the others around the table agreed with him.'

'Except you?'

Lord Oakford smiled. 'I said that Hitler was an evil man and he had to be stopped. But that war was a last resort. When they asked me how I thought I could stop him without a war and without doing a deal with him, I said we had to stand firm by Czechoslovakia and force him to back down. They weren't impressed. And, more importantly, they are pretty confident Neville is committed to bringing Herr Hitler to the conference table and making whatever concessions he asks for.'

'But if General Beck and the others get rid of him, there won't be anyone to give concessions to.'

'You know that, and I know that. They don't.'

There was a pause. 'Thank you for listening to me, Father.'

'You were pretty bloody rude. I don't think anyone has ever called me a coward before.'

'I know, I'm sorry. It was the only way I could get through to you. I needed to make the point.'

Lord Oakford smiled. 'And actually you did it in exactly the right way. I knew what you meant; I knew I was taking the easy way out by clinging to appeasement at all costs, that's what made me so angry.' He smiled. 'Your mother put me straight, as always. If you ever get married again, marry someone with more sense than you. It can be very useful sometimes.'

Conrad found himself thinking immediately of Anneliese. Then he stopped. He was still married to someone else, someone with considerably less sense than himself. He glanced at his father. There was a twinkle in his eye, as if he could read Conrad's mind. Conrad felt himself reddening and changed the subject to cover his confusion. 'So what do you think Chamberlain will do? Now he knows about the coup he must stand by Czechoslovakia, surely?'

'I really don't know,' said Lord Oakford. 'Neville is quite committed to appeasement.'

'I can't believe he would pass up such an opportunity!' Conrad frowned. He had assumed that the British government would go along with von Kleist's suggestion, once they had satisfied themselves that he was credible. 'If Chamberlain does let Hitler walk into Czechoslovakia unopposed, will the Cabinet follow him?'

'Some probably won't – Duff Cooper, for example. Some will, come what may – Kingsley Wood, Sam Hoare. But I think the others will follow Edward. Although he's toeing the appeasement line at the moment, he's not an out-and-out appeaser at all costs. If he comes to believe that Hitler can't be trusted or that there is another way of stopping him, he might withdraw his support for the Prime Minister. And say what you like about Edward, he does have a reputation for integrity. He could swing the majority of the Cabinet against Neville if he was absolutely convinced Neville was wrong.'

'So it's all down to Lord Halifax,' said Conrad.

'I think so,' said his father. 'Let's hope he takes the right decision.'

Twenty-six

Conrad looked down upon the clear white V cutting across Lake Havel as a passenger ferry made its way south towards Potsdam. A pocket of warm air rose up from the Grunewald and struck the descending aeroplane, causing it to lurch alarmingly. Conrad gripped the armrests of his seat as the Ju-52 lowered itself on to the runway at Tempelhof.

It wasn't the landing that bothered him, but what would happen afterwards. Whenever he had crossed the borders of the Third Reich before, his luggage had been diligently searched, but his personal correspondence had never been read. He had stuffed Churchill's letter to von Kleist into the middle of a sheaf of old love letters from Veronica. As long as he was treated as any other passenger he had nothing to fear, but if Klaus had somehow learned of his return to Germany and decided to have him searched thoroughly, he would be in big trouble. He had cabled ahead to Theo to meet him at the aerodrome, so all he needed to do was to get through customs safely and he could hand the letter over and be done with it.

He was about twenty people back from the front of the queue in the terminal building. It was moving slowly: the German border police ahead were being thorough, but not suspiciously over-diligent.

Suddenly he felt as much as saw the queue stiffen. Two border policemen were walking purposefully towards the waiting passengers. Everyone looked around, trying to decide whether it was they or their neighbour that the police were approaching. The palms of Conrad's hands became instantly clammy. He looked straight ahead, and then, realizing that this set him apart from the rest of the queue, joined in with those staring at the policemen.

They walked right up to him. 'Herr de Lancey?'

He nodded.

'Come this way please!'

The policemen's faces were stiff and correct; Conrad couldn't read them. Thoughts scrambled around his brain as he tried to think of what he would say to Klaus if the letter were discovered. In it Churchill made the point that if the Germans invaded Czechoslovakia a long and bloody war with Britain and France would result, but he didn't mention von Kleist's name or his activities, other than to note that the recipient had recently paid him a visit. The letter was addressed to 'My dear Sir'. Conrad decided that his best bet was to claim that Churchill had written the letter to him, and that he was keeping it as a memento from a celebrated politician on an important subject.

Would Klaus believe that? Somehow, Conrad doubted it.

Under the curious gaze of his fellow passengers, Conrad was led through a door into a small office.

There, in uniform, was a figure he recognized.

'Theo! What the devil are you playing at?'

Theo grinned and shook Conrad's hand. He nodded to the two policemen, dismissing them. 'You don't think I could let you go through carrying that letter, do you?'

'You could have warned me you would be meeting me on this side of customs. I had quite a fright when those policemen came for me.'

'Keeps you on your toes,' said Theo, clapping Conrad on

the back. 'Now, come on. Once we are in the car, you can tell me all about it.'

Theo and Conrad slipped out of a side door from the little office, out of sight of the other passengers. Theo's Horch was parked outside and in a few moments they were heading through the Kreuzberg to Conrad's flat.

'Have you seen von Kleist since he got back to Germany?' Conrad asked.

'Yes, I have.'

'Is he happy with his trip?'

'I think so. He feels he made his point and that Churchill especially listened to him. He is still disappointed he didn't meet anyone actually in government. Have you got the letter?'

Conrad rummaged through his suitcase and handed Theo Churchill's letter. 'It's not from the Prime Minister, but I hope it will do.'

'But will he get the message?' Theo asked.

'Oh, definitely. Halifax has had a full report already. Chamberlain is in Scotland fishing, but he'll find out all about it soon enough.'

'What will his reaction be?'

'I have no idea. But my father will keep his ear to the ground. What's all this?'

Theo's car was stopped at a junction while a seemingly endless line of trucks crammed with soldiers drove past.

'There's a parade in honour of Admiral Horthy, the Hungarian regent. It's supposed to be one of the biggest yet. It's playing havoc with the traffic.'

Conrad stared at the soldiers, hundreds of them, thousands of them. It seemed like a whole division. 'If the British listen to von Kleist's message and stand by Czechoslovakia, do you think General Beck will keep his promise to lead a revolt?'

'General Beck has resigned.'

'He's what!' Conrad turned towards Theo who was staring straight ahead at the column of trucks.

'He submitted his resignation yesterday. We tried to stop him, but he insisted.'

'So who will lead the coup?'

Theo sighed. 'That's a very good question. His successor is almost certain to be General Halder, his deputy.'

'Will he do it?'

'I don't know,' said Theo. 'We'll see.'

Conrad shook his head. 'So Uncle Ewald's trip was a waste of time.'

'No, it wasn't!' said Theo. Anger mixed with determination in his voice. 'There are enough of us who are determined to act. Trust me. We *will* get rid of that maniac.'

Conrad smiled at his friend. 'Good. And I will do all I can to help you.'

Eventually Theo battled his way through the mayhem and dropped Conrad at his flat. Conrad was anxious to see Anneliese. True, he had promised Theo that they would stay away from each other to avoid provoking Klaus unnecessarily, but he thought he could risk dropping in on her during the day for a short period. He remembered that she was on an early shift that day and should be home by four. Since he had a couple of hours until then, he decided to walk, and watch the parade on the way.

Unter den Linden was packed, as was the Victory Avenue through the Tiergarten. Conrad found himself a spot near the Brandenburg Gate to watch the procession. Infantry marched past with a rapid goose-step; Prussian cavalry mounted on fine chargers trotted along, looking vulnerable in front of the armoured monstrosities clanking behind them. Bandsmen in many different uniforms played the same martial music. Looking down on it all was the Quadriga, the sculpture of Victory driving a four-horse chariot perched atop the Brandenburg Gate. The crowd were cheering wildly, not just the men but the women too, their faces lit up with excitement and pride. Arms were raised everywhere in the Nazi salute. When a giant gun passed by carried by four trucks, a gun bigger than Conrad had ever seen or even imagined, the crowd erupted into ecstasies of militaristic joy. Conrad wondered whether Uncle Ewald was right; it seemed to him at that moment that the German people were straining to march into a war, smiling and laughing to the sound of the bands playing *Deutschland über Alles*.

Beck's resignation was clearly a blow to Theo and his conspirators. But it was equally clear that something drastic had to be done to stop the Nazi juggernaut smashing over Europe. Conrad hoped that there were enough Germans who thought like Theo to do it.

It was impossible to cross the never-ending line of soldiers, and so Conrad doubled back to take the U-Bahn underneath them to the Scheunenviertel. He spent twenty minutes loitering in the streets around Anneliese's building, checking for watchers. It was five o'clock by the time he finally rang the bell to her building. Frau Goldstein answered the door.

When she saw him, she burst into tears.

'What is it?' asked Conrad. 'Where's Anneliese?'

'Oh, Herr de Lancey, it's so terrible. I was hoping you would come so I could tell you—'

'Where is she?' Conrad repeated more urgently, only just managing to restrain himself from shaking the woman.

'It was last night they came. They took her away.'

'Who? Who took her away?'

'The Gestapo.'

'Was it Schalke?'

'No. But it was another one I recognized. The one with red hair who arrested you.'

'Dressel. Where did they take her?'

'I don't know. I asked them, but all they said was: "You won't be seeing her for a long while."'

Conrad closed his eyes. He had never anticipated that Anneliese would be arrested before he could get her out of the country. How foolish he had been! 'Did they hurt her?'

'I don't think so. But she looked very frightened.' The landlady sniffed. 'She did shout something to me.'

'What was that?'

'She said, "Tell Herr de Lancey I love him." So I am telling you that now. Oh, Herr de Lancey, do you think they have taken her to a camp?'

'I don't know,' said Conrad. 'I just don't know.'

Conrad reeled out on to the street. Klaus! Klaus must have been behind it; he had sent his henchman Dressel because he didn't have the guts to arrest Anneliese face-to-face.

But why? Why would he harm her when he was so obsessed with her? Perhaps it was some bizarre kidnap attempt. Perhaps love had turned to hate. Conrad had no idea: it was yet another example of the illogical behaviour of this insane country. Perhaps they had already let her go and she was making her way back home. Or perhaps she was at that moment locked up in a concentration camp.

Conrad felt a surge of hot anger rush through his body. Klaus was playing with Anneliese's life, toying with it. He had no damn right to do that! Impotence and frustration stoked up his rage. He stumbled towards Oranienburger Strasse in search of a cab. He would go straight to Prinz-Albrecht-Strasse and confront Klaus, demand Anneliese's release. He didn't care what the Gestapo did to him, he had to show them that they couldn't push around the little people with impunity, that Klaus couldn't hurt Anneliese, his Anneliese, and get away with it.

After a minute or so of frantic waving, a taxi stopped and Conrad climbed in and flopped into the back seat.

'Where to, chief?' the driver asked in his Berliner accent.

Conrad took a deep breath and tried to calm himself down. He had to think this through. Anneliese's life was too important to jeopardize through his desire to make a point. Going to Gestapo HQ was a waste of time; he knew that. It might make him feel better, but that wasn't important. What was important was to find out where Anneliese was and get her out of there.

'Chief?'

'Tiergartenstrasse,' Conrad said. 'Number seventeen.'

Foley would be able to discover where the Gestapo had taken Anneliese, or at least he would know whom Conrad could speak to to find out.

The parade had finished, but it took the taxi half an hour to fight its way through the crowds of people streaming home, their faces still flushed with the exhilaration of the afternoon. It was early evening, so there were no queues outside the Passport Control Office, but inside the building there was chaos. Foley was carrying a box stuffed full of papers through the entrance hall. When he saw Conrad, he put the box down. 'De Lancey! You catch us at a very bad moment. But I'm glad you're here, I need a quick word with you. Come on through.'

Conrad followed Foley into his office, which was strewn with more papers, tea chests and boxes.

'What's going on here?'

'Some of us are leaving,' Foley said. 'In a hurry.'

'Why?'

'Did you see something in the paper about a British diplomat arrested in Austria? A Captain Kendrick?'

'Yes, I did.'

'He was our Passport Control Officer in Vienna.'

'You mean...'

'I mean he had the same hobby as me and all the other British Passport Control Officers in Europe. The Germans and everyone else have known for years that the title is just a cover for other activities, but London are concerned that now they are going to round some of us up. So we have been recalled immediately. We'll leave a skeleton staff of genuine passport officials to deal with the mess here.'

'Will you be coming back?'

'Your guess is as good as mine. If everything blows over, perhaps. But if Germany invades Czechoslovakia and the balloon goes up, probably not. Which is why I wanted to speak to you.'

'Oh, yes?'

'Yes. No one staying on here knows anything about intelligence work. But if you come across anything you think I should know, look me up when you are in London. Your father will be able to find me.'

'My father?'

'He's well connected, he'll know how to track me down.'

'I suppose so. Look, Captain Foley, I know you're frantically busy, but Anneliese has been arrested by the Gestapo. I don't know where she has been taken, and I hoped you could find out.'

Foley frowned. 'I'm sorry to hear that, de Lancey. As you can see, I can't help you myself.'

'What do you want me to do with the Mayer file?' Conrad turned to see a young secretary at the door clutching a thick manila folder. 'Oh, I'm sorry, Captain Foley, I didn't know you were with someone.'

'That should go in the diplomatic bag, thank you, Margaret,' said Foley. 'Give us a couple of minutes.'

'Certainly, Captain Foley,' the woman said and withdrew.

'I'll tell you what,' said Foley. 'You can try this man.' He scribbled a name on a piece of paper and passed it to Conrad. *Wilfrid Israel.* 'You can find him at N. Israel.'

N. Israel was one of Berlin's smartest department stores. Remarkably, it was still open despite its obviously Jewish name. 'I take it he owns the place?'

'He does. He helps me arrange things. Tell him I sent you. Oh, and when you do find Anneliese, the people here should still be able to issue her a visa for Britain, once she gets her papers together. There's a note in her file.'

'Thank you, Captain Foley.'

'Anyway, must be getting on.'

Conrad left the Passport Control Office, crossed the road and went into the Tiergarten. There were still people making their way home from the parade along the main paths. He soon found himself at the Rosengarten, where he had been so many times before with Anneliese. He couldn't bear the thought of her in a concentration camp. He remembered when she had first told him that she had been inside one and how inhuman it had been. Later she had recounted little anecdotes about her time there. Although the stories had had a certain black humour, there was always the background of starvation, sadism, torture and despair. He knew there were tens of thousands of Germans in the camps, but at that moment he only cared about one of them.

He sat on a bench in front of a yellow rose Anneliese particularly liked, and savoured the heavy scent of the blossom. A white butterfly skipped between the blooms, revelling in its freedom. He remembered her shouted message to Frau Goldstein. He couldn't let her down.

But he felt despair close in around him. What chance did the ordinary person have in this new world of the Third Reich? Someone like Klaus Schalke, with his twisted obsessions, had the untrammelled power of the state at his disposal to toy with the lives of Conrad and Anneliese as he wished. Faced with such brazen evil, the German people had grumbled and then acquiesced. And what Klaus was doing to Anneliese, Hitler was doing to whole countries. The leaders of the other European powers, decent, nervous men who played by the rules, were setting themselves up to do the same thing: grumble and then acquiesce. Hitler understood this; he was counting on it.

There *were* some brave men scattered around Europe who were prepared to do something. Theo. Ewald von Kleist. Winston Churchill. Conrad knew then he had to do all he possibly could to help them. That way he had some hope of extracting Anneliese from the madness.

But if Hitler did invade Czechoslovakia at the end of September there could well be war. Conrad would have to return to England, leaving Anneliese in Germany to God knows what fate.

That was only five weeks away.

PART THREE

Late August 1938

Twenty-seven

'So what shall we do about Czechoslovakia, Edward?'

Neville Chamberlain was happiest sharing the unrelenting burden of running the British Empire with his closest supporters and confidants deep within No. 10 Downing Street. Once he had agreed a policy with them, then he would set about presenting the case to the wider Cabinet, knowing what outcome he was aiming to achieve. He was sixty-nine, at the end of a moderately distinguished political career, which had been overshadowed by the greater figures of his father Joseph and his brother Austen. Now, suddenly, he found himself Prime Minister, a position neither of them had been able to achieve. Not only that, but he held that office at one of the most difficult points in his country's history. His achievements to date had been as Minister of Health and then as Chancellor of the Exchequer and he knew nothing about foreign affairs. But he was determined to prove himself up to the challenge. The Czech crisis had been brewing all summer, and he had been racking his brains for a solution. Now he thought he had one, and he was looking forward to telling his colleagues about it. It was quite brilliant.

There were three other men around the table: Sir John Simon, the Chancellor of the Exchequer, Lord Halifax, the Foreign Secretary, and Sir Horace Wilson, a civil servant who had been responsible for negotiating a solution to the General Strike in 1926 and who had helped smooth the abdication of

Edward VIII two years before. Just the man to deal with a tricky customer like Herr Hitler.

Lord Halifax's long face was grimmer than usual as he replied. 'The only deterrent likely to be effective in preventing Hitler invading the Sudetenland is an announcement that Britain will declare war on Germany if he does.' Halifax pronounced the words 'detewent' and 'pwevent': he couldn't say his 'r's properly. 'There are two problems with this. One is that a significant proportion of public opinion both here and in the Empire is against such a course of action.'

'And the other?'

'The other is that if Hitler ignores us and invades Czechoslovakia anyway we would face a dilemma. Either we fight a war which will almost certainly result in the loss of Czechoslovakia, or we back down, in which case all our diplomatic credibility will be destroyed.'

Heads nodded around the table in understanding. That, in a nutshell, was the difficulty with which Hitler was constantly presenting them.

Halifax continued. 'We have received representations from some senior figures in Germany that they will launch a revolution against Hitler if he invades Czechoslovakia, but I am not sure how much weight we should give to that.'

Chamberlain snorted. 'None at all. I am sure that this Herr von Kleist is personally opposed to Hitler and is trying to stir things up. He reminds me of the Jacobites at the court of France in King William's time. I think we can discount a lot of what he says.'

'Van is suspicious of him,' Halifax said. 'He thinks there wouldn't be much difference between a Germany run by nationalist monarchists and one run by Hitler. But Winston seems to feel that if we stand by Czechoslovakia, von Kleist and his friends will bring about a swift change of government and guarantee stability.'

'Winston!' Chamberlain muttered with impatience. 'And what's your view, Edward?'

'I have my reservations.'

'So do I,' murmured Chamberlain.

'It's a question of whether it is justifiable to fight a certain war in order to forestall a possible war later,' Halifax said. 'Perhaps we should keep Hitler guessing.'

The time had come for Chamberlain's plan. 'I have been giving the matter much thought,' he began. 'And I have an idea. Let us call it Plan Z.' He smiled at the small moment of melodrama. 'It will come into operation only in certain circumstances, and for it to be effective it must be a complete surprise. So until then nothing should be said about it, even to Cabinet.'

Halifax raised his eyebrows. 'And what is this Plan Z?'

Chamberlain could barely contain his excitement. 'When it looks as if an invasion of Czechoslovakia is imminent, I fly to Germany, without any warning, and have talks with Herr Hitler, during which I force him to commit to peace. He will have no choice but to respond to such a dramatic gesture: the leader of one country cutting through all the diplomatic protocol and flying to see the leader of another. Once we are speaking man to man I'm sure we can hammer out a compromise; indeed I am determined that we shall. We shall secure peace in Europe for the foreseeable future. Eh, Edward?'

Lord Halifax's jaw had dropped. 'It's certainly a bold idea, Prime Minister.'

'Of course it is! And that's why it will work. But not a word to anyone. As I said, it must be a total surprise.'

* * *

Theo's first impression of General of Artillery Halder was not a good one. Short, with pince-nez spectacles, close-cropped grey hair and a stubbly moustache, he looked more like a fastidious schoolteacher than a German general. There he was, sitting in Beck's chair, watched by the forbidding portrait of von Moltke, the fourth potential leader of a coup. Von Fritsch had been crushed by the humiliation of trumped-up charges, Beck had resigned in a fit of self-righteousness and von Brauchitsch took indecision to an art form. Now it was Halder's turn. Not for the first time Theo wished that Oster was a general and not a lowly colonel.

The lowly colonel had arranged the meeting, bringing Theo along with him. The schoolmaster lost no time in getting to the point. 'Well, Oster, may I speak frankly?'

'Absolutely, Herr General. Lieutenant von Hertenberg is totally trustworthy. He has been involved in all our planning to date.'

Halder threw Theo a sharp, suspicious glance. For a moment Theo felt as if he had forgotten his Latin homework.

'Very good,' the new Chief of the General Staff said reluctantly. 'General Beck has told me something of what you have been up to. The time for memoranda is over; now it is time for action. I have been working on the details of Case Green, and I can tell you Hitler is serious. The German army will invade Czechoslovakia and, if the British and French stand by the Czechs, that means war.'

'*If* the British and French stand by the Czechs,' said Oster. 'We sent someone over to speak to the British government. We have a letter from Churchill which states that he thinks a world war would very probably follow an invasion of Czechoslovakia, but Churchill isn't the government. We don't know what Chamberlain is thinking.'

'They *must* support the Czechs,' said Halder. 'Can't they see that that is the only way of stopping the madman?' The general got to his feet and began pacing. 'Hitler is a fool!' he said, his voice loaded with contempt and anger. 'Not just a fool but a criminal. The man thrives on blood. He is mad, you know, criminally insane. I think a psychologist would have a field day with him; I believe he is sexually pathological. He has no idea of military strategy and his methods are inhuman. He must be stopped, and stopped soon, before he can drag Germany into a war we shall surely lose.'

Theo was impressed: the schoolmaster had a temper, although he wasn't sure what he meant by 'sexually pathological'.

'So you would be prepared to lead a coup?' asked Oster.

'Absolutely,' said Halder. 'It is my duty as a German officer to do so.'

'What about General von Brauchitsch?' Oster asked.

'Let's leave him out of it for now,' said Halder. 'I will approach him when we are ready. Present him with a *fait accompli* when the easiest thing for him to do will be to go along with us. Now, tell me about von Witzleben?'

Von Witzleben was the general in command of Army District III, which encompassed Berlin. His active support was key to the success of any coup.

'I have spoken to him in the broadest terms,' said Oster. 'He is sympathetic. But we haven't discussed detailed plans yet.'

'Well, we should. And the Berlin police?'

'That's a bit more difficult. We think they will support us, but we don't know for sure.'

'We must find out. Who are you suggesting would lead a new government? We need a civilian; it can't be a general.'

'Hjalmar Schacht,' said Oster.

Halder nodded his approval. Schacht was probably the most respected politician in the Third Reich. Until the previous November he had been Minister of Economics and he was still President of the Reichsbank. It was he who was credited with taming the hyperinflation of the 1920s, and dragging Germany out of the economic quagmire that had pulled it down at the beginning of the 1930s. His wizardry had brought about full employment and had financed Hitler's rearmament programme. He commanded respect both inside Germany and abroad. 'I would like to meet him,' the general said.

'Hertenberg will arrange it,' said Oster.

'Very good.' Halder stopped pacing and stared at Oster. 'The one thing that concerns me about this whole idea is that we must avoid creating a "Hitler myth".'

'What do you mean?' asked Oster.

'I mean that it must be absolutely clear that Hitler's removal is necessary. If he is overthrown in peacetime by a group of generals, his followers will claim he was stabbed in the back, just as they claim the Kaiser was stabbed in the back in 1918. We must wait until he has actually taken the country to war. No one in Germany wants another war; only then will they understand that he must be deposed.'

Oster winced. 'But surely it would be better to act before that? Then we retain control of events. If we wait for war to be declared we are at the mercy of decisions taken by Hitler and by Chamberlain. And who knows how the army will act when guns are being fired and soldiers are dying and Hitler is urging them to fight for their fatherland?'

Halder shook his head. 'I am very firm on this point. We cannot act until the country is on the brink of disaster.'

There was silence in the room. Then Theo broke it. 'You

are familiar with Case Green, Herr General. Is there a window when it will be clear that Hitler has irrevocably launched an invasion, but before war has actually been declared?'

Halder frowned. 'Yes. Yes, there is. Case Green requires forty-eight hours' notice before the Czech border is actually crossed.'

'Perhaps that is when we strike,' said Theo. 'As soon Hitler has given the order to move.'

Halder nodded. 'Yes, that will work.' He smiled and rubbed his hands. 'Well, Oster, Hertenberg. We have some work to do.'

The Nazis had yet to eradicate all signs of Judaism from Berlin, and even in 1938 the words 'N. Israel' shone bold and large from a five-storey building of steel and glass opposite the town hall. This was Israel's department store. Although not quite as large as Wertheim's, it had a long history of serving the Prussian and Brandenburg landed families during their seasonal trips to Berlin. It was a store where good service was everything, and nothing was too much trouble to obtain; it was held in great affection by Berlin's upper classes.

It was early evening, and Conrad asked for the office of the proprietor, Wilfrid Israel. To reach it he passed through the linen department, an elaborately decorated hall from which staircases and wrought-iron balconies rose up on all sides to a domed roof of stained glass. There he was shown into a lift and taken up to the fifth floor, where he was met by a tall, slim man of about forty, with thinning fair hair and a pale, fragile complexion. He had an air of elegant refinement about him; to Conrad he had the appearance of an art collector rather than a businessman or a shopkeeper. Indeed, modern expensive-looking paintings adorned the walls of his office, and a glass cabinet displayed a collection of oriental statues. A frail pink orchid bloomed in a pot behind his desk.

'Ah, Mr de Lancey, what a pleasure to meet you,' Israel said in good English.

'Thank you for seeing me,' said Conrad.

'Not at all,' said Israel. 'Captain Foley sent me a note to expect you just before he left for London.' He smiled. 'I'm always eager to help Captain Foley if I can.'

A butler came in with some coffee on a tray. Israel sipped his, exposing jade cufflinks as he did so. His suit, Conrad was sure, came from Savile Row, not his own shop.

'You know I met your father on a number of occasions, Mr de Lancey?'

'Really?' Conrad was used to people telling him they knew his father, but this man surprised him. 'Where was that?'

'It was just after the war. I was working with the Quaker Emergency Committee trying to get powdered milk to babies in Germany. Your father was very helpful. Of course I was only a young man then, young and idealistic, but I like to think that he and I got on rather well.'

'He always believed that the Allies treated the Germans rather shabbily after the war. As do I.'

'Fortunately, I missed the war. I was just old enough, but my health wasn't very good then. It still isn't,' said Israel. 'Anyway, how can I help you?'

'I have a friend who has been taken into protective custody. Or at least I think she has.' Conrad briefly explained what had happened to Anneliese, and described her relationship to Klaus and to himself.

'Ah, yes, I remember her. Her father was the Jewish doctor arrested for giving blood to a gentile, wasn't he? I helped get him out of Sachsenhausen.'

'Can you help me find her?'

'Probably,' said Israel. 'Most women from Berlin are sent

to Lichtenburg, but my understanding is that it's almost full now and they are taking some women to the men's camp at Sachsenhausen while they build a new all-female camp nearby. I can have a word with some of my contacts.'

'And if you find her, can you get her out?'

'If she is in Sachsenhausen we have a good chance. The camp commandant has unlimited credit at Israel's. It's his wife's favourite store.'

'I can give you some money to cover expenses,' said Conrad.

Israel smiled. 'I seem to remember your father is a banker, isn't he?'

'That's right.'

'Well, what we really need is foreign currency. If you speak to Lionel de Rothschild in London, he'll tell you where a donation can be of most use.'

'I'll do that,' said Conrad.

Israel put down his coffee cup. 'I'm afraid I have a lot to attend to these days.' He shook Conrad's hand. 'I'll see what I can do for Anneliese. And don't give up. There's always hope. However bad things look, however mad the world seems to have become, there is always hope.'

Conrad closed his eyes, sat back on the bench and let the soft late-afternoon sunlight caress his cheeks. He could hear the distant hum of the city around him, the chirp of a blackbird going about its business in the bushes, the gentle murmur and occasional girlish laugh of the lovers on other benches around the Rosengarten. A breath of gentle breeze brought with it the blended scent of a dozen different varieties of rose. With his eyes shut, he could almost feel Anneliese next to him, silent, smiling gently to herself, happy.

His meeting with Wilfrid Israel had encouraged him; the

man exuded a quiet confidence. But all Conrad could do now was wait. Wait and think of Anneliese. If he closed his eyes he could hear her voice, her laugh, even her silence. For a few moments a feeling of calm would overwhelm him. And then it would be dispelled by a tumult of violent emotions: anxiety for Anneliese amidst the unknown horrors of a concentration camp; anger at Klaus who he was sure was responsible for her arrest; anger with the whole Nazi edifice which locked up people like her for simply being who they were; guilt that it was his relationship with her that had roused Klaus's jealousy. But unlike in July, when bitterness had caused him to hide in the Stabi and deny the evil that was swirling around him, this time he was determined to do something, to get Anneliese out of whatever concentration camp she was in and then out of the country, and to do whatever he could, however small, to help Theo and his friends rid Germany of Hitler.

According to Theo, the plans for the coup were developing; support was hardening within the army and without. The conspirators had appreciated Churchill's letter, but they needed a firmer commitment from someone in government. Conrad had suggested that they focus on Lord Halifax, and a meeting between Theo Kordt, an official at the German Embassy in London, and the British Foreign Secretary was being arranged.

It was very difficult for Conrad to control his agitation. If things went according to plan, within a month Anneliese would be out of the concentration camp and Hitler would be out of power. If things didn't, well, he would never see her again.

Klaus walked rapidly through the familiar streets of Halle from the train station to the town hall. His colleagues at Prinz-Albrecht-Strasse thought he was in Magdeburg, and indeed he would drop into the Gestapo office there on his way back to

Berlin. It was vital that no one should know he was in his old home town.

He felt better now that Anneliese was safe in Sachsenhausen. He had found it unbearable when she was free, free to see de Lancey whenever she wanted. She was probably suffering in the camp, but that would be as nothing compared to all the suffering she had put him through. He wasn't sure how long he should keep her there. At least until de Lancey was out of the way.

De Lancey's continued existence troubled Klaus. Direct action against him was out of the question now he had Canaris's protection; Heydrich would never stand for it. Unless, that is, Heydrich came to believe that de Lancey was a threat, not in some general way to the Third Reich, but to Heydrich personally. Which was why Klaus was in Halle. But Heydrich would be suspicious of Klaus, so it was important that doubts about de Lancey were planted indirectly.

Klaus reached the medieval Market Square, dominated by its massive gothic Red Tower, and slipped into the town hall, where he asked for a Herr Eckert. Klaus and Herr Eckert had spent quite a lot of time together three years before when Klaus was doing some sensitive work for Heydrich. Now he wanted Herr Eckert to perform a further small task for him. On the train down to Halle Klaus had mulled over what encouragement he would give to Herr Eckert to ensure his cooperation. He decided that the threat of a painful death should be simple and effective enough.

An hour later, Klaus took the train to Magdeburg to drop in on the Gestapo office there and establish his alibi, and then back to Berlin. There he lurked outside de Lancey's apartment until he saw him leave, whereupon he nipped inside and had a quick word with the superintendent of the building. Using the superintendent's keys he let himself into de Lancey's apartment. Five minutes later, pausing only to issue pointed threats to the superintendent if he should breathe a word of Klaus's presence to anyone, he was gone.

Anneliese felt light-headed as she stood in the queue for the lavatories. There were only two of them for a hundred women, and there was always a rush for them first thing in the morning before roll call. She was worried that she was getting sick; it was never a good idea to get sick in a camp. She hoped it was just the hunger.

She had been in Sachsenhausen now for just over a week and it was definitely tougher than Moringen, the women-only camp near Hanover she had been sent to in 1933. There the guards were drawn from the local Nazi Women's League. They had seemed harsh enough, but the Sachsenhausen overseers had been recruited directly by the SS for their brutality. A temporary women's sub-camp had been erected near the main men's camp: the male prisoners were busy building a more permanent complex for the women at Ravensbrück. The two largest groups of inmates were the Jehovah's Witnesses and the communists, although the number of Jewish women prisoners was increasing fast. There were also prostitutes, drunkards, vagrants and petty thieves. At Moringen, Anneliese had been labelled a communist. This time, a yellow triangle sown on the left arm of her dress identified her as a Jew.

The queue was moving slowly, despite the urging of the waiting women. No one wanted to be late for roll call. At last Anneliese's turn came, and she just made it out to the yard before the guard, whom the prisoners nicknamed the Scorpion, read out the roll. Anneliese was finding it difficult to stand, and could barely shout her response to her name loudly enough.

As the prisoners were dismissed to go to their breakfast of stale bread and turnip jam, she and two other women were asked to stay behind. The Scorpion – none of the inmates knew her real name – was a thin woman of about thirty with a long ugly nose. She always seemed to pick the same three women for punishment: Anneliese, a petite blonde communist named Andrea, and Sylvia, a statuesque Jehovah's Witness whose head had been shaved because she had been discovered with lice. The other two had told Anneliese that before her arrival in the camp the Scorpion used to pick on another Jewish girl, pretty and defiant. The girl had stood it well at first, but then had committed suicide. Anneliese was her replacement.

Anneliese was impressed with the strength of both women. The Jehovah's Witnesses had openly defied Hitler from the outset: in their eyes the Nazi salutes and greetings were words of Satan, and they said so. Three years before, the movement had been outlawed and most of the members carted off to concentration camps, where they continued to defy Nazi authority, quoting passages from the Bible at their captors at every opportunity. The faith of Andrea, the communist, was just as strong, but in her case it was the unswerving belief that the Nazi regime would crumble at any moment and the proletariat would take over Germany and set the concentration-camp inmates free. Anneliese's belief in God was much more hesitant, and her faith in communism had been shaken when she had noted the similarities between the state-controlled society in Nazi Germany and the state-controlled society of the communist ideal. But she was just as determined to survive her time in Sachsenhausen, for the sake of Conrad, for the sake of her parents, and to show the Nazi bastards, including Klaus – especially Klaus – that they couldn't break her.

Except now her head felt light and the queasiness was

increasing. She needed food badly. She felt hot – perhaps she had a temperature.

'You three were late for roll call as usual,' the Scorpion said in her broad Berliner accent. She was holding a cane, and two male SS guards and an Alsatian looked on. 'The camp rules are simple yet you insist on wilfully disobeying them. Your behaviour is intolerable. You will stand facing the wall until work.'

The three of them had been made to do this two days before, missing breakfast. Not a good way to start a twelve-hour day working in the camp laundry, but bearable if you were fit and healthy. That morning, Anneliese was neither.

The wall in question was built of white-painted brick and served as a perimeter between the men's and women's sections of the camp. The women lined up facing it. The guard prodded each of them in the back. 'Straight! Stand up straight!'

Then she gave a brisk command to the Alsatian, which immediately placed itself in front of the three prisoners and began barking and growling. Anneliese had never been afraid of dogs before she had arrived at Sachsenhausen. Now she was petrified of them.

It was still only five-thirty, and not yet light. Although it was early September, the temperature was low at this time of the morning. The prisoners' feet were bare and very cold. It began to rain, at first a few cold drops, then a steady drizzle. After a few minutes the cold water seeped through to Anneliese's skin. By now her temperature was raging, so for the first few seconds the rainwater was wonderfully cooling. Then she began to shiver.

'Straight! I said straight!' came the cry from the Scorpion, who had taken shelter in a doorway a few metres away.

'I'm not sure I can stand this,' Anneliese said out of the corner of her mouth.

'"Blessed are you when men hate you, when they exclude you and insult you and reject your name as evil,"' Sylvia said. 'Luke six, verse twenty-two.'

'Are you ill?' Andrea asked, somewhat more helpfully.

'I think I might be.'

'Don't admit it to her,' said Sylvia.

'She'll take it as a sign of weakness; she won't let you go,' said Andrea.

'Shush! She's coming!' Sylvia had heard her footsteps. Anneliese couldn't hear anything but a buzzing in her ears.

'You must stand up straight!' a voice shouted behind her. Anneliese realized she was swaying. 'Listen to me!'

She barely heard the swish but she felt a sharp pain at the back of her thighs. Then another blow across her back made her pitch forward. Her head banged hard against the wall, and everything went black.

Twenty-eight

Theo's silver Horch sped through the woods on its way back to Berlin. Next to him sat General von Witzleben, commander of Army District III. Theo liked him: he had served with Theo's father, and he was an altogether simpler, less complicated soldier than either Beck or Halder. He, too, had insisted on seeing Schacht, and Theo and he had just spent the Sunday afternoon with the President of the Reichsbank at his country house. The politician and the soldier had got on very well, each respecting the other's discipline. Schacht repeated to von Witzleben what he had told General Halder, that he would be willing to lead a civilian government after a coup.

'We'll need a detailed list of targets, Hertenberg,' the general said. 'SS barracks, telephone exchanges, police stations. They will all have to be taken on the first day. In the first few hours, even.'

'Yes, Herr General,' replied Theo. 'I have made a provisional list. It has proven quite difficult to pin down where exactly all the SS barracks are. But I have a contact in the police who I hope will be able to help me.'

'We must be sure of the police,' said von Witzleben. 'If they oppose us, the coup will be impossible to pull off.'

'I know, Herr General.' Theo and Oster had good contacts in the police, but the chief of the Berlin police force, Count Helldorf, was one of the original members of the Nazi Party, and an unknown quantity. Theo would have to get to know him soon.

The general stared at the trees flashing past. 'I don't profess to know about politics, indeed I believe generals should stay well clear of politicians. But Hitler wants a war, he is doing everything he can to provoke it and it will be the end of Germany. He has to go. Tell Oster he can count on me.'

Theo smiled. 'I am very glad to hear that, Herr General.'

Theo slept poorly that night, plans rolling around his brain in disjointed confusion. But eventually he must have drifted off, because he was wakened by the jarring sound of the telephone bell. He rolled out of bed, padded barefoot into the hallway of his apartment and picked up the receiver. 'Hertenberg.'

He heard three guttural coughs, and then the line went dead.

Theo blinked and put down the receiver. He dressed hurriedly, let himself out of the apartment and started up his car. He drove south-west towards the wealthy suburbs of Berlin, passing through Lichterfelde to Zehlendorf. At the corner of two small residential roads he saw a man waiting for him. He slowed, and the man jumped in.

'Left here,' he said. Theo obeyed, turning into a narrow residential street. His passenger was always careful, very careful, and Theo followed his instructions to the letter.

They wound a complicated route through the silent back streets of Zehlendorf before pulling up by a small lake at the southern extremity of the Grunewald.

Theo switched off the car engine and they sat in silence for a full minute, listening, before his companion pulled out a pistol and crept around the car, poking into bushes. Then he motioned for Theo to follow him through the trees down to the shore of the lake. The moon was three-quarters full and shone off the still water. They were alone and out of range of any microphones.

'Well?' said Theo.

'I have the list,' said the man, passing Theo an envelope. He was a grizzled old policeman with thin lips, shrewd eyes under bushy eyebrows and a large broad nose. His name was Artur Nebe, and he had built up a reputation as Berlin's foremost detective. Now he was head of the Kripo, the civilian sister-organization of the Gestapo. He and Theo met occasionally, always in the utmost secrecy; of all the conspirators Nebe was the most obsessively careful. 'All the SS barracks in the country. It was a nightmare to put together. It's only because every newly opened brothel must be reported to the local police that I could get the information at all.' Nebe grinned. 'You can't have an SS barracks without a brothel.'

Theo took the envelope. 'Thank you,' he said. 'I will need to approach Helldorf very soon.'

'Good luck,' said Nebe. 'Just don't mention I'm involved.'

'Don't you trust him?'

The grizzled policeman smiled. 'I trust no one, Hertenberg. That's why I am still alive.'

Theo grasped the nettle and went round to police headquarters in the Alexanderplatz the following morning. He was nervous. Count Helldorf might be an aristocrat, but he was the kind of aristocrat of whom Theo was most suspicious. In addition to being a member of the Nazi Party since 1925, von Helldorf was leader of the SA in Berlin. The man was a Nazi through and through, with a reputation for toughness and a fearsome temper.

Theo well understood that the more people who became aware of the plot, the greater the risk that it would be exposed. He was confident of the loyalty of the tight network of Prussian families of which he was a part, and of Artur Nebe and the small number of generals in whom they had confided. But von Helldorf? Von Helldorf might be a conspirator too far.

Without the support, or at least the neutrality, of the Chief of Police in Berlin, the coup would fail. Theo had been assured by an old friend of his family's, the Deputy Chief of Police Count Schulenburg, that von Helldorf would respond positively to an approach. Theo just had to trust him.

Von Helldorf was about forty, clean-shaven with tight lips, hard eyes and a duelling scar above his left eye. He listened impassively as Theo spoke.

'A friend suggested I contact you about ideas that some of the officers in the army have been discussing,' Theo began.

'Go on,' said von Helldorf.

Theo realized there was no point in beating about the bush. 'There is a plan afoot to remove Hitler,' he said. 'As soon as he orders the invasion of Czechoslovakia, which we think he will very shortly, the army will take over Berlin and he will be arrested.' Theo watched von Helldorf for a reaction, but he didn't get one. 'In those circumstances the attitude of the Berlin police will be vital. If you oppose the army, there will be a bloodbath.'

Count Helldorf sat back in his chair, examining Theo. For a moment Theo thought he had made a dreadful mistake.

But then von Helldorf's thin lips formed a smile. 'It's about time someone did something. Tell me, Lieutenant von Herten-berg, how can we help?'

'*Heil Hitler*,' Klaus drawled casually as he entered Heydrich's office.

'*Heil Hitler*,' Heydrich replied. He signed a letter in front of him and placed it firmly in his out tray, smiling to himself as he did so. Heydrich's signature was an important weapon of power in the Third Reich, an instrument of life and death, and its owner enjoyed wielding that power.

He looked up at Klaus. 'A couple of things, Schalke. We have just received an interesting rumour: a high-up German politician has recently visited London. We don't know when exactly he went, but we think it might have been last month. He had unofficial talks with the British.'

'Any idea who it might be?'

'No. Have you?'

Klaus thought a moment. 'No, I haven't. But we can look through our files, see who has travelled out of the country recently.'

'Do that. I will check with our Abwehr friends.'

'Is there a chance it might have something to do with Conrad de Lancey?' asked Klaus hopefully.

'There's no evidence for that,' said Heydrich. 'But I do want to discuss de Lancey with you.'

'Oh, yes?'

'It seems that he has been seen in Halle asking questions about my family.'

'Oh, really?'

'He spoke to a man named Eckert at the town hall. Eckert said de Lancey seemed to have a detailed knowledge about my ancestry, knowledge that I thought was safely buried.' Heydrich stared at Klaus, the man who had buried it.

'Do we know who he is working for?' said Klaus.

'Despite what the Abwehr say, he must be working for the British. I wouldn't put it past the Abwehr to check on my background – we check up on theirs, after all – but I don't see why they would use a British citizen for that kind of work.'

'It would not be a good thing if the British secret service got hold of any...' Klaus hesitated, '...erroneous information about you, Herr Gruppenführer.'

'No, it wouldn't. Which is why I want you to take some men and search de Lancey's flat. Take Kriminalrat Huber with you. And Huber leads the search.'

'Is that necessary?' Klaus asked.

Heydrich smiled. 'I know about your personal feelings towards Herr de Lancey, and I don't want them to get in the way of the investigation. But if Huber finds anything, he gives it to you and only you.'

'Yes, Herr Gruppenführer!' There was no one in the Gestapo who knew as much about Heydrich's ancestry as Klaus, including Heydrich himself, and Heydrich was eager to keep it that way.

Three-quarters of an hour later Huber and three Gestapo agents were methodically combing Conrad's flat, carefully replacing everything they moved. Klaus watched. The superintendent had done a good job of showing surprise at their arrival, but Klaus lagged behind the others as they climbed the stairs, just to make sure that the man was suitably frightened. He was.

It didn't take them long. One of the floorboards under a rug in the bedroom creaked. When Klaus had investigated it, it had been easy to remove, revealing a hiding place that had obviously been used before. Klaus doubted Conrad knew anything about it; the superintendent had told him that the previous occupant was a Jewish architect who was much more likely to have had need of it. The Gestapo found it in five minutes.

Klaus watched closely as Huber was handed a single sheet of paper. He gave it the merest glance and then passed it on to Klaus. There, in handwriting that Klaus had ensured closely resembled Conrad's, was a family tree of one Reinhard

Heydrich, extensively annotated. Klaus nodded at Huber, who ordered his men to make sure that the flat was left exactly as they had found it. Five minutes more and they were gone.

Heydrich paled as he read the scrap of paper. 'Damn it!' he said. 'These are lies, all lies! Schalke, you know these are lies. I am no more Jewish than the Führer.'

'Of course, Herr Gruppenführer,' Klaus said, thinking that that was one claim it would be very foolish to try to verify for all sorts of reasons. 'But they are lies we don't want the British to see.'

Heydrich glanced at Klaus. 'So what do you suggest we do?'

'Kill him,' Klaus said.

'You're just jealous of him because of your Jewish tart, aren't you?'

'The Jewish tart is in a concentration camp,' Klaus said calmly.

'I'm very pleased to hear it.'

'But yes, I would be happy to see Conrad de Lancey die. In fact, I will see to it personally, if you wish.'

'The Abwehr would never stand for it.'

'Let's do it and tell them afterwards. Say we have evidence that de Lancey was spying on senior members of the Gestapo for the British.'

Heydrich frowned, thinking. 'Yes, that might work. The Abwehr would never want to admit to being involved in anything like that.'

'De Lancey has hoodwinked them,' said Klaus. 'They'll be as upset about him as we are. But I'm sure they would be fascinated by what he has discovered, if we ever let them get their hands on him. Which I suggest we don't.'

'All right, Schalke. Arrest him, find out who he's working for and then kill him. But do it fast, and do it somewhere where the Abwehr won't be able to find him. Nowhere official.'

'Yes, Herr Gruppenführer!'

Twenty-nine

The taxi dropped Conrad outside his flat. He scanned the square and saw Warren Sumner waiting for him on a low wall under the old chestnut tree. The American waved and ambled over, carrying a bag.

'Sorry I'm a bit late,' Conrad said, shaking his hand. 'I hope you haven't been waiting long?'

'Ten minutes, that's all. It's good to see you.'

'And you too.' And it was. Warren's friendly smile and his American accent were a breath of fresh air to Conrad, bringing signs of an outside world removed from the increasingly tense atmosphere of Berlin on the brink of war.

'Are you sure you don't mind me staying the next couple of nights?'

'Not at all,' said Conrad. 'I could do with the company.' He led Warren into his building and they climbed the stairs. 'What is it exactly you are doing back here? I thought they needed you in Prague?'

'Vernon Sherritt, our Berlin correspondent, has to go back to the States to sort out some family business. His father is very ill – he won't last more than a few days. The paper doesn't want to leave the Berlin office unstaffed, so they sent me back, at least until Vernon returns. I start next week.'

'Interesting time to be here,' said Conrad, unlocking the door to his flat.

'It sure is. Vernon is going to try to return by the end of the month. That's when the balloon goes up, apparently.'

'So you'll be back in Prague when the German tanks roll in?'

'I'm not convinced they will,' Warren said, dumping his bag in Conrad's spare room.

'Really? You don't think Hitler will invade?'

'You bet he will. But your military attaché in Prague thinks the Czechs can hold out for six months, maybe more. You should have seen the Czech army when they mobilized in May. They're very professional and their weapons are all modern. I've been out and seen the border fortifications; they are as good as anything on the Maginot Line.'

'But doesn't the British government think the Czechs have no chance?'

'That's the Ambassador's view. He says they'll be overrun in days. He's just as bad as Henderson here in Berlin. And for some reason your government listens to the diplomat rather than the soldier when it comes to assessing military capabilities. You know, you really should get yourself a new government some time. Do you still have elections in your country?'

'We do, but they don't seem to change anything,' said Conrad. 'Can I get you a drink?'

'Here – I brought you some real whisky,' said Warren. He disappeared to his room and reappeared with a bottle of Johnnie Walker Black Label.

'Excellent,' said Conrad, and poured them each a glass, adding a splash from his soda siphon.

'So, how is Anneliese?' Warren asked, sipping his whisky. 'I hope I'll get to see her.'

'I'm afraid you won't,' said Conrad grimly. 'She's in Sachsen-hausen.'

Warren frowned. 'Oh God, I am sorry. Boy, it doesn't take

you long to realize you are back in the Thousand Year Reich. Why did they take her there? Or was it just one of those random round-ups?

'It was my fault. Her old boyfriend, the Gestapo officer, got jealous of us and had her locked up. But I've just seen someone who thinks he can get her out in the next few days.'

'Is she OK? Have you heard from her?'

'No, I haven't. But I've been told she has a head injury.' He frowned. 'It's quite serious.'

'Is she going to be all right?'

'I hope so,' Conrad said. 'I have to believe so. But in a camp, who knows?' The reason that Conrad had been late to meet Warren was that he had just seen Wilfrid Israel again. Good news had been mixed with bad. The head injury worried Conrad.

Warren shook his head. 'Good luck with that. The sooner you get her out the better.' A thought seemed to strike him. 'Say, I thought I saw some Gestapo boys in this square when the cab dropped me off.'

'What!'

'They weren't in uniform, but I can still identify them a mile off.'

'Were they watching this building?'

'It's hard to say. Why, are you expecting a visit from them?'

'They've picked me up twice so far,' Conrad said. 'I suspect third time is unlucky.' He sprang to his feet and moved over to the window. 'I can't see anyone in the square.' He looked closely at the church, the chestnut tree, the parked cars, the doorways. 'Of course they might be in one of the flats. Wait a moment, I think there's someone in that car!'

'Take it easy. They are probably after someone else.'

'Believe me, Warren, it's never a good idea to take it easy these days. Christ, here they come!'

Two Mercedes drove rapidly into the square and stopped outside Conrad's building. Several men got out, including a large figure Conrad recognized. The door of the car Conrad had spotted opened and the watcher hurried over to the group.

Conrad thought rapidly. He only had a minute at most before the Gestapo reached his flat. Hiding there was impossible. He could try hammering on the door of another occupant of the building, but the Gestapo would be sure to search the whole building if they didn't find him in his own flat. The only way out was the back window, which overlooked a small courtyard. The Gestapo probably didn't have a man in there. Yet.

'Look, Warren. When they come in, say that I left the flat a couple of minutes ago to buy some cigarettes. They'll think I'm hiding out somewhere else in the building.' He moved over to the rear-facing window and opened it. 'Shut this behind me, will you?'

'Sure,' said Warren, still bemused.

'And Warren?'

'Yes?'

'You're welcome to stay here for the next few days. In fact I'd appreciate it if you looked after the place. I might be gone for a while.'

With that he clambered out of the window. Outside was a small ornamental iron balcony, no more than six inches deep, and scarcely wider than the window itself. There was nowhere to crouch out of sight; he would have to move on, and move on fast.

Conrad had spent a few summers in his teens climbing in the Alps with his elder brother, Edward. He was agile and strong and had no fear of heights. But the wall of the building was smooth, the balcony was four floors up and there was nowhere to go. Except perhaps the next balcony along. It would require a leap and a stretch, and then, most importantly, the strength to grab the railings and hang on. Conrad thought he could leap the distance, but wasn't sure he had the strength of grip required. Also the gaps between the bars of the next balcony were quite narrow. He would have to judge it perfectly. There was a chance, a good chance, that he would fall.

He considered the odds. He had wriggled out of Gestapo interrogations twice in the past, couldn't he do it again? On balance, he thought it highly unlikely. Schalke wasn't here to play games with him. He was here to kill him, Conrad was sure of it.

So he jumped.

Arms outstretched, his fingers slipped through the gap in the bars and wrapped around the iron. As his body swung under the balcony, its weight tore at his wrists and hands, and his grip almost broke. But it held. It required all the strength in his forearms to heave himself up on to the balcony. He heard a short scream from within, and through the window recognized one of his neighbours, a woman in her thirties whose husband put on a brown uniform on Sundays. Not the kind of neighbour to hide him from the Gestapo. In fact, as soon as they knocked on her door they would know where he was.

He moved fast. Another balcony. And another. His wrists and forearms were on fire. He wasn't sure whether he had the strength for many more. Fortunately a drainpipe ran down the wall right beside the next balcony. He jumped and his grip held. The drainpipe looked easy to climb, either up or down. Down below was the courtyard with no direct opening out on to the street. The Gestapo would be out there any moment. Up was the roof.

Conrad shinned upwards.

He came to the eaves when he heard a window opening below. He swung himself up on to the tiles. Keeping to the reverse slope of the roof away from the street, he stumbled along for thirty or forty yards until he came to a corner. Another twenty yards, and he slid over the gable of the roof on to the slope facing the street, a small road leading off the square. He could see no Gestapo below, but he could hear the sound of tiles slipping off behind him. They were on the roof.

He searched for a likely drainpipe, but couldn't immediately see one. But there was a plane tree whose branches reached almost to the eaves. Another leap, another scramble and he was hanging from a branch. It seemed to take forever to get down the tree. Any moment the Gestapo might crawl over the gable of the roof and spot him. He jumped the last eight feet on to the pavement, and then ran as silently as he could along the narrow street.

He turned into Bülowstrasse, a larger thoroughfare, and slowed to a rapid walk. A running man was just too conspicuous, but a walking man was too slow. He was debating what to do when a tram swished past him and then ground to a halt at a stop not far ahead. He hopped on just as the doors were closing. Through the window he glimpsed the Gestapo men spilling out on to the street, and swiftly found a seat on the opposite side, away from the pavement, where they wouldn't be able to see him. He took the tram all the way up to the Kurfürstendamm and then changed on to a bus heading east towards Hohenzollernstrasse.

He needed Theo's help.

Ten minutes later he was in Theo's flat, glass of whisky in hand, recounting the story of his escape. Theo listened closely.

'Stay here tonight,' he said. 'I'll speak to Canaris tomorrow, I'm sure he can sort this out. I can't believe the Gestapo would arrest someone they know is one of our agents.'

'That seems to be what they are trying to do,' said Conrad. 'Perhaps Schalke is acting on his own initiative.'

'If he is, he'll be in big trouble,' Theo said. 'That's not a wise thing to do in this country. More whisky?'

He poured out two more glasses of Scotch from a decanter. They were still speculating on what the Gestapo were up to when the doorbell rang. Theo raised his eyebrows, found his belt and buckled it on. With his pistol at his hip, he went downstairs to where the door to his flat opened out on to the street.

There was Schalke with three men behind him. 'Lieutenant von Hertenberg, please let us in,' said Schalke.

Theo stood up straight. 'Why?'

'We are searching for a British spy. A friend of yours.'

'A friend of mine? I don't know any British spy.'

'Conrad de Lancey.'

'You are correct, Herr de Lancey *is* a friend of mine. And, as you know, he is doing some confidential work for the Abwehr.'

'Spying on the Gestapo?'

'What do you mean?' said Theo.

'We have evidence that de Lancey has been spying against senior members of the Gestapo.'

'Ridiculous,' said Theo.

'We went to his flat and he evaded arrest half an hour ago. We think it is possible that he is here.'

'Well, he isn't.'

'Let's see,' said Schalke and raised a hand to push Theo out of the way.

In an instant Theo had pushed him back into the street and drawn his pistol. 'How dare you try to force your way into my home!' Theo screamed. 'I give you my word as a German officer that de Lancey is not in here, and that should be enough. I know what this is all about, you ignorant pig!' Spittle was flying from his lips now and his face was going red, the scar on his jaw showing up a livid white. 'You are jealous of him because he became friendly with your Jewish girlfriend.' Schalke stiffened at the word 'Jewish'. 'The problem with swine like you is that you think with your dick, not with your brains.' Theo's eyes were bulging, and Schalke took two steps back. 'I will permit you to enter my flat if, and only if, I receive a direct order from Admiral Canaris requiring me too. Until then, piss off, the lot of you!'

Tall as Theo was, Schalke was two centimetres taller, yet he was intimidated by the pistol and by the fury. For a moment he looked as if he would stand and argue, then he turned on his heel and, with a quick order to his henchmen, he got into the car and drove slowly off.

'Whew,' said Theo when he returned to Conrad in the flat. 'That certainly got the circulation going.'

'Very impressive,' said Conrad. 'Your face is still red, you know.'

'It's the Prussian breeding,' said Theo. 'Von Hertenbergs have been screaming at ignorant dogs like that for centuries.'

'Well, I'm glad they took your word as a German officer.'

Theo smiled. 'Don't tell Father.'

'Did they leave?'

'Just around the corner. You can be sure they will be watching this place like hawks.' Theo corrected himself. 'Or like cats around a mouse hole.'

'Did he say why they are after me?' Conrad asked.

'Yes. Something about you spying on senior Gestapo officers. Do you know what that is about?'

'No,' said Conrad. 'No idea.'

'Are you sure?' Theo looked at his friend closely. 'No secret mission for our friend Foley?'

'No,' said Conrad. 'And please don't scream at me.'

Theo smiled. 'All right, I won't. It could cause a problem, though. If the Gestapo have a convincing story about you spying on them, it will be difficult for Canaris to stand up for you without provoking a showdown with Heydrich. Which is something he will wish to avoid, at least for the next few weeks until things are resolved one way or the other.'

'So what do I do?' said Conrad.

'Let me think.'

Four hours later, at about midnight, a tall upright figure in the uniform of a lieutenant of the Wehrmacht, cap pulled down over his eyes and carrying a small case, left Theo's flat, strode smartly over to his car, started it up, and pulled off. A minute later four Gestapo officers, led by Klaus Schalke, broke down the door of Theo's apartment and rushed in. Barely two minutes after that they were retreating back on to the street, Theo's invective raining down on them.

Conrad drove the Horch to a street a couple of blocks from the U-Bahn station at Dahlem, an affluent suburb on the Grunewald's eastern edge. Having parked the car, Conrad pulled out his shirt and trousers from the case and changed out of Theo's uniform. He locked the case and the uniform in the boot, and after checking to make sure no one was watching, placed the key behind the rear tyre. Then, glancing at the torn square of map he had brought with him, he tramped the leafy streets of Dahlem until three in the morning. There was no one around, no one to see him. Finally he approached a small, white-painted cottage with a thatched roof that backed on to the forest itself, and knocked softly. A short young man came to the door in his pyjamas. He fumbled for his spectacles and scanned the note Conrad had brought him from Theo and let him in.

* * *

They were three tourists driving around Berlin looking at the sights: a middle-aged woman at the wheel of the powerful Hispano-Suiza with a young man, just a little too old to be her son, sitting next to her, and a middle-aged gentleman in the back. The young man was Theo, the woman was Elisabeth Strünck, a wealthy friend of Oster's, and the gentleman in the back seat was General Count Brockdorff-Ahlefeldt, the commander of the 23rd Division based at Potsdam and General von Witzleben's right-hand man. They had driven slowly up and down Wilhelmstrasse, past the Reich Chancellery, Prinz-Albrecht-Strasse and Göring's Air Ministry, and were now en route to the SS barracks at Lichterfelde. Theo was busy scribbling his notes as von Brockdorff identified the strengths and weaknesses of each building – points which were vulnerable to attack, escape routes that needed to be cut off, estimates of how many men would be required to capture and hold it.

Theo had almost cancelled the outing. The Gestapo's sudden interest in Conrad had disrupted things. The morning after Conrad had slipped through the Gestapo's net, Theo had spoken to Canaris, who in turn had spoken to Heydrich. Heydrich had told Canaris about the rumours of a German politician reaching London, and also that the Gestapo had evidence that Conrad had been seen in Halle spying on them. The admiral decided it was time for the Abwehr to drop its support for Conrad, at least in the eyes of the Gestapo. To Heydrich he had sounded troubled and promised to try to find out what Conrad had been up to and where he was now. And he told Theo to make sure that Conrad laid low and stayed out of the way.

All the agitation meant that Theo was now under Gestapo surveillance. He had shaken off his tail by going for a ride in the

Tiergarten with a friend in the early morning, galloping to the other side of the park and leaving his horse at a stables there. The Gestapo had not yet perfected a technique for surveillance on horseback. Theo had then taken the U-Bahn, and met General von Brockdorff at Yorckstrasse station, where Frau Strünck had picked them both up in her car.

After a hesitant start, plans for the coup were coming together well. Oster was coordinating everything, with Theo supporting him from below and Canaris from above. Halder was still committed to leading the coup, and Beck was helping in the background. Generals von Witzleben and von Brockdorff would deliver the army units around Berlin, and General Hoepner's First Light Division, based in Thuringia, was prepared to cut off the Leibstandarte SS Adolf Hitler Division should it march on Berlin from its position on the Czech border.

The plotters had kept the circle of officers who knew the specifics of their plans to a minimum, but they had a list of those generals, like General Adam on the West Wall, on whom they could count. Theo had drafted detailed orders to be sent out as soon as the coup was launched to the leader of each military district, specifying which buildings were to be secured and who was to be arrested. They wouldn't know how many of the generals would obey these orders until the day of the coup itself, but Oster was optimistic that it would be most of them.

Even the consciences of the conspirators had been taken care of. General Beck had arranged for a number of them to visit the canon of St Hedwig's Cathedral, Father Bernhard Lichtenberg, a persistent critic of the Nazis' treatment of the Jews. The deeply Protestant officers listened to the Catholic as he justified the oath-breaking and even assassination that they were contemplating. For men whose primary motivation was a sense of duty, it was an important preparation.

Politicians, police, army, lawyers, civil servants: they were all ready.

Because of Halder's insistence that they should wait until the country was on the brink of war, the timing of the coup was entirely in the hands of Hitler. The conspirators judged that the most likely date was 14 September, only three days away. The Nuremberg Party rally was in progress, and Hitler was due to make the closing speech on 12 September. There was a good chance that he would use the opportunity to provoke war with Czechoslovakia. Göring had already ranted about a 'miserable pygmy race without culture' that was 'oppressing a cultured people' with 'Moscow and the eternal mask of the Jew devil' behind it. If Hitler decided to act, the conspirators had to be ready to move as soon as he returned to Berlin and ordered the commencement of Case Green.

The sightseers spent a whole day on their tour, visiting all the principal strongpoints that would have to be seized. By the time they had finished, Theo and von Brockdorff had a clear idea of what needed to be done. They were optimistic: it would require more troops than they had initially estimated, but with the tacit support of the police, control of Berlin could be theirs.

Confident that he had no Gestapo tail, Theo went on to Dahlem to see Conrad and the people he had sent him to without warning. The house belonged to an old friend of his from Prussia, Hans-Jürgen von Wedemeyer, and his Swedish wife Elsa. Hans-Jürgen was a lawyer and Elsa was seven months pregnant. Theo had some explaining to do.

Hans-Jürgen greeted Theo at the door. 'Your friend's upstairs, in the attic.'

'I'm so sorry for imposing him on you like this. He was in a bit of a tight spot. You were the best people I could think of.'

'Not at all,' said Hans-Jürgen, although he looked nervous. 'How long will he be staying?'

'A week perhaps? I don't know, we'll have to see.'

'A week?' Hans-Jürgen said dubiously.

'He can stay as long as he wants.' Elsa had appeared, her belly thrusting forward in her summer dress. 'As long as he's careful. He's a charming man, although we've decided we shouldn't know his real name. We call him Jan.'

Theo climbed up the narrow stairs into what was little more than a roof space. There he found Conrad squatting on the floor with a copy of *The Magic Mountain* by Thomas Mann.

'Isn't that banned?' Theo asked.

'I knew there was a reason the Gestapo were after me.'

'How are you doing?'

'Bored to tears. But your friends are nice people. Are the Gestapo still chasing me or did your admiral call them off?'

'I'm afraid he hasn't. In fact, as far as the Gestapo are concerned, the Abwehr are after you too.' Theo explained what Heydrich had said: that Conrad had been seen in Halle spying on the Gestapo.

'Halle? I've never been there in my life. Schalke has set me up,' said Conrad.

'Well, you won't be able to show your face around Berlin any more. We can probably work out an escape route for you back to England.'

'I'd rather stay here until the coup. It should only be a couple of weeks now, shouldn't it?'

'Probably less, if Hitler starts the ball rolling at Nuremberg tomorrow. We're ready.'

'Excellent! I'm happy to help, Theo. I'd like to be involved. Perhaps you'll need someone to talk to the British government?'

'We'll see.'

'Can you track down Warren for me? Tell him to let my family know I'm all right. And can you also ask him to get in touch with Wilfrid Israel and see if he has any news for me?'

'The owner of the department store?' Conrad hadn't mentioned Wilfrid to Theo before.

'That's right. He might have news about Anneliese.'

'All right, I'll speak to him.' Theo began to climb down the stairs. 'I probably won't come here again myself; I don't want to risk leading the Gestapo to you. But I will send a message when I have news. Be patient, Conrad. And please be careful. These are old friends, I would hate them to be caught hiding you.'

Thirty

It was 12 September, the seventh and last day of the Nuremberg rally, the annual celebration of the National Socialist Workers' Party. For a week the Gothic façades and gabled roofs of the medieval town had been draped in crimson flags as tens of thousands – no, hundreds of thousands of men and women marched back and forth in the multitude of uniforms of the Third Reich. There were speeches and music everywhere: Beethoven's *Egmont* overture, the overture to Wagner's *Die Meistersinger*, Hitler's favourite, 'Do You See the Sun Rise in the East?', 'The Heathlands of Brandenburg' and countless other marches. Trains converged on the city from all over Germany bringing eager participants and spectators, and during the frenetic week the crowds and the marchers merged into one: '*Ein Volk*'. Among the goose-stepping thousands strutted the Nazi leaders, accompanied this year for the first time by swaggering Italians in white uniforms and gold tassels.

The last day was 'Army Day', when, three miles outside the city on the Zeppelin Field Stadium, recently built by Albert Speer, infantry, tanks and artillery dashed about amidst bangs and flashes. Overhead the Luftwaffe flew in relentless formations, wave upon wave of modern monoplanes. From one rally to the next the people had seen their country grow more powerful. The tanks were sleeker, faster, bigger, as were the aeroplanes: the old biplanes were banished from the skies.

The Arbeitsdienst, the massed ranks of young labourers goose-stepping along with shovels glinting on their shoulders were still there, but the crowd knew that in a matter of days they would be re-equipped with rifles and ready to fight for their fatherland.

At the end of the day, tens of thousands were gathered to hear the Führer speak, their hearts full of the excitement, the glory, the promise of the Third Reich. On the platform were the Nazi leaders: Goebbels, Göring, Hess, Himmler and the generals who had spent the day watching the army manoeuvres. Behind them were foreign dignitaries, including Lords Brocket and McGowan, and Unity Mitford, Diana Guinness's younger sister, and her mother, Lady Redesdale.

Sitting next to Unity was Veronica de Lancey.

Diana had been to the Nuremberg rallies many times before, but was unable to attend this one because she was seven months pregnant with Oswald Mosley's child. But Veronica had heard so much about it that she wanted to go. It was Unity who had first successfully stalked Hitler in the Carlton Terrace Tea House in Munich and who had introduced Diana to 'Uncle Wolf'. Unity was absolutely besotted by the Führer, so much so that Diana was worried about her mental stability. War with Britain, which seemed inevitable, would tear her apart.

Veronica had arrived in Nuremberg as a detached observer, but her diffident cynicism had been worn away by the rousing music, the pageantry and the handsome men in their stylish uniforms. She hadn't understood a word of the speeches, but the euphoria of the crowd, the mass of thousand upon thousand of ecstatic Germans, had affected her, sweeping her along so that she awaited the appearance of the Führer with as much eagerness as everyone else in the stadium.

The Führer was late; the crowd wasn't restless – he was always late, they knew that – but the anticipation grew. Finally, the catchy 'Badenweiler March' flowed out over the loudspeaker system, and Adolf Hitler appeared on the platform in a blaze of white light, a small man with a long shadow surveying the tens of thousands of upturned, expectant faces. For what seemed an age he saluted the cheering crowd and the wheeling, goose-stepping formations in front of him.

And then he began to speak, very quietly at first, so quietly that every ear in that huge field strained to hear him. The speech grew in volume, as Hitler used every rhetorical device in his armoury. His voice, whether low and halting or loud and insistent, was laden with emotion, an emotion that was reflected and magnified by his audience a hundredfold. His Viennese-suburban accent, which on first hearing had sounded mildly unpleasant to his German listeners, was now familiar and intoxicating. As the speech rolled towards its end, he turned his attention to Czechoslovakia.

'The misery of the Sudeten Germans is indescribable. The Czech state has sought to annihilate them. As human beings they are oppressed and scandalously treated in an intolerable fashion.'

Horror and outrage rippled through the crowd.

'I have not demanded that Germany should subjugate three and a half million Frenchmen, or that we should sub-jugate three and a half million Englishmen: my demand is that the subjugation of three and a half million Germans in Czechoslovakia shall stop, and that in its place they will have the free right of self-determination. If the English and the French support the continued subjugation of the Sudeten Germans, then their decision will have serious consequences! I serve peace best if I leave no one in any doubt on this point.'

Then, his face flushed and his eyes bulging, his voice rose to a crescendo as he bellowed: 'The German Reich has been asleep for long enough! The German people are now awake and are stepping forward to accept their rightful crown of the millennium!'

The crowd erupted into a surge of *Sieg Heil*s as the speech echoed around the stadium and beyond, across Germany, across the continent of Europe to Paris, London and Prague.

They heard it in the Sudetenland. Spontaneous riots, long planned by the Sudeten German Party under the leadership of Konrad Henlein, broke out all over the region. But it rained, hard and long and cold. The Czechs declared martial law, but showed restraint and discipline. There was no massacre of Sudeten Germans; in fact casualties were low on both sides. The revolt spluttered and fizzled out.

In Paris, the Cabinet was split on whether to stand by France's treaty obligation to the Czechs in the event of a German invasion. Georges Bonnet, the Foreign Minister, argued forcefully that peace should be preserved at any price. Édouard Daladier, the Prime Minister, dithered. Telegrams were sent to Moscow, to Washington and to London.

In London, Chamberlain knew that Britain was entering a decisive phase in its history, and it was incumbent on him as Prime Minister to be decisive. German troops were massed on the Czech border, and it seemed highly likely that German tanks would roll into the Sudetenland within days, perhaps within hours.

The information he had was frustratingly contradictory. Both Britain and Germany were rearming rapidly. The assessment of the majority of his advisers was that Britain needed another year at least to be ready for war, and that in an early war the German Luftwaffe would bomb Prague, Paris and London to obliteration within sixty days. Others thought that, on the contrary, Germany was still too weak to overwhelm the combined forces of Britain, France and Czechoslovakia.

It looked as if the plot to overthrow Hitler that von Kleist had revealed to the British government was more real than Chamberlain had originally thought. All over Europe, from Moscow to The Hague, German military attachés and diplomats were whispering to their British counterparts that Britain must stand by Czechoslovakia. Two more emissaries, a retired colonel named Böhm-Tettelbach and Theo Kordt, the diplomat at the German Embassy in London, had had quiet discussions with British officials, Kordt even speaking to Lord Halifax himself in 10 Downing Street. Indications were that the coup could be launched at any time, according to some reports possibly even that very day.

But relying on disaffected generals to save Europe from war seemed extremely risky to Chamberlain. Who knew what would happen if their coup were allowed to proceed? Chamberlain at least believed he could deal with Hitler; he did not relish the prospect of negotiating with unknown generals, traitors, throwbacks to the warmongering imperial Germany of the last war. He could not permit the plotters to throw a spanner in the works now: the time had come for him to seize the initiative. He, and he alone, could win peace for Europe.

It was time for Plan Z.

Unfortunately, Sir Nevile Henderson had counselled against Chamberlain's original plan of flying unannounced to Berlin. There were all kinds of practical problems, one being that his aeroplane might be shot down by the Luftwaffe, and the other that Hitler was planning to go to Berchtesgaden after the Nuremberg rally, so he wouldn't be in Berlin to receive him. So, after frantic discussions among those few members of government that knew of Plan Z's existence, a telegram was drafted for Hitler:

IN VIEW OF THE INCREASINGLY CRITICAL SITUATION,
I PROPOSE TO COME OVER AT ONCE TO SEE YOU WITH
A VIEW TO TRYING TO FIND A PEACEFUL SOLUTION. I
PROPOSE TO COME ACROSS BY AIR AND AM READY TO
START TOMORROW. PLEASE INDICATE EARLIEST TIME YOU
COULD SEE ME AND SUGGEST PLACE OF MEETING. SHOULD
BE GRATEFUL FOR YOUR EARLY REPLY.

NEVILLE CHAMBERLAIN

The reply came the next afternoon. The Führer would be happy to receive the Prime Minister at the Berghof, his mountain retreat in Bavaria, the following day, 15 September, and he was invited to bring Mrs Chamberlain if he so wished. Chamberlain informed the King, the Cabinet, and then the people what he was about to do.

The plotters were ready. Canaris and his inner core of advisers, including Oster and Theo, were waiting at the Abwehr's offices. They expected Case Green to be put into motion that afternoon, the 14th. This would be followed by Hitler's return to Berlin from Bavaria, at which point the coup would be launched, General von Witzleben would arrest Hitler and the carefully prepared legal case against him would be put in motion. The army, the police, the lawyers, the politicians: they were all ready to undertake their assigned rolls.

It was a long afternoon. Theo checked and double-checked the orders that were to be sent out to the regional commands of the Wehrmacht and the police the moment that the coup was announced. Oster found it impossible to sit still and paced around the offices trying to keep himself busy. Only Canaris remained calm.

By eight o'clock there was no news and so the Abwehr officers stayed on to dinner at the Tirpitzufer. The conversation was stilted; any subject seemed irrelevant compared to the enormity of what lay ahead of them. In twenty-four hours, forty-eight at the most, the tyrant would be overthrown.

Dinner was interrupted by a message for Canaris from the War Ministry next door. All eyes were on him: was this the announcement they had all been waiting for? Canaris opened the envelope and scanned the sheet of paper within. His already pale face went white.

'What is it, excellency?' asked Oster.

'Chamberlain has announced that he will fly to see Hitler at the Berghof tomorrow to discuss a solution to the Czechoslovak situation.'

It took a moment for the news to sink in. 'A solution?' Theo said. 'You mean he's going to give up the Sudetenland without a fight.'

'It sounds very much as if he is,' the admiral agreed, putting down his knife and fork. 'I'm sorry. I seem to have lost my appetite.'

Chamberlain flew to Munich the next day in a silver Lockheed Electra. It was the first time he had ever been in an aeroplane, and he took no agenda, no interpreter and no wife, just his special adviser Sir Horace Wilson, his umbrella and the conviction that peace was achievable. Henderson and von Ribbentrop, the German Foreign Minister, met him at the airport and joined him on the train to Berchtesgaden. Chamberlain was gratified by his reception by the crowd in the small Bavarian town; it confirmed his hunch that he was popular in Germany. The Berghof was high above the town on the slopes of the Obersalzberg, a mountain dividing Germany from Austria. Unfortunately that day the spectacular views were shrouded in cloud.

Chamberlain thought his visit a success. Although he found Hitler the commonest little dog, he felt that his temperament was one of excitability rather than insanity. The British Prime Minister prided himself on his ability to understand the common man, and he was quite sure that he had made a favourable impression on the Führer. To Hitler's assertion that he would start a world war if necessary to save the Sudeten Germans from Czech oppression, Chamberlain had said that he would need to consult with his colleagues, but for himself it was immaterial whether the Sudeten Germans stayed in Czechoslovakia or were included in Germany. In doing this he had held out the prospect of negotiations for Herr Hitler, negotiations that would meet Germany's most important demands and that would thus bring peace.

Hitler thought Chamberlain was *'ein Arschloch'*.

Thirty-one

Klaus was trembling with excitement as he entered Heydrich's office. What he had to tell him should make the chief sit up and take notice.

'Ah, Schalke, any luck with the German politician who went to London?'

'Not directly, Herr Gruppenführer. We haven't been able to find a record of any politician leaving the country whose movements cannot be verified. But...'

'But?'

'But I have stumbled upon something that might be connected. A source whom I feel sure is reliable tells me that there is a conspiracy afoot to remove Hitler as soon as he orders the invasion of Czechoslovakia.'

Heydrich frowned. 'Who is this source?'

Klaus told him.

Heydrich shook his head. 'It is just a rumour. If we jumped every time we heard a rumour that someone was unhappy with the Führer, we'd have the whole country locked up by now.'

'There are more details,' Klaus said. 'The plans are at a very advanced stage. The army is involved, and the Abwehr, and the Foreign Office.'

'And who is the leader of this revolt?'

'We don't know,' Klaus admitted. 'But Lieutenant von

Hertenberg of the Abwehr is involved. As is Conrad de Lancey, the British spy we are searching for.'

'Why am I not surprised to hear that name?' Heydrich said.

'We know de Lancey is a spy,' Klaus replied. 'Now we know what he's really up to.'

'I thought he was investigating my ancestry? I don't see what that has to do with a plot against the Führer.'

'He seems to be involved in all kinds of things.'

'Is Göring involved in this plot?'

'Not from what I've heard. I think de Lancey might have been pulling the wool over our eyes with that one.'

'Or over the Abwehr's eyes. Admiral Canaris more or less admitted to me that de Lancey had deceived them. They are looking for him as hard as we are.'

'My understanding is that the Abwehr are involved in the plot too.'

'Admiral Canaris?'

'I don't know how high up it goes,' Klaus admitted.

'You don't know much, do you?'

Klaus's excitement had turned to frustration. 'But what if this information is accurate? We're not talking about a lone nutcase here. This is a widespread conspiracy against the Reich. We can't just ignore it.'

'What do you want me to do, Schalke?' said Heydrich, his own frustration showing. 'Throw every general into jail? Arrest Canaris? Even arresting Hertenberg would cause a stink. We were lucky to get away with the Fritsch case. The Führer needs the army now – he's just about to start a world war, if you hadn't noticed. The last thing he will want is us storming around the Bendlerstrasse locking up everyone in sight.'

'If there is a putsch and the Führer is removed, you know what will happen to the Gestapo,' Klaus said.

Heydrich steepled his long fingers. 'All right, Schalke. Get me some more evidence, something in writing, preferably. I want specifics: names, dates, plans. And find this spy de Lancey. I am beginning to share your distaste for the man.'

Theo paid another visit to the Wedemeyers in Dahlem. There was no way of avoiding it: he had an important message for Conrad and he had to deliver it himself. He had used the same manoeuvre with his horse in the Tiergarten to lose the two Gestapo whom he had spotted on his tail. He had then taken a roundabout route, backtracking several times on the U-Bahn, before ending up at the Wedemeyers' house. It all took a long time.

Elsa let Theo in and once again he climbed the stairs to the attic. Conrad was lying on his tiny bed. *The Magic Mountain* was a thick book, but Conrad had nearly finished it.

'How are things?' Theo asked.

'Still bored. Elsa is teaching me Swedish. It's not that different from Danish, so I am picking it up fairly quickly.'

'I didn't know you spoke Danish?'

'It's hard to understand the Schleswig-Holstein question without it.'

'I'm sure,' said Theo. 'Have you stayed here the whole time?'

'I go out for long nocturnal walks in the forest,' said Conrad. 'Otherwise I'd go insane.'

'I hope you are being careful?'

'Very careful. I'm keeping well clear of the gardener: apparently he's the local *Blockwart*.'

'You've been in this country long enough not to underestimate the danger of the nosey neighbour,' Theo said. 'I told you these people are my friends.'

'I know. Have you seen Warren?' Conrad asked.

'A couple of times. The Gestapo picked him up after you ran off, but they didn't rough him up. They are careful with foreign journalists, especially Americans. He's decided to stay in your flat while he is in Berlin. I hope that's all right with you?'

'Absolutely. That's good of him. Has he had a chance to speak to Wilfrid Israel?'

'Yes,' said Theo.

Conrad could tell from the way Theo enunciated that one word that there was something wrong. 'What is it, Theo? It's Anneliese, isn't it? He can't get her out.'

'It's worse than that,' said Theo.

'Her head?'

Theo nodded. 'She's dead, I'm afraid, Conrad. Wilfrid Israel heard it from the camp commandant at Sachsenhausen. I'm sorry.'

Ever since Conrad had heard about Anneliese's head injury he had feared this. His face froze, but he was crumbling inside. He couldn't speak; he was fighting to contain his emotion in front of Theo.

Theo touched his arm. The sympathy in that touch was over-powering: Conrad almost cracked. He tried to say something, but couldn't. He needed to be alone so he could deal with this; he didn't want to fall apart with Theo watching him.

Theo understood. 'Would you like me to go?'

Conrad nodded, blinking.

'I'll try and see you this evening, if I can. She was a wonderful woman.'

Conrad nodded again, and Theo was gone.

Tears streamed down his cheeks. Conrad couldn't remember the time he had last cried – however miserable he had felt after the mess with Veronica he had held it together. But not now. Not now.

He swore softly to himself, and then louder and louder. He

hit the bed, pounding the mattress so hard that the bed creaked and the springs rang out.

He had to get out of there. He put on his shoes and stumbled downstairs, past Elsa and out of the sitting room, through the French windows into the garden. He strode across the lawn to the fence, climbed over and plunged into the forest.

He didn't look where he was going, he just charged deeper into the woods, head down. Where there was a choice of paths, he took the smaller one. It had rained overnight, and there was still the smell of damp leaves in the air as the wood dried out under the September sunshine. Occasionally he passed purposeful walkers who offered him a cheery 'Heil Hitler'. He ignored them.

How had she died? Beaten by some SS bully? Her head staved in with the butt of a rifle? A fist? His imagination conjured up images of a broken and bleeding Anneliese, lying helpless on the dusty ground of a concentration camp.

And then he thought of her as he had known her. The hours piled upon hours that they had spent together, talking. How being with someone had never felt so right to him before. He remembered the way she stood; her hair, her smile, her green eyes, her smell; her irony – how she teased him gently, invigorating him. He remembered how her skin felt cool under his hot touch. He remembered her vitality, her spirit and also the vulnerability that she so jealously guarded and that he alone was allowed to see. At that moment he could remember everything about her with total clarity. He wanted to hold the moment forever; he had a terrible fear that from now on his memory of her would fade and fray until only scraps remained.

Of course it was his fault that she had died. The second that they had realized exactly how obsessed Klaus Schalke was with her he should have backed off. Somehow he could have arranged for her to leave Germany; and even if he hadn't succeeded she would still be alive. He was too selfish; he had simply wanted to spend as much time with her as possible and now he was paying the price.

What was he thinking? She was the one who had paid the price.

He wanted to get right away from Berlin. From England too. Start a new life. Find a hole a long way away that he could crawl into. America, perhaps? No, that wasn't far enough. India? New Zealand – now that was a long long way away.

Then, almost as if he could hear her, he thought about what Anneliese would have made of the situation. Do something practical, she would have said, something that would make a difference. While there was a chance that he could help Theo and his friends get rid of Hitler, he couldn't run away. He had to help in any way he could: if necessary he would kill the dictator himself. His pulse quickened at the thought.

Ultimately one man was responsible for Anneliese's death, and for the deaths of thousands of other Germans. Adolf Hitler. For most of his life, Conrad had shied away from killing, but now he remembered Anneliese's words when they were discussing whether he should help von Kleist. It was his duty: to himself, to Anneliese, to humanity.

Someone had to kill Hitler, and kill him soon before the whole of Europe was engulfed in his evil. Conrad was determined that that person should be he.

And, while he was at it, he would get even with Klaus Schalke as well.

Otto Barsch admired the climbing rose he had just cut back. The rose had had a wonderful summer, and had now conquered the whole length of the arbour at the back of the garden. The garden was not Otto's; it belonged to a civil servant in the Transport Ministry. When Otto had started working in the garden four years before, the two boys of the house had still spent most of their summer holidays there with their friends. Now they were older they went further afield for their fun.

Otto hadn't always been a gardener. He came from Breslau in Silesia. He had fought in the war, displaying the commonplace bravery of the ordinary soldier who managed somehow to keep his sanity in the hell of flying metal, mud and death. Afterwards he had taken a job in a factory manufacturing lifting equipment for the coal mines, but in 1930 he, along with all his colleagues, had been thrown out on to the street. He had migrated to Berlin, and had spent a couple of years near starvation before securing odd jobs as a gardener in this quarter of Dahlem. He had discovered a natural talent, and the householders seemed to like his air of steady reliability and his genial but respectful conversation, so he now worked for most of the people on that particular road. He didn't earn much money, scarcely enough to keep his wife and his daughter in their tiny tenement room.

The tough couple of years of the early thirties had been brightened by membership of the Nazi Party and the SA. Although not a violent man by nature, he couldn't help but be invigorated by the street battles with the communists, and when Hitler came to power in January 1933, his happiness knew no bounds. With his brown uniform, which he religiously wore on Sundays and at every other opportunity, came a certain power and status that gave Otto a much-needed boost. But after the initial euphoria, things had not gone quite so well for him. The SA had been humiliated during the Night of the Long Knives in 1934, and the rearmament boom of the 1930s had somehow left him behind, barely scratching a living among the tulips, roses and hydrangeas of the suburban gardens.

He took his duty as a Nazi and a German seriously, and he was proud to be the *Blockwart* for the street. This was a semi-official position, the holder of which had a duty to pass on any suspicious or anti-social behaviour in his block to higher authorities. This caused him some anguish, as he liked the people he worked for. When a young clerk had been whisked away after Otto had overheard him listening to the BBC, Otto had felt rotten. In particular he liked the Wedemeyers, and Frau von Wedemeyer, who, although not a German, was looking the picture of a good Aryan mother-to-be, with her blonde plaited hair, her rosy cheeks and her full belly.

So he hadn't said anything when he had spotted the footprints by the fence at the back of the garden, or the light on in the attic. But when he peered through the beech hedge to the next-door garden and saw a young athletic man brazenly walk out of the house and leap over the back fence in broad daylight, he decided he ought to report it. It was his duty.

Theo felt terrible as he left the Dahlem house. Conrad had had a very rough time since he had come to Germany. Theo liked Anneliese, admired her even, in a way he could never admire Sophie. For a short spell, far too brief, Conrad had been a lucky man. This madness could not be allowed to continue. Perhaps Chamberlain's negotiations with Hitler would fail, or he would miraculously change his mind, and the coup could go ahead. Theo desperately hoped so.

He took the U-Bahn across the city to a small café around the corner from St Hedwig's Hospital, where he had arranged to meet Sophie. He was forty minutes late, but she was still waiting for him, as he knew she would be, in her crisp nurse's uniform with a cup of coffee and a newspaper in front of her.

'I'm sorry, Sophie,' he said. 'Things are frantic at the War Office. I hope you're not late for work.'

Sophie smiled, pleased to see him. 'I've got ten minutes, and it sounded important.' She tapped the newspaper she was reading, the *Berliner Tageblatt*. 'I'm sure things are busy, with everything that's going on in the Sudetenland.'

Theo took the paper. Women and children mown down by Czech armoured cars, screamed the headline.

He tossed it back on the table. 'I don't know how they can write this rubbish.'

'Don't you believe it's true?'

'Of course it's not.'

Sophie frowned. 'What about that one, then?' The headline on the abandoned paper at the table next to them was clearly visible. *Bloody regime – new Czech murders of Germans.* 'And I have heard Henlein on the wireless. He says he has *seen* the Czech army committing atrocities. And he's there.'

'Of course he does,' said Theo impatiently. 'And anyway, he's not there any more, he's run away back to Germany. The truth is the Sudeten uprising has fizzled out in the rain. And from what we are hearing, the Czechs have actually shown restraint.'

'So the newspapers are lying?' Sophie's big blue eyes showed confusion, but also a hint of anger.

'Basically, yes.'

'Theo, sometimes I think you are too clever,' she said. 'You don't see the things that are right in front of your nose. The Sudetenland is German; it's full of Germans, who just want to be a part of their own country. We have to help them. My father thinks we should invade Czechoslovakia, and I think he's right. It's only justice.'

'So your father is an expert on international relations, is

he?' said Theo. 'Why does he care? There aren't many fish in Czechoslovakia, you know.'

Sophie reddened. 'He may be a fishmonger, but he is an intelligent man who is interested in these things. Yes, he's just an ordinary German, he's not a general like your father, but he has common sense. And he fought for his country in the war. In a trench, not in a *Schloss* thirty kilometres behind the lines.'

Theo bit back his anger. 'I've told you before, Sophie, you can't believe what you read in the papers. Especially these days.'

'I'm going to be late,' said Sophie. 'You said you had something to tell me. Is that it?'

'Anneliese is dead,' Theo said baldly. As soon as the words were out of his mouth, he regretted their bluntness.

Sophie froze. She blinked, and a tear leaked out of first one eye and then the other. 'Oh, no.' It wasn't a cry. It was little more than a whisper.

Theo reached over the table and held her hand in his.

'She wasn't even Jewish,' Sophie said, the tears flowing freely. 'She was a Christian, really. They made a mistake. A dreadful mistake.'

Theo withdrew his hand. 'So it would have been OK if she was one hundred per cent Jewish?'

Anger flashed in Sophie's moist eyes. 'She was my friend, Theo. Leave me alone!'

Theo let her blunder out of the café, thinking he should have handled her better. But sometimes he just didn't have the patience to put up with the ignorance he saw all around him. He fought the temptation to order a quick brandy, paid the bill and left.

Twenty metres down the street from the café a man stepped out of the doorway and set off after Theo. He had picked Theo up that morning, catching him as he brought his horse into the

Tattersalls' stables by the zoo in the Tiergarten. The Abwehr officer really had been foolish to think the same dodge would work twice.

Thirty-two

Lord Oakford emerged from the Travellers' Club in Pall Mall and decided to walk all the way home across Green Park, Hyde Park and Kensington Gardens. He had a lot to think about. He had just had luncheon with Sir Robert Vansittart, who had filled him in on the comings and goings between London and Germany, and just as important, between Whitehall and No. 10. Both Van and Lord Oakford had been at Eton with Lord Halifax. Van had shone in comparison to Wood, as Halifax was known then, being a member of 'Pop', the exclusive club for the most popular boys, and an Oppidan Scholar. Although Halifax had caught up later on – he had after all won a fellowship to All Souls College in Oxford – Van had never quite got out of the habit of looking down his nose at the six-foot-eight-inch peer, something that had not helped their relationship when Halifax was Foreign Secretary and Van was his adviser. But Van knew Halifax well, and what he had had to say about him had made Lord Oakford think.

London was alive with preparations for war. Hyde Park resembled a building site, with soldiers energetically digging trenches everywhere. Barrage balloons were floating up and down the Thames from the most unlikely places, and the snouts of anti-aircraft guns pointed skywards. Extra editions of the newspapers were whipped from vendors within minutes of their being delivered. These announced government plans to issue gas masks to every adult, child and baby in the land.

Lord Oakford wished that he could speak to his son about what he had just heard over luncheon. He had no idea where Conrad was: only that he was in hiding somewhere in or around Berlin. Lord Oakford had a feeling that something could still be done to save the situation but it would have to be done rapidly, and Conrad was the man to do it. Through Warren Sumner he had a means of communicating with him, but he really needed to discuss things face-to-face. For a mad moment he thought of flying over to Berlin himself. But that would attract too much attention. Also, he would have to ask the government's permission, which would be exceedingly awkward, and almost certainly wouldn't be granted.

But someone had to make contact with Conrad. Someone whom both he and Conrad trusted, who was intelligent enough to pass on complicated messages, and above all who wouldn't raise the suspicions of the German authorities. The answer came to him as he passed the round pond in Kensington Gardens. As soon as he reached the house in Kensington Square he telephoned Chilton Coombe and spoke to Millie, telling her to come to London by the first available train and to bring her passport.

The follow-up meeting between Chamberlain and Hitler took place at Bad Godesberg, on the Rhine, on 22 September. It all started well enough. Chamberlain was met at Cologne Aerodrome by a guard of honour and a fine band playing 'God Save the King'. He was driven from there to the Petersberg Hotel, one of the most luxurious in Germany. Each room had its own bathroom filled with the products of Cologne: scent, soap, bath salts and shaving equipment. A balcony ran the length of the hotel, and Chamberlain and Henderson spent the following morning admiring the view of the Rhine, glimmering in the warm Indian summer sunshine, and discussing the forthcoming talks.

Hitler had taken up residence in the Hotel Dreesen on the other side of the river, and at five o'clock in the afternoon Chamberlain, Henderson and Ivone Kirkpatrick crossed the Rhine by ferry under the eyes of thousands of onlookers lining the banks. It felt rather like Henley or the University Boat Race. Hitler met Chamberlain at the entrance of the hotel, and proceedings began without delay.

Chamberlain started by laying out all that he had achieved since their meeting at Berchtesgaden. He had managed to obtain the agreement of the British Cabinet, the French government and most crucially the Czech government on the peaceful transfer of the Sudetenland to Germany. Now all that remained was to discuss how to achieve this transfer, and once that had been settled to put in place guarantees for peace in Europe.

Then things went wrong.

Hitler announced that everything Chamberlain had done so far, all his efforts at finding a compromise over Czecho-slovakia, were now of no use. Chamberlain was shocked. Having worked so hard to accede to Hitler's demands he was being told that he hadn't gone far enough. Hitler went on to explain that his friendship with Hungary and Poland demanded that their claims on Czechoslovakia must be met also.

This was plainly ridiculous, but Chamberlain wasn't about to give up. He had come to Bad Godesberg to secure peace for Europe, and he wasn't going to let Hitler's intransigence sway him from that goal. A long, tough twenty-four hours of negotiations lay ahead for the two leaders.

Klaus polished his glasses for the tenth time that morning. Two things preoccupied him. One was how to obtain written proof from his informant about the planned coup. The other was to find de Lancey. He strongly suspected the two problems might be linked. He had mixed feelings about this: on the one hand he was gratified that de Lancey did seem to be a genuine danger to the Reich and hence a legitimate target; on the other it meant that if Klaus found him he would be expected to interrogate him. Klaus didn't want to take the risk. If he found de Lancey, he would shoot him there and then and deal with the consequences later. He didn't want to give de Lancey the slightest chance of slipping away yet again.

On his desk was the report from the single Gestapo agent who had managed to stick to von Hertenberg two days before. Klaus suspected that the answer to one if not both his problems lay with the Abwehr officer. The agent had done well, but hadn't seen von Hertenberg meet de Lancey or any of the possible conspirators. Von Hertenberg had visited Count Helldorf, the Chief of the Berlin Police and a good Nazi. That must certainly be on Abwehr business. He had also visited a young couple, the Wedemeyers, in Dahlem. Von Wedemeyer, like von Hertenberg, was the son of a Pomeranian Junker. He was a mild-mannered civil servant with a clean bill of health, but it might be worth doing more checks on him.

There was a light tap on the door.

'Enter!'

The door opened and the mousy figure of Gertrude Lüttgen crept in. '*Heil Hitler*, Herr Kriminalrat.'

Klaus smiled. '*Heil Hitler*. What have you got for me?'

'It's probably nothing, Herr Kriminalrat, but I was just wondering whether this report from a *Blockwart* in Dahlem might interest you.'

Klaus replaced his glasses and quickly scanned the sheet of paper and grinned. He reached for the telephone. 'Dressel? Get four men and meet me outside immediately. I think we have found de Lancey.'

* * *

A number of small lakes were dotted around the Grunewald. At the edge of one of these, Conrad waited, sitting with his back against a tree just a few yards off the path. He hoped that he was inconspicuous without giving the impression to a passer-by who spotted him that he was actually hiding. Hans-Jürgen von Wedemeyer had arrived home from work the previous evening with a message from Theo that he wanted to meet Conrad at this spot rather than risk seeing him at the house again. Conrad was curious about why Theo wanted to see him. But his thoughts kept turning back to Anneliese.

At one o'clock precisely Conrad heard some jaunty whistling in the distance. It was a tune he recognized, 'The Lincolnshire Poacher', sounding so English in the middle of this German forest. He scrambled to his feet and when he emerged on to the path he saw Theo strolling along next to the tall, rangy figure of his sister.

'Millie!' He gave her a hug. 'What on earth are you doing here?'

'I thought this was the perfect time for a holiday,' said Millie. 'What with no tourists around on account of the world war.'

'*Auf Deutsch*,' admonished Theo, but he was smiling.

'Sorry,' said Conrad in that language. There was no one else around, but Theo was quite right. And Millie's German was almost as good as his. 'But seriously, Millie, this is not a good time for an English girl to be in Germany.'

'I know. When I got my visa from the German Embassy in London, I had to tell them I was visiting a very sick aunt in Hamburg. So I flew there and took the train. Aeroplanes are just as dreadful as I thought they would be. And do you know what they call the Hamburg to Berlin express? The *Flying*

Hamburger. It doesn't quite have the same ring as the *Flying Scotsman,* does it?'

'Father sent you.'

'That's right. He would have come himself, but that would have been too obvious. But how are you? Herr von Hertenberg says you are on the run from the Gestapo?'

'They haven't caught me yet.'

'Well, do be careful.' Millie's expression was full of concern. 'Isn't there any way you can get out of the country?'

'I want to stay for a bit. There's some business I have to sort out first. So what did Father want to tell me?'

Millie glanced at Theo and blushed.

'It's all right, you can speak in front of Theo.'

Millie smiled sweetly at Theo. 'I'm sorry, Herr von Hertenberg, but my father was quite explicit. I must speak to my brother alone.'

'I quite understand,' said Theo with his most charming smile. 'I'll walk around the lake.'

Conrad and Millie found a bench on a small patch of sand next to the lake and watched Theo stride out around the perimeter. The water was dark and silent, and the reflection of an old white hunting lodge glimmered dully near the far shore. Through the trees and the reed beds they caught glimpses of a couple of other walkers, but there was no one within earshot.

'Father has been talking to his friends in Whitehall,' Millie began. 'He says that Chamberlain is determined to negotiate with Hitler, come what may, and to give away whatever is required to secure peace. Father says he can't be dissuaded but he might be overruled.'

'Overruled. How?'

'In Cabinet. A majority of the Cabinet has been in favour of appeasement, but that majority is shaky. Some members are beginning to wonder whether Chamberlain's trust in Hitler is misplaced. In particular, Father's old friend Lord Halifax.'

'I thought he was an appeaser through and through, just like Chamberlain?'

'There's no doubt he wants peace. But in the last couple of weeks he has been suggesting a tougher stand on Czechoslovakia. Two weeks ago, while Hitler was at the Nuremberg rally, Halifax persuaded the Prime Minister to allow him to send a strongly worded warning to Hitler that if Germany were to invade Czechoslovakia, war with Britain and France would inevitably result.'

'Excellent!' said Conrad.

'I'm afraid it's not,' said Millie. 'Apparently, when the message reached the British Ambassador to Berlin, a dreadful chap called Henderson, he refused to deliver it!'

'I've met Henderson,' said Conrad. 'He is awful.'

'He said Halifax's message would tip Hitler over the edge. Chamberlain was all too happy to go along with Henderson. But Halifax is in two minds and Father believes that the rest of the Cabinet are looking to him for a lead. If he opposes Chamberlain, then they will too.'

'Is there any chance of that?'

'I don't know if you have seen the newspapers, but Chamberlain flew to Bad Godesberg yesterday to talk to Hitler. Just as I was leaving London, Father was hearing rumours that the meeting had gone very badly. Hitler has been moving the goalposts; as soon as Chamberlain makes a concession, Hitler refuses to be satisfied and asks for more. This is causing some disquiet in the Cabinet.'

'So it should,' said Conrad.

Millie glanced at her brother nervously. 'Now, Father tells me that there is some secret plot to ditch Hitler.'

'There is,' said Conrad. 'Theo is involved. He was in on it from the beginning.'

'Well, our government doesn't know what to make of this. Chamberlain doesn't want anything to do with it, but Father believes that Halifax can be convinced that if Britain stands by Czechoslovakia, Hitler will be overthrown.'

'What will it take to convince him?'

'That's why I'm here,' said Millie. 'All kinds of Germans have been talking to the British government at different levels, but they are all too junior. Father thinks that if one of the leaders of the plot spoke to Lord Halifax directly, in secret, then he might well be convinced. But it must be a leader. Someone with credibility, someone Halifax will have heard of, someone who is giving the orders, not another message boy.'

'I'll talk to them about it.'

'Father says that if an unannounced aeroplane tries to land at Manston Aerodrome in Kent at night in the next week it won't be shot down. If you can fix something up, get Warren Sumner to send him a telegram mentioning the day you expect whoever it is to arrive. But do it as soon as you can. There are some very important decisions to be taken over the next few days.'

Conrad walked back through the forest towards the Wedemeyers' house. He felt invigorated. It had been good to see Millie, and to hear the news from his father. He felt that he was once again contributing something to the effort, doing something for Anneliese. Theo was taking Millie back to the station so she could return to Hamburg. Her intention was to take the first flight she could back to London; if anyone asked, she would say that her aunt had staged an unexpected recovery. Theo planned to meet Conrad by the lake again at six o'clock to take him to see his boss, Colonel Oster. Conrad decided to risk sneaking back into the house during daylight, although Theo once again warned him to be careful.

The warning worked. As Conrad drew near to the back fence of the garden, he thought he had better just check that the gardener wasn't working there or in either of the neighbouring properties. The Wedemeyers' house was clear, as was the house to the left, but as he crept along the trees to the right he heard a familiar voice.

Klaus Schalke.

Conrad didn't stop to look. He just slipped away.

He spent the afternoon lurking in the bushes by the lake, his thoughts lurching from Anneliese to Elsa and her husband and baby. He knew Elsa was in the house when he left; she would almost certainly have been arrested by now for harbouring him. He remembered what had happened to Joachim: they wouldn't treat a pregnant woman like that, would they?

Of course they would.

How had they found out about him? Perhaps the notorious gardener had seen him after all. It was all very well putting himself in danger, but not the Wedemeyers: they were innocent people, brave people who had helped out a friend of a friend.

Twice he saw Gestapo walk rapidly past; once he recognized the red hair of Dressel, Schalke's sidekick. He felt safe in the bushes; it would take an infantry division to search the whole of the Grunewald. It was only after he had been sitting there smugly for two hours that the thought of dogs occurred to him. Fortunately he saw nothing more threatening than a couple of dachshunds out for their afternoon walk.

Theo was furious when Conrad told him about the Gestapo. 'I told you to be careful!'

'I was!'

'Then how did Schalke find you?'

'How am I suppose to know? Perhaps he followed you to the Wedemeyers' house.'

'There was no one on my tail, I checked.'

'You can never be sure of that.'

'How do you know? Are you some kind of expert on surveillance?' Theo realized he had raised his voice, and tried to control himself. 'They will probably be in Gestapo cells as we speak. Elsa might lose the baby. Hell, she might lose her husband!'

'I know,' said Conrad. He took a deep breath. 'Look. If it was me who gave them away, I'm very sorry, more sorry than I can say. I will always be grateful for their generosity and their courage.'

Theo pursed his lips. 'With luck, they'll be all right. I told them if they were arrested to admit that I had asked them to hide you, and to say that they thought I was some kind of spy for the German government and so they thought they were helping the Reich. It has the merit of being the truth.'

'Let's hope it works.'

'Come on,' said Theo. 'Follow me.' They crept further into the woods, avoiding the paths, until they emerged at a bridleway. It was getting dark. Theo checked his watch.

'Oster should be here in six minutes. We'll wait a few metres off the path.'

They found a thick bush, and squatted behind it.

'We can't see him from here,' Conrad said.

'We'll hear him,' said Theo. 'He's coming on horseback.

They sat in silence for a minute, waiting.

'The last time I saw your sister she was only fifteen,' Theo said. 'She was pretty then. But now... I love her accent, by the way.'

'Careful,' Conrad said. 'She's much too good for you.'

'I'm sure she is,' said Theo. 'I expect she has men swarming around her like flies.'

'She does rather,' said Conrad. 'But she does a good job of swatting them away.'

'Hmm.'

Conrad grinned. But he wasn't sure about Theo wooing Millie. His friend had many good points, but Conrad didn't like the way Theo took Sophie for granted, and although he would probably treat Millie with more respect because of her class, it was the kind of respect that was only skin deep.

'What are you going to do with Hitler?' Conrad asked. 'When you have captured him.'

In the grey light of dusk Conrad could see Theo smile. 'There has been some discussion on that subject. Admiral Canaris is anxious that he shouldn't be killed. And so are Generals Beck and Halder. They won't countenance what they call murder. One of the Abwehr lawyers has been working on the legal case for the arrest, and Canaris's plan is that once Hitler is captured he will undergo a psychiatric assessment by Professor Bonhoeffer. He's the father of the pastor at that wedding in Pomerania we went to. He will certify him insane.'

'But if he's still alive then his supporters will try to free him, won't they? You have to assassinate him, surely?'

'That's my view. And Colonel Oster's.'

'The others won't listen?'

'No.' Conrad could feel as much as see that Theo wanted to say more. 'So Colonel Oster and I have decided to make sure that he does die.'

'How?'

'The raiding party that will go into the Chancellery to grab him will be led by a man called Heinz. He's a tough nut from the old *Freikorps* days.' The *Freikorps* were gangs of ex-soldiers who had terrorized Germany in the years following the last war. 'Colonel Oster has asked him to shoot Hitler in the panic immediately following his arrest. If for some reason Heinz can't do it, I will. Canaris doesn't know about this.'

'That's good,' said Conrad.

Theo cocked his head. 'Here comes Oster.'

Sure enough, Conrad could feel as much as hear a horse's hooves approaching at a trot.

'Stay here,' said Theo, and he pushed his way past the bush towards the path. He returned a moment later with a slightly built, elegant colonel of about fifty, wearing an Iron Cross First Class and a Knight's Cross on his impeccable uniform.

'You must be Herr de Lancey,' the officer said, holding out his hand. 'I'm glad to meet you, finally.'

'And you, Colonel Oster,' said Conrad, shaking it.

'Hertenberg tells me that your sister had some interesting information for us.'

There, among the bushes, Conrad repeated everything Millie had told him, emphasizing the need to persuade Halifax and that only a personal visit by one of the leaders of the plot could achieve that.

Oster frowned. 'That will have to be General Halder. Admiral Canaris is no good; no one knows him.'

'Will Halder do it?' Theo asked.

'I don't know,' said Oster. 'It's difficult to ask a serving chief of general staff to fly to a potential enemy's country in secret.'

'What about General Beck?' said Conrad. 'I understand he has resigned, but he was the Chief of the General Staff for many years, wasn't he? I'm sure he would impress Lord Halifax.'

'And he would be more persuasive than Halder,' said Theo.

'Provided he doesn't write any more of those damned memoranda,' said Oster. 'You're right. I'll ask Beck.'

'My father says that an aeroplane arriving at Manston Aerodrome in Kent will be allowed to land. He suggested a nocturnal visit.'

'How soon?' asked Oster.

'As soon as possible. If Halifax is to be persuaded, we should do it now, before Chamberlain has had a chance to tie Czechoslovakia up in a ribbon and hand it to Hitler.'

'You mean this week?'

'I mean tomorrow night.'

Oster smiled. 'I'll go straight to Beck's house now. It's not far. And if he agrees, which knowing him I think he will, I'll telephone you at home, Hertenberg, and you can arrange things. I don't think General Beck speaks English. Could you accompany him, Herr de Lancey?'

'With pleasure,' said Conrad.

'We should plan a very quick visit,' said Oster. 'Fly there, speak to Lord Halifax, fly back.' He frowned. 'But will there be time to make an appointment to see him? And will he want to see General Beck late at night?'

'My father is an old school friend of Lord Halifax's,' Conrad said. 'I'm sure he will get Halifax to see us if we arrive on his doorstep.'

'The famous English old-school tie,' said Oster.

'I used to hate it, but it does have its uses,' said Conrad.

'We will need to use an airfield somewhere near the North Sea coast. Hertenberg can drive General Beck and you up there tomorrow.'

Theo nodded.

'If we succeed, and the British government stands by Czechoslovakia, is there a chance that Hitler will back down?' Conrad asked.

'Very little,' said Oster. 'Hitler is determined to march into

Prague ahead of his tanks and his flags and he doesn't want Chamberlain to spoil his fun by meeting his demands, which is why he is making them more outrageous by the day. He wants a war.'

'If we can just persuade Halifax to stand by Czechoslovakia, we'll stop Hitler before he has a chance to start one,' said Theo, a gleam in his eye.

'Thank you for all you are doing to help us, Herr de Lancey,' said Oster.

'It's a pleasure, believe me.'

'Tell me,' said Oster, his eyes sharp. 'Why are you helping us? Are you doing it for your country? Or for our country?'

Conrad was a little taken aback by the question, but it deserved a straight answer. 'In a way, for both. It's not really a question of obedience; as you know my government and yours are happily waltzing their way to a war and don't want us to interrupt them. It's just that I know that Hitler is wrong and he has to be stopped. And my government is wrong not to stop him.'

On the path, through the bushes, they heard the horse utter a gentle whinny and stamp its feet. Oster smiled. 'Good luck tomorrow,' he said, and turned to go.

'Herr Oster?' Conrad said.

The Abwehr colonel paused.

'I have a question for you.'

'Yes?'

'I understand that a raiding party is being put together to arrest Hitler?'

Oster looked at Theo, who shrugged.

'Possibly,' he said carefully.

'Would you consider me for that raiding party?'

'And why should I do that?'

'I have done a lot to help you over the last few weeks and I would like to do more. I'd like to be there at the end. I think I've earned it.'

Oster glanced at Theo, who nodded.

'I'll think about it,' said the colonel.

Klaus arrived early at the meeting place, the statue of a long-dead composer of whom he had never heard, by one of the small ponds in the Tiergarten. It was after ten o'clock and the park was empty. Klaus checked his watch. His inform-ant was late, twenty minutes now. He ground his teeth in impatience.

Then he heard the gentle crunch of heels on gravel as she approached the statue.

'Klaus?'

'Over here!' A loud whisper.

The small, elfin figure of Sophie emerged from the shadows.

'Cigarette?'

Sophie gratefully accepted one, and they both lit up. 'I told you I can't help you any more, now Anneliese is dead.'

'Poor Anneliese,' said Klaus. 'I know how much she meant to you; how much she meant to both of us. I was just on the point of securing her release as well. One more day and she would have been free.'

'Who locked her up?'

'Heydrich. He has a thing about racial defilement.'

Sophie shook her head. 'It makes me wonder about the govern-ment. If the Führer knew what people were doing in his name, he wouldn't allow it. I mean, I never think of Anneliese as Jewish.'

'Neither did I,' said Klaus, employing the correct tense.

'She went to church, didn't she? If that doesn't make you a Christian, then what does?'

They stood in silence for a few moments, smoking.

'Sophie, I need some more evidence. About the plot. Written evidence.'

Sophie shook her head. 'I've told you, I'm not giving you anything else.'

'I tried to get Anneliese out,' Klaus said.

'But you didn't succeed, did you?'

'Theo's in trouble,' Klaus said.

'You said you would protect him!' There was a note of panic in Sophie's voice.

'It will be difficult,' said Klaus. 'We know he has been hiding de Lancey.'

'Has he?'

'Do you know where de Lancey is?'

'No. I heard he escaped from the Gestapo and he's on the run. I don't think Theo has anything to do with him.'

'He has. He hid him with some friends in Dahlem. A man named Hans-Jürgen von Wedemeyer and his wife. They are in custody now, but de Lancey has slipped away. Again.'

'I'm sure Theo has nothing to do with it,' said Sophie.

'I can do my best for Theo,' said Klaus. 'I can't promise to keep him out of jail, but I can make sure he isn't shot, and that's something.'

'No!' said Sophie.

'He could be arrested at any time. I need evidence, Sophie. Written evidence.'

'I said I wouldn't help you.'

'It's not just me you are helping. It's the Führer. Unless you and I do something, there will be a putsch and he will be captured, humiliated and probably killed. He is the greatest man Germany has ever produced. If he lives he will lead us all to glory. But if you allow this plot to go ahead, you will be responsible for his death. Do you want that?'

Sophie sucked hard on her cigarette. 'Why do you need written evidence?'

'Accusing the army of planning to overthrow the Führer is very serious. We need hard evidence, not just rumour. Can you get me anything?'

'Theo has a notebook. I once had a peek in it, that's where I learned about the coup against the Führer in the first place. He only brings it home occasionally, and when he does he is very careful with it.'

'Can you get it for me?'

'Perhaps. If he brings it home with him. But if I take it, he'll know it's gone straightaway.'

Klaus thought a moment. 'I have an idea.'

Sophie listened doubtfully as he explained it. 'I can try,' she said. 'But I will need a few days for the right opportunity.'

'How many days?'

'Give me four. But I can't guarantee it. If he doesn't bring the notebook home there is nothing I can do.'

'All right,' said Klaus. 'I'll meet you here in four days' time.'

'And you will do your best to keep Theo out of trouble?'

'I'll do all I can. And I'll make sure the Führer knows what you have done.'

For the first time that evening, Sophie smiled, her white teeth gleaming in the moonlight.

Thirty-three

Theo and Colonel Oster had only a few hours to arrange the flight to England. Fortunately, false papers, visas and currency wouldn't be needed for such a short trip. The Abwehr had a Fiesler Storch at permanent readiness should they need it in a hurry. To be certain of reaching Kent it would have to take off from somewhere in the north-west of Germany, which meant that Theo would have to set off from Berlin with his passengers at about lunchtime.

In the morning, he got a colleague to check on the Wedemeyers and it was with huge relief that he heard that they had been released from Gestapo headquarters. At eleven o'clock, he started on the hour-long dance to lose his Gestapo watchers. Even though he couldn't see anyone, he had to assume that they were there somewhere. He took an indirect route on the U-Bahn to the Kurfürstendamm station, timing his emergence to meet a BMW driven by Captain von Both, a former adjutant of General von Fritsch. Conrad was crouching in the back. Theo had taken Conrad to von Both's apartment the previous night, with the idea that Conrad would pose as a soldier visiting his friend in Berlin on leave for a couple of days.

Von Both drove off rapidly, leaving any unseen foot-bound watchers behind. Theo checked for pursuing taxis, but couldn't spot any. They stopped at Warren's office, where von Both left them and Theo told Warren to send an immediate cable to Lord

Oakford mentioning the word 'today'. Theo was uncomfortable about involving Warren in the plot, but it was clear that Warren thought that the message referred to Conrad's escape from the Gestapo and nothing more.

Theo drove on to a rendezvous with General Beck by the Landwehr Canal. Half an hour later the BMW was barrelling along the new autobahn towards Hamburg and then Wilhelms-haven, where the Storch would be waiting for them.

That morning, 24 September, Chamberlain returned to London from Bad Godesberg. It had been a much tougher meeting than he had expected. There was no doubt that Herr Hitler was a tricky negotiator, but Chamberlain was convinced that he and the German Chancellor had built up a personal rapport. At one point Hitler had said: 'You are the only man to whom I have ever made a concession.' It was going to be exceedingly difficult winning over the Cabinet and the Czechs, but Chamberlain was still certain that his concept of personal diplomacy was working. Peace was in his grasp.

The Cabinet met at five-thirty that afternoon to discuss the negotiations. At the end of the previous day's discussion in Bad Godesberg, Hitler had produced a document outlining his new demands. These were that the Czech government should begin evacuation of the Sudetenland on 26 September, only two days away, and complete it by 28 September. This document had been circulated to the ministers around the long table.

Chamberlain spoke for an hour. When he had finished des-cribing what had happened on the banks of the Rhine, he looked around the table to ensure he had the attention of the whole Cabinet. He did.

'I admit that I was shocked initially by the hardening of Herr Hitler's position. The German Chancellor has a narrow mind and he is violently prejudiced on certain subjects. But Herr Hitler has certain standards: he will not deceive a man whom he respects and I am sure that Herr Hitler respects me. I am confident that he is speaking the truth when he says Germany has no more territorial ambitions in Europe once the Sudetenland question is settled and that such a settlement will be a turning point in Anglo-German relations.'

He cleared his throat. 'This morning, I flew up the river over London. I imagined a German bomber flying the same course, and I asked myself what degree of protection we can afford to the thousands of homes I saw stretched out below me. At that moment I felt we were in no position to justify waging a war today in order to prevent a war hereafter. I believe we should accept Herr Hitler's terms, and we should persuade the Czech government to do so as well.'

There followed a few minutes of aimless discussion until Duff Cooper spoke. One of the youngest ministers around the table, he was First Lord of the Admiralty and a friend of Winston Churchill's. Chamberlain had expected trouble from him.

'Prime Minister, I must object most strongly to the course of action you suggest. It appears to me that the Germans must still be convinced that under no circumstances will this country fight. There is one method, and one method only, of persuading them to the contrary, and that is by instantly declaring full mobilization. I am sure that public opinion will eventually compel us to go to the assistance of the Czechs. Hitherto, we have been faced with the unpleasant alternatives of peace with dishonour, or war. I now foresee a third possibility: namely a war with dishonour.'

Duff Cooper's words made an impression. Hore-Belisha, Lord Winterton, Oliver Stanley, Lord de la Warr and Walter Elliot all supported him. But, crucially, Sir John Simon, the

Chancellor of the Exchequer, and Lord Halifax, the Foreign Secretary, did not. The Cabinet was bad-tempered as it broke up, agreeing to discuss the matter the following morning when everyone had had a chance to read through Hitler's terms again.

Later that evening Halifax was driven home from Downing Street, where he had dined with the Prime Minister, by Alec Cadogan, the Permanent Under-Secretary at the Foreign Office. Cadogan was incensed by Hitler's proposals; he felt that the British government was in danger of behaving with dishonour, and he spent the short car trip haranguing Halifax with these views. Halifax ignored him.

Cadogan dropped Halifax off at his house at 88 Eaton Square and bade him goodnight. It was ten-thirty, and Halifax was tired, but he took the memorandum of Hitler's terms with him into his study.

Half an hour later, his butler interrupted him. 'Lord Oakford is here, my lord. He wishes to speak to you.'

'Oakford! What time is it?'

'Eleven o'clock, my lord.'

For the previous few weeks Halifax had been besieged by friends and enemies pressing their own points of view about peace and war upon him, foremost of whom had been Winston Churchill. Halifax was heartily sick of this lobbying: he was Foreign Secretary, and he would make up his own mind based on a reasoned assessment of the information available to the government.

'Lord Oakford is accompanied by his son and a man who claims to be a German general.' Disapproval seeped from the butler's words.

'What!' Halifax rubbed first one eye and then the other with his good hand. What on earth was Oakford up to? 'All right, Thompson, send them in.'

* * *

There was tension around the Cabinet table in 10 Downing Street when the ministers reconvened at ten-thirty the following morning, 25 September. The Prime Minister took his place in front of the marble fireplace at the centre of the table, his lean, anxious expression and sober dress contrasting with the portrait behind him of a confident and somewhat corpulent Sir Robert Walpole in all his Georgian finery. He opened proceedings, answering specific points arising from the German memorandum, and then Oliver Stanley raised the key question: should the Cabinet advise the Czechoslovak government to accept Hitler's proposals?

Halifax was first to answer. He spoke in a low voice, laden with emotion. His long face showed signs of both fatigue and determination. Everyone around the table could tell that something had changed.

'Yesterday I felt that acceptance of the scheme put forward for the Sudetenland did not involve a new acceptance of principle. But now I am not quite so sure. Last night, I could not sleep, and in the watches of the night I came to change my mind. I cannot rid my mind of the fact that Herr Hitler has given us nothing, and that he is dictating terms just as though he has won a war without having to fight. The ultimate end that I wish to see accomplished is the destruction of Nazism. So long as Nazism lasts, peace will be uncertain.'

Halifax glanced around the table at his Cabinet colleagues, although he avoided Chamberlain's eye. 'For these reasons, I do not think it would be wise for us to advise the Czech government to accept Germany's ultimatum. We should lay the case before them. If they reject it, I imagine that France will join in, and if the French go in, we should join them.

'I remember Herr Hitler saying that he gained power by words not by bayonets. I wonder whether we can be quite sure that he has not gained power by words in the present instance. We should not forget that if he is driven to war, the result might be the downfall of the Nazi regime.

'I have worked most closely with the Prime Minister throughout this long crisis, but now I am not quite sure that our minds are still altogether at one. Nevertheless, I think it right to expose my own hesitations with complete frankness.'

There was stunned silence as the members of the Cabinet took in Halifax's change of heart. As Lord Hailsham produced an article from the *Daily Telegraph* outlining all the previous occasions when Hitler had made promises and broken them, Chamberlain scribbled a note to his Foreign Secretary:

> *Your complete change of view since I saw you last night is a horrible blow to me, but of course you must form your opinions for yourself. However it remains to see what the French say.*
> *If they say they will go in, thereby dragging us in I do not think I could accept responsibility for the decision.*
> *But I don't want to anticipate what has not yet arisen.*
> *N.C.*

Halifax replied:

> *I feel a brute – but I lay awake most of the night, tormenting myself and did not feel I could reach any other conclusion at this moment, on the point of co-ercing CZ.*
> *E.*

He couldn't mention the real reason he had changed his mind, even to the Prime Minister – especially to the Prime

Minister. The night before, General Beck had left Halifax in absolutely no doubt that the prospect of a coup in Berlin was real if Britain stood by Czechoslovakia. Halifax had been impressed by the intense general, with his intelligent eyes, his thoughtful, academic way of speaking and his obvious sincerity. The conspiracy wasn't just the disgruntled mutterings of a few junior reactionaries, it was much more than that. But Lord Oakford had put Halifax in a very difficult position. Halifax knew that if he spoke to the Prime Minister in confidence it would make little difference to Chamberlain's opinion, and if he mentioned his meeting of the night before in Cabinet it would be impossible to keep quiet the fact that he had spoken to one of the most senior generals in the German army. Besides, Beck had demanded nothing more of him than that he listen and keep the meeting confidential. Halifax had given no other undertakings, no assurances.

Beck had also been convincing on Hitler's aims: on his absolute determination to march into Prague. After speaking to the general, it was clear to Halifax that when Hitler told Chamberlain that he had no more territorial claims in Europe than the Sudetenland, it was a barefaced lie. The dictator could not be trusted. After Beck, Oakford and his son de Lancey had left him, Halifax had indeed found it impossible to sleep. As dawn came, he had decided on two things: grant General Beck's request to stay silent about his visit, and show Hitler that Britain would stand by the Czechs. It might mean revolution in Germany; it might even mean war. But Duff Cooper and Alec Cadogan were right – it was the only way of proceeding with honour.

Chamberlain read Halifax's slip and scribbled a quick response on it.

Night conclusions are seldom taken in the right perspective.
N.C.

But as he sent the note back to Halifax he knew that peace, his peace, was slipping away.

The north German plain was covered in a torn blanket of mist as the Storch flew towards the rising sun. Conrad was amazed that the pilot could find the airfield, and only part of the runway was visible between the wisps of grey as they touched down. Theo was there to meet them; he had spent the night in Wilhelmshaven.

'A successful trip, Herr General?'

'I think so,' said General Beck. 'Lord Oakford managed to secure an audience for us. I found Halifax very stiff, but he did seem to listen to me.'

'I think you were persuasive, Herr General,' said Conrad. 'Halifax said the Cabinet is discussing Czechoslovakia this morning. I just hope we have done enough to change his mind.'

Conrad sat in the front of the BMW, next to Theo, and General Beck sat in the back. Once they were on the autobahn, the general fell asleep.

'Aren't you tired?' Theo asked Conrad.

'I am. I got hardly any sleep on the aeroplane: I can't stop thinking about what happened to Anneliese. But after being cooped up in that house in Dahlem it was good to do something. And I'm so glad the Wedemeyers have been let go.'

'So am I. I feel very bad about putting them in danger like that.'

'And you? You say the Gestapo are following you all the time; why don't they pick you up?'

'It would start a civil war. I'm sure Heydrich will have a word with Canaris about me soon, but he knows he has to tread carefully.'

'With luck, in a couple of days it won't really matter where he treads.'

Theo hooted at a small Opel blocking the outside lane of the autobahn and cursed. The Opel moved, and the BMW sped on.

Theo glanced over his shoulder at the sleeping general, and spoke in a low voice, in English. 'So you came back.'

'Didn't you think I would?'

'You could have stayed in England. You would have been safe there.'

'I want to see this through. Did Oster say whether he would let me join the raiding party?'

'He will. I'll get you a uniform and some papers and introduce you to Heinz.'

Conrad smiled. Finally he was to be allowed the chance to do something real to right the wrongs of the Third Reich. He appreciated the enormity of what he had volunteered to do: it would change the course of history, he hoped and prayed, for the better.

Because Conrad's intention wasn't just to help Theo and his compatriots storm the Chancellery. Oster's plan was that in the confusion of the arrest, someone would shoot Hitler. Conrad was determined that he would be that someone, even if he lost his life in the process.

Thirty-four

Theo's alarm went off at six o'clock. As he rolled over to turn it off, his nostrils caught a trace of Sophie's perfume on his pillow. She had come around unexpectedly the night before and had stayed a few hours. There had been something unusually passionate, almost desperate, about their lovemaking. Theo smiled at the memory of it. Sophie really was a sexy little thing. Pity she was so dumb.

He hauled himself out of bed. He had a busy day ahead of him. General Beck's nocturnal discussion with Lord Halifax seemed to have done the trick. In the two days since the general's visit, British resolve had hardened, making it almost certain that Hitler would order Case Green for the invasion of Czechoslovakia the following day, the 28th. And when he did, the conspirators would be ready.

Theo washed, pulled on his uniform and, just before leaving his apartment, dug out his briefcase from the bottom drawer of the sideboard, where it nestled underneath a folded tablecloth. He pulled out a small key from his trouser pocket and unlocked it. The notebook was still there, where he had put it the previous night when he had finished working on it. Comforted, he snapped the case shut and left for Abwehr HQ.

While the rest of the world prepared for war, Conrad had spent the two days cooped up in Captain von Both's apartment. When the superintendent of the building asked the captain about his visitor, von Both used the story about Conrad being a friend on leave. He embellished it by saying that Conrad was recovering from an illness, which was why he spent so much time indoors instead of enjoying the sights of Berlin, or indeed returning to his regiment, when every other soldier in Germany was on the move.

The enforced solitude gave Conrad time to think. He thought of Anneliese, but also how, with a lot of luck, he might soon be able to avenge her and the thousands like her who had been destroyed by Hitler. He found it hard to control his impatience, to just sit and wait.

But there was another thought that troubled him, something harking back to his first days in Berlin.

Theo came to see him at about eleven in the morning with a uniform and some papers.

'Here you are. Lieutenant Eiche, 14th Artillery Regiment. Born in Hamburg, 1911.'

'A gunner? I know nothing about artillery.'

'You know nothing about anything military. If you are going to be a German soldier you will have to walk around as if you have a ruler crammed up your arse. Seriously, for the next couple of days you had better concentrate on standing up straight.'

'When do I join the raiding party?'

'This afternoon. I'll take you there; Captain Heinz is expecting you. It looks like we move tomorrow.'

Conrad smiled. 'Excellent.'

'I'll see you about two o'clock, then,' said Theo.

'Theo, before you go. I've been thinking about something these last few days, something that bothers me.'

'What is it?'

'Joachim. We never really satisfied ourselves about who spoke to Schalke about him. I thought it was you; then I suspected Anneliese. Both of those suspicions were wrong.'

'I see what you mean,' said Theo thoughtfully. 'So who else can it have been?'

'Well, that's what I have been thinking. What about Sophie?'

'No,' said Theo firmly.

'Why not?'

'Two reasons. Firstly, she definitely doesn't speak English. And secondly, she was in the Ladies when Joachim was talking about the plot.'

'Are her family Nazis?'

'Perhaps,' said Theo. 'I have scarcely ever met them. But yes, I suspect that her father is. But then so are many millions of people in Germany. And believe me, Sophie has no interest in politics.'

'Does she know that you are involved in the plot?'

'Of course not!' said Theo indignantly. 'She knows I'm doing something secret, but I've told her that I'm working on war plans. She's happy with that. Look here, Conrad, this is absurd. She wasn't there, so how could she possibly know what Joachim said?'

'Perhaps Anneliese told her afterwards.'

'Anneliese? Why should she do that?'

'They were friends. At that stage Anneliese had no idea that you were really involved in anything. It was interesting gossip. Why shouldn't she tell Sophie all about it?' Conrad sighed. 'I just wish it was still possible to ask her.'

Theo shook his head, his lips pursed in anger.

'I remember thinking it was a coincidence that it was Klaus Schalke who arrested Joachim and me,' Conrad went on. 'At the time I was suspicious of Anneliese, because of course she knew Schalke. Anneliese told me that the two people who stood by her after her boyfriend was killed in the concentration camp were Sophie and Schalke.'

'Which means?'

'Which means that they almost certainly know each other. Which means that when Sophie heard about Joachim's rumour she turned to the one Gestapo officer she already knew and trusted: Klaus Schalke.'

'Now you really are stretching your imagination.'

'And which also means that if Sophie discovers there really is a plot, she might go and talk to Schalke about it again.'

'Totally ridiculous!' Theo said, raising his voice. 'I know Sophie. If she did overhear something I was doing, she wouldn't trouble herself to worry about what it was. She has no interest in what I do. And she wouldn't betray me.'

'Are you sure, Theo?'

'Quite sure,' said Theo. He turned to leave, and then hesitated.

'What is it?' asked Conrad.

'It's nothing.'

'Theo?'

'Well... I have a notebook. It contains all our plans. There's too much to memorize; I have to write the details down somewhere. I'm very careful with it: I keep it in a filing cabinet in the Abwehr HQ, and when I take it home I keep it locked in my briefcase.'

'Have you lost it?'

'No. But I took it home last night, and this morning when I got to the office and opened it, I found a hair stuck in one of the pages. A blonde hair.'

'Sophie's?'

Theo shrugged.

'Was Sophie with you last night?'

Theo glanced at Conrad, his brow furrowed in concern. 'Yes. Yes, she was.'

Warren turned the corner from Unter den Linden on to Wilhelmstrasse, and hurried to secure himself a good vantage point in the Wilhelmplatz from which he could see the balcony of the Chancellery. It was a starkly modern building, less than ten years old, but already the present Chancellor had outgrown it. For nine months workmen had been building a newer, grander Chancellery next door, and it was nearly finished. The cost was rumoured to be three hundred million marks.

Poor Vernon Sherritt's father had clung on to life longer than expected, and so Vernon had been delayed. He wasn't sailing from New York until the following day. This meant that when war was declared, Warren would be his newspaper's correspondent in Berlin rather than back in Prague. Although sorry for his boss, Warren was happy with this turn of events. Unlike Hitler, he thought it would take months, not days, before the Germans marched into Prague.

War looked to be a certainty. In the last few days, follow-ing Hitler's unreasonable demands at Bad Godesberg, the British government had found its backbone at last. The journalist rumour mill was working at maximum speed as newspapermen in London and Berlin pieced together what was happening. The day before, Lord Halifax had issued a press release, apparently with the assistance of Churchill, in which he stated baldly that if the Germans attacked Czechoslovakia the immediate result would be that France would come to her assistance, and Britain would stand by France. Sir Horace Wilson, Chamberlain's shadowy adviser, had travelled to Berlin to bring Hitler the news that the Czechs had rejected his demands. Hitler had tried to storm out of his own office in fury, but realizing this was pretty silly, threw Wilson out instead. The previous evening Warren had seen the Führer give a speech at the Sportpalast, where he had worked himself up into the worst paroxysm of fury that Warren had ever witnessed. He had promised that if the Czechs didn't hand over the Sudetenland by 1 October, Germany would take it by force. The French had mobilized fourteen divisions, and the first rumours were just coming through from London that the Royal Navy had been mobilized too.

It was war.

But for some reason, overnight, the German people seemed to have lost all their belligerence. The jaunty air of anticipation had left the streets, to be replaced with sullen caution. People walked differently. Faces that had been purposeful the day before were now anxious.

The Wehrmacht's divisions were on the move, and Warren knew that one of them had been ordered to march through the city at five o'clock, the time when the streets were thronged with Berliners going home from work. Ordinarily large crowds would have gathered to watch, but this time there were only a couple of hundred people standing outside the Chancellery. Warren was in a good spot to view the balcony, just outside the Kaiserhof Hotel. He spotted Bill Shirer, the CBS correspondent, and one or two other foreign journalists, but for once they seemed more excited than the natives.

The troops arrived, on foot, on horseback, in trucks, an endless stream of young men staring straight ahead towards war. The crowd, such as it was, remained absolutely silent. The tramp of feet, the clopping of hooves, the grinding of engines seemed unnaturally loud without its usual accompaniment of cheering. Warren saw the doors up on the balcony of the Chancellery open, and Hitler appeared, bare-headed. He gazed at the troops marching along on the street below, and at the small gathering of people opposite. Not an arm was raised in salute. There was not a *Sieg Heil* to be heard. The crowd looked away, as if embarrassed. Hitler turned sharply on his heel and withdrew.

It was one of the most extraordinary sights Warren had seen since he had been in Berlin. Perhaps the most bellicose people in Europe didn't want war after all.

As Warren made his way back to his apartment, he became aware of an envelope sticking out of his jacket pocket, bearing his name in familiar handwriting. He opened it. Inside was a note and another, smaller envelope, addressed to Lord Oakford in Kensington Square in London.

He scanned the note. It was from Conrad asking him to ensure that the envelope was delivered to his father without the German censors seeing it.

Conrad! How the hell had the envelope got into his jacket pocket? Warren glanced rapidly around him, but all he saw was a mass of Berliners hurrying home, their faces pinched with worry.

For a moment the journalist in him was tempted to steam open the envelope: he had no idea what the contents were, but he knew they would be interesting. But he resisted the temptation. He was probably the only person in Berlin Conrad could trust, and he wasn't going to let him down.

Thirty-five

The Kakadu was nearly empty; Berlin wasn't in the mood to go out and dance that night. Conrad hadn't been there since that fateful evening in June. The blonde and brunette barmaids chatted idly to each other. The band played listlessly, and only two couples occupied the dance floor, by the look of them Eintänzer, employees who were paid to dance with customers. There were some drinkers dotted around the tables, and one of them was Theo.

Conrad threaded his way through the tables towards his friend, feeling conspicuous in the uniform he had been wearing for the last five hours.

'Ah, Lieutenant Eiche, good evening. Have some champagne.' Theo, too, was wearing uniform. He poured Conrad a glass of 'champagne', the mildly alcoholic sparkling apple juice that the Kakadu had resorted to in those times of shortage. 'How was Captain Heinz?'

'He seems very capable,' Conrad said. 'And very tough.' He had spent the evening with Heinz and about forty young German officers, going through the plans for the following day. 'The others are all staying in various flats around Wilhelm-strasse tonight. I'm going back there after this. Are you joining us tomorrow?'

'Yes,' said Theo. 'I'll meet you at army headquarters at six a.m.'

'Are you certain it's going ahead?'

'Oh, yes,' said Theo. 'Hitler has publicly committed himself to invading before 1 October. Case Green calls for two days' preparation before the invasion. If he intends to invade on the thirtieth, that means he must issue the orders tomorrow, the twenty-eighth. And he told the British that he expects to hear back from the Czechs by two p.m. on the twenty-eighth.'

'What if the British give in? Or the Czechs?'

'They won't. The British have just given the order to mobilize their fleet. Your father was right: Halifax was the man to persuade. And the Czechs are brave. As for Hitler, he's equally determined.' Theo smiled. 'No, tomorrow is the day.'

Conrad sipped his champagne. He didn't want to drink too much: he hadn't had much sleep over the last couple of days, and it was unlikely he would get much that night. 'Are you sure you want me here when you talk to her?'

'Yes. And I think this is the right place. I know Sophie. This will bring back Joachim. By the way, she told me she wouldn't be able to meet me until eleven because her shift at the hospital finished at ten. I checked. She was off at four.'

'So where has she been?'

'That's something else I will ask her. Look out, here she comes.'

Conrad's back was towards the entrance of the bar, and he didn't turn around. He heard Sophie's light step draw near behind them. 'Hello, darling,' she said, and kissed Theo on the cheek. She turned to greet the stranger, and then stopped when she saw Conrad.

'Hello, Sophie,' he said.

'Conrad! I thought the Gestapo were after you?'

'They are.'

'And what are you doing in that uniform?'

'Conrad is doing me a favour, darling,' Theo said.

Sophie reddened and sat down. 'Pour me some champagne, please, Theo.'

Theo obliged and she took a large gulp.

'Where have you been?' Theo asked mildly.

'At the hospital, I told you.'

'That's funny, they said you finished at four when I went round there today.'

'Oh,' said Sophie, blushing again. 'Um... I had to cover for Susanne. Her mother is ill.'

'I see.' Theo's voice was still reasonable, almost kind. 'And did you read anything interesting in my notebook?'

'What notebook?'

'The one I write my plans in.'

'Your war plans?'

'No, my coup plans.'

Sophie looked at Theo and Conrad in panic. 'I have to go,' she said and scrambled to her feet.

'Sit, Sophie,' said Theo, his voice firm, but still not threatening. 'Sit and tell me all about it.'

A tear rolled down Sophie's cheek. 'Oh, I'm sorry, Theo. I'm so sorry.'

'Why did you do it, Sophie?'

'I did it for the Führer. I had to do it. I couldn't allow him to be kidnapped or killed. You must understand that.'

'I didn't know you cared a fig about him,' Theo said.

'I always have,' said Sophie. 'Ever since I first saw him with my father in 1931. He's an amazing man, Theo, a wonderful man. Just to hear him speak is incredible. He understands us, all of us. I don't know how you could never see that.'

Now it was Theo's turn to look shocked. 'You never told me you felt this way.'

'Of course not. You wouldn't have understood. Neither would Anneliese. Sometimes you intellectuals are just too clever for your own good; you can't see the obvious.'

'The obvious?'

'That the Führer has saved Germany. That he will lead us to a glorious future if only we follow him.'

'Did you talk to Klaus Schalke about Joachim and his idiotic rumour?'

Sophie nodded. 'Anneliese told me what she had overheard. She said he was planning to assassinate the Führer.'

'And so Klaus killed him.'

'Klaus said it was an accident. He said Joachim had a heart attack.'

'While he was being drowned by Gestapo gorillas.'

Sophie put her head in her hands. 'I know. I feel very bad about that.'

'And yet you spoke to Klaus again, didn't you? Recently. About me.'

Sophie looked directly at Theo. 'I had to, don't you see? I read your notebook. I knew what you were planning. And Klaus promised that you would be kept out of trouble. He also said he would get Anneliese out of the concentration camp.'

'He was the one who put her in there,' muttered Conrad.

'But how could you do that to me?' Theo said, his voice an angry growl. 'I thought you loved me?'

'Oh, I do, Theo, I do. It was the hardest decision I've ever had to make. For days I did nothing. But I couldn't let you destroy the Führer. Then I thought: What would you do? I mean, if you had to choose between me and what you thought was your duty. I knew the answer and I made my decision.'

Conrad could see that Theo was fighting to maintain his self-control. 'So where have you just been, Sophie?' he asked quietly.

Sophie looked down. 'With Klaus. Last night I took your keys and got out your briefcase. I copied out your notes, or some of them anyway, and then put everything back as I had found it. I gave my copy to him.'

Theo closed his eyes.

'What's in it?' Conrad asked.

'Everything,' Theo answered. 'Timings, targets, participants, although I have used codenames for those.'

'Will Klaus be able to break the code?'

'Probably.' Theo glared at Sophie, his eyes full of fury. 'You ignorant, stupid bitch! You know you have consigned all those people to death? Including me and Conrad and probably yourself?'

Sophie's eyes flashed with anger. 'That's what you've always thought of me, isn't it? That I'm ignorant? That I'm stupid? That I'm a bitch? I've loved you totally, completely, and you've taken me for granted. Of course I put up with it – I was desperate not to lose you, so I put up with it. But I have my opinions too! I did what I thought was right. You of all people should respect that.'

'What you thought was right?' Theo sneered.

Conrad reached out a hand and grabbed his arm. 'Theo! Stay calm. You *must* stay calm. We have to work out what to do.'

Theo shut up, but his eyes were burning. Sophie crumbled as her anger turned to misery. She covered her face with her hands and slumped in her chair, head down, sobbing. A group of Luftwaffe officers a couple of tables away turned to look.

'We have to get Sophie's notes back, before Klaus shows them to his bosses,' Conrad said in a low voice. 'There's still time for the Gestapo to thwart the coup.'

'It's probably too late,' muttered Theo.

'Not necessarily,' said Conrad. 'Sophie, what did you copy Theo's notes into?'

'A school copybook I bought a few days ago,' Sophie said between sobs. 'It's blue.'

'And you gave this copybook to Klaus?'

'Yes. Only half an hour ago. In the Tiergarten. I came straight here afterwards.'

'Was this the first time you told him about the plot?'

'No. I told him a few days ago, but he said he needed written evidence. It sounded as if he had to convince someone.'

'And how much is written in there?'

'Several pages,' Sophie said. 'I spent nearly two hours doing it, in the kitchen, while Theo was asleep.'

Conrad was thinking. 'Right. If Klaus has to convince someone that the plot is real, he will want to read the notes carefully before he shows it to anyone. Perhaps try to work out who the codenames refer to. We might still have some time, if we can find him. Sophie, do you know where he lives?'

'No,' said Sophie. 'But I have his telephone number at home and at Gestapo headquarters.'

'Even if we could track him down, what if he is at Gestapo HQ poring over the notes right now?' Theo said. 'We could never get at him in there.'

'We need to lure him out.' Conrad tapped his chin, thinking rapidly. 'Sophie, will you help us?'

'Help you do what?'

'Get the notes back.'

'No,' Sophie said. 'No. I gave them to Klaus for a reason. To save the Führer.'

'Sophie,' Conrad said softly. 'Sophie, listen to me.'

Sophie sniffed, but her large moist eyes were on Conrad.

'Tomorrow, the Führer is going to order the preparations

for the German army to attack Czechoslovakia. The British and the French will stand by the Czechs. Do you know what that means?'

'The Sudeten Germans will be freed?' Sophie answered.

'There will be a war, Sophie. A world war. As big as the last one, perhaps bigger. The Führer wants a war. You know he does, you've seen him speak.'

'But if there is a war, we will win it.'

'Perhaps,' said Conrad. 'But hundreds of thousands of people will die first. It won't be glorious, it will be bloody. You don't want that, do you?'

Sophie didn't answer.

'The reason that Theo is planning to do what he is planning is that he wants to arrest the Führer before he has a chance to start this war.' Conrad could see doubt in Sophie's eyes. 'Trust him. Trust me. Trust Anneliese.'

'I can't,' said Sophie, shaking her head slowly. 'I can't help you.'

'You know they'll execute me,' said Theo quietly.

'No they won't. Klaus promised me they wouldn't.'

'Klaus is a Gestapo officer. You can't trust his promise. You know that, don't you, Sophie?'

Sophie closed her eyes and, as she did so, more tears ran down her cheeks.

'Don't you, Sophie?' Theo's voice was more insistent.

Sophie nodded.

'It's as though you have tied the noose yourself,' Theo said. 'They'll probably hang me for treason. Unless they decide to behead me as a spy.'

'Can't you just run away?' said Sophie, her eyes open wide, pleading. 'Just leave now. Run to Britain or somewhere. Conrad will help you.'

Theo slowly shook his head. 'You know me. You know I can't run away. Only you can save me.'

Sophie bit her lip.

'If we can get the notebook back from Schalke I might live.'

Sophie started to say something. Her lip trembled.

'I know you loved me yesterday. Do you still love me today?'

Sophie muttered something so quiet that neither Theo nor Conrad could hear it.

'What was that?'

'Yes. I said yes,' said Sophie. 'But I've just betrayed you. You must hate me.'

'If you help us get the notebook back from Conrad, I will forgive you.'

'Will you really?' said Sophie, hope in her eyes. She was desperate to believe him.

Theo nodded.

'But what if the Führer is killed?' Sophie said. 'I can't be responsible for that.'

'He won't be,' Conrad said. 'The idea is to arrest him and keep him safe until the Czech crisis can be solved peacefully.'

'Are you sure?'

Conrad could see the doubt in her eyes. He *had* to convince her. 'I give you my word.' His eyes held hers. That was when he discovered he was a very good liar.

Sophie turned back to Theo. Conrad could see that despite all her doubts she wanted more than anything else to believe him, to trust him, to save his life.

Finally she sniffed, wiped the tears from her eyes and smiled. 'All right,' she said. 'What do you want me to do?'

Thirty-six

Klaus's hands were shaking, literally shaking, as he leafed through the blue copybook, its pages covered in Sophie's clear schoolgirl handwriting. He was in his office at 8 Prinz-Albrecht-Strasse. He wasn't quite the only man in the building; the Gestapo were hard-working and there were always cases to be caught up on. But he knew that what he had in front of him was for Heydrich's eyes only, and he knew Heydrich was at home in Schlachtensee.

Twice he reached for the telephone, but both times he hesitated. As he read it became clear that the likely timing for the coup was 28 September, the very next day. He knew that he had to move fast. But before he spoke to Heydrich he needed to answer the most important question: who was involved in the plot? Von Hertenberg had used codenames for the plotters. Some of them were obvious, others more difficult.

He pulled out some sheets of typing paper and made notes, trying to pull it all together. As he worked, the codenames became clearer. Hertenberg himself was 'Eagle.' Oster was 'Owl'. Canaris was 'Lion'. Canaris! So the conspiracy went right to the top of the Abwehr. 'Jaguar' was a general, probably Beck, possibly Fritsch. But then there were others, including 'Zebra', who was going to lead the government once Hitler was overthrown. Klaus had a feeling that Zebra might be Göring. It would be just like him to turn the army against the SS, overthrow Hitler and then take power himself. Or it could even be Goebbels. It would be vital for Heydrich to know whom he was up against before he reacted to the news Klaus was going to bring him.

He decided to see how much he could work out in an hour and then call Heydrich.

The telephone rang. He picked it up. 'Schalke.'

'I've found something else.' Klaus recognized Sophie's urgent whisper. 'It's a list of animals with names next to it. Meet me at the same place in twenty minutes and I'll give it to you.'

Klaus's heartbeat quickened. 'Wonderful. Perhaps you could just read them out over the telephone. Who is Zebra?'

'I have to go! Meet me there.' The telephone went dead.

Klaus rubbed his hands and checked his watch. It was half past midnight. It was a shame Sophie couldn't just have read out the vital codenames, but she was obviously under pressure. He should be able to meet her, get the list and call Heydrich by three o'clock. That would still give the Gestapo time to respond before the coup was launched. He picked up the copybook and hesitated as his eyes fell on the mess of paper on his desk. He stuffed all the notes in a drawer and locked it, putting the key in his trousers. Then he grabbed his coat and headed for the Tiergarten.

Ten minutes later, Kriminal Assistant Fischer made his way along the corridor to Klaus's office. He couldn't stop yawning. He hated late nights, but he had promised Klaus the report on Wilfrid Israel by the following morning.

Klaus was worth pleasing. Fischer had joined the Gestapo the year before as a young policeman from the Prenzlauer Berg suburb of Berlin and an idealistic Nazi. He had imagined that he would be rooting out hardened conspirators against the regime.

The reality, that he spent most of his time persecuting the weak and the mildly dishonest who had been denounced by jealous colleagues, had been a bit of a shock. But he was ambitious, and he realized two things were needed to get on in the Gestapo: to be more ruthless than the next man, and to latch yourself to a patron who could protect you. Fischer had chosen Klaus: he was intelligent, and he had a good relationship with the most important patron of all, Heydrich.

Klaus's office was unlocked but empty; Fischer had seen him in there only twenty minutes before, hunched over some papers in intense concentration. Fischer dropped the report, sealed in an envelope, on Klaus's desk. He was about to leave when he noticed a single sheet of paper lying under the desk, covered with Klaus's scrawl. Unlike Klaus, Fischer didn't like mess. He picked up the sheet and glanced at it to decide whether to throw it into the waste-paper basket.

A word and a date caught Fischer's eye. The word was *coup*, and the date was *28 September*. Fischer read. Stunned, his fatigue forgotten for the moment, he sat in Klaus's chair and read some more.

No wonder Klaus was working so late!

He checked his watch. It was half past one. Fischer had an appointment with the Nazi Labour Front representative in Israel's department store first thing in the morning, where he planned to spend a couple of hours interviewing shopwalkers and buying clerks.

He placed the sheet of paper carefully in the centre of the desk where Klaus would be sure to see it when he came in the next morning, and went home.

Conrad and Theo squatted behind a rhododendron bush about twenty yards away from the statue of the composer, Albert

Lortzing. There was a half-moon, and the marble glimmered in the darkness. Both men were in uniform and both were armed with Lugers. Sophie was standing in front of the statue nervously smoking a cigarette. In her handbag was a fake list of codenames that Theo had quickly drawn up a few minutes before.

Although it had been a warm day, this near to autumn the temperature cooled down during the night, and it was cold crouching in the bushes. No one else was about. The moon added a blue tinge to the dark, silent waters of the pond opposite the statue. A willow tree's long fingers reached down to tickle the still surface. Ten years earlier the woods would have been alive with prostitutes and drug dealers, and customers for both. In these days of *Ordnung*, the few that were left ignored the park.

They heard the sound of footsteps on the gravel. The unmistakable silhouette of Klaus Schalke emerged along the path into the clearing by the statue. He saw Sophie and headed towards her.

Conrad raised his Luger; it had been decided that he should do the honours. But just as he was about to squeeze the trigger, he hesitated. Sophie had moved in front of his line of fire, so that she was standing between him and Klaus, but Klaus was so tall that Conrad had a clear shot of his head. He had never used a Luger before and he didn't want to hit Sophie by mistake.

'Get on with it!' whispered Theo.

'Hang on,' said Conrad. 'I'll get a better shot in a moment.'

But he didn't get his moment. Metal clicked softly a couple of feet behind his skull: the sound of a safety catch being released. 'Drop your guns. Both of you.'

Conrad recognized the voice of Dressel. He hesitated. Should he shoot Klaus anyway and take the consequences?

'You heard me.'

There was no point. Dressel would find Sophie's notes if he didn't know about them already. Conrad dropped his gun. And so did Theo.

'Schalke! Over here! Look what I've found.'

Klaus started and then lumbered over towards them. Conrad noticed he was clutching a copybook. 'Well done, Dressel! I knew it was a good idea to get you out of bed.' He smiled at Conrad. 'Well, well. A British civilian in a German army uniform! Confirmation you are a spy if ever I needed it.'

'Shall I shoot him?' asked Dressel, hopefully.

'Not yet,' said Klaus. 'And Hertenberg. You must be a spy too. A traitor. Oh, dear.'

'Run, Sophie!' Theo shouted.

Sophie hesitated and Klaus launched himself towards her. She turned to run, but Klaus grabbed her by the arm and threw her to the ground. Dressel hit Theo hard over the head, and he crumpled. Conrad dropped to his knees to check on his friend, but Dressel ordered him to stand up straight.

'Theo!' Sophie shouted, and tried to run over to him, but Klaus's grip was strong.

'Still! Keep still!' he commanded, jerking her arm.

Sophie stood still.

'Do you have the list of codenames?'

Sophie glared at Klaus, but began to open her small handbag.

'Slowly!' warned Dressel, pointing his pistol directly at her.

She hesitated and then carefully drew out a small sheet of paper, which she handed to Klaus.

Klaus smiled. 'Thank you. Now, move over there, with your boyfriend!'

Sophie rushed over to Theo, who was clutching his head and groaning. Dressel covered all three expertly with his pistol. Klaus produced a small torch and read the list.

'Hah! Goebbels. I thought so.' He scanned some more lines. 'Wait a moment. Himmler? Heydrich? But Lion is Canaris, surely.' He glanced at Theo, sitting on the ground.

'This isn't the real list, is it?' Theo didn't answer. Klaus examined it again. 'It's a fresh sheet of paper. You wrote this tonight.' He shook his head, screwed the list into a ball and dropped it on the grass.

'Shall we take them back to headquarters, boss?' Dressel asked. 'Or do we just shoot them?'

'We need to find out the real codenames.'

Still on the ground, Theo let out a sharp cry of pain as Dressel kicked him hard in the kidneys. 'Do you want me to work on them here?'

'No time.' Klaus hesitated and then drew his own pistol and pointed it at Sophie. 'Come here!'

Sophie took three hesitant steps forward. Klaus held the pistol to her head. 'Look at Hertenberg!' he commanded. Sophie turned towards Theo, her eyes, unnaturally large at the best of times, were even wider with fear.

'Now, Hertenberg. Tell me the codenames, or I will shoot her.'

Theo rose stiffly to his feet. He looked down at the ground. 'Go ahead,' he said. 'I don't care about her. She betrayed me.'

Sophie let out a whimper.

'Of course you care about her,' Klaus said. 'You have been lovers for a year.'

Theo slowly raised his eyes to Sophie's. 'All right,' he said, in a soft voice. 'I do care about her. In fact, I love her. I have never really told her that before: I should have done.'

'Then give me the codenames. Who is Lion? And who is Zebra?'

Theo shook his head. 'No. You will kill Sophie and me

anyway. I am not going to betray any more brave men.'

Klaus hesitated. He needed another plan. 'Sophie? Do you know any of the codenames?'

'I worked some of them out myself.' Her voice was shaking with fear.

'Don't tell him!' said Theo.

Dressel struck Theo again, somewhere painful, and Theo let out a grunt.

'Sophie, if you tell me the names, I can stop the coup,' Klaus urged. 'I can save the Führer and arrest the traitors who want to overthrow him.'

Sophie bit her trembling lip, hesitating.

'This is the man who killed Anneliese,' Conrad said. 'You can't trust him!'

Dressel was about to strike Conrad when Klaus held up his hand to restrain him. 'Anneliese is alive,' he said.

'What?' said Sophie.

'She's alive. I had her moved from Sachsenhausen before de Lancey could get her released. She's in another camp. And once de Lancey is dead, I will free her.'

'How can I believe that?'

'I've kept her safe,' Klaus said. 'You know how I feel about her. I would never let any harm come to her.'

'Don't believe him!' said Conrad. 'He's lying!'

This time Dressel whacked him with the pistol and Conrad clutched his mouth, from which blood was leaking.

Sophie looked from Conrad to Theo, and then to Klaus. 'All right,' she said. 'Show me the list.'

Klaus smiled and lowered his gun, and put it back in its holster. He picked up the ball of paper and smoothed it out. He pulled out his torch and Sophie stood next to him as he shone the torch on the names.

'Eagle is Theo. And Leopard is Conrad.'

'Yes, yes,' said Klaus impatiently. 'But what about Zebra?'

'Zebra. I don't know,' said Sophie. 'Let me ask Theo.'

'How are you going to do that?' said Klaus.

'Watch,' said Sophie.

She moved slowly towards Theo, pursing her lips. Theo looked the other way. Conrad saw something flash in the moonlight in Sophie's bag. A needle. A hypodermic needle. A nurse's weapon. Sophie had come to her rendezvous with Klaus armed.

Conrad tensed, ready to move.

As Sophie raised herself on her toes to kiss Theo, she moved her right hand to her bag. Theo stared angrily off in the other direction. Dressel watched Theo.

As Sophie pressed herself up to him, Theo pushed her away in disgust. She seemed to slip and fall into Dressel, who took two steps back, his gun waving off target. She twisted and with lightning speed plunged the hypodermic into Dressel's wrist. He yelped in pain and the pistol fell to the ground. Conrad leaped. In one motion he grabbed the gun, turned it on Dressel, pointed it at his head and pulled the trigger.

Dressel died instantly, but at such close range that his skull was a mess. Sophie screamed and recoiled. Conrad turned his gun on Klaus, but Klaus was already moving behind Sophie. As Conrad looked for a clear shot, Klaus grabbed her and pulled out his own gun, holding it to her temple.

'Stay there!' shouted Klaus as he backed away.

Conrad hesitated. He glanced at Theo, who was rooted to the spot.

Sophie stared at Conrad, her eyes wide with fear. Her cheek was spattered with Dressel's blood. 'Theo,' she whimpered. She closed her eyes.

Klaus could not be allowed to escape; it was as simple as that.

And Theo shouldn't have to take the decision. Conrad hoped that if he hit Klaus in the forehead, he would die instantly, before he had a chance to press the trigger of his own weapon.

Conrad aimed carefully. Fired.

His hope was misplaced. The two shots rang out almost simultaneously, and Klaus and Sophie crumpled to the ground. Klaus must have been watching Conrad's trigger finger rather than waiting for the sound of the shot before firing his own gun.

'Come on, Theo,' said Conrad dully to his blood-spattered friend, who cradled Sophie in his arms.

Theo looked up at him. There were tears in his eyes. 'She was so brave. She died so bravely.'

'Let's go,' Conrad said. He picked up the blue copybook, lying on the grass a few feet away from Klaus's body, and took Theo gently by the arm. 'Someone might have heard the shots. We have to go. We still have things to do.'

Thirty-seven

Chamberlain woke early on the morning of 28 September knowing he had until two o'clock that afternoon to stop a war. He was exhausted. The day before had been long and frustrating, the worst of the crisis. He had sent last-minute appeals to Hitler requesting that he reconsider his position, and to Roosevelt asking him to intervene. With Horace Wilson, just back from his latest failed mission to Berlin, he had drafted a telegram to the Czech government insisting that they accede to Germany's demands, but this had been scotched by Halifax, who remained firm that they could not press the Czechs to do something that the British government believed to be wrong. Chamberlain knew he would have a Cabinet revolt on his hands if he persisted, and so he gave up. At eight o'clock, exhausted, he had given a radio broadcast to the nation, preparing them for war. He knew it had not been an inspirational address; he had not felt inspired. Then, to cap it all, he had been awoken that morning by a letter from Hitler rejecting the pleas Wilson had made in Berlin to change his mind.

He would have one more try. He drafted a message to Hitler proposing a five-power conference of Germany, Britain, France, Italy and Czechoslovakia to discuss the question. Then, following the suggestion of the British Ambassador in Rome, he wrote a similar message to Mussolini. The messages had been dispatched to His Majesty's respective Ambassadors in Berlin and Rome by ten o'clock.

* * *

Gertrude Lüttgen came in to work very early that morning. She knew that Klaus was interested in Wilfrid Israel, and she had just remembered that he had been seen with Adam von Trott, someone else the Gestapo had suspicions about. She knocked on Klaus's door and carried in the Trott file.

Klaus's office was empty, which didn't surprise her this early in the morning. On the desk, next to an envelope with Klaus's name on it in Kriminal Assistant Fischer's handwriting, was a single sheet of paper. Curiosity was what had made Gertrude one of the Gestapo's best clerks. She couldn't resist picking up the sheet and reading it.

It was not yet dawn when Conrad and Theo met the other members of the raiding party at army headquarters in the Bendlerstrasse. They had each managed a couple of hours' sleep, Conrad in one of the flats commandeered by the raiding party, Theo in his own apartment. Captain Heinz handed out guns, ammunition and grenades and again ran through the plan to take the Chancellery. Security there was poor, especially in the current crisis when all kinds of people were coming and going, and there were only thirteen SS guards on duty. Oster had arranged for a friend in the Foreign Ministry to unlock the big double doors behind the guards, and it was through here that the assault would be made.

Most of the members of the raiding party knew Theo and knew each other. They were Prussian army officers, student leaders, writers and young aristocrats. Captain Heinz, the former soldier from the Great War who had fought in the dirty street battles of the 1920s, was older and more battle-hardened than his men. But there was no lack of courage in the tense young faces as they waited for the order to move. Despite his flawless accent, they knew that Conrad was not a German soldier, but they were comforted by the fact that Theo and Heinz seemed to have confidence in him. For Conrad's part, he was proud to be among them, and determined not to fail in his chosen task. To shoot and kill Hitler.

The raiding party dispersed back to the three flats near the Chancellery to wait.

'Theo?'

'What is it?' Conrad and Theo were hurrying along the streets towards their rendezvous. The raiding party were moving in twos and threes so as not to attract attention.

'I wonder what will happen when they find the bodies?'

'They'll start an investigation. Once they realize who Klaus is, the police will call in the Gestapo.'

'Will they discover what Klaus was working on?'

'It will take them some time. We know that Klaus didn't have any concrete evidence, which is why he wanted my notes. And we've got those back now.'

'So you don't think they will piece it together?'

'Not before two o'clock this afternoon,' said Theo. 'And after that it will be too late.'

Gertrude, usually so diligent, found it impossible to concentrate on her work that morning. She was an intelligent woman; she understood what she had read. There were highly detailed plans to launch a coup against the Führer as soon as he mobilized for war against Czechoslovakia. And that mobilization was expected this very day!

What surprised Gertrude, shocked her even, was that she found she hoped the coup would succeed. She was a good Nazi: she had joined the League of German Girls, the female equivalent of the Hitler Youth, at sixteen, soon after Hitler had come to power. She enjoyed her job, she was good at it, and she liked working for Klaus. But things happened in Prinz-Albrecht-Strasse that horrified her, things that she would never dream of telling her father, the pastor at St Mark's Church. Six months before, she had begun to lose files or misplace information in cases where the story of one of the Gestapo's victims seemed particularly poignant. Never with Jews, she had no sympathy at all with Jews. But there were some people, decent, hard-working Germans, who had been caught up in the Third Reich's machinery through no fault of their own. These people she helped.

She knew deep in her heart that the Third Reich had gone wrong somewhere; not only that, she could see it was set on a path of ever-increasing violence and depravity. Nothing could stop it, except perhaps a world war.

Or a coup.

'Have you heard the news, Gertrude?'

Gertrude was jolted out of her reverie to see Claudia, a colleague in her department, her face flushed with a mixture of excitement and horror.

Gertrude's heart skipped a beat. Was this it? The coup?

'Kriminalrat Schalke has been found shot in the Tiergarten! With Dressel. And a woman. All dead!'

The news hit Gertrude hard. She liked working for Klaus; he appreciated her skills and he was less cruel than many of his colleagues. But she knew immediately what she had to do. She grabbed the Trott file from her desk and strode into Klaus's office. She placed some of the papers in the file on his desk and scooped up the single page of Klaus's notes, stuffing it back into that same folder. She was just in time; on the way back to her own office she passed Kriminalrat Huber and two of his men marching determinedly along the corridor.

* * *

In the Bendlerstrasse, General von Witzleben and Colonel Oster gathered in the office of General Halder. Oster handed the Chief of the General Staff a letter.

'What's this?' asked Halder.

'Two days ago, Horace Wilson, who is a special adviser to Chamberlain, delivered an offer of further discussions to Hitler,' said Oster. 'This is a copy of Hitler's reply.'

Halder read the note, his face reddening as he did so. 'This proves it,' he said. 'Despite everything he has told me over the last few days, it is clear Hitler is determined to invade Czechoslovakia whatever the British do.'

'That's what I thought,' said General von Witzleben.

Halder glanced at his co-conspirators. 'The time has come to bring in General von Brauchitsch,' he said.

'But what if he doesn't respond?' said von Witzleben.

'Then we move without him. Wait here.'

With that, Halder strode out of his office, clutching the copy of Hitler's reply to Chamberlain.

He was back five minutes later, a smile on his face.

'Will he do it?' von Witzleben asked.

'Yes. But he wants to go to the Chancellery just to make sure that Hitler really is bent on war. He will call us from there with the order to move.'

'But should we wait, Herr General?' asked von Witzleben.

'We wait,' said Halder. 'I believe von Brauchitsch is convinced. And the coup will have much more legitimacy if the commander-in-chief of the army gives the order.'

Von Witzleben hurried off to Army District III headquarters in the Hohenzollerndamm, where he waited by the telephone ready to give von Brockdorff's 23rd Infantry Division its orders to march from Potsdam, only a few kilometres outside Berlin. Before he left, he assured Oster that if von Brauchitsch dithered, he would give the order to launch the coup himself.

Oster sat at his desk in Abwehr headquarters, ready to telephone Heinz. Canaris, Schacht, Count Helldorf, Beck and dozens of other conspirators knew what they had to do. Everything was in place. Everyone was waiting.

It was after eleven o'clock by the time Fischer got back to Gestapo headquarters. His interviews with the staff of N. Israel had been disappointing. Even the Party members had shown an unusual determination not to incriminate their boss.

He headed straight for Klaus's office, ostensibly to check that Klaus had received his report, but also to ask some indirect questions about the sheet of notes he had seen. Was there really going to be a coup attempt that day, he wondered? Perhaps Klaus would be out of the office doing something about it.

Long before he got there, he heard the news. He hurried on, and found a Gestapo agent going through Klaus's desk.

'Have you found his notes on the coup?' Fischer said.

'What notes?' said the agent.

'A single sheet of paper. I found it on the floor in his office and left it on his desk. At the top of the sheet was the word "Coup" and today's date. There were notes about a plan for a putsch: an attack on the Chancellery and a military takeover of Berlin.

'I haven't seen anything like that.'

'Are you sure? Let me look.' Fischer shoved the agent out of the way and quickly glanced through the papers on Klaus's desk. He found some documents related to a man named Adam von Trott, and his own report on Wilfrid Israel still sealed in its envelope, but nothing about a coup.

'Who's in charge of the investigation?' Fischer snapped.

'Kriminalrat Huber.'

'Do you know where he is?'

'I think he's reporting to Gruppenführer Heydrich.'

The small apartment was filled with the smell of sweat and cigarette smoke; there was so much cigarette smoke that it was difficult to see. Twenty men were crammed in there. Some of them spoke softly to each other, some played skat or back-gammon, some just stared into space. All of them smoked.

Conrad sat next to Theo on the floor in the kitchen and thought about what he was about to do. Assassinating a world leader was a major step, the enormity of which was only now sinking in. He thought of other assassins, the killer of Abraham Lincoln – who was that? – John Wilkes Booth. And then of course there was Gavrilo Princip, the man who had shot the Archduke Franz Ferdinand at Sarajevo and started the most terrible war the world had known. To date. Princip had believed totally in the cause of Serb nationalism, but Conrad didn't share his ideological certainty. Since the age of eighteen Conrad had espoused the cause of pacifism, but in the last couple of years his faith in that cause had been shaken as all his assumptions had been proved too simplistic. Now, though, there was something simple he could do to prevent millions of men killing each other.

He knew that by taking it upon himself to shoot Hitler he was greatly reducing his chances of survival. Every one of the Führer's bodyguard that remained standing would instantly point his weapon at him.

If he succeeded, his action would certainly make its mark in the history books. But his name wouldn't be associated with it: a mysterious Lieutenant Eiche would take the credit. Conrad didn't mind; he wasn't looking for a place in history. There was only one person whom he wanted to know what he had done: his father. He hoped Warren had found a way of safely delivering his letter.

For a pacifist, Conrad had killed a lot of people. There was one of the Republican soldiers whom he and David Griffiths had caught raping the nuns in Spain. There were others in Spain too; he hadn't counted how many he had shot in his eight months there. A dozen perhaps? Twenty? Then there were Klaus, Dressel and Sophie. He had really killed Sophie.

'I'm sorry about Sophie, Theo.'

Theo didn't answer at first. He just stared at the small potted fern on the windowsill of the kitchen. 'I was a fool. An arrogant fool.'

Conrad didn't say anything. He agreed with Theo and Theo knew it.

'She was absolutely right that I took her for granted, Conrad. I thought I knew her so well, I thought she was so shallow, but I didn't understand her at all. I never would have suspected she was a *Nazisse*. I never suspected she was anything much.'

Still Conrad didn't answer.

'You know, when I said I loved her, at the end, I only said that to make her feel better.'

'I know.'

'But in the end she died for me. For us. For what we are doing.'

They sat in silence for a minute.

'Got another cigarette?' Conrad asked. Theo handed him one and he lit it. 'Did you hear what Klaus said about Anneliese?'

'About how he had whisked her away to another camp?'

'Yes. Do you believe it?'

'Honestly?'

'Yes, honestly.'

'No,' said Theo. 'Klaus would have said anything to get Sophie to give him the names on that list. What about you?'

Conrad pulled angrily at his cigarette. 'No.'

'I'm sorry,' said Theo. 'Sophie. Anneliese. Both...'

'Killed by the Nazis.'

'Yes,' said Theo.

'That might happen to us,' said Conrad. 'In an hour or two.'

'Yes,' said Theo. 'But at least we will die fighting the swine.'

Heydrich listened to Huber's report of the investigation into Klaus's murder. Death rarely upset Heydrich, but this one did. He realized he had liked his shambling assistant. He would miss his cunning insights, and his company at the Salon Kitty.

Huber had already made progress. Footprints of two men had been found at the scene of the crime: soldiers, or at least men wearing army-issued boots. The girl had been identified as Sophie Pohlmann, who was the girlfriend of Lieutenant Theo von Hertenberg, who worked at the War Ministry. As far as Huber was aware, Klaus was working on an investigation of Wilfrid Israel, the owner of the department store. And Huber had found an interesting scrap of paper crunched into a ball a few metres from the bodies.

He handed it to Heydrich.

It was a list. Of animals. Beside each animal was the name of a leading Nazi figure.

'What do you think this is?' asked Heydrich.

'I don't know,' said Huber. 'The writing isn't Schalke's. Perhaps it's an assassination list? That's just a guess.'

'And an interesting one,' said Heydrich.

'Do you have anything you can add, Herr Gruppenführer?' Huber asked. 'I know that Schalke often did special work for you directly.'

'Possibly,' said Heydrich. 'Theo von Hertenberg is an officer in the Abwehr. I'm sure Schalke will have had a file on him. And Schalke had heard a rumour about a coup, although he had no hard evidence. You know how many rumours there are, Huber?'

'Certainly.'

'And you are correct, Schalke was doing some special work for me. Work that I would like to remain confidential.'

'Was that related to the search of the Englishman de Lancey's apartment?' Huber remembered the other scrap of paper he had found there, which he had passed on to Klaus unread. Now he wished he had looked at it more closely. Although there were some things it was better not to know.

'Yes, it was.'

'Do you think the killing might be related?'

'I don't know,' said Heydrich. 'Perhaps. Hertenberg and de Lancey are old friends. Let me call Admiral Canaris. I want to see if he knows anything about this. Wait outside.'

'Yes, Herr Gruppenführer!'

Heydrich mulled over the possibilities in his mind. He knew Schalke had been obsessed with that Jewish girl, and as a result was obsessed with de Lancey. On the other hand, he had also been looking for hard evidence of a coup and the names on the list did look like targets. Canaris would know. He picked up the telephone.

Admiral Canaris had cleared his desk. He was waiting, ready to react to whatever the day's events might bring. It really did look as if this would be the last day of the Thousand Year Reich.

His telephone rang. 'Gruppenführer Heydrich for you, excellency.'

'Thank you.' In the moments while his secretary connected the head of the Gestapo, all Canaris's senses sharpened.

'Admiral, I would like your opinion on something.'

'Of course, Reinhard, what is it?' Canaris kept his voice level, friendly.

'Two of my officers were murdered last night in the Tiergarten, together with a woman. The woman's name is Sophie Pohlmann, and the officers were Schalke and Dressel. Pohlmann is the girlfriend of one of your officers, Lieutenant von Hertenberg. Do you know anything about this?'

'No, I don't,' said Canaris, inwardly cursing Theo for not keeping him informed. This was dangerous.

'A list was found at the scene of the crime.'

'A list? Who was on it?'

'Senior party officials. Göring, Goebbels, myself. Not you.'

At least that wasn't a genuine list of members of the conspiracy then, thought Canaris with relief. 'Is the Führer's name on the list?' he asked, not caring what the answer was. He wanted time to think.

'No.'

He didn't need much time. Canaris was a quick thinker and a master of deception. Heydrich needed an answer immediately, an answer that would put the Gestapo off the scent.

'Was Conrad de Lancey involved?' Canaris asked, groping his way towards that answer.

'We don't know,' Heydrich replied. 'I do know Schalke was actively investigating him.'

Canaris remembered that Conrad had claimed when under arrest by the Gestapo that he was an Abwehr agent investigating British attempts to use Göring as a spy. This claim had been discredited when the Gestapo alleged that de Lancey had been spying on their senior officers in Halle, an allegation that de Lancey denied. Canaris knew Heydrich's file by heart. He was from Halle. And there were rumours that his ancestry was Jewish. An idea flashed into the spy chief's mind.

'Ignore the list,' Canaris said. 'It's a figment of de Lancey's imagination. You were right; he is a British spy. But the assassination list is just a cover.'

'A cover? For what?'

'For some investigations he was making into your background, Reinhard. Something to do with your ancestry. We found some documents he had copied.'

There was a pause. 'What have you done with them?'

Canaris laughed. 'Why, destroyed them of course. I didn't believe a word of them. And don't worry, only myself and Hertenberg have seen them. And of course your man Schalke. De Lancey must have killed him.'

'And where is de Lancey now?' Heydrich asked.

'Somewhere he won't cause you any more trouble,' Canaris answered as ambiguously as possible. 'If you can keep this quiet at your end, I assure you we can here.'

There was silence on the telephone as Heydrich thought this offer over. 'Thank you, Admiral.'

'It was no trouble,' said Canaris. He smiled as he put down the receiver, pleased that he could still think quickly under pressure. That should buy them a few more hours.

And that was all they needed.

Thirty-eight

Lord Perth, the British Ambassador in Rome, rushed to the Palazzo Chigi, where he spoke to Count Ciano, the Italian Foreign Minister, pleading for Mussolini to take up the role of mediator. Ciano hurried to see the Duce, who was enthusiastic about his proposed role as European peacemaker, much more enthusiastic than he was at the idea of being sucked into a war with France and Britain over Czechoslovakia. Mussolini picked up the telephone and called Count Attolico, the Italian Ambassador to Germany, telling him to see Hitler immediately and suggest that he delay hostilities for twenty-four hours while Mussolini convened a conference to discuss the situation.

In Berlin, Sir Nevile Henderson was having much more difficulty getting his message through to Hitler. The Reich Chancellery was chaos. The corridors were full of ministers, generals, Party officials and foreign diplomats, each with his entourage of hangers-on, each craving an audience with Hitler. The Führer himself was in a state of great excitement, moving from room to room, haranguing whoever would listen on the subject of the evil Czechs and listening to no one. The members of the Leibstandarte SS Adolf Hitler, Hitler's personal bodyguard, had lost control; they too were caught up in the excitement.

Henderson could not get near Hitler, despite having made an appointment, but the French Ambassador, André François-

Poncet, somehow managed to force himself in front of the German Chancellor, armed with a map of Europe, large sections of which had been coloured red to signify German control. 'Why should you take the risk of war when your essential demands could be met without it?' he asked in fluent German. For the first time that morning, Hitler seemed to be listening.

Count Attolico arrived breathless in the Red Room, the antechamber outside the Chancellor's office, neatly bypassing the waiting Henderson. He accosted the SS adjutant at the door. 'I have a personal message for the Führer from the Duce and I must see him quick, quick, quick,' he said in excitable English; Attolico spoke no German. The adjutant interrupted François-Poncet to give Hitler the message, and Hitler, together with his interpreter, left François-Poncet to speak to the Italian Ambassador in the corridor.

Chamberlain had been persuaded to call an emergency session of Parliament to debate Czechoslovakia. The House of Commons was packed, with MPs listening closely to the Prime Minister's every word as he gave a detailed account of the events of the crisis. Ambassadors, bishops and even Queen Mary were crammed into the visitors' galleries, watching the last few hours of peace dribble away.

Then Lord Halifax, in the Peers' Gallery, was handed a note by Alec Cadogan. He scanned it, and hurried down behind the Speaker's Chair, where he sent it on to Lord Dunglass, the Prime Minister's Parliamentary Private Secretary. Dunglass passed it to Sir John Simon, who did his best to attract the attention of the Prime Minister, who was still on his feet.

Eventually Chamberlain noticed Simon's frantic signals. He stopped speaking and read the note slowly, betraying no emotion on his face. The House watched in silence. The seconds ticked by. He glanced at his Chancellor of the Exchequer.

'Shall I tell them now?' he asked in a whisper that could be heard throughout the chamber.

Simon nodded.

Chamberlain looked up. 'I have something further to say to the House. I have now been informed by Herr Hitler that he invites me to meet him in Munich tomorrow morning. He has also invited Signor Mussolini and Monsieur Daladier. I need not say what my answer will be.'

The House erupted in cheering.

Chamberlain waited for quiet and then continued. 'We are all patriots and there can be no honourable member of this House who does not feel his heart leap that the crisis has been postponed to give us once more the opportunity to try what reason and good will and discussion will do to settle a problem which is already within sight of settlement.'

This time there was no stopping the cheering. Almost to a man, and a woman, the House stood to applaud their prime minister. Almost. Winston Churchill remained firmly in his seat, his head sunk in his shoulders, his expression a mixture of anger and despair.

General von Brauchitsch was caught up in the chaos at the Chancellery. Before he had fought his way to the front of the queue to speak to Hitler, it was clear that something momentous had occurred.

He never telephoned von Witzleben.

Oster heard it from Erich Kordt, the civil servant in the Foreign Ministry who had promised to unlock the double doors in the Chancellery, and whose brother, Theo Kordt, was in the German Embassy in London.

'Hans, the invasion is on hold.'

'What's happened?'

'Mussolini has offered to host a Five-Power Conference at Munich and Hitler has accepted. It means he will almost certainly get the Sudetenland without a war.'

'I don't believe it,' said Oster.

'Does this mean our plans are cancelled?'

Oster took a deep breath. 'I don't know. I'll have to think about it. Talk to some people.'

He put down the phone and hurried to General von Witzleben's headquarters only a few minutes' walk away.

'Have you heard?' The question was unnecessary; he could see from the general's face that he had.

'I can't believe it. So close!'

'Can we go ahead anyway?'

'Von Brauchitsch will never order a coup now. Neither will Halder, for that matter. He has always insisted that the country needs to be on the brink of war before we move.'

'But what about you, Herr General? You said you would act if von Brauchitsch and Halder faltered.'

The general shook his head. 'Don't you see?' he said. 'To this poor foolish nation, Hitler is once again our dearly beloved führer: unique, sent by God. And we are nothing more than a little pile of reactionary officers and politicians who dare to put pebbles in the way of the greatest statesman of all times at the moment of his greatest triumph.' The general smiled wryly. 'If we try to do something now, history, and not just German history, will have nothing more to say about us than that we refused to serve the greatest German when he was at his greatest.'

'So it's over?'

Von Witzleben nodded. 'It's over.'

As Oster walked back to his own office on the Tirpitzufer,

the anger boiled up inside him. How could Chamberlain have been so stupid? After the Sudetenland, Hitler would take the rest of Czechoslovakia. And then the Danzig Corridor, and probably the whole of Poland. This was the best chance the British had to stop him! How many times had they been told that the German army would remove Hitler if he launched an invasion of Czechoslovakia? Yet they hadn't listened.

If only Chamberlain had stood firm, Hitler would have been dead before the day was out.

Thirty-nine

The telephone rang in the smoke-filled apartment and there was instant silence. All eyes were on Heinz as he answered. The young men in uniform around him stiffened. Hands clutched weapons.

Heinz's face was impassive, but there was perhaps a slight drooping of the shoulders as he listened. His face was grim as he turned to face his men.

'It's off,' he said. 'Hitler has agreed to meet the British Prime Minister in Munich to discuss the future of Czechoslovakia. The British and French have caved in. There will be no invasion of Czechoslovakia. There will be no coup.'

There was an uproar of groans and shouted questions, most of which Heinz was unable to answer.

'This can't be true,' said Conrad.

'I'm going to talk to Oster,' said Theo. He got to his feet and squeezed past the crush of people to get to the telephone. A minute later he was back.

'It is true,' he said.

'Can't we go ahead anyway?'

'I suggested that to Oster, but he says no. The generals won't do it and Canaris won't do it. Oster ordered me to stand down with the others.'

'But he can't order me,' said Conrad.

'What do you mean?'

'I mean that I am going to the Chancellery right now to shoot Adolf Hitler myself.'

'You're mad.'

'No I'm not. Heinz said it was chaos in there. I know where I can get in. I'm going.'

With that Conrad laid the Schmeisser machine pistol he had been issued with on to the floor and sidled towards the door. He'd never get into the Chancellery with the machine pistol, and his Luger sidearm should be enough to do the job.

Theo followed him. 'I'm coming with you.'

Heinz calmed his raiding party and organized them to disperse. A couple of minutes later he realized Eiche and Hertenberg were absent. Someone said he had seen them slip out. Heinz thought for a moment and then telephoned Oster.

Fischer dashed round to the next-door building. He found Huber leaving Heydrich's office, scowling.

'Herr Kriminalrat, I have some information about the Schalke case.'

'Put it in a report and send it to me,' snapped Huber angrily. He didn't stop, but walked rapidly towards the stairs.

Fischer hurried to keep up with him. 'Last night I saw some notes on Schalke's desk. About a coup. A plan to storm the Chancellery today. The twenty-eighth!'

'Didn't you hear me?' said Huber, not breaking his stride. 'Write it down in a report for me.'

Fischer grabbed his superior officer's sleeve. 'But if there really is a coup planned for today—'

Huber stopped and glared at Fischer. 'Get your hands off me!'

Fischer dropped his hands to his side.

'Kriminal Assistant Fischer, let me make something clear.

The Gruppenführer knows about the so-called coup. He believes that it is a fiction. He also knows why Schalke was killed, but for his own reasons he doesn't want anyone else to know, including Schalke's own colleagues. The Gruppenführer has made himself very clear on this point, and when the Gruppenführer makes himself clear, it is best to listen. Do you understand?'

Fischer nodded. 'Yes, Herr Kriminalrat!'

Conrad and Theo walked smartly along the streets the short distance to the Chancellery, two Wehrmacht officers in a hurry in a city full of Wehrmacht officers in a hurry.

Conrad was appalled by what Chamberlain had done. The British Prime Minister had known that Hitler's days were numbered. All he had had to do was to show some concrete support for Czechoslovakia and the most evil and dangerous leader in European history would have been overthrown by his own people. But Chamberlain didn't even have the courage for that.

Conrad thought of all the risks brave, honourable Germans like Ewald von Kleist and Theo and General Beck and countless others that Conrad didn't even know had taken to enlist the help of the British government. Chamberlain had ignored them all.

Well, Conrad wouldn't. He would do what he was sure was right.

'You don't have to come,' he said to Theo. 'This is different to a coup. We are very unlikely to survive this.'

'I know.' Theo's voice was unnaturally hoarse. He coughed, trying to clear his throat. 'I got you into this, Conrad, and I'm going through it with you. Wherever it leads.'

Conrad smiled at his friend. Theo looked nervous. Nervous and courageous. For all his military ancestry, he had never been this close to death before. It struck Conrad that he and Theo were quite similar after all. With embarrassment he remembered his suspicions of Theo when he had first arrived in Berlin. They had been way off the mark: all the time Theo had been dealing with the violence, cruelty and fear of life under the Nazis. But ultimately, both Conrad and Theo had come to the same conclusion: they would do what they must to stand up to Nazism, even if it meant death.

Theo caught Conrad's glance and straightened, throwing back his shoulders. 'Besides which, you'll need me to get you to Hitler. I can tell the guards I have a message for him from Admiral Canaris.'

Conrad *had* been this close to death before. The fear spurred him on; it felt good to be acting, not waiting. His senses were alive. He picked out the different sounds of the street noises: the rumble and roar of the motor cars; the jangle of tram bells; the swish of bicycle tyres; the subdued click of pedestrians' heels on the pavements. His nostrils took in the cool sharpness of the early autumnal Berlin air, tinged with petrol fumes and the scent of two smartly dressed ladies whom he and Theo pushed past.

He knew he only had a few more minutes to live, but that knowledge made him walk faster towards the Chancellery and his destiny. Was it destiny? Was it duty? He didn't know, but he did know that there was no choice but to go through with it. Hitler had ruined so many lives, and taken so many others – including Anneliese's – and he had only just started. It had fallen to Conrad to do something about it, and he wasn't going to shirk that responsibility.

He remembered his father describing how he had stumbled towards the German trenches at Passchendaele, knowing he would die, but also knowing that he didn't want to kill any more human beings before he did so. Well, Conrad had one more human being to kill. His father's war to end all wars had been a sham. But one death to avert one more world war would be worthwhile.

Three deaths if you included himself and Theo.

They arrived at the Wilhelmplatz in front of the Reich Chancellery. There were plenty of people milling about the entrance. As they watched, von Ribbentrop hurried out, followed by a small entourage, passing a diplomat in winged collar and morning suit hurrying in. Two black-uniformed SS guards stood at attention watching the comings and goings out of the corners of their eyes.

Conrad glanced at Theo. Once they had walked into that building, they would not walk out alive.

'Ready?'

Theo nodded.

'Then let's go.'

Fischer's mind span in confusion as he left the Prinz-Albrecht-Palais on Wilhelmstrasse. He pulled out a cigarette and lit it. Rather than go straight back to Gestapo headquarters next door, he decided to stroll up the street to try to get his thoughts in order.

Huber could say what he liked, but the notes Fischer had read suggested that Schalke took the threat of the coup seriously. So why had Heydrich shut the investigation down? It was clear that Huber didn't know. It must be a personal reason. Perhaps Heydrich was involved with the coup? Perhaps the SS and the Gestapo were planning to take over the government? But the notes suggested that the Wehrmacht were planning to move *against* the Gestapo, not with them.

It made no sense.

He crossed Leipziger Strasse and passed the Kaiserhof Hotel. He dropped his cigarette stub and was about to turn back towards his office when he saw a face he recognized. Two faces.

They were two men he had trailed on and off for Klaus. Conrad de Lancey and Theo von Hertenberg. And de Lancey was wearing the uniform of an officer in the Wehrmacht! He watched as the two men exchanged words and set off across the road to the Reich Chancellery. Fischer followed them.

Conrad and Theo walked straight past the Chancellery entrance on Wilhelmstrasse and turned into a small courtyard where there were two double doors. These were unguarded, presumably because the guards assumed they were locked. Without pausing, Theo turned the heavy iron handle of one of the doors and pushed. The door moved; Oster's Foreign Ministry friend had done as he had promised.

The lobby of the building was full of people jostling, protesting, hurrying to and fro. The black-uniformed SS guards with their white gloves were busy by the main entrance stopping visitors, too busy to notice Conrad and Theo. A small bespectacled man did see them and turned the other way. Oster's friend, perhaps.

Theo led Conrad to the foot of the grand staircase. Neither of them had been inside before, although both of them had studied the plans Heinz had shown them. There were more SS guards on the staircase, but they were being jostled by anxious-looking officers, diplomats and civil servants rushing up and down the stairs.

Conrad glanced up and saw a figure he recognized bearing down on him: Sir Nevile Henderson, His Majesty's Ambassador to Germany, looking preoccupied. Conrad lowered his head as he climbed the stairs, hoping that his uniform would confuse the Ambassador. And so it did, until the last instant when out of the corner of his eye, Conrad saw Henderson hesitate on the bottom step.

'De Lancey?' the Ambassador enquired in a doubtful voice.

Conrad kept going, trusting in Henderson's desire not to make an embarrassing scene and his fear of being proven mistaken if he did. It worked.

They hurried along a corridor at the top of the stairs until they reached an opened door, guarded by a tall SS man. Theo barked that he had to see the Führer urgently with a message from Admiral Canaris. The guard waved him into a red-plush antechamber. An impatient crowd was gathered at one end of the room, outside the door to Hitler's office. An SS adjutant acted as gatekeeper.

'*Heil Hitler!*' said Theo, raising his arm. 'We have an important message for the Führer from Admiral Canaris.'

'Everyone here wishes to speak to the Führer,' said the SS officer.

'But I must speak to him at once,' said Theo. 'Tell him the Abwehr has uncovered a British secret-service plot to destabilize the High Command. They are planning to put it into action at any minute.'

The SS officer glanced doubtfully at Theo. 'Then why doesn't Admiral Canaris come himself?'

'He's trying to deal with the plot now!' said Theo. 'We don't have much time.'

In a day of surprise and counter-surprise, this proposition did not seem as incredible as it might otherwise have done. 'Very well,' said the SS officer. 'The Führer is speaking to Field Marshal Göring now. I will interrupt him.'

Fischer ran across the road and up the steps to the entrance, where he was promptly stopped by the two SS guards. He gabbled his explanation, but they wouldn't listen. A delegation of Italian diplomats pulled up in a long Mercedes and hurried up the steps. The guards, who recognized them, let them through.

Fischer gave up and dodged into the courtyard to the door he had seen de Lancey and Hertenberg use. It pushed open easily. There was a reception desk in the lobby, and he rushed over to it.

'There are intruders in the building!' he said to the harassed SS guard at the desk.

'Who are you?'

'They are planning to shoot the Führer.'

The guard raised an eyebrow. 'I said, who are you?'

'Kriminal Assistant Fischer, Gestapo.' Fischer pulled out his Party badge.

At that moment the Italian delegation arrived and launched into a tirade in English, Italian and German at the guard. The guard ignored Fischer's badge and dealt with the visitors.

'The Führer's life is in danger!' Fischer shouted in frustration.

The Italians ignored him. The guard snapped at him to wait. It took a minute to sign all the Italians in, and then they were on their way.

'There are two men in the building dressed as Wehrmacht officers,' Fischer said. 'I have information at Gestapo head-quarters that suggests there is a plan to overthrow the Führer today. I believe that these men intend to kill him in the next few minutes.' Now the guard was listening. 'I must speak to your superior officer at once!' Fischer urged. 'If the Führer dies, it will be your responsibility!'

The guard picked up the telephone and dialled a number. Fischer noticed a Wehrmacht colonel slip through the double doors from which he had just come a moment earlier. 'The adjutant is just coming,' the guard said, passing the receiver to the excitable Gestapo officer. Fischer decided to ignore the colonel. The important thing was to get through to the guards around Hitler before it was too late.

Two diplomats, a civil servant and a general scowled at Theo and Conrad as they waited. Through the window, Conrad could see the garden behind the Chancellery and the men calmly working on the new building next door, oblivious to the drama unfolding so close to them.

Conrad scanned the two SS guards. Tall, fit, young, inexperienced, they were distracted by all the excitement and the hubbub around them. They would respond to a rapid movement, but if he surreptitiously slipped his Luger from out of his holster, they probably wouldn't notice. There was plenty to keep them occupied.

There was a bustle outside the room and the sound of English being spoken in a heavy Italian accent echoed down the corridor. 'The Duce wishes me to speak to the Führer now. Now, I say.'

A stumpy man with a short bristle of iron-grey hair and thick-lensed glasses burst into the Red Room and pushed himself in front of Conrad and Theo just as the door to the Chancellor's office opened.

There, six feet in front of Conrad, listening to the Italian Ambassador haranguing him in English, was Adolf Hitler.

Conrad had never seen the dictator so close. The little moustache and the lock of fine dark hair hanging down over the forehead were instantly recognizable. Lord Halifax had described him as commonplace and vulgar, but to Conrad he was the most powerful and dangerous man in Europe. An air of suppressed tension seemed to surround him, and caused those waiting for him to stiffen in anticipation. Close to, Conrad noticed that Hitler's skin was soft and pale, and flecked with drops of sweat, as were the bristles of his moustache. His right shoulder twitched in an angry tic. Blue eyes bulging from dark sockets stared at the Italian Ambassador in front of him as his interpreter translated.

Conrad slowly moved his hand to the Luger at his side. In a moment, the dictator would be dead. In another moment, in all probability, so would Conrad. He didn't care; it would be worth it. No one noticed Conrad; everyone's eyes were on the Führer.

Or not quite everyone's.

'Don't do it, Herr de Lancey. I order you not to shoot.'

The voice, little more than a whisper came from a foot behind Conrad.

Conrad turned to see Colonel Oster standing behind him, unarmed. 'You can't order me, remember, Oster. That's why I'm here.'

'I can order Hertenberg to shoot you.'

'He won't. At least not until it is too late.' Conrad slipped his pistol from its holster and rested it in front of his belt, under his cap which he clutched with his other hand. Still no one had noticed.

'Everything has changed,' said Oster. 'This morning, you were assisting a legitimate revolution, an attempt to bring democracy back to Germany. Now you are a lone assassin. Before, you were going to stop a war. Now, if you shoot Hitler, you will start one.'

'He's evil, Oster. You know that. How many Germans have to die before you realize how evil he is?'

'You will make him a martyr. The German people will demand revenge on the British, the Czechs, the French, all of Europe.'

Conrad hesitated.

'Hertenberg. Shoot de Lancey.'

Conrad waited. At the first movement Theo made towards his pistol, Conrad would shoot Hitler.

As Theo looked from his friend to his mentor, Conrad could see the excitement, the desire to seize the moment, overcome by Theo's innate respect for authority – and for reason.

'We don't want to start a war, Conrad,' said Theo. 'Remember Algy.'

Conrad thought of Algernon Pendleton who had lost his life at Ypres in 1916. And he thought of Gavrilo Princip whose assassin's bullet two years before had led to Algy's death, and millions of others like him.

'This is too big a decision for you and me to take,' said Theo. 'Let's go.'

Conrad felt the weight of history bearing down on his shoulders. He had spent years of his life studying German history. He, of all people, should know that the consequences of what he was about to do would be impossible to predict and could be truly disastrous. He had thought long and hard before he had convinced himself that the coup was the best way to bring peace.

Oster was right; an assassination was different. At that moment Conrad realized that he was being driven by hatred and a desire for revenge, rather than a sober calculation of the balance between right and wrong, peace and war.

He returned his Luger to its holster and turned to Theo.

'Don't worry. You don't have to shoot me.'

The SS adjutant took his time to get to the telephone, there were so many people clamouring for his attention. When he eventually picked up the receiver, he was bombarded by frantic warnings from an overwrought Gestapo agent. He was getting weary of these histrionics.

He glanced up to see the two Wehrmacht officers leaving the antechamber, accompanied by a colonel.

'Don't waste my time, Fischer,' he snapped. 'I can see the men now. They are leaving the building.'

Forty

The next day, Chamberlain flew to Munich, armed with his neatly furled umbrella. The leaders of Britain, France, Italy and Germany discussed the future of Czechoslovakia in the Brown House, the Nazi Party headquarters. The Five-Power Conference had become a Four-Power Conference: the Czech delegation was left skulking in the corridors outside. Inside, the four governments decided that the Czechs should allow German troops to march into the Sudetenland by 10 October. The text of this agreement was handed to the Czech Foreign Minister at 1.30 a.m.; he was told that a response from his government was not required. Without the Sudetenland and its line of fortifications the rest of Czechoslovakia was defence-less. As the Czech Prime Minister put it: 'We were given the choice of being murdered or committing suicide.'

The following morning, Chamberlain wrote out a brief note on a piece of paper and persuaded Hitler to sign it. This Hitler did quickly, and without much thought. The note stated:

> *We, the German Führer and Chancellor and the British Prime Minister, have had a further meeting today and are agreed in recognizing that the question of Anglo-German relations is of the first importance for the two countries and for Europe.*
>
> *We regard the agreement signed last night and the*

Anglo-German Naval Agreement as symbolic of the desire
of our two peoples never to go to war with one another
again.

We are resolved that the method of consultation shall be
the method adopted to deal with any other questions that
may concern our two countries, and we are determined to
continue our efforts to remove possible sources of difference
and thus to contribute to assure the peace of Europe.

It was this declaration that Chamberlain had been working so tirelessly to secure. This was the goal of Plan Z; it was for this that he had let Hitler remain in power. This was the piece of paper he waved to the cheering crowd at Heston Airport later that day on his return to London. This it was that guaranteed 'peace in our time'.

Three days later, Hjalmar Schacht, Colonel Oster, Theo and Generals von Witzleben and Beck all met at von Witzleben's house. There they tossed all their plans for the coup into the fire, including Theo's notebook. Perhaps one day in the future Hitler would overreach himself and give them another opportunity to act, but for now they had to watch an ecstatic populace cheer their führer as he absorbed the Sudetenland into the Reich without a drop of blood being shed.

The debate on the Munich Agreement in the House of Commons lasted three days. Duff Cooper duly resigned, but the prevailing tone was in favour of the Prime Minister who had preserved peace. At the end of the debate, Winston Churchill gave his own summary of what had happened:

'One pound was demanded at the pistol's point. When it was given, two pounds were demanded at the pistol's point. Finally, the dictator consented to take one pound, seventeen shillings and sixpence and the rest in promises of goodwill for the future.'

* * *

The traffic in the Potsdamer Platz was as busy as ever and, with the threat of war suddenly removed, crowds thronged towards Wertheim's department store on the far side of the square from the Café Josty. Theo and Conrad toyed with small cups of coffee each. Throughout 1938 the quality of coffee available in Berlin's cafés had deteriorated steadily, but however bad it was Berliners were still in the habit of drinking it.

'Are you sure this is safe?' Conrad asked.

'Quite sure,' said Theo. 'The last thing the Gestapo wants to do is find you. For some reason, Heydrich is convinced that you have been spending your free time in Halle checking up on his ancestry. It didn't take much for us to hint that Klaus Schalke's death was connected to that somehow. It was amazing how quickly the Gestapo dropped their investigation.'

'I'm sorry I couldn't come to Sophie's funeral.'

'It was sad. The saddest thing was that her father insisted on all the Nazi paraphernalia. But I don't believe she died a Nazi.'

'She didn't,' said Conrad.

'Hey, fellas!' They looked around to see Warren striding towards them, white teeth flashing. 'Conrad! I didn't expect to find you here. But I'm glad to see you are still in one piece.'

'My name is Lars. Dr Lars Bendixen.' The Abwehr had given him new papers to replace those of Lieutenant Eiche.

'Whatever you say, doctor. But I'm not going to put up with that cod-Danish accent all afternoon.'

'All right,' said Conrad, 'let's speak German, then,' although he persisted with the Danish accent in that language.

'That's better,' said Warren. 'So, doc, I've got this pain in my back. Have you got anything for it?'

'Doctor of history, you imbecile. At the University of Copenhagen.'

'Shame. I thought you might have learned something useful
for a change.'

'Are you returning to Prague soon?'

'Next week. Vernon arrived back in Berlin yesterday. It will
be interesting. From what I understand the Czechs are hopping
mad.'

'That doesn't surprise me.'

'I shipped all your things back to your family in England,
by the way. Just in time, too. The Gestapo showed up at your
apartment to confiscate them the day afterwards.'

'Thank you, Warren.'

'What shall I do with the place?'

'Just leave it. I'll write to the owner in Paris to explain what
has happened. If I send him a big enough cheque, I'm sure he
will understand.'

Warren ordered a cup of coffee. 'Oh, and I got a friend who
was flying to Paris to post that letter to your father from there.'

Conrad smiled. 'I knew I could rely on you. I thought you
would be in front of the Chancellery to watch the parade. I was
lucky there were so few other people there so I could find you.'

'I didn't spot you,' said Warren.

Conrad glanced at Theo, who was frowning. He hadn't told
him of his quick escapade the afternoon before the coup to get
a message to his father. Come to think of it, the poor man must
be mystified. 'Could you do me one more favour, Warren? Could
you just let him know that I am alive?'

'OK,' said Warren. 'Say, with all this toing and froing to
Munich and places, did I miss a story?'

Conrad and Theo exchanged glances and grinned. 'I would
say that you did,' Conrad said.

'Am I going to hear about it now?'

'One day,' said Theo. 'One day, I hope.'

Warren frowned. Then he looked over towards the door of the café. 'Isn't that Captain Foley?'

Sure enough the unassuming Englishman was making his way towards their table. Behind him was a woman, walking awkwardly in clothes that were too big for her thin body.

Anneliese.

Her face was pinched and pale, the skin drawn tight over her cheekbones. But there was nothing unfamiliar about her smile when she saw Conrad.

She sat in the empty chair next to him.

'Captain Foley says I am not to kiss you,' she said to Conrad. 'But consider yourself kissed.'

'And you. It's so good to see you! I thought I would never see you again.'

'I look dreadful, though, don't I?'

'No,' said Conrad. 'You look wonderful.'

'We only have a few minutes,' said Foley. 'Anneliese has to leave the country tonight, so we must catch a train.'

'Do you want anything to eat?' asked Theo.

'Captain Foley gave me lunch on the way from Lichtenburg. But I'll have a Menzeltorte.'

The Menzeltorte was a Café Josty speciality. It was a square pastry with a hard layer of iced chocolate, underneath which was soft cream in lighter chocolate, then a crisp base.

'I know I'll only be able to manage a couple of mouthfuls, but I've been dreaming of it for the last six weeks.'

'Are you... all right?' Conrad asked.

'You mean, what was it like?'

'I suppose I do.'

'It was worse than last time. I had been in the camp a couple of weeks when I knocked myself out, falling against a wall. I spent a day in the infirmary, and after that I was in solitary confinement, first at Sachsenhausen, and then in Lichtenburg Castle. I had no idea why, until Captain Foley explained it to me.'

'Klaus wanted to hide you away.'

'So you couldn't have me.'

'I've got you now.' Their eyes met and Anneliese smiled. The café was crowded and noisy and Theo, Warren and Foley were carrying on a lively conversation right next to them, but Conrad didn't care. As far as he was concerned, Anneliese and he were the only two people there.

'You know he's dead now?' Conrad said after a few moments.

'Yes. Captain Foley told me that too. He also said that it was thanks to your persistence that they found me.'

'Before he died, Klaus said that you hadn't been killed, that he had whisked you away to another camp. Frankly, I didn't believe him, but I couldn't leave Germany until I had found out for sure. So I pestered a friend of Foley's called Israel, who pestered the commandant at Sachsenhausen, who admitted that Klaus had told him to announce that you were dead and transfer you somewhere else. It took a few days, but Israel was able to track you down to Lichtenburg. We owe him a lot.'

'Oh, Conrad, it's awful in those places, cut off from the outside world, not even knowing if the people you love know you are there. Not knowing whether you will ever get out.'

'Well, after Munich they decided Berlin was safe enough for Foley to return. So he came back here and got you out.'

'Munich? What happened in Munich?'

'There was nearly a war when you were in the camp. Munich was the conference that stopped it. Or delayed it. You can read all about it when you get a newspaper.'

'And Theo's little scheme?' Anneliese glanced at the Abwehr officer.

Conrad shrugged. 'Nothing came of it.'

'That's a shame.'

'It is. One day, perhaps.' Conrad hesitated, not wishing to add to Anneliese's troubles, but he couldn't hide what he had to say from her, either. 'Sophie's dead.'

Anneliese closed her eyes, and seemed to slump forward. Despite Foley's strictures about no signs of affection, Conrad reached out a hand to steady her.

'Let me guess. Klaus?'

Conrad nodded.

A tear ran down Anneliese's cheek. She wiped it away. 'I can't wait to get out of this country.'

The Menzeltorte came, and Anneliese took two bites, pushing it aside. 'What a shame. My poor stomach: it's far too rich. Any more and I think I will be sick.'

'Never mind,' said Conrad. 'Next week I'll take you to the Ritz for tea.'

Anneliese smiled. 'It will be so good to see my parents. But I'm nervous about England. I've never been there: I've no idea what I will do.'

Conrad fished a scrap of paper out of his pocket and scribbled down an address. 'I know you will be staying with your parents, but if you need anything, get in touch with my mother. She will help you, and she speaks German of course.'

'I hope my brother will be all right. He says the Luftwaffe need every pilot they can get and so they won't ask him any difficult questions.'

Conrad wondered whether in a year or two Anneliese's brother would be dropping bombs on his parents in England, but he kept that thought to himself.

'Will you be coming to London soon?' Anneliese asked.

'Very soon,' said Conrad. 'My papers say I'm a Danish academic, so I have to go to Copenhagen first. But I'll be home in a few days.'

'I can't wait.'

'All right,' announced Foley. 'I'm afraid it's time for us to dash. We certainly don't want Anneliese to miss her train.' He shook Warren's hand, and then Theo's. 'Good to meet you, Hertenberg. If ever you want a quiet chat—'

Theo grinned. 'There is absolutely no chance of that, Captain Foley. I am a loyal German.'

'Of course, of course.' He turned to Conrad. 'As for you, de Lancey. Don't be surprised if some friends of mine get in touch.'

'If they do, I'll tell them where to go,' said Conrad. 'But thank you for all your help, Foley.'

'Not at all, old boy.'

Conrad, Theo and Warren watched the small man and the frail woman make their way across the Potsdamer Platz. Warren stayed only a couple of minutes more, and then he hurried off too, chasing the news.

For a long time Conrad and Theo sat in silence, watching Berlin swirl in front of them.

'Do you think I was right?' Conrad asked. 'Not to shoot him?'

'We'll never know,' said Theo. 'If you had, war might have been declared already.'

'My bet is that you and I will be at war within a year anyway,' said Conrad.

Theo grimaced. Suddenly he sat up and beckoned to a waitress. 'Two schnapps, please.'

'It's a bit early, isn't it?' Conrad said.

'No. It's the right time.'

The waitress reappeared a minute later with the glasses. Theo raised his. 'To Algy.'

Conrad smiled.

'To Algy.'

Author's Note

There really was a plot to overthrow Hitler in September 1938. It was the first of many involving a number of senior German army officers, which culminated in the failed attempt on Hitler's life in his bunker at Rastenburg on 20 July 1944. The existence of the 1938 plot was transmitted to the British government in the summer by Ewald von Kleist with the help of a young, well-connected British journalist named Ian Colvin. Chamberlain knew that if he stood firm with Czechoslovakia the German generals would attempt a coup. Indeed, on the morning of 28 September, a raiding party under Captain Heinz was waiting for the order to take the Chancellery and arrest the Führer. But after Hitler accepted Mussolini and Chamberlain's offer of talks at Munich at around noon that day, the order never came. Chamberlain had saved Hitler.

The senior representative of the British secret service in Berlin in the 1930s was Captain Foley, who held the post of Chief Passport Control Officer as cover. A quiet, self-effacing but extremely hard-working man, he was responsible for the passage of thousands of Jews from Germany to Britain, Palestine and the Empire in the face of stiff opposition from the British and German bureaucracies. In 1959 a grove of 2,200 pine trees was planted outside Jerusalem to commemorate him, each one paid for by someone he had saved from the concentration camps.

Most of the major characters in this book are fictional. Although Conrad de Lancey plays the same role as Colvin did in real life, he is not Ian Colvin. Neither does Theo von Hertenberg represent a real historical figure, although he shares some of the characteristics of a number of extremely courageous young German lawyers who were given great responsibility during this and subsequent plots against Hitler, including Fabian von Schlabrendorff, Adam von Trott, Hans-Bernd Gisevius and Helmuth von Moltke.

See my website www.michaelridpath.com for a fuller discussion of what is fiction and what is fact, as well as the sources I used to research the book.

I would like to thank a number of people for their help over the many years it took to write this novel: my agents Carole Blake and Oli Munson at Blake Friedmann, Nic Cheetham, Laura Palmer and Becci Sharpe at Head of Zeus, Richenda Todd, Allan and Stephanie Walker, Toby Wyles, Virginia Manzer, Sir Ronald Harwood, Frances Fyfield, Bruce Hunter, Hilma Roest, Chris and Sheila Murphy, James Holland, Christopher Appleton, Michael Johnson, Christine Sieger, Simon Petherick, Jan Dopheide, Nick Gay of Berlin Walks and of course my wife, Barbara.